THE COLONY

THE COLONY

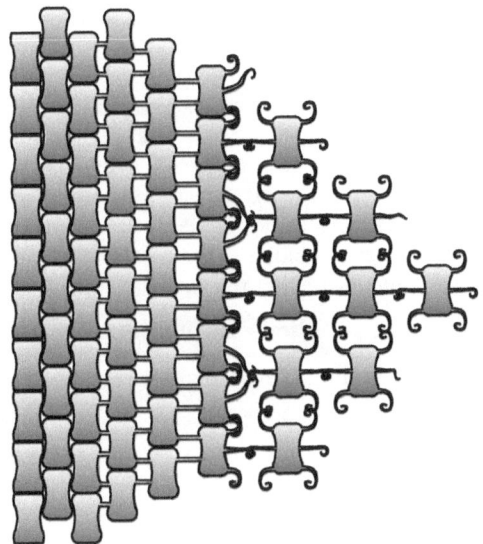

Blaine C. Readler

Full Arc
Press

THE COLONY

Published by Full Arc Press

Visit us at: http://www.readler.com

E-mail: blaine@readler.com

ISBN: 978-0-9834973-3-2

Printed in the United States of America

First Edition: 2012

Dedicated to Ray Bradbury, whose seminal visions showed us the splendors and horrors of a world we believe so normal.

ACKNOWLEDGEMENTS

Inestimable (but greater than much) thanks to Chris Wilson, Tim O'Lena, and Trey Alexander for proofing the first copies and flagging parades of gaffes.

And, as always, the story would be barely readable without MTB's steady hand—I didn't marry her specifically for her proficiency at editing, and she hasn't yet divorced me because of it.

God is in the detail.
—architect Ludwig Mies

The devil is in the details.
—everybody who overlooked them.

PART I

DISCOVERY

Chapter 1

Kiel came upon the colony by accident. Of course, to say accident can mean either by chance or calamity, but for Kiel it was both. The calamity was broad-based and had been part of his life as a drifter long enough to be subsumed into the daily fabric. He remembered reading how it was possible for black holes to be as large as entire galaxies; you could be inside one and not even know it. That's how it felt sometimes, except that he was always aware, every waking second and many sleeping ones as well. It was what had set him on the road months before, abandoning his suburban life and all its consumer comforts.

The accidental aspect comprised a curious twelve-year-old boy and his younger sister. Kiel had made his way west and north to Wisconsin as spring had bloomed into summer, seeking quiet farming communities where events rarely gained wider visibility than the weekly community paper—a place where anonymity was assumed rather than achieved. He had taken for granted that the climate would be congenial for open-road traveling, and on this count he'd met an unpleasant surprise. The climate upsets that accompany global warming rained down on him in a wet, chilling drizzle pattering endlessly on his soaked cotton hat. June was supposed to be sunny and pleasant here at the cloistered top of the heartland. Judging by the sullen faces of the Wisconsinites he'd met, he surmised that a week-long cold rain was a climate upset for them as well.

Kiel had been keeping a low profile ever since an uncomfortable lunch conversation with an inquisitive sheriff's deputy in Waukesha County five days before. This meant sticking to franchise fast food and dive motels that accepted an extra off-ledger twenty dollars in lieu of a credit card deposit. He hadn't seen accommodations of any kind, though, since the morning before as he hitched his way across the endless flat farmland of America's settled torso. Now evening was massing above the already dark blanket overcast and he held little hope that the next hour of fading light would be any different than the previous dozen as he slouched along the highway with his thumb outstretched.

His fingers were wrinkled from being soaked so long, and the whole-body shivering was starting to rattle his teeth. It was time to accept that he'd be spending another night in the rain.

He peered around through the mist of drizzle that limited his view to a few hundred yards. Somewhere off across the fields there would be a farmhouse—in Wisconsin, you were always standing on somebody's farm. The question was which direction? It wasn't a farmhouse per se that he sought—it didn't even occur to him to ask for lodging—but a barn. He was desperate enough to take a tool shed. Hell, he'd crawl in with the chickens if they'd let him.

He shouldered his heavy, dripping backpack and trudged up the highway. Twice that day he'd walked nearly a mile between farmer's lanes. He came to a dirt road, but the grassy middle and absence of mailbox implied that this was just an access entrance, probably just leading off to remote fields. Kiel stared ahead along the highway. Suddenly a pickup truck whooshed by, slapping his face with a wash of cold spray. He realized that he couldn't take the highway another minute. It didn't matter if he was standing in one spot or shuffling along the shoulder; just being on the highway was destitution. He turned and slogged along the muddy access road. Now at least he wasn't by inference begging for anything, he was just homeless.

Water squished and sloshed in his boots, and his water-logged socks sagged around his ankles. His spare pair was probably still dry, wrapped inside the green garbage bag in his pack, but dry clothes were just an abstract notion until he could find shelter. He hated the thought of pitching his tent. It was so tiny, and he was so wet, there was nothing in the idea that included dry. He might as well just crawl under a bush.

Off to his left, a line of brush and young trees angled towards him as he slogged along. As it closed in, he saw that it was a stream—a small river almost, swelled from days of rain, rushing along with earnest purpose. Under the looming darkness, the rapid impatience of it seemed desperate, as though the rapid flow urgently wanted to get where it was going before total darkness settled in. Kiel felt left behind in his heavy, leaden boots, abandoned to drown in the interminable fall of rain.

He had no choice. He staggered on. Ahead, bulky shapes formed from out of the deepening gray drizzle. It was another line of trees intersecting the stream at right angles. Kiel took this to be another stream. He stopped and stared. His vision shook as his shivering teeth rattled away uncontrollably. This couldn't be another stream. Streams don't cross each other like roads. The fact that he had held this thought, if even for just a moment, troubled Kiel. He understood the effects of hypothermia, and knew that plenty of people died each year from doing stupid things long before their bodies actually shut down from cold.

As he came closer, though, he saw that he wasn't so far off after all. Streams don't cross other streams, but roads do. The rutted access road he was trudging ended at the line of trees. Between two rows of tall, mature maples and oaks lay the skeleton of an abandoned road. Weeds and small brush sprouted haphazardly, but among the riot of returning nature, Kiel could see patches of macadam—the old kind, slick with worn, polished tar. He guessed that this was the original highway, replaced by the wide two-lane artery a quarter mile behind him. Why they had moved it, he couldn't even venture a guess. Maybe it was easier than cutting down all these big trees. There; he'd ventured a guess after all. Or maybe this one hadn't been aimed right—maybe it missed the next town by a small margin.

Kiel shook his head, sending thick drops flying from his nose. Nutty thoughts like that spelled the beginning of the end.

He had to find shelter and get warm.

Darkness was falling fast, settling in at an alarming advance. It looked like it would have to be the tiny tent after all. He wouldn't attempt to change clothes; that would be futile. He would just curl in on himself and try to wait it out. There wasn't much opportunity for stupidity to kill him huddled under a flimsy bit of synthetic cloth.

It would help if he could find a bit of higher ground. The road was flat, as were the fields on both sides. As he gazed around, though, he noticed that the bridge that spanned the swollen stream was still intact. It was a trestle matrix assembled from hefty rusting members of half-inch thick I-beams, built in a time when America was proud of its dominance of steel production, when US Steel was the largest corporation in the world. This was a bridge that boasted of steel enough to squander, standing the test of time and feeling relaxed about it.

The bridge was perhaps a serendipitous bonanza, a last desperate possibility for a bit of dry dirt. He slogged over and at first his heart sank when he saw that the wild rush of water lapped against the cement foundation. But then he saw a three-foot hole in the road where it met the waffle grid surface of the bridge. Peering down, he could tell that previous floods had washed out a large cavity, and the road had collapsed into it. The interior was nearly black in the fast-fading light. He had a small flashlight stashed somewhere in his pack, but was too tired to look for it. He squatted down, reached in, and waved his arm around, realizing too late that this was probably one of those stupid decisions that hypothermia could induce. What if a raccoon or badger was using it as a lair? What if it hosted a nest of rattlesnakes?

He yanked his arm out with a little yelp. Grumbling, he took off his pack and let it fall with a slap in the water pooled on the ancient macadam. The little LED light wasn't where he thought he'd stashed it, nor was it where he should have stashed it. By the time he'd located it, half his possessions were scattered about getting wet. It was typical of life lived out of a bag; half his existence seemed to comprise either rooting around or re-packing.

Leaving his things lying in the rain, he flicked on the light, peered into the hole, and was gratified with the sight. The previous flood had washed out a little cave two feet high and perhaps five wide. Rain dripped down in a continuous shower from the waffle grid in front of him, but on each side and behind him, the solid layer of thick macadam provided a dry roof. There were no badgers or snakes, just the gentle scurry of what he assumed were mice, gone before his beam could find them.

Without waiting to even think about it, Kiel started jamming his things into the pack, but quickly decided that this was a waste of time, and lowered the half-full bag down the hole, shoved it to one side, then collected the rest of his things and tossed them down as well. With one last glance at a sky that seemed to glower even darker at his escape, Kiel eased himself down, pushing his legs ahead of him in order to fit in horizontally. It was a tight fit. His boots extended below the dribble falling from the waffle grid, and rain fell through the hole and splattered to the ground inches from his face, but the rest of him was dry. Well, the rest of him was still soaked, but not getting any wetter. Most importantly, the cold rain wasn't continually carrying away his warmth.

He gathered together his loose items, caked now with dirt morphing into smearing mud, and stashed them safely behind the pack, which he settled into place to use as a pillow.

He sighed with relief. He still shivered uncontrollably, but already warmth was returning. He was hungry—famished. Any bit of spare energy left to root for a power bar, though, had been extinguished. He would eat after he'd rested awhile and gotten warm. He turned off the light, and after a moment's thought, kept it clutched in his fist, which he placed under his cheek. He felt the gritty mud that coated his fingers mash against his face. That was his last sensation.

ж ж ж

Kiel woke to a sound. The stream gurgled in haste a couple of feet away, and the restless whoosh of wind flicked cool and refreshing across his face. But it wasn't these that had woken him. A pale white light streamed through the hole to illuminate the mud-caked bottom of his pack. The moon. And the wind. The weather was breaking. A front was blowing through, tearing apart and dragging away the hateful rain clouds.

There! The sound. It was difficult to place—a squeal, like a young girl screaming in terror in the distance. Or maybe chalk on a blackboard. He turned his head, ignoring the resisting stiff neck, trying to locate it. It wasn't a far-away ear-splitting scream, but a tiny screech close by. Very close, in fact.

He still had the flashlight in his hand, and he turned it on. He wasn't sure what he would find, maybe a mouse caught in his bootlaces. He played the small beam around his little cave, but there was nothing to explain it.

It came again, and this time he could tell that it was above him. The flashlight revealed just the dark underside of the macadam road. No, the sound was more to the left. There! Massed among the waffle grid was . . . what? It looked like silver mold, or maybe a thin foam coating of metallic paint.

His flinched when he realized that there was movement. The foam wasn't a continuous coating, but a myriad of tightly packed . . . things. He could now discern individual components, like a giant crowd of bald men as viewed from a thousand feet above. Kiel saw that the sound coincided with a shiver that flowed in a path through the crowd.

He had no clue what he was looking at. He guessed that it must be some type of social insect, perhaps a subterranean ant species whose coloring had become superfluous after millions of years evolving in darkness. There was an ominous element in the inscrutable alienness, but Kiel was drawn by the mystery of the squeals. Were they perhaps executing miscreant members in some macabre insect ritual under the waning gibbous moon? He shivered, and not from the cold. He watched the silver mob and wondered. The insect elements seemed to pack tighter, and the squeals became more frequent. He saw that the shiver that accompanied each squeal flowed continuously along the bottom of a waffle rib all the way to the edge of the grid, where it disappeared up and away, as though news of the latest execution was being passed along to the ant king sitting in a throne on the broken, abandoned road above.

Curiosity finally overpowered caution, and Kiel reached up with his outstretched finger. Were they really individual elements, or like slime mold, a continuum of substance? He paused before the tip of his finger actually touched the crowd. He thought that he could see them straining to keep away. The squeals and all flowing shivers stopped as only the blustery wind outside remained animated. Kiel intended to pull away, to leave them undisturbed, but the curious part of him couldn't resist. He eased his finger upward. Suddenly, as though the pause button had been released, the entire mass surged along the waffle grid, disappearing in an upside-down waterfall upwards at the edge. Simultaneously, Kiel felt a sharp bite on the tip of his finger. Holy shit! A half-dozen tiny sliver crabs clung there chewing on him!

Kiel yelped and shook his hand, but the little bastards clung fast, and the pain only intensified. Goddamn! He scraped the fingertip along the dirt, and when that didn't work, across the rough fabric of his backpack. This did the trick, and they fell off and rolled away. His finger still hurt like hell. He examined it and saw that one micro-crab had chewed its way in and was almost buried. Kiel cried out in despair and tried to pick it out with his other hand, but couldn't get a grip using his stub-chewed nails. In a panic, he bit the tip of his finger, and when he felt something tiny wiggling on his tongue, he spit. And spit again. He thrashed around with the flashlight, looking for the crablets that had fallen off the pack, but they were gone, fled or buried in the dirt.

He lay back and held still, his senses tingling with hyper-alertness for any movement. Nothing.

He shuddered at the horror of it. The waffle grid above was completely empty of organisms. Exposed now, the metal looked decayed, as though eaten away by acid.

As soon as he was satisfied that none had crawled into his clothes, Kiel decided to leave the hell-hole. He hesitated, though. The blustery wind whipped about up there, and he was still wet through-and-through. He'd be shivering and cold the rest of the night. If he wasn't going to sleep anyway, he might as well not sleep here where it was at least warm. And he had no idea where the crab-mold went anyway. How did he know he would be safe from them up there?

With another shiver, he sucked his wounded finger tip and lay with the flashlight aimed at the edge of the grid where the mass had disappeared. These were his last batteries, but he was damned if he was going to lay in the dark waiting for them to return.

Wisconsin. Thomas Jefferson should have sold the territory to Canada for a hundred dollars. Mrs. Jefferson could have bought some nice drapes for the new White House.

ж ж ж

Kiel opened his eyes and saw sunlight shining on dirt. He remembered. He had crawled under the road. The tip of his finger had been chewed up—

He jerked his head around. "Shit!" he exclaimed in surprise.

Two faces peered down at him through the hole. They were young faces—a serious boy perhaps twelve years old watching him cautiously, and a younger girl, her thick brown hair falling down around a dainty, proud little mouth and eyes wide with wonder.

"Where'd you come from?" Kiel blurted.

The boy raised one eyebrow, as though the irony of the question was too obvious to elaborate. "We came from our house."

The boy emphasized "house" just enough to point out the contrast to Kiel's temporary residence.

"Cam, maybe—" the girl started, but the boy shook his head impatiently, never taking his eyes from Kiel.

The little girl apparently decided she didn't need Cam's permission. "You're not strange, are you mister?" she asked.

Kiel looked at her and blinked. He burst out laughing. "I'm not exactly in a position to argue my side of that debate."

The little girl's face closed up in anger, embarrassed by his reaction.

It occurred to Kiel what she meant. "Your mom told you not to talk to strange men, didn't she?" he said.

The girl just pouted, her pride hurt.

"Don't be such a dummy, Nicki," the boy admonished. "Mom meant not to talk to men we don't know—strangers, not men that are strange."

"You're talking to him, and you don't know him," Nicki accused in counterattack.

The boy sighed. "Like he said, he's not in much of a position to do anything."

"Still. You're talking to him, and you don't know him. I'm telling Mom."

"Fine. Tell Mom." To Kiel, the boy named Cam said, "You okay, mister?"

"I'm fine compared to people running from a grizzly," he replied, maneuvering his arm to get his hand free, which wasn't easy in the confined space. "Hi," he added, reaching up, "I'm Kiel."

Cam looked at it as though he'd never seen a handshake before.

Kiel noticed that he was extending a hand that was essentially caked mud in the shape of fingers and a thumb. Dried blood added a touch of drama. "Sorry," he said, retracting the mummy appendage. "I'm going to extricate myself—you might want to back up."

Extrication was not straightforward. Kiel wondered how he had gotten in there in the first place. He wasn't designed to bend in the places needed to slip out. He yanked his pack forward to lean against as he tried to scoot up and out. After a moment's hesitation, Cam reached his hand out to help, but Kiel declined, explaining that he didn't want both of them trapped in the hole. In the end, Kiel accidentally broke off a large section of macadam while pulling on it, and then there was plenty of room to crawl out.

"He ruined it!" Nicki complained.

"Don't be rude!" her brother admonished. "He didn't ruin it. He just widened the door a little."

Kiel reached down and gathered his pack and loose possessions from the mud and dirt. Spread out on the abandoned road, it could have been the remains from the bottom of a Katrina flood closet.

Cam was smallish. His speech and manner was that of preteen, but his height and frame would have blended easily with an average elementary school crowd. He stood next to Kiel as they surveyed the sad mess. "Are you going to keep all of it?" Cam asked.

Kiel shrugged. "I don't have much choice."

The swollen stream still rushed along in bloated haste, but under the bright morning sun, the wild gray torrent of the night before now sparkled with bright sun-jewels and suggested nature's ambition rather than her anger.

Kiel carried his things to the edge where the waves lapped the weeds and grass that lay flat in submission.

"You're washing your muddy things in muddy water," Nicki observed, perplexed.

"Nicki!" Cam started. "I told you not to be—"

"It's okay," Kiel assured as he squatted down to start the rinsing process. "The water looks really dirty, honey, but it's much cleaner than my clothes. You'll see in a minute."

"He called me 'honey,'" Nicki protested to her brother, who just shrugged.

Kiel froze, holding a sock waving in the rushing water. Panic clenched his chest. What had he done? The trap was waiting, ready to spring wherever he went.

"Sorry," he forced himself to say. He turned to her. "Your name is Nicki, right? That's what I'll call you."

"It's just a nickname," Cam said, annoyed, "like when the mailman calls you 'Peaches.'"

"I know that. I'm not stupid. But that's what Daddy used to call Mom."

Her brother looked at her a moment and then explained to Kiel, "Our parents are separated."

"Cam!" Nicki shrieked.

He rolled his eyes. "We're not supposed to tell anybody," he told Kiel, and then to his sister he said, "Mr. . . . Kiel doesn't live around here. It doesn't matter."

"That's my first name," Kiel offered, resuming his washing. "You can call me just Kiel."

"What's your last name?" Nicki asked. She seemed suspicious, as though she might get one up on her older brother.

Kiel didn't look up as he lay the other sock aside and shoved a shirt into the stream. "Martin," he said. He stopped and looked at her. "My name is Kiel Martin."

She watched him through cautious eyes. "You promise not to tell anybody?" she demanded.

He smiled. "I promise." He held up his hand. "Scout's honor."

Behind his smile, Kiel felt vaguely nauseous. Lies everywhere. He'd been using Martin since South Bend. It was probably time to change it. For today, though, here in the farm heartland of Wisconsin, he was Mr. Kiel Martin.

Lies begat lies.

He hadn't started it, though.

The Colony

Chapter 2

"What brought you guys out here this morning?" Kiel asked as he spread the wet clothes along the bank to dry. Cam was helping, but Nicki refused, responding with just "Yuk!" to her brother's suggestion.

"I wanted to check out some animals we've been watching," Cam said. "See how they managed with the rain."

"What animals?"

"The calves," Nicki answered. She had dropped her belligerence. She didn't want to miss out on any action.

"That's what Nicki calls them," Cam explained. "They're about a thousand times too small for calves." He shrugged and shook his head as though sharing with Kiel the knowledge that women were inscrutable.

"They *look* like calves," she affirmed.

"They look about as much like calves as I do," her brother retorted. To Kiel, he explained, "She thinks that they're like cows because they always seem to be in herds."

"And they graze," Nicki added. "Just like calves."

"On what?" Kiel asked, probing through his pack to make sure he'd gotten all the dirty or wet things out.

"On the bridge," Nicki said.

Kiel stopped and looked at her. He remembered the nightmare in the dark hole.

"She doesn't know that for a fact," Cam corrected.

"You said so yourself!" Nicki protested.

"I said it *looked* like they were. You're just like the girls in my class—always jumping to conclusions. A fact has to be proven."

"You just can't take—"

"Hold it," Kiel interrupted, standing up. "You're talking about those crab things? Silver—about the size of an ant?"

Both kids nodded. "You saw them?" Cam asked.

In answer, Kiel held out his raw, wounded finger.

Cam held up his thumb. The backside was scabbed, as though healing from a nasty fall off his bike.

"You probably tried to hurt them," Nicki accused.

"I only tried to touch them," Kiel countered.

"They didn't know that."

"They're dangerous," he declared. "What are they?"

The brother and sister shrugged together.

"Where'd they come from?"

They lifted their shoulders and held them—supplications of ignorance.

"I thought they were some kind of insect unique to Wisconsin," Kiel said. "Maybe termites that mutated after eating too much cheese."

"A cheese joke," Nicki noted.

"Mr. Dickson—the science teacher—was going to come and look, but he was too busy," Cam said.

"You thought that he tried to come, but got lost," Nicki corrected.

Cam returned her glare dourly.

"He likes Mr. Dickson," Nicki revealed.

"Because he knows about science!" Cam objected.

"You said he was nice."

"Well, yeah. So what? Would you rather he was mean?"

"I'm just saying that you like him, that's all."

"Yeah, but you make it sound like—"

"Yo!" Kiel called.

They looked at him in surprise.

"Look, Nicki, Cam can like anybody he pleases—"

"I don't *like* him like that—"

"No, I know. I mean—Nicki, it's like your brother said: you shouldn't jump to conclusions about things people say."

"You're sticking up for him because you're a boy."

"I'm sticking up for him because he's right."

Under her breath, she reiterated, "He likes Mr. Dickson."

Kiel let it go. "Okay, kids. I'd love to stick around and debate social philosophy, but I have to eat. And all I have left are two soggy power bars. Do you know where there's a restaurant around here? Or even a convenience store?"

"Sure," Cam answered. "It's the local market. People go to Oshkosh for most of their groceries, but the One Stop sells stuff like chips and bread and cold meat."

"Sounds perfect. Where?"

"Um, from here . . ." He thought about it, then pointed back the way Kiel had come. "You go to the highway and turn right."

"How far?"

Cam shrugged. He didn't drive. "I dunno. Seven miles—maybe ten."

Kiel groaned. "Nothing closer? Not even a gas station?"

Cam thought about it.

"You can eat at Gamma's," Nicki offered.

"What's Gambas?"

"Not 'Gambas,' " Nicki corrected, "Gam-ma's."

"It's our grandmother," Cam explained. "We're staying there."

"But you can't tell anybody," Nicki reminded. "You promised."

"Ah, I see," Kiel said.

This was probably their mom's mother. Cam looked unhappy at his sister's offer. "That's very generous," Kiel said, "but I'm not sure your Gamma would appreciate a surprise guest—particularly one who looks like he just staggered out from a nuclear test site."

"Gamma likes visitors," Nicki confirmed.

"She likes visitors when she's invited them," Cam corrected. The boy chewed his lip a moment. "I know—we'll run back and tell her you're coming, and then we'll come back and get you."

Kiel smiled at the two kids. "I appreciate your kindness, I really do. But I wouldn't feel right basically inviting myself in."

"You're not inviting yourself," Cam persisted, "we're inviting you."

"It's not really your prerogative to invite people to your grandmother's house, is it?"

"Does he mean that it's not our house?" Nicki asked her brother.

"In a way," Cam replied. He pointed at Kiel's hand. "You need to get that cleaned and bandaged. It'll get infected."

"That's true. But I expect they'll have what I need at the One Stop."

Cam's mouth was set as he glanced around. "You're going to re-pack all your wet stuff and walk ten miles, when you can relax and have a nice cup of coffee right here?"

Kiel looked at him a moment and burst out laughing. "Cam, you might be interested in science, but you could make your fortune in sales. Okay. Run tell your Gamma that a dirty bum is coming for breakfast."

The two kids trotted away, and Kiel sat down with his back against one of the bridge supports, enjoying the warm summer sun. After a few minutes, he pulled his pack over and lay back, using it to rest his head on.

He woke from a dream where silver crayfish were trying to crawl up his pant legs. He looked up to find a man dressed in a denim shirt and jeans gazing down at him. A conservative, no-nonsense mustache and precisely trimmed salt-and-pepper sideburns conveyed a disciplined life. If it weren't for the faded clothes and thick, calloused working hands, Kiel could have taken him for a career military man. Kiel had the sense that he had just said something.

"Er, hi," Kiel sputtered, pulling himself up into a sitting position. "I was just passing through, and I—"

"I know," the man assured. "The kids told me."

The man stood studying him, and Kiel felt swelling anxiety with each second of scrutiny. He wanted to explain in minute detail that the three of them had only talked—absolutely nothing else. The man broke the mounting tension by grunting and pointing at the pack. "Doing some traveling, eh?"

"Yeah," Kiel replied, getting to his feet. "Off to see the spacious skies, amber waves of grain, and purple mountain majesties."

The man's mouth turned in the slightest of grins. Kiel had the impression that this was as jovial as it got.

"Plenty of grain around here, but no mountain majesties, unless you count Chippewa Ridge there," the man commented, pointing off across the field. Kiel looked for something substantial, like the Appalachians he had grown up in, but he realized the man meant a low line of hills just a quarter mile away. In Altoona these would have been called speed bumps.

"Where you headed?" the man asked.

Good question. "California, eventually. Taking in the sights along the way."

The man eyed him. "You look a little old to be just settling down."

The guy was probing—checking him out. He would have done the same. "I'm sort of settling down for a second time. Changing jobs, and taking the opportunity for a little time off. I'm a teacher—a science teacher."

A science teacher? Where the hell did he pull that from? Probably from Cam.

The man nodded. "Where're you from?"

"I was born in Albany, but grew up in Baltimore."

Lies! All lies!

The man eyed him a moment, then extended his hand. "Daniel—Daniel Bakke."

"Kiel . . . Martin," he returned, and then felt himself blushing as he shook hands. He was tired from sleeping in a wet hole, and he'd forgotten for a split second whether he'd changed his name yet.

Daniel stared at him a second, and then turned and started walking away. "Well, we'd better get back. Mom hates to warm up food in the microwave."

Kiel hesitated. Maybe the smeared mud had hid his blushing.

Daniel stopped and turned around. "You might as well leave your stuff here to dry. Nobody'll bother it."

Kiel nodded, but grabbed his pack. His wallet and toothbrush were inside. "I take it that Gamma is your mother-in-law?" he said as they walked together towards a house and barn that appeared as they rounded a stand of trees.

Actually, that wouldn't make sense, since Cam had said his parents were separated.

Daniel confirmed this. "She's my mother-in-mother. I'm the kids' uncle."

He explained that he worked the farm and would soon own it, once the paperwork went through. His father had died suddenly the year before, and it had taken this long before his mother was up to facing the legal details. Once the deed was officially signed over, of course, he'd be in debt to Julie for half the inheritance.

"Julie?" Kiel said. "Is that Cam and Nicki's mother?"

Daniel nodded. "She's staying with Mom for the time being—the time 'being' indefinitely."

"Right," Kiel agreed. "Cam explained that his parents were separated—oh shit!"

Daniel's mouth turned up in that minimal micro-smile. "I didn't hear that."

"Crap! I promised!"

The farmer gave him an odd look. "It's not like I don't know."

"Sure—but *I'm* not supposed to know."

"You would have figured it out after about five minutes. Don't worry. Besides I don't think you pose a threat to Brandon."

"Brandon?"

Daniel grunted. "The S-O-B who got Julie pregnant with Cam, and then demonstrated how magnanimous he was by marrying her."

He went on to explain that the story was that Julie was staying with their mom to take care of her through her debilitating grief after their father died—this was supposed to explain why she and the kids weren't with Brandon in Oshkosh.

"Why the big secret?" Kiel asked. "Everybody gets divorced. It's probably more common than marriage."

"Not candidates running for Senator."

"State legislature?"

"Nope. The big time. He wants to get his ass out of Wisconsin and move to DC."

"I see. Yeah. We like to pretend that our elected leaders are the better parts of us."

"If you can't keep your family together, how can you expect to do any better with the country?"

Kiel wasn't sure if Daniel was mocking American naiveté, or stating an honest opinion. He figured he'd better just lie low until he got a feel for the territory.

"Brandon comes by about once a week," Daniel went on. "Supposedly to spend quality time with his precious loved ones, but more likely it's to work on old Tagget—he owns the farm just north of us. Most of the Chippewa Ridge is his. Brandon's trying to buy some of his property. Claims he wants to protect and expand the Bakke homestead."

"You don't believe him?"

"Bah! If he had the least interest in the Bakke homestead, he'd take Julie and the kids back with him to Oskosh."

"He, uh, kicked them out?"

"The opposite. Julie left him, but he knows how to get her back."

"What's that?"

Daniel glanced at him. "Stop being an S-O-B. It's not complicated."

They had arrived at the house, or at least the house that appeared to be associated with the farm. A covered porch wrapped around two sides, but only the main entrance and a swing next to it wasn't occupied by broken furniture and potted plants—some green, some long dead. There was even an aquarium, although the fish inside didn't look very tropical; in fact, they looked like fingerling trout.

Behind this large, two-story house, almost an afterthought, was a manufactured home—the kind that's delivered and assembled as two big halves. Contrasted with the original house, this one was just one story and looked about as cozy as living in retail space.

Daniel saw him looking at the insta-home. "That's where we live—Peggy, Tanya, and me. Tanya's away at college. At least she's supposed to be attending U-W—University of Wisconsin—but I think she's basically just hanging out and enjoying herself."

Kiel assumed that one of the women was his wife, and the other a daughter, but he didn't have a chance to ask, as an elderly woman in a faded cotton dress and new running shoes came through the door. "Get in here and get washed up!" she called. "The food's getting cold."

She turned and went back inside, letting the screen door slam behind her.

"That's Mom—Gamma to the kids," Daniel explained.

They passed the front door by, and walked around to the back and directly into the kitchen, which was almost as big as the entire first floor of the house that Kiel had abandoned in Altoona.

His host was at the stove and turned around, wiping her hands on her apron. She looked at him a moment, and then said, "I'd shake your hand, but then nobody'd want to eat my food. You look like you just crawled out of a septic tank. Bathroom's right down the hall. Do what you can to get presentable, but be quick about it. Pancakes don't re-heat."

She turned back to the stove and Daniel said, "Mom doesn't go much for social niceties."

"Waste of time!" she called without turning around.

After he'd made a mess of the bathroom by transferring his dirt to the sink top and towel, he came back to the kitchen to find Cam and Nicki already sitting at the table on each side of a woman he assumed to be their mother. She stood up and extended her hand. It was a delicate, smooth hand, the hand of an equally delicate woman. As far as Kiel could tell, she wore no makeup, and he couldn't imagine it improving on the original perfection. The old cliché about natural country-girl beauty had found new life.

"Kiel Martin," he said, taking her hand and remembering his last name. "Pleased to meet you, ma'am."

She smiled at him and it was a smile full of expression: it suggested *I might just be glad to meet somebody new, and I wonder if you are as interesting as your hobo appearance suggests.* What she actually said was, "I'm not ready yet to be a ma'am. I'm Julie, and I'm pleased to meet you . . . Kiel, you said?"

"That's right, er, Julie."

"That's a very unusual name. What's the origin?"

Luckily he'd been using his real first name, so he knew. "My father liked the fact that at the end of World War I German sailors mutinied in the city, believing that the mission they were being sent out on against England was suicide. It sparked a wider revolution that brought down the last German monarch and formed the first republic."

"So, you're named after a German city?"

"It could be worse."

"Like being named after a movie actress."

"Julie Andrews? *The Sound of Music?*"

"Julie Christie—Lara in *Doctor Zhivago*. Dad had a crush on her after seeing the movie."

"He did not," her mother stated from the stove with her back to them. "He was impressed with her acting."

"Dan," Julie said to her brother, "am I right, or am I right?"

He held up his hands. "Don't get me involved." He sidled towards the door. "I have to check the west-side drainage pump." The door slammed behind him before anybody could object.

Julie held her hand to the side of her mouth, pretending that this would prevent her mother from hearing. "Dad hung a movie poster of her in the milk shed."

Mrs. Bakke turned around, holding a spatula like a club. "Your father was in love with exactly two things: me and six dozen head of cattle—and most of the time I came out on top." She stopped, realizing what she'd said. "I know what you're thinking, and you should be ashamed."

Kiel thought that this did not seem like a woman debilitated with grief.

"I don't understand," Nicki complained to her mother.

"You're not supposed to, my dear," Julie said, smoothing her hair.

The girl leaned forward and asked her brother, "Do *you* know what she meant?"

"Sure," Cam said, glancing nervously between his mother and Gamma.

"You'd better not," Julie reproved, and the boy blushed red.

"Yo-hoo!" came a perky female voice through the screen door.

"That woman could smell sausage a mile away," Mrs. Bakke muttered loud enough for everyone to hear, including the new visitor.

If Daniel's wife had heard, she pretended ignorance. She was plump and made-up as though ready for Sunday morning mega-church. Kiel wondered if perhaps she'd suddenly decided to try all of her makeup at one time. The layered contours brought to mind a clown trying to disguise herself as a normal person.

"Gee, Peggy," Mrs. Bakke said, with feigned enthusiasm as she turned back to the stove, "just in time for another breakfast."

She emphasized "another" with enough force that Kiel glanced at Peggy, but the woman seemed not to hear. Kiel suspected that Peggy breezed through life mastering a honed ability to not hear.

"You must be Kiel," Peggy sang, holding out her hand, fingers dangling as though expecting him to gently press his lips against them.

He resisted and simply shook her offered limp hand. It was like handling a dead squid.

"Oh my!" she exclaimed, putting her free hand to her mouth. "You're wounded!"

He looked at the raw tip of his finger. He'd forgotten about it. "That's actually interesting," he remarked, letting go of the squid. "It happened last night while I was sleeping in a hole. I saw these weird little things . . . er, probably mice."

He had noticed that Cam and Nicki were making alarmed faces, aghast that he was talking about the micro-crabs. Evidently it was a secret, but the secret itself was apparently a secret, since they hadn't told him to keep quiet.

"Mice!" Peggy shrieked. "You could have rabies!"

Mrs. Bakke had come to the table carrying a huge plate of pancakes. "You can't catch rabies from shaking hands," she reproved.

Peggy had been surreptitiously wiping her hand on her dress, but now quickly hid it behind her back.

"Well, sit down," Mrs. Bakke barked at her. "We all know that's why you're here."

Peggy sat down, smiling gaily, bringing her practiced talent to bear. As far as Kiel could tell, she had heard only the first sentence.

Chapter 3

Kiel had forgotten how famished he was, but it came back with resounding clarity when Mrs. Bakke laid the cornucopia out on the table. Despite himself, his hands kept his mouth continuously full, even as he fielded a barrage of questions lobbed at him. He replied with the truth when he could, but the lies were piling up in an intricate interconnected matrix that was becoming precarious in its complexity. He made a mental note to write it all down in his notebook. When the subject of his profession rolled around, he paused. He had to be careful with this, since it would define him, and he'd be expected to be knowledgeable henceforth. He decided that for once the truth was best.

"I have a degree in engineering—" *Oops!* He remembered what he had told Daniel. So much for the truth. "But I went on to get my teaching credits. I teach high school science."

Cam was looking at him funny. He was probably surprised that Kiel hadn't brought this up when they were talking about *his* science teacher.

Julie's eyes brightened. "I studied biology at U-W for two years. Do you teach that?"

Time to dance. "Physics. The extent of my biology knowledge is that prokaryote cells have a nucleus, and eukaryotes don't."

Julie raised one eyebrow.

"Er, I got it backwards, didn't I? See? Now you understand why they don't let me near the bio lab."

Kiel did actually know a fair amount of physics. He had started out with that as his major, but switched to engineering when he'd met Maria. He didn't think that she would stay interested for very long in a guy who planned to be in school for the better part of a decade before landing a job that could buy a house and new car.

"Well," Peggy chimed in. "We'll have to introduce you to Mr. Dickson. Cameron always talks so highly of him."

Cam rolled his eyes.

The subject was wandering a little too close to home. Kiel had learned that the art of lying included misdirection. "Mrs. Bakke," he effused, gesturing at the walls of the kitchen, "I love your house. This is a place where you can really feel at home—room to stretch out."

Mrs. Bakke gave Peggy a hard look, but the self-invited guest pretended not to see. "Room to stretch out," the plump woman observed, "but lots of room needs a lot of cleaning and maintenance. That's one advantage of our house—the cozy one out back—although it's cramped for a whole family, it is easy to clean. Everything on one floor, too."

The food on the others' plates suddenly required focused attention. Mrs. Bakke, however, sat watching Peggy with a sour mouth. "Let it go, Peg," she urged irritably. "You'll have the house soon enough. Once we get Julie and the kids settled, you can start dragging your furniture across the yard. Besides, there's just three of you, and Tanya's hardly ever there anyway."

Kiel guessed that Daniel had bought the manufactured home as a temporary residence until the generation wheels of the farm turned another cog. He'd seen it happen on almost all the farms in Pennsylvania. Where once the younger family would have lived under the same roof as the aging parents, manufactured housing was now cheap enough to allow the in-laws their own space. The inferior quality of their own space, though, was forever made obvious sitting next to the heritage house.

Julie moved her eggs back and forth across her plate. Kiel imagined that she must feel uncomfortable, a burden. "I'll bet it's good to spend some time back where you grew up," he said to her.

"I think we often take our roots for granted. There's a lot of people in the world who don't have that advantage, a place where they belong—really belong."

Mrs. Bakke seemed to catch what he was getting at. She reached over and patted her daughter's hand. "This house is as much yours as mine or Daniel's," she assured in what seemed to Kiel unusual softness. She then looked Peggy in the eye, snorted, and went back to eating.

For once the mascara-caked woman seemed unable to ignore the dig. She patted her mouth daintily, stood up, and declared that she supposed she'd had enough to eat. With a dramatic show of insincere politeness, she thanked Mrs. Bakke and took her leave, back to her manufactured own space.

"Daniel's a smart boy," Mrs. Bakke declared when the door had closed, "but everybody makes a mistake now and again."

When Kiel realized that he couldn't stuff another bite into his mouth, he thanked Mrs. Bakke for her kind hospitality and announced that he should probably be on his way.

"You might as well take a bath before you go," she said. "Start off again nice and fresh."

"Thanks, but I think I've imposed enough already."

"It's not a matter of hospitality," she warned. "The sheriff's libel to pick you up as a threat to community health."

He grinned and stood up, placing the napkin next to his empty plate. "I hope I'm not so ripe that I disturbed your appetites."

"You smell like Pappa's leached field," Nicki proclaimed.

Julie giggled and put her hand to her mouth. "That's not nice, sweetie."

Mrs. Bakke laughed out loud. "Count on a child to call a spade a spade."

Kiel shook his head in confusion. "I don't understand."

It was up to Cam to explain. "Pappa's septic tank got blocked once, and the sewage ran over the top of the ground. That's the leach field, where the . . . stuff is normally decomposed by germs under the ground."

"By bacteria, actually," his mother elaborated. "Mr. Martin, I'm so sorry. I'm sure that Nicki didn't mean to be impolite."

"That's quite alright. This is the sort of thing a man needs to know. Also, I think I'm not ready to be 'Mr. Martin' to a young woman. How about just Kiel."

While he took a shower, Cam ran across to his Aunt Peggy's to borrow some of his uncle's clothes until they could wash Kiel's own meager selection. Mrs. Bakke offered something from her deceased husband's closet, but he had been a hefty man—Kiel would have suggested obese. She completely disappeared behind his pants when she held them up, arms outstretched as far as she could reach.

When Kiel emerged from the bathroom toweling his hair and feeling a little awkward wearing another man's clothes, he was met by Cam and Nicki, faces flushed with some victory. "Mom says you can stay over," Nicki blurted, beating Cam to the honor.

"Well, that's very generous of her, but I—"

"She said you'd resist," Cam interrupted, "but Gamma says that you now have to earn the meal you just ate."

Kiel looked at the two of them. "She did, eh? Was that her idea?"

"It was Cam's," Nicki answered. "He thought of it."

"Shut up!" her brother complained, poking her with his elbow. "It doesn't matter whose idea it was. Gamma says you have to stay."

Kiel and the kids came to the kitchen where Mrs. Bakke and Julie had finished loading the dishwasher and were wiping the counters. "I understand I've been remanded to a sentence of servitude," he said.

"That's right," Mrs. Bakke agreed. "No free lunches in this house."

"I see. Well, I'm glad for the chance to earn my meal—what do you have for me?"

She shook out the dish towel she'd been using, hung it on the stove handle, and then turned to him. "I'll think of something. In the meantime, I need you to keep these two rapscallions out of our hair while Julie and me change all the bedclothes—Monday's are wash days."

Kiel eyed the two kids. "It will be my pleasure."

"Yeah? Well, we'll see if you're singing the same tune in a couple of hours. In fact, come to think of it, chaperoning these two not only pays for your breakfast, but earns you dinner and a bed as well."

Once outside on the porch, Kiel said to them, "You don't really give your grandmother a hard time, do you?"

Nicki shook her head "no," and Cam shrugged and nodded. "She can be a dictator sometimes."

"Like Caesar?"

"More like Hitler. She thinks kids are being spoiled if they're, like, not always doing some kind of chores."

"Well then, we'd better get away before she thinks of some."

Cam's face lit up. "Let's go back to the bridge. Maybe we can—"

"Yoo-hoo!" Peggy called from her front door. "You want to work on my puzzle with me?"

Cam groaned and Nicki pouted. "It's all she does," Cam whispered. "There's nothing more boring in the whole world—watching her put together her jigsaw puzzles."

Kiel put his hand to his mouth and called back, "Thanks! It sounds like fun, but we have an errand we have to take care of."

"What errand?" she asked.

He glanced down at the kids. "The calves! We have to see how they came through all the rain!"

"Calves?" Peggy repeated as Kiel quickly herded Cam and Nicki off the porch and down the lane. "Daniel didn't mention a problem."

"It's complicated!" Kiel called back, and then trotted them away.

Once out of earshot of the houses they slowed to a walk. The productive put-putter of Daniel's tractor droned somewhere out of sight. Kiel would have thought the fields too muddy to work, but he guessed that a farmer couldn't afford any idle time during the growing season.

"I gather that the calves—the bridge calves—are a secret?" Kiel asked.

"You mean the little spider things?"

"I thought they looked and felt more like crabs, but yes."

They shuffled along a while before Cam finally replied. "Uncle Daniel can be like Gamma sometimes." The boy seemed to lose the words to go on.

"In what way?" Kiel asked.

Nicki chimed in. "He says that Cam is getting too old to be playing around with fantasies. Uncle Daniel says that Cam should be either in school, or learning a trade."

"Learning a trade?" Kiel repeated incredulously. "You're in—what—fifth grade?"

"Sixth. Starting sixth this fall."

"Does he want you to maybe be a chimney sweep?"

Cam looked at him, perplexed. Nicki said, "What's that?"

Kiel chuckled. "Fireplaces are used now for occasional entertainment instead of every day for heat. When used a lot, a chimney builds up soot. If it gets too thick, the chimney can catch on fire. A chimney sweep is a person who goes down to clean it. In old England they used young boys because they were the only ones that could fit down the tight space."

"Not little girls?" Nicki asked.

"Not little girls. Little girls worked in clothes factories."

Cam seemed to shudder thinking about being dropped down a chimney.

"Well, today I'll be the fall guy," Kiel offered. "We'll goof off, and I'll take the heat."

When they came to the old bridge, they stood around the hole in the road, looking into the darkness. Kiel was very aware of his bandaged finger and the scabs on Cam's thumb. "I didn't think to bring my flashlight," he said.

Cam reached into his pocket and pulled out a key ring. A small light was attached by a fine chain. He handed it to Kiel.

"Well, that's unfortunate. It was my only good excuse."

He got down on his hands and knees, telling himself that they were just tiny . . . things. How much harm could they do? How much harm could a scorpion do? A black widow? A whole crowd of black widows?

Better not think about that. They hadn't done any more harm than a cornered mouse might. Yet.

He leaned in, being careful to keep his head away from the edges. He swung the little beam around, and breathed relief that nothing tiny and silver reflected the light. He looked everywhere, making sure that none were hiding. Satisfied, he straightened up and lowered his feet into the hole. Now that he'd broken off part of the edge getting out, he had room to squat with his knees against his chin. From this angle, he could study the bottom side of the bridge I-beams. The sections eaten away—for that is exactly what it looked like—shone and sparkled like jewels. These were metal surfaces that had very recently been exposed—there hadn't been enough time to begin oxidation. The eaten cavities were speckled with a myriad of tiny concave cavities, as though a beehive had been sliced in half and then shrunk by a factor of ten. Whether the tiny excavations had been made by some sort of dissolving acid, or mechanical scooping was difficult to tell, although Kiel suspected that acid would not leave such a mirror-perfect smooth surface.

"They must be nocturnal," he concluded crawling out and handing Cam back his light.

The boy shook his head. "We've always seen them during the day. Mom wouldn't let us come after dark."

Kiel smiled. "Would you have come if she'd let you?"

Cam thought about it for perhaps two seconds, and then shook his head vigorously.

"I would," Nicki, piped. "I'm not afraid."

"That's easy to say now," her brother countered. "You'd change your tune if it was pitch dark outside."

The little girl folded her arms across her chest and stared defiantly at the two of them.

"Well," Kiel continued, "if they're not nocturnal, then I guess I must have spooked them. Maybe they're gone for good."

Cam mulled this. "I don't think so. There were a couple of days when they weren't here, at least not in the hole."

"You've seen them someplace else?"

Cam hesitated. "I'm not sure. I think so."

He led Kiel along the bank a short distance to where a small section of the dirt had collapsed into the stream. Kiel would have guessed that it was maybe a muskrat den that had been flooded by the rising water. Cam stopped ten feet away, put his finger to his lips, and then squatted down. Kiel squatted quietly next to him, but Nicki stayed back, sitting on the ground.

"I think they sometimes come out that hole," Cam whispered.

"You saw them?" Kiel whispered back.

The boy looked conflicted. "I think so. They were . . . different."

"Different? In what—"

Cam had put his hand on Kiel's arm. The boy pointed towards the hole. Kiel was looking for tiny ant-sized crabs, and so didn't notice at first what Cam was referring to. Then he saw it: a three-inch section of the ground near the collapse heaved ever so slightly, as though a buried muskrat had woken up and taken a deep breath. Kiel didn't understand how tiny ant-sized creatures could move so much dirt. The ground settled back and then was still.

"Let's wait," Cam whispered, and Kiel nodded consent, sitting back on his rear to be more comfortable.

After a few minutes, Nicki crawled up and tried to whisper, but she wasn't very proficient, and her words came out almost as loud as if she hadn't tried. "I'm bored. I want to go back to Gamma's."

Cam rolled his eyes and sighed. "Go ahead, then," he whispered harshly.

"I want somebody to walk with me."

"What? Are you scared?"

She first shook her head, and then nodded.

"I thought you weren't afraid to come out here even in the dark—oh, never mind."

Cam started to get up, and Kiel, not thinking, said, "I'll take her back."

Instantly he regretted it. It was so easy to forget. *Never, ever allow yourself to be alone with a young child.* Did he need to tattoo it on the back of his hand? "Actually," he whispered, "maybe you should, Cam."

The boy shrugged and stood up a second time.

"I, uh, don't want to get caught by your aunt Peggy," Kiel explained.

Cam shrugged again and headed off with his sister.

Lame. Totally lame. It was the only thing that had come to mind.

Kiel thought he saw the ground move a bit once before Cam came back, but he couldn't be sure. His observation partner settled down next to him without a word, and they began their watchful vigilance.

Kiel was impressed with the boy's patience. He sat squatting on his heels for twenty minutes before sitting back and wrapping his arms around his knees. He didn't move for another half hour.

Their patience was rewarded when the herd of miniature calves finally emerged.

The herd, though, had cooperated and collected together into a single, coordinated entity. It had been bizarre enough to witness the individual tiny creatures at work harvesting iron, but to see them operating together to create a complex organism was downright unnerving. It was as though Kiel was witnessing millions of years of evolution, from free-floating single-celled life, to highly functional multi-cellular vertebrates, in a matter of minutes. The silvery structure pushed up through the loose dirt, and at first looked like a mass of crushed tinfoil. But as it pushed farther above the surface, it morphed before Kiel's eyes, forming and taking shape. He could just discern the thousands upon thousands of individual crab creatures grasping each other with their many entwined legs, each pulling and turning against its neighbors like the cells of a muscle, extending an upright appendage here, and pushing out a leg there. Within the span of one of Kiel's held breaths, the mass of miniature crabs had emerged and completed the metamorphosis. A complete, unified creature sat in the freshly turned dirt, composing itself after the self-birth. It shook once, and then twice, shrugging off loose earth.

It looked to Kiel like perhaps a caricature of a rabbit, huddled on four legs, elongated, oversized ears thrust skyward. But the transformation wasn't quite complete. The general form had been established, and now the various parts extended into functional action. The ears snaked outwards, flattened and cupped, like a cobra puffing before a strike. Kiel thought the thing had lost control when it began to flail mindlessly in a frantic dance of chaotic motion. He saw, though, that there was a pattern to the complex dance. He imagined that two hawks bound together at their feet might make similar flapping, groping motions.

His analogy found life, for through the swirling cloud of dust raised by the whirling ears-cum-wings, Kiel caught glimpses of the creature rising into the air. Five feet above the ground, it seemed to falter and hover a moment, as though finding its balance, before continuing its vertical ascent. Above the swirling dust cloud, level with the tops of the trees along the bank, it paused again. It moved sideways a few feet towards them, and then both Cam and Kiel cried out and fell back as it dove straight at them. Kiel recovered to find the thing looming over them. It was no bigger than a large crow, but the franticly whirring wings created an angry burring wail that seemed to clutch hungrily at his heart. He had the horrifying sense that ten thousand tiny crabs were all studying him in unison, collectively deciding his fate. An instant later, it rose up and away, pausing some hundred feet above before shooting off in a straight line towards Chippewa Ridge. Kiel and Cam sat gaping, dumbly staring as the otherworldly apparition disappeared into the distance.

They sat frozen, mute. The cicadas had gone silent, and now slowly, one-by-one took up their song of summer and heat.

"What is it?" Cam finally whispered, as though afraid it might hear and return.

"I don't know," Kiel replied. "But I guess we were lucky to be here at just the right time."

Cam turned to stare at him with wide, stunned eyes. "We were lucky?" The boy gazed off towards the low line of hills, and a goofy grin spread across his face. He looked at Kiel. "Yeah! We were lucky!"

Chapter 4

"We have to tell somebody," Kiel said, "maybe the science department of a local college."

Cam moved a little pile of dirt around idly with his toe. He gave one quick shrug.

The collective corporeal beast had departed some minutes before, and Kiel was recovering from the shock. "You don't want anybody else involved, do you?" he ventured.

Cam seemed about to comment, but instead just shrugged again.

Kiel realized that before he had shown up, these strange creatures had been the sole domain of Cam and his sister. The tiny-crab herd—the "calves"—had revealed themselves to be even stranger than suspected, downright monstrous in fact. But the crablets had been *their* monsters. Cam had welcomed Kiel into the fold, but did he now have the prerogative to usurp control just because he was the adult?

He had an idea. "Hey! Your mom studied biology in college. She might have some ideas."

That just seemed to trouble Cam even more and he sighed and sat down on the ground. "She'd just make me stay away."

"That doesn't sound like a bad idea. I was thinking the same thing—for myself!"

"Besides," Cam went on, ignoring Kiel's comment, "if they do turn out to be dangerous somehow—"

"If?"

"If they do, then that would just be more ammunition for my dad."

"I don't understand."

Cam looked him in the eye, as though gauging his trustworthiness. "My dad is threatening to take us—Nicki and me—if my mom doesn't come back, or at least do exactly what he says."

"You think he could get a judge to give him custody just because your mom lets you get too close to some weird little animals?"

Cam shrugged. He communicated a lot with those. "My dad's a lawyer."

"Ah. I guess that says it all. Well, we'll keep it our secret for now. But we'll have to come up with a plan."

What Kiel was thinking was that as the adult maybe he not only had the prerogative but in fact the duty to wield some control.

It could be so difficult. Kiel wondered whether perhaps he shouldn't just stay away from kids altogether—all kids.

ж ж ж

Kiel sat on the porch swing watching the barn cats tussle with a frayed length of rope as the sun slid towards evening amber. He decided that he could get used to this life. He'd come back from their Close Encounter to rest a few minutes on the sofa, and woke a couple of hours later to find that he'd had himself a nice long nap. The night spent in the hole had been a long interrupted series of thin, troubled layers of sleep, almost worse than no sleep at all. After his nap he felt much better, and even endured an hour helping Peggy with her farm-scene jigsaw puzzle. There was irony in the choice of puzzle, but Kiel's mood was too good to contemplate it.

Now, his stomach full of Mrs. Bakke's hearty dinner, the porch swing seemed exactly the proper place for him in the universe's scheme of harmony and balance. He knew that hospitality can turn to hostility after a few days when everybody but the guest is working to earn their keep. For now, however, he was going to enjoy it while it lasted.

The screen door swung open, and he caught a whiff of Julie's perfume. "Nothing like a Wisconsin sunset," she observed, sprinkling fish food into the aquarium of baby trout.

He looked at her and grinned. "Beauty by contrast?"

She threw him a quick glance and smiled when she saw that he was joking. "I suppose a sunset would appear more majestic when set against an unremarkable horizon," she agreed.

She sat down on the steps and wrapped her arms around her shins so that her chin rested on her knees.

"I'm just used to a landscape full of rolling mountains," he explained.

"In Baltimore?" She looked at him. "Daniel told me that you grew up there."

Lies! He hated always being on guard to keep everything straight. "The Appalachians aren't very far west of the city. We lived for a while closer to them."

He scrolled through maps in his mind to confirm that this was true.

"In Fredericksburg, maybe?" she asked. "I have some cousins who moved there."

"Fredericksburg—yeah, pretty close to there."

"Wait! Not Fredericksburg," she corrected, "that's south of D.C. I meant Frederick. That's the town west of Baltimore."

"Oh, yeah. Frederick, not Fredericksburg. I still get them mixed up."

He hated the lies! She seemed not to notice his stumble. She just gazed tranquilly at the deepening crimson sky.

She turned her zenful gaze to him. "Thanks, by the way, for the support at lunch."

He looked at her quizzically.

"You stuck up for me when Peggy started in again with the clumsy hints about wanting the house. I was about ready to use my stun gun on her."

"You have one of those tasers?"

"It's just a wand. Cam bought it for me. I'm not sure for whom he thinks I might need it. Anyway," she said, placing her hand lightly on his for emphasis, "thanks for sticking up for me."

He'd already forgotten the incident. "It was your mom who came to the rescue. She's one sharp cookie."

"It's easier to seem sharp when you don't let propriety get in the way of your opinions. But, yes, she is a sharp cookie. Daniel and I could never get anything over on her." She looked at him. "What? What are you smiling about?"

"Earlier you used 'whom,' and just now you said 'Daniel and I.' That's not very Wisconsinian. Most people would just say 'Daniel and me.' "

She tilted her head, humbly shrugging off the compliment. "Daniel and I used to read a lot when we were kids. We were voracious. We used to challenge each other with grammar and pronunciation—our own best teachers." She sighed. "I don't have much time for reading now. Daniel hardly reads at all anymore. Running a farm is a fulltime job twice over."

She watched the growing sunset glory a second and then turned back. "And that's Wisconsinitian, not Wisconsinian."

"Is that the proper Native American pronunciation?"

"As close as we can get to the original Algonquian, I guess. Or hope."

After a few moments of quiet, she asked, "Is that where you live now—Frederick?"

He looked into her eyes, and he felt a palpable pain at the thought of uttering one more lie to this kind and lovely woman. He took a deep breath. *To hell with it.* "No. Altoona. That's in central Pennsylvania. Right in the heart of the Appalachians, in fact. At least, that's where I was living before I took off."

"That's where you taught high school science?"

He stared at the frayed rope sprawled forlornly in the fading light, abandoned by the cats for some evening prowling. The science teacher lie was already out there. He gave the tiniest of nods and shrugged. He decided that implying assent but not actually saying the words wasn't as evil.

"It doesn't seem like a happy memory," she suggested gently.

He shrugged again. If he opened his mouth to speak, he'd have to lie.

She extended her legs down the steps and leaned back onto her elbows. "Do you know that I'm separated from my husband?" she asked so quietly that he wasn't sure she was even talking to him.

"Brandon," he affirmed. He glanced at her. "I got that from Daniel, not the kids."

That part was actually true. They hadn't told him their father's name.

She chuckled. "Good for them." Her face turned serious again. "It's a difficult situation. He's pretty much calling all the shots."

"He's running for U.S. Senator."

She nodded soberly. "He's a man with many powerful connections. Not one to be trifled with."

Kiel tried to think of some way to bring up the custody issue without giving away that Cam had already divulged it. "At least you've got the kids."

She seemed to sink into herself. "For now."

She sat up and covered her face with her hands.

Oh shit! Now he'd done it. "I'm sorry . . . I didn't mean to—"

"No, it's okay," she reassured, straightening up and taking a deep, cleansing breath. "He won't get them. I have to believe that. I'll do whatever it takes—whatever." She said this like a Mafioso delivering a non-too-subtle threat. "I handed him the first round, but now the gloves are off."

"The first round—by choosing to leave?"

"Well, that as well; I guess I actually handed him the first two rounds. I was talking about something I screwed up earlier. It was a minor mistake, but he's managed to blow it up all out of proportion."

Kiel nodded. Politeness dissuaded him from begging her to go on with more details. "I understand he's a lawyer. They're probably very good at that. It's sort of their job—to exaggerate and blow things out of proportion."

She gave him a sardonic grin. "Marrying a lawyer is like taking in a baby tiger for a pet. It's perfectly safe as long as it wants to be."

She looked at him a moment, blinked, and then studied her clasped hands. "In my second year at college—before I met Brandon—I was arrested for possession of cocaine."

She glanced up at him and he realized he probably looked shocked. "It happens," he assured.

It happens? He'd been taken off guard.

"The stupid, tragic part is that I didn't even *have* any. I'd never even tried the stuff—probably never would. I was in Milwaukee with some friends. We were driving around and it turned out that they each had some on them. I pretty much knew they were using, but I didn't know that one of them was a small-time dealer. The city vice cops had been watching him, and it was my bad luck that they grabbed him while I was there visiting."

"Don't they actually have to find some on you—I mean physically on you?"

"You'd think. It was my car, though."

"Oops. Still, if your friends had stuck up for you—you know, testified that you didn't even know they had it—"

"Maybe. It all comes down to a good lawyer, though, and mine was a public defender."

"Why? Didn't your mom and dad—"

"Pop's philosophy was that if you hung out with friends that were criminals, you were a criminal. In retrospect, I think he may have regretted not helping, but he'd never admit it. I was just one of dozens of cases for this public defender, and the fifteen minutes he had to spare got me a suspended sentence on a plea bargain."

"So at least you didn't go to jail."

"No, but I was now a felon. From that point forward I couldn't work in a government research lab, nor would I even be able to teach school. That's a big reason I dropped out of college. What was the point?"

"Yikes."

"Yikes indeed. But I haven't even gotten to the stupid part yet. A few months ago one of those very same friends came to visit in Oshkosh. Guess what she had concealed in her purse?"

"Coke?"

"Nope. Less than twenty grams of pot."

"And she didn't have medical permission?"

"Yes, she did. She was careful about that. She had all the paperwork. Small quantities of medical marijuana are legal, but only according to local ordinance. Federal law still says it's a crime. That time, and maybe that time only, the Oshkosh police decided to abide by federal law."

"I don't get it. Why would they—" She was giving him another sardonic grin. "Uh-oh. You mean that your husband *arranged* the bust?"

She just raised her eyebrows.

"That's crazy! You'd already left him?"

She shook her head. "No, but he guessed the truth, that I was preparing. He's smart. And he's ruthless. Blackmail is a very effective means of control. He knew I could do a lot of damage to his chances at Senator."

Kiel absorbed this. "It was your car again? You were also charged with possession?"

"Not at all. But I was on record as associating with a known two-time drug felon. My friend will now probably go to jail."

Kiel shook his head. "I still don't get it. Surely you're not on probation anymore. What law have you broken by associating with a known felon?"

She sighed. "Now we come full circle."

It took Kiel a moment to remember how they'd started. "The kids!"

"Yep."

"If it comes to a custody battle, he'll use this against you."

"He'll try to prove that I'm an unfit mother. Not only might he get custody, but I could be forced into a controlled visitation situation. Effectively, I won't be their mom anymore."

Kiel took a deep breath and let it out slowly. "It is a mess, isn't it?"

"It is a mess indeed." She glanced around and lowered her voice. "And the worst of it is that I don't think he really even wants custody, other than as a weapon against me, and that it looks good on his political resume."

"I'm . . . sorry."

It sounded lame. But what could he say?

She unclasped her hands, touched the fingertips together in contemplation a moment, and then smoothed her jeans, as though preparing to get up and walk away, perhaps from the bad vibes. She didn't though. Instead, she placed her palms on the porch behind her, leaned back, and asked, "Do you have a special someone waiting back in Altoona?"

It had to come up eventually. He had prepared a story that he'd been using since Akron, but he decided instead to tell her the truth. Or at least a small part. "I had—past tense. I told Daniel that I was between jobs, but in fact I have no job waiting. I'm just running—running away."

He felt his pulse quicken. Getting this close to the actual truth terrified him.

"Running from what?" she asked, turning to him now, giving him her complete attention.

He felt the tip of the knife touch against his Adam's Apple, and he knew that he was too chicken to press it farther. He stuck to the half-truth. "From that special someone."

"It didn't work out?"

"If it were that simple, that it just didn't work out, I wouldn't have quit my job and taken off. Working it out or not working it out implies that the two parties either find the balance to live together, or go their separate ways. In our case there wasn't two separate paths for us to separate onto."

Her brows were knitted together. "I don't understand."

"I wouldn't expect you to. I'm being obtuse. I'm sorry. It's just . . . hard to face the truth. Her name is Maria. She's sick, and I couldn't take it anymore."

Kiel felt like he was suffocating. His chest muscles seemed paralyzed. He'd never spoken those words before, and saying them aloud was like hearing a judge announce the death penalty.

"Kiel!" Julie exclaimed. "Are you okay?"

He realized that he'd stopped swinging and was just sitting, staring into the gathering darkness. He shook his head to clear it. "I've never admitted it before."

Julie was watching him, concerned. "Is she . . . bed-ridden? Requiring constant care?"

Kiel stared at her. What was she talking about? "No! Oh no. I could handle that. She's schizophrenic. Most of the time, she's perfectly normal. But sometimes, she just goes nuts. And when she does, I mean she's *really* nuts. I thought I could hang in there, just weather through the crazy bouts, but I was wrong. It wore me down, and I . . . I just couldn't take it anymore. So I ran away."

They sat in silence. The trees were now just silhouettes against a blue-black sky. Thin wisps of high pink cirrus clouds had faded to dull, dark gray smudges. Platoons of crickets, waking to the night darkness they inhabited, joined together in a syncopated hypnotic chorus.

"You never married?" Julie asked.

"No. God no. We weren't even living together."

Julie spoke softly, like she didn't want to disturb the cricket anthem. "You're not her caregiver, Kiel."

He didn't say anything. His mind felt numb.

"If you were her brother, or father, or even a close cousin . . . just because you date someone, doesn't automatically make you responsible forever. That's what marriage vows are for."

It would be so easy to let it all go if that were the whole truth.

If only Maria had seen that it wasn't going to work out. If only she'd just let him go.

Chapter 5

Kiel woke to bright sunshine streaming through a crack in the curtains. Like a spotlight, the brilliant light splashed across a photo on a small table. The picture centered on a burly man who seemed barely cooperative about being captured. He held two children, each by a hand. All three were dressed in their Sunday best. Kiel assumed the boy, perhaps Cam's age, to be Daniel, although it wasn't obvious. The younger girl, however, was clearly Julie. The little half-smile that invited you to join in on some privately held fun, the soft brown hair falling casually across her forehead to rest precariously above one eyebrow, ready with a little shake to fall and conceal inner secrets, the delicate shoulders that called out to be hugged, all were miniature, doll-sized features of the woman he'd met less that twenty-four hours before.

"Ki-el!"

He jerked his head around, and he realized that Cam, standing there with his hands on his hips, had addressed him once already from some place in his sleep.

"Wa?" Kiel mumbled, "Is it time to get up?"

The boy sighed impatiently. "It's, like, eight-thirty. Gamma says that you can stay in bed, but if you take any longer, you'll be getting up for lunch instead of breakfast."

Cam was dressed, and had obviously been up for awhile. They had shared the room, with Kiel sleeping in the twin bed that Cam's sister normally used. Nicki had been relegated to sleep with her mom.

"Right. I'm up. Er, I'll have to get dressed."

Cam nodded, and after a moment caught the message. "I'll be downstairs," he said, closing the door behind him.

Kiel had no pajamas and had slept in one of his two pairs of undershorts. Both had developed holes while on the road, and some people of a more puritan sense would consider the resulting view to render him effectively naked.

He was still yawning when he entered the kitchen to find that Mrs. Bakke had been given advance warning. Breakfast had already been prepared, served, and cleared away (this was a working farm, after all), but his host motioned for him to sit down at the table as she took a plate of eggs, sausage, home fries, and pancakes from the microwave. "Had to nuke it," she grumbled, dropping it down in front of him with little regard for decorum or even several cubes of potatoes bouncing off the plate and across the table. "The pancakes are going to feel like rubber."

Kiel had the sense that he'd ruined an opportunity for her to properly perform her job. "I'm, uh, normally an early riser," he explained as she busied herself cleaning a counter that looked already spotless. "I guess that sleeping in a hole in the rain the night before threw me off."

She whipped the washcloth over the sink like Indiana Jones.

"Sorry," he added.

She seemed to finally relent. "Oh, don't fret. Nobody would be up until noon if I didn't crack the whip around here."

"Or the washcloth," he added.

She gave him a puzzled look.

"I was up at 5:30, Mom," Julie said, coming in to pour a cup of coffee.

"And I was already in the kitchen waiting," her mother reminded her.

"But you also went to bed at 9:30."

"Like decent folk do."

"Sleep wars," Kiel observed, trying to talk around a mouthful of pancakes.

He stopped chewing when he realized that both women were staring at him.

Suddenly Julie burst out laughing. "You said 'sleep wars.' I thought you said, 'sheep roars.' "

"I thought he was talking about strip bars," Mrs. Bakke added chuckling.

Kiel swallowed. "I guess there was a good reason why we got scolded for talking with our mouths full."

Julie sat at the table across from Kiel. She looked mostly at the coffee in her cup and the view out the window, only now and then glancing over at him. He had the idea that she normally wouldn't sit down and relax over a mid-morning cup of coffee.

Cam came in and plopped down next to his mom. He seemed impatient about something, fidgeting and sighing dramatically. Nicki called several times from the next room for him to come join her, and he finally yelled back, suggesting that she shut up already.

"Is that what you want?" Julie asked him gently. "Do you want her to ignore you?"

He shook his head grudgingly. The boy glanced up at Kiel. "Mom says that when you tell somebody to shut up, you're giving them permission to pretend you don't exist," he explained.

"But, why?" she pressed.

He sighed. "Because it's a very rude thing to do. You are basically telling them that they don't count. And if they don't count, then they might as well not exist. So when they ignore you, they are simply doing what you asked in the first place."

Kiel looked from the son to the mother. He wasn't sure whether to be more impressed with her lesson or her son's ability to absorb it.

"So, where will be you off to next?" Julie asked, looking at him.

With his plate only half eaten, and the memory of a soft mattress and clean sheets still fresh in his mind, Kiel found it difficult to think about a next destination that, as likely as not, would be another wet field somewhere. "I was making for Green Bay when the rain derailed me."

Sloppy! He never revealed his plans.

"Really? Why there?"

"An old college buddy."

He would normally have gone on to describe in detail this fictional character, but he didn't have the heart for it with Julie. The truth was that he was planning on spending a few days at the library there doing research—preparing his case, getting some background on the laws related to his charge, maybe even contact a lawyer. The fact that he'd run away was going to be a huge hurdle. He suspected that a lawyer probably wasn't even allowed to work with him while he was a fugitive.

"Well, what do you know!" Julie enthused. "I have a college friend that lives there as well."

Kiel wasn't sure where this was heading; it was going to get sticky if she offered to give him a ride and take the opportunity to visit her friend.

Mrs. Bakke saved him, but he almost regretted being saved. "You're welcome to stay on here awhile," she offered, finally sitting down with a cup of coffee herself. "But one day's the limit as a guest. From here on out you'll be a boarder."

"Er, sure. I'd be happy to pay my—"

"Nobody's talking money. We got chores aplenty."

He nodded. He had no revenue, and although not a problem yet, his stash of money would eventually run out. Any way to save it was welcomed.

"You can start with some weeding. The truck patch looks like it wants to be a jungle when it grows up. All this rain will've softened the ground—should be easy pulling."

"I have a good relationship with mud. Sounds right up my alley."

"First I need you to do some babysitting, though."

"Gamma!" Cam protested.

"Oh, you know it's just an expression." To Kiel, she continued, "Julie and me, we have to go to the church and help get ready for the bake sale. I'd normally ask Peg, but, well it'd be nice not to have to."

Kiel understood completely, but gathered that this was an unspoken elaboration.

Cam seemed not to know what to do with himself. If he wasn't sprawled on the living room floor, he was lounging on the porch swing, idly flipping pages of a comic book. He didn't seem to be able to remain in one place more than five minutes.

It was when Julie and her mother climbed in the sedan and drove off down the lane that it became clear that the boy had been just waiting for them to leave. "We've got at least two hours," he declared, all action and energy now. He glanced in the house where his sister was playing with a set of Legos. "She'll be all right here."

"Whoa!" Kiel exclaimed. "What are you talking about?"

The boy screwed up his mouth, considering. "The colony. I think they migrate about the same time every day."

The name seemed perfectly suited. The boy was on the ball. "What makes you think this?"

"It was about the same time when Nicki and I first saw them leave the remote station."

"Remote station?"

"The hole," he explained. He seemed impatient that Kiel didn't already know this. "Where they took off from yesterday."

"Two times doesn't prove a pattern."

"It's one hundred percent of known examples so far."

"True . . . why do you call it the remote station?"

"It's obvious. That's not their permanent home."

"Why?"

"Why would they collect together and fly off?"

"I don't know—maybe to visit their actual remote station?"

"Why would they go someplace else and then come back?"

"Turn it around: why would they be here—at the hole—only temporarily?"

Cam grinned. He was holding a full house. "To mine iron."

Kiel stared at him. The kid was right. He had to be. The eaten-away cavities of the bridge. The shiny, non-corroded surface—recently exposed. The screeching sound he'd heard—it had been the crablets scrapping away thin layers of the bridge. "Where would they be taking it?"

Tumbling one after another in Kiel's mind came a crowd of other questions: Why did they need metal? How could tiny insect-like creatures scrape layers of metal from a bridge? What in God's name *were* they?

"To their home base," Cam said, answering the only verbalized question. "Which is why we have to GO! NOW! Before it's too late!"

Kiel nodded vaguely, dazed with the concept of a colony of unimagined creatures mining iron from an old bridge and then incorporating into some kind of collective flying beast to carry it home.

Cam disappeared into the house and came back with a small backpack that he was stuffing a camera into. "Let's go," he urged, swinging his arm in an arc and trotting off down the dirt track.

"Hold on!" Kiel called, coming to his senses.

Cam stopped reluctantly and turned.

"Nicki is NOT all right by herself. We can't leave her."

The boy scowled, looking off into the distance where the old bridge lay and then back to Kiel. "Fine! Stay here with her. I'll go by myself!"

"You can't go by yourself! I'm supposed to watch you—both of you!"

And you can't leave me here alone with her, he added to himself. But he also knew how much this meant to Cam. "Okay!" he called. "Wait just a minute. We'll take Nicki along."

Cam started to protest, but Kiel ignored him and went into the house. Nicki wasn't thrilled about going. It was boring. Kiel had to promise to play a game with her when they got back.

Like Dorothy and her anthropomorphic entourage, the three of them trouped off to see the Wizard. They stopped a hundred feet from the bridge. "We need to set up watch stations," Cam directed, rooting through his pack. He pulled out a walkie-talkie and handed it to Kiel, then studied the bridge. "I couldn't tell which side they followed last time. Could you?" he asked.

"Mmm, not really. If I had to guess, I'd say the other bank."

The stream wound its way out from the hills of the Chippewa Ridge in the near distance. It wasn't obvious which side the colony collective would follow . . . if it flew at all today.

"Come on," Cam ordered, starting forward towards the bridge.

"Cam!" Kiel called.

The boy stopped and turned.

"Stay here with your sister a minute. Let me check it out."

The pre-teen didn't seem happy about being relegated to a chaperone, but complied.

Kiel found that the hole looked the same as they'd left it the day before. He hadn't thought to bring his flashlight. He could ask Cam for his little keychain light, but he was pretty confident about the situation. He found a stick and, leaning carefully down into the hole, swept it around along the underside. Nothing seemed to fall. Commending himself on his bravery, he gingerly felt along the underside of the I-beam. Nothing. He couldn't tell if more of the metal was missing.

He stood up and brushed the dirt from his knees. The exit point along the bank was next. He was more nervous about this part. Taking each step slowly and softly, he approached the bank of the stream. Either things had changed, or he just hadn't taken note of everything the day before. He remembered just one hole next to the water, which had now significantly receded. Before him, the ground seemed to have been plowed up in a three-foot radius, as though there had been a number of exits since yesterday.

Maybe there was a chance to see something after all.

"Okay," he said quietly to Cam when he came back. "How do you want to do this?"

Cam took them across the bridge, nearly black with rust, but still sound. They scolded Nicki when she started jumping in the middle in order to create a little storm of rust flakes that fell, to be quickly swept away in the stream.

On the far side, the old highway wandered off to destinations unknown, but the trio left it immediately to make their way along the stream towards Chippewa Ridge. The field on this side had been left fallow, and the going was slow as they worked their way through tangles of weeds. Nicki had the worst of it, and Kiel picked her up and carried her on his shoulder, hoping that she'd soon get tired of calling out "Giddy-up!" and "Gallop, boy!" She didn't, but luckily the fallow field ended after a couple of hundred yards when they came to a stone fence, where rocks of all sizes had been piled in neat, knee-high walls along the perimeters of the fields. They had been gathered when the fields had first been worked untold decades before. Thick brush and small trees grew along both sides where the ploughs didn't reach.

A path, made either by deer or people, led across the fence, and Cam crossed over. Kiel put Nicki down and they followed.

The field on the other side, although not planted, was devoid of most weeds, carpeted instead with thick, heavy grass, clumped and intertwined. Passage would be almost as difficult as the fallow field. Here Cam paused. "You stay here with Nicki," he instructed and showed Kiel how to turn on the walkie-talkie. "Call me if you see anything coming."

The boy started off, stepping high to navigate the sea of grass.

"I thought this was the end of Uncle Daniels land!" Nicki called to her brother.

He lifted his arm and waved off her concern without turning around.

"Cam!" Kiel called.

The boy stopped, paused, and then turned, giving Nicki a hard look.

"Is this true?" Kiel asked.

The boy let out a frustrated breath. "Old Tagget won't mind."

"You're sure?"

"Sure I'm sure."

Tagget. He'd heard that name before. He remembered. Daniel had said that Brandon wanted to buy some land from him. Maybe this field was part of it.

"Tagget's mean," Nicki said.

"He won't mind!" Cam repeated forcefully. "Anyway, he never even comes back here!"

The boy turned and started off again, practically leaping along, getting away quickly before Kiel could object.

Kiel let him go. What harm were they doing? It was one thing to trespass in somebody's back yard, but they couldn't even see Tagget's house.

He and Nicki sat down on appropriately sized rocks and watched until Cam reached the far side of the field and disappeared after crossing that stone fence. After a few minutes, Kiel thumbed the "talk" button on the walkie-talkie. "Cam, can you hear me?"

After some seconds there was a pop of static and Cam's voice said, "Yeah. Just fine."

"How far are you going?"

Static. "I'm almost there—the edge of this field."

Kiel wasn't sure if "this field" was the next one, or another farther still. "Call me when you're in place."

"Roger."

"Who's Roger?" Nicki asked.

"That's just something we say to indicate that we understand," he explained.

"I know that. But who is he?"

Kiel laughed. "I don't know. I don't think it's actually a person."

"Then, why do we say it?"

"Umm, why do we say any word? It's just something we all agree on the meaning of."

"Why not just say 'okay,' or 'understood'?"

Kiel looked at her. "Do you really want to know, or do you just want to hear me talk?"

She sat, pouting at his reprimand. He didn't mean to make her feel bad. "Sometimes we use whole words when we're talking about letters of the alphabet—so that the other person will know what we mean. The letters D and T sound very similar when we say them, so we might say 'D as in dog,' and 'T as in tattoo.' Maybe the word 'roger' was used in the military for the letter R."

She looked up at him defiantly. "So, what does the R stand for?"

He grinned. Time to take it out. "R stands for 'received,' as in 'I have received your transmission.' Are you satisfied?"

Kiel had no idea if this was true, but it sounded good.

"Why didn't you just say that—"

She was interrupted by Cam. "Okay," his voice said over the walkie-talkie. "I'm in position. The far edge of the second field."

"So now we wait."

A pop of static. "Roger."

"If R stands for received—"

"Shh," Kiel urged. "We have to listen for them. In fact, your ears are probably much better than mine," he lied. "I want you to stand up on that big rock and tell me if you hear anything."

She took her job seriously, turning her head slowly back and forth like a little human radar system, and Kiel was glad for the peace it provided him.

The morning was getting warm, and he swatted at flies that seemed intent on crawling up his nose. When they were back at the bridge, Chippewa Ridge had seemed distant, but he now saw that the hills—the Altoona speed bumps—weren't even as big as he had thought. They'd already come nearly half-way to the beginnings. He had been fooled by the thick covering of brush that he'd mistaken for a full forest of trees. He guessed that the soil must be thin on the ridge, otherwise there *would* be trees. Towards the top of the hill, something glinted in the sun. Kiel guessed at first that it was a piece of broken bottle or discarded foil wrapper. The point of light shone brilliant and constant, though. He remembered seeing it earlier, in fact. He doubted that something as small as a piece of bottle or wrapper would reflect so intensely and consistently over such a wide distance. Maybe it was a large piece of glass or mirror. Maybe it was the wreckage of a small, private airplane.

Maybe he should reign in his imagination, he decided.

The buzzing drone of the flies was hypnotic, and probably would have eventually put him to sleep if he didn't have to keep slapping at them. Suddenly, Nicki said, "It's coming."

Kiel waited. Let her realize her mistake. She climbed down off the rock. "Aren't you going to call Cam?" she asked.

"What do they sound like?"

But then he heard it himself, an aggressive burring roar, like some giant mutant bee. He didn't remember it being so loud the day before.

He thumbed the walkie-talkie. "Cam, it's coming."

Static pop. "Really?"

"Yeah, I think so."

Then he saw it . . . but there were two—no, three! They glided over the brush and small trees that lined each side of the stream. The ear-wings were blurs of motion. At a glance, they looked like a miniature version of an army helicopter patrol. The movie *Apocalypse Now* came to mind.

He realized that Nicki was huddled next to him; she was clasping his arm in her little hand. "I'm scared!" she wailed.

"There's nothing to be scared about. They won't hurt you."

The squadron of incorporated crablets was now parallel with them, not fifty feet away, following the stream as though searching for miniature enemy gunboats.

Suddenly one of them veered off course, right towards them. Nicki screamed and tried to bury her head in his armpit. He wrapped his arms protectively around the little girl and watched the approaching enigma. It paused ten feet away. The breeze it produced fluttered his hair. Those whirring ear-wings alone would make a formidable mincing weapon. It dawned on him that he might have been wrong when he told Nicki that they wouldn't hurt them. The multi-creatured beast seemed to study them, even though Kiel could discern no recognizable eyes. The lack of familiar features such as an eye or beak or even a talon rendered the thing eerily abominable. The alien apparition rose a few inches, and then circled them slowly, deliberately. Finally, as suddenly as it had decided to veer off course to investigate them, it took off to catch up to its companions, now nearly out of sight along the stream.

Cam!

He let go of Nicki and jumped up, thumbing the walkie-talkie. "Cam, hide! Do you hear me? Hide!"

Nothing.

Shit!

Nicki was crying hysterically next to him, hugging his leg.

He took Nicki firmly by the shoulders. "Listen," he urged, trying to sound calm, "I'm going to go see about your brother. Stay here."

This set her to wailing even louder.

He crouched down and peered into her tear-soaked face. "Nicki, do you want me to help Cam?"

She continued crying loudly, but nodded vigorously.

"Then you have to stay here. Lie down and stay quiet. They're gone, and they won't come back. I promise."

A lie, but he had no choice.

She looked at him through the most pitiful fear he'd ever seen, but she nodded and threw herself to the ground, curling into a fetal ball.

He sprinted off towards Cam, and immediately stumbled, feeling his ankle wrench in a grasping mound of grass. He ran on, lifting his knees high as he'd seen Cam do. He scrambled over the next stone fence, only to find another empty field waiting—no sign of Cam or the incorporated beasts.

He jumped down and continued on. Cam had said that he was at the edge of the second field. Maybe he had meant that he had positioned himself on the far side of the second fence. At the next fence Kiel found no obvious path, so he plunged through, stumbling clumsily on loose stones and feeling twigs and thorns scratch at his face and arms. He beat his way out the other side, pulling the brush aside forcefully.

No Cam! Just an abandoned walkie-talkie lying in the grass. *Damn it!*

Wait! He saw him—the boy was sprinting away at least a hundred yards farther on. *"Cam!"* he called. "CAM!"

The boy didn't hear, or chose to ignore him.

This was the end of the worked fields. From here, the ground tumbled on in an uneven gently climbing slope up to the base of the ridge. Cam was almost to the first steep step of the ridge proper.

And then Kiel saw the beasts. Three tiny specs flying in formation ahead of Cam. They disappeared, as though melting into the side of the ridge. Seconds later, Cam disappeared as well.

Kiel took off again. He was wheezing, out of breath. It seemed to take forever to climb the shallow slope. As he drew near, he saw why Cam and the beasts had seemed to disappear. It was an illusion. A slanting indentation fell away to the left, invisible from a distance. He rounded the corner and found himself in a short, steep canyon. The formation didn't fit with the rest of the terrain in this part of Wisconsin, where everything was flat or eroded to worn, undramatic smoothness. Cam stood farther in, facing the head of the little canyon where fallen rubble had created an uneven ramp up to the face of the inner cliff. He turned when he heard Kiel, and just pointed ahead to the ramp of riprap.

Kiel trotted the rest of the distance. "Where are they?" he asked quietly, still breathing heavily.

Cam pointed again. "They flew into that hole."

Kiel now saw it. Perhaps five feet wide, and a foot high, a black mouth opened into the face of the cliff just where the top of the ramp met the canyon wall. It looked like there had previously been a much larger hole that was now almost completely covered by the fallen rocks.

Cam started forward, and Kiel caught him by the upper arm. "Wait," he said.

"Why?"

"We don't know what they are, what they might do. One of them . . . came over to study us."

"It didn't hurt you?"

It was as much a reminder as a question.

"No, but think about it. What animal—an animal the size of a rat—would go out of its way to get close to people and then carefully circle them as though they were specimens under glass?"

Cam shrugged. "So?"

"They're not afraid of us, not even cautious."

"Neither are ants or flies."

"True, but an ant or a fly can't rip off your face with spinning blades."

This seemed to give the boy pause. But only for a moment. He carefully removed Kiel's hand from his arm. "I'm going to take a look."

Kiel was saved from having to get all adult on the youngster. In the distance, but clear enough that it was impossible to miss, a high-pitched horn blared. It sounded like the hand-held air horns boaters use.

The distant blaring had an immediate and disconcerting effect on the boy. "Oh, crap!" he cried as he sprinted off back the way they'd come.

Kiel, just beginning to finally catch his breath, took off after him. "What's wrong?" he called.

Without turning around, Cam yelled back, "We shouldn't be here!"

Kiel pounded on a few steps before shouting, "*Now* you tell me?"

PART II

PREPARATION

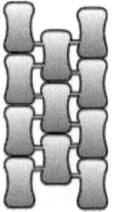

Blaine C. Readler

Chapter 6

Kiel was fairly wet with sweat when they finally arrived back at the farmhouse. It had been at least twenty minutes since the to-me horn had sounded, and Julie was sitting on the porch swing with a man that Kiel had never seen before. A Lexus sedan sat parked in front of the house.

"Daddy!" Nicki cried when she saw him, and ran ahead, up the porch steps and practically leaped into his open arms.

Brandon was handsome and well-dressed in clean, casual slacks and a soft, pale-blue polo shirt. He seemed like the kind of guy who might do some work that got him dirty just for the experience. His jet-black hair fell into a natural part that perfectly framed his dark olive face.

Julie got up and came down the steps to meet Kiel and Cam. "Where were you?" she asked, doing a poor job of hiding her concern.

"We saw what looked like a strange bird, and were curious," Kiel replied.

They had talked it over, and he had compromised with Cam who wanted to keep it all secret. This wasn't a complete lie. The beast did fly—not exactly like a bird, but it did fly.

"It's been nearly a half-hour since Mom sounded the horn," she chided.

"We were on the other side of the stream. I'm sorry. I shouldn't have taken the kids so far. We were having such an exciting time, though."

He'd almost said a fun time, and that would definitely have been a lie.

Julie seemed to relax, having done her duty to reprimand him, for that is what Kiel assumed had happened. This was about as harsh as she got.

"Look at you!" she exclaimed, licking her finger and wiping at the smudges on Cam's face while he squirmed to keep away. "What have you been doing? Mining for coal?"

Kiel noticed that Nicki was babbling on to her father about the beast, how it had dove at her and tried to carry her away. Brandon smiled and nodded. He was obviously not even listening. Kiel glanced at Cam, and the boy was glaring at his sister.

"What are you talking about?" Julie asked, coming back to the steps.

Nicki looked at Kiel, probably remembering that they had agreed that it might be best not to worry her mom about the adventure quite yet, but the temptation to deliver a fantastic story was too much for the little girl. "There was this flying animal—it's a whole bunch of little crab-things—I called them calves—that swooped down at me!" With this, she made a dramatic arc with both arms. "It would have carried me away, but Kiel made it go away—and then he ran after Cam—all the way to the ridge—they said that there was an old cave there that—"

"You went across Tagget's land to Chippewa Ridge?" Brandon cut in. He didn't sound happy about their excursion.

"It's my fault," Kiel confessed. "I shouldn't have taken them so far."

Brandon just looked at him. Kiel felt as though he was being measured, categorized for future reference.

"Old Tagget didn't see us," Cam defended. "He never comes around there."

Kiel had the impression that Cam often defended himself to his father.

"That doesn't matter," Brandon said. "I told you to stay off his land." The debonair man let his disapproving gaze work its acid a moment. Then, in a more conversational tone, he asked, "What sort of cave did you find?"

"It was hard to tell—" Kiel started, but Cam cut him off.

"It was just a hole. Nicki exaggerates everything."

"*You* said it was a cave," she accused.

Cam rolled his eyes as though implying that it was no use arguing with an infant.

Brandon looked from Cam back to Nicki. "Well, which was it? A hole or a cave?"

Both kids started defending their positions as Daniel appeared around the corner wiping his hands with a rag. "Came back to harass old Tagget?" he asked.

Julie's husband seemed not to hear, continuing to watch his offspring arguing.

Daniel walked around the front of the porch. "I understand the county treasurer's reviewing his back taxes. Now ain't that convenient for you?"

Brandon turned to his brother-in-law, obviously having heard everything he'd said. "I had nothing to do with that."

"Oh, you didn't did you? That's not what I heard from Phil."

The visitor turned his attention back to Cam and Nicki. "I don't even live in this county. Phil might want to be careful with accusations."

"Oh, yeah," Daniel said feigning surprised remembrance, "you're a litigation lawyer."

Brandon ignored him. "Okay!" he exclaimed brightly, getting up and cutting off the kid's argument. "I came to take you guys for ice-cream. We don't have much time left, so we'd better get to it."

Nicki jumped up and down, singing a little joyful tune, but Cam looked unimpressed. He whispered something to his mom, but she just looked at him and shook her head. Not happy with the response, he loped along sullenly behind his father and sister to the car.

After Brandon pulled away, spitting gravel and dust, Daniel joined his sister on the swing, and Kiel, not sure what to do, sat on the steps.

"It's true, you know," Daniel said, presumably to Julie.

"That Brandon occasionally takes litigation cases?" she asked innocently with a teasing grin.

Daniel snorted. "He took a law degree just so that he could harass people. No, I mean the word is that he got somebody in Winnebago County to nudge somebody else in our tax assessment department. That's how the big shot good-ol-boys get things done; they trade nudges—no paper trail, no accountability."

"Seems to me that there's not a whole lot of accountability passing around gossip at the gas station either," Julie remarked amiably.

Daniel looked at her and shook his head. "Why do you defend him? You wouldn't be here if you believed he was defendable."

"Cam wouldn't let you get away with that kind of logic. There's very good reasons why I don't want to be married to Brandon, and I'm not saying his ethics are pure. But that doesn't mean he's guilty of every rumor that gets into the mill."

Her brother grunted reluctant agreement.

"Besides, why in the world would Brandon go to such trouble just to get Tagget to lower the price of his land? The difference can't be worth that much, certainly not worth using up a nudge."

Daniel smirked. "I talked to Tagget the other day. Brandon's not trying to get him to lower his price; he's just trying to get the old coot to sell in the first place."

"What's changed? Tagget was looking for a buyer just a year ago."

"What's changed is how much land's involved. Tagget wants to unload just the ten acre strip along our border. Brandon wants to buy something like two-hundred acres."

Julie looked skeptical. "That doesn't make sense. That would be half of Tagget's farm."

Her brother shook his head, the smirk broadening. "I didn't say two-hundred acres of cultivatable land."

Julie just stared at him.

"He wants Chippewa Ridge."

Her brows scrunched together. "Why, for heaven's sake?"

"You tell me. He's your husband."

"For the time being." Her face grew hard. "Oh, poo! I don't even want to know what that man's up to. I'm through with all that."

"Watch your potty mouth," Mrs. Bakke warned opening the screen door.

"He deserves it. Poo, poo, poo. And then some more poo all over his face."

"Can't argue with that assessment. But for you, young man," she directed, pointing a bony finger at Kiel, "it's time to commune with some weeds."

He stood up, glad to escape from the uncomfortable airing of family grievances.

ж ж ж

Kiel wished he was back on the porch steps listening to Julie describe how she wanted to smear poo on Brandon's face. Her mother had fed him, and then chained him out in the blistering sun to expire. There was no physical chain, and the sun wasn't actually hot enough to raise blisters, but after an hour pulling weed after vile weed, sometimes squatting, sometimes on his hands and knees, Kiel was almost ready to return to Altoona and turn himself in.

Where were the illegal aliens when you needed them?

He came to the end of the row of peas he'd been working, and stood up to survey what lay beyond: a veritable forest of weeds waiting to wrestle with his sore fingers. In fact, now that he studied the last five feet of the garden, he wasn't sure there was anything even planted among the weeds. One hearty wide-leafed variety seemed to have flourished and taken over the anarchy.

He dove in anyway, figuring he could earn extra points for effort. He assumed that he'd eventually uncover some recognizable vegetable, and he was a good four feet into the swath when Mrs. Bakke cried from behind him, "What on earth's gotten into you, boy! Have you gone mad?"

He stood up and looked at her and then down at the clean patch of soil he'd defoliated. "It's dirt," he said, pointing at the freshly exposed ground. "I thought that's what we wanted."

"You're massacring my potatoes!" She reached down, picked up one of the broad-leafed bullies he'd tossed aside, and held it out in her open palm like it was a dead kitten.

"Oops!"

She tks-tsk'd him and told him to stay put as she hurried off. A couple of minutes later she returned with a shovel and bucket. "They're about ready anyways," she remarked, handing him the shovel. "Be careful you don't split them. Go in about a foot to the side of the plant, and work inwards. Just dig up the ones you beheaded." She started back towards the house, but turned around. "You don't need to weed potatoes. They're already members of the gang, and natural leaders at that."

After an hour of pulling weeds, Kiel found that digging up potatoes was actually fun. It was like hunting for buried treasure. He filled up the bucket and had to go and get a second before he reached the untouched wild zone.

He washed up and sat down in the kitchen with a cup of tea and cookies that Mrs. Bakke set before him. Cam and Nicki were still out with their father, and he could hear the vacuum cleaner upstairs, where Julie was presumably cleaning. He finished, washed his dishes and sat back down to watch his hostess cut up a chicken. After a few minutes, she stopped and looked at him. "I'm not used to a man watching while I work," she remarked. "To tell you the truth, it makes me nervous. Why don't you take a nap? That's what all the other men I know do when they have any free time."

He ambled outside and sat on the porch swing watching the bees wander from dandelion to dandelion, like they just couldn't make up their minds. He didn't feel like a nap and guessed that, despite his near-death experience with weeds, this was because he simply didn't work as hard as the other men in Mrs. Bakke's life.

He decided to take a walk and his feet followed the paths with which they were already familiar. Five minutes later he found himself standing at the abandoned bridge. He avoided the fresh, broken dirt at the bank's edge, and crossed the bridge instead.

He was intrigued with what they had seen and the talk about old Tagget not wanting to give up Chippewa Ridge. It was a lot easier retracing their previous steps without the kids to worry about. He crossed the fallow field that belonged to the Bakkes, and paused at the beginning of Tagget's land. Like Cam had said, the old man never comes down this way. He pressed on, through the sea of jumbled grass and then the final field before the approach to the ridge. Here he paused again. Moving onto and up the gentle slope seemed a more distinct transition than crossing from Bakke's land to Tagget's. Even though the fields behind him were owned by different men, they were both fields that belonged to men. This boulder-strewn expanse ahead of him did not. In theory it belonged to Tagget, but that was just an abstract notion bolstered by some documents filed with the county. It was not worked by man, and thus still belonged to nature.

The sudden sound of buzzing startled Kiel. He peered back along the stream, but saw no squadron of bizarre incorporated crablets. The sound was a nearby cicada, firing up its song after going silent with Kiel's approach.

Drawn on by curiosity, Kiel climbed the slope. It wasn't far, barely a hundred yards, but seemed to recede constantly before him—an illusion, he presumed, caused by the much steeper slope of the bluff ahead forming the near side of the ridge.

He finally came to the little canyon angling off to the left, into which Cam and the beasts had seemed to disappear. Ahead of him was the ramp of rubble sloping up to the jet-black, mouth-shaped hole. He walked closer, each footstep echoing among the sheer, smooth walls. He tried walking more softly, and filled the canyon with the amplified sound of a man walking softly. When he came to the foot of the rubble ramp, he stepped gingerly onto the loose stones. He was expecting them to roll and slide beneath him, and was surprised that they seemed set into cement. He supposed that they'd had years to settle and find their most stable position as later rocks fell like hammer blows.

He hadn't intended to go all the way to the top, but the ease of climb was irresistible, as if all those years of settling would be wasted, otherwise. When he finally arrived at the hole, he felt wafts of cool air wash across his face from within. He would have thought that the air from a cave large enough to produce wafts would be . . . he wasn't sure—musty, maybe. But these brief drafts felt refreshing, like walking outside into the night from a stuffy building. In fact, he thought he caught the faint odor of fresh laundry, which seemed ridiculous. But there it was.

He heard the buzzing sound again, but this was no cicada. He was suddenly filled with panic, like hearing the enraged shout of his neighbor Mr. Womback when he and his friend were caught soaping the cranky man's windows at Halloween. He didn't even bother to look behind him, but scrambled off to the side; he knew he didn't have time to make it off the ramp. Not knowing what else to do, he lay down among the rubble against the face of the cliff, trying to look inanimate.

Sharp edges dug painfully into his ribcage and hip as he saw two beasts approaching at eye-level. The burring roar swelled and seemed to vibrate the very canyon walls. *They're only as big as rats,* he told himself. *But so are rattlesnakes, and they don't even fly.* The duo flew in line, one after another, perhaps twenty feet apart. The lead beast disappeared into the face of the cliff without pausing or adjusting its course. Kiel thought he was home free until he realized that the second beast was slowing as it approached. It swerved and headed directly for Kiel. He heard a high, thin whine, which he recognized as coming from himself. He wanted to close his eyes tight, but fear froze them open. The incorporated beast hovered, inches above his chest. Staring, petrified, Kiel felt horror crawl along his spine as he realized that he was indeed looking at thousands of crablets all intertwined, all cooperating to form this multi-unit organism of the air. He cowered under the overwhelming sense that he was observing something completely alien to everything he knew and understood.

The beast, or rather the thousands of tiny beasts, decided they'd seen enough, and backed off. A moment later, the burring drone was fading into the interior.

Kiel lay listening. The sound of the beast faded slowly, slowly.

The cave was big.

Chapter 7

Mrs. Bakke served potatoes au gratin that night for dinner. When she set the steaming-hot baking dish on the table, Kiel looked at her. "Yes, folks," she announced to the table, "our starch dish this evening is served thanks to the ambitious harvesting of our guest."

Admiring the carefully arranged layers of sliced potato and cheese, Kiel replied, "All I did was drag them out of the ground; you performed the magic that turned the tubers into a culinary work of art."

"Flattery will get you everywhere, Mr. Martin. Or at least another night in a bed. Did you kids enjoy your ice cream?" she asked, sitting down.

Nicki sighed demonstratively. "It was just the One Stop."

Her grandmother guffawed. "You thought he was going to take you to the diner in Rapon?"

"Factory ice cream from the One Stop is so pleedian," the little girl declared.

The silence was broken by Julie. "I think you mean plebian, dear."

Nicki's mouth pursed in anger and embarrassment. "That's how Cam said it."

"I did not," he refuted irritably without looking up.

"He's mad because Daddy yelled at him when he said that."

"He didn't yell. He just asked whether I wanted him to come and visit or not."

"And Cam said not if he was just going to drag us around while he does his own business."

The boy put his fork down and glared at her.

"That's when Daddy yelled," she concluded.

"Okay," Julie concluded. "That's enough."

"I've got news for you, my dear," Mrs. Bakke said to her granddaughter. "The ice cream at the Rapon diner is made in a factory too."

Nicki stared at her belligerently, but decided to quit while ahead.

"What business did Daddy take you on?" Julie asked. The conversational tone sounded to Kiel just a little affected.

"He stopped to talk to old Tagget," Cam replied.

"I know that's what you hear some of us say," his mother said. "But I want you to just call him Mr. Tagget."

"He is old—but I get it."

"Was that the only business? Just talking with Mr. Tagget?"

"That was enough. We were there, like, two hours."

"Two hours? You were hardly gone longer than that."

"It felt that long, sitting in the car while he and Tagget drank whiskey."

"You know that?"

"Ye-ah! You could smell it on his breath."

"It smelled like sourballs," Nicki added helpfully.

Their mother studied them. She took a little breath, as though about to say something, but thought better of it and took up a forkful of au gratin potatoes instead.

"Did he receive any calls?" she asked off-handily after she'd chewed and swallowed.

"You're fishing, Mom," Cam accused.

She took another little breath, and then smiled. "Perhaps I was. That's not fair, and I apologize."

"That's okay. He was fishing also."

She raised one eyebrow. "Really? I guess I should have expected that. What did he ask about?"

68

Cam hesitated. "He asked about Kiel."

This seemed to surprise Julie. She sighed. "I should have seen that coming as well. What did you tell him?"

The boy shrugged and dabbed at his food. "The truth. I told Dad that Kiel was a guest of Gammas. He was going to help out around the place."

"Good. That's good, Cam," she enthused.

"It's the truth!" he protested, as though she were in fact complimenting him on a good lie.

Julie looked surprised. "Of course it is, honey."

He pushed his food around some more. "He asked if Kiel talked about stuff like drugs."

"Oh?" Julie responded, seeming to want more, but hesitating to blatantly fish.

"That's when Daddy yelled at Cam again," Nicki reported.

Julie looked at Cam expectantly.

The boy put his fork down and snorted. "All I said was that Kiel would never do drugs, and anyway that was his own business if he did."

"You also said that Daddy was just trying to get levage on Mom," Nicki reminded. To her mother she explained, "That's when Daddy yelled at Cam again."

"That's lev-er-age, honey—not lev-age," Julie corrected automatically. To her son she said, "It's very, very sweet of you to try to defend me, Cam, but I don't need it. Everything will be fine." She returned her attention to the meal. "Just fine."

Somehow, Kiel didn't think she was paying quite as much respect to absolute truth as her son.

Ж Ж Ж

Kiel was helping clean up after dinner when Daniel stopped by. He didn't look happy. He motioned to Julie, who wiped her hands and followed him outside.

Kiel took over her job of accepting the washed dishes from Mrs. Bakke to dry and put away, but kept an eye and ear on the front door for news. "I expect we'll know soon enough what's up," his hostess remarked, glancing at him knowingly.

Sometimes Kiel wanted to reach up and feel if there was a little door in his head that had popped open.

After fifteen minutes, Julie came back in alone and practically fell into a chair looking dazed. "He's filed," she uttered, as if to invisible people sitting around her at the table. "Daniel found out from a friend in Oshkosh."

Mrs. Bakke wiped her hands and sat down next to her daughter. "He's filed for divorce?"

Julie nodded, still staring at invisible people.

"Isn't this good news? Isn't this what you want?"

Julie shook her head as though waking from a trance. "He's claiming grounds of abandonment and irredeemable criminal character. He's setting the stage to . . . you know."

"Take the kids. The swine!"

Julie nodded slowly, a deep, universal acknowledgement.

"It doesn't make sense," her mother mused. "What happened to his candidacy? The whole separation was supposed to be a big secret!"

"I know. That's what scares me. What could be so important that he'd jeopardize the election?"

Mrs. Bakke reached out and clasped her daughter's hand. "Maybe it is the kids. Maybe they're more important than being Senator."

Julie rolled her eyes. She seemed to be coming back to life. "Mom, please. Do you really believe that?"

"No. But I figured that idea might sit better than fear of the unknown."

They finished cleaning up the kitchen, and Mrs. Bakke went off to read some bedtime stories to Cam and Nicki. Kiel took a shower, and when he came back down, Julie was sitting at the kitchen table, surrounded by small piles of folders and papers.

Kiel sat down opposite her. "It's a little late in the year for getting your taxes together," he quipped, kicking himself for such a lame attempt at humor.

She smiled, seeming happy to have his company. "A little investigative research."

He turned the closest sheet around and saw that it was a memo written on Brandon's law office letterhead. He glanced at others and whistled. "How did you get all this?"

"I left the house in Oshkosh in a hurry. I grabbed this box of his records by mistake. If I knew what a jerk he was going to be I would have loaded up a U-haul."

"In Wisconsin you say 'jerk.' In Altoona we would say 'bastard,' or perhaps 'prick.'"

"Those are appropriate Wisconsin names for Brandon as well. I have a pocketful of even stronger ones I'd gladly pull out if I didn't have to set an example for the kids."

"So, they don't have access to the internet?"

She grinned. "I know they see those and a lot more, but maybe with some self-restraint I can give them a feel for when they're appropriate."

Kiel nodded at the paper-spread. "Looking for something to use in defense?"

"Defense, heck—offense. I'm going for his throat. Like I said before, the gloves are now off. Unfortunately, there doesn't seem to be much of any use here. It's mostly just receipts and non case-related memos. I wouldn't expect him to leave sensitive material lying around the house."

Kiel looked through some of the piles. He didn't really think he could add anything of value, but he enjoyed helping her, even if it was just in a notional sense.

He remembered something from earlier. "Does he often drink in the middle of the day? Whisky is just another kind of drug. Driving his kids around while under the influence should surely count for something."

Julie shook her head sadly. "No, I can't remember him ever having a drink before five o'clock. He's not really a drinker. I guess that just goes to show how important this deal with Tagget is."

Kiel turned his attention back to the scattered papers. It was like going through discarded raffle tickets—there was a finite possibility that you would find a winner, but there were also a dozen more fruitful things you could do instead. He came to one, though, that caught his attention. "What's this?" he asked, handing to her.

"A notice of stock purchase . . ." She looked up at him. "Are you familiar with this company?"

He shrugged and shook his head.

She looked at the sheet again. "Tandem-dyne," she read. It was her turn to whistle. "He bought ten-thousand shares at twelve dollars a share—son-of-a-bitch!" she hissed, and then glanced around to make sure the kids hadn't heard. "That's over a hundred thousand dollars!"

"I take it you didn't know about this?"

"Heck, no! No wonder he's always haranguing about staying within the family budget—he's been robbing the piggy bank!"

"So, is this something you can use?"

She looked it over again, and shook her head. "I doubt it. From a court's perspective, he's just investing the family money. It's not like he lost it in a poker game. Even if it was a stupid investment, it's not grounds for divorce."

"And we don't even know if it was a stupid investment."

She stood up and shook the paper. "Well, let's find out!"

They went upstairs to her bedroom where she kept her laptop, and Kiel found that he was self-conscious about being there. It wasn't like there was any suggestion of hanky-panky in the least, but just being in the room where she got undressed at night, where she kept the garments that nobody but Brandon ever saw, made him feel tingly. He was embarrassed by the tingle.

"It's dial-up," she remarked gesturing towards the laptop. "Do you remember what that is?"

The connection was indeed snail-slow. Accessing modern graphics-rich websites via a telephone line was like filling a bathtub through a straw. It took several minutes just to download the Tandem-dyne logo. Slowly, s-l-o-w-l-y, the company's home page began to form and fill out. Most of it was the usual hyperbole hype with handsome male and female models pretending to do various interesting jobs. The company seemed to be a defense contractor, apparently supplying consulting expertise as third-party support on complex equipment development. One line caught Kiel's eye, though: *compression, channel multiplexing, and encryption comprise complete downlink bundling for unmanned drones.*

"Hmm," he mused.

"What?" she asked.

He pointed to the line on the screen.

She glanced at him. "Do you understand what all that means?"

"Only vaguely. It's the unmanned drone development that caught my eye."

She nodded in agreement. "They're in the news a lot. I've heard that even with the military spending cutbacks, the drone programs are actually expanding. So . . . you're thinking that he might have made a good investment after all?"

He was making the association that was obvious to him: unmanned military drones, and strange autonomous flying contraptions unlike anything else on Earth. She knew nothing of the latter, though, and he wasn't ready to bring her into the fold, not without talking to Cam first. "Maybe. I think it depends on the business side of the company as much as what the company does—who the CEO is, and who he knows."

"Well, if it comes down to how well the company's executives are tied into the good-ol-boy network, then Brandon has a leg-up. He lives, breathes, and sucks at the teat of that crowd."

"Which you also need if you want to run for U.S. Senator," he observed.

"And which he seems to have forfeited."

"All so that he could come out on top in a divorce fight."

"And take my kids in the process."

Kiel let the sequence stop there. He didn't want to cause her more pain.

Certainly not in the same room where her undergarments lived.

ж ж ж

"I'm sure my dad wants Tagget's land for something bad," Cam insisted.

They'd finished breakfast, and the boy was taking Kiel to the barn to show him the go-kart he was building with some help from his uncle.

"You're 'sure.' " Kiel challenged. "Wouldn't it be more accurate to say that you're confident, or maybe even that you just believe it?"

"Now you definitely sound like Mr. Dickson."

"He must be a very smart man."

"Okay, I'm confident."

"Which implies that you have evidence."

"Ye-ah—my Dad!"

"Er, I think he's the accused. You can't use him as evidence. That's the Fifth Amendment."

"No, I mean he's always looking to cheat somebody, or take advantage no matter what."

"Sounds to me like you're a prejudiced witness yourself."

"Can we cut the courtroom stuff? I'm serious. He's going to take Nicki and me if we don't do something."

Kiel didn't say anything for a minute. "Is that what you think?"

"Come on, Kiel. I'm not stupid. I have ears."

"Does Nicki know?"

"I don't think so. At least, she hasn't said anything to me."

They'd arrived at the barn, and Cam put his weight against the huge door, sliding it aside on its hanging rollers. They walked into darkness. Kiel reveled in the heady mix of odors—musty old hay, manure, creosote—while he waited for his eyes to adjust.

"What do you want to do?" Kiel asked.

"I want to find out why my dad wants Tagget's land."

"Your uncle told me that he just wants to expand the Bakke property."

"My dad couldn't care less about the Bakke property."

"Your uncle told me that as well."

"I'm sure that if we can find out why my dad wants Tagget's land, we can get Mom off the hook."

"There you go with that 'sure' again."

"Why are you just giving me a hard time?"

Kiel squatted down in front of the boy. He'd meant to be level with his eyes, but in the dim light filtering through hundreds of cracks in the walls, he found that he was actually now looking up. "Listen, I want to help your mother the same as you. I just want to be very careful. If we screw something up, it might work to your dad's advantage. We could shoot ourselves in the foot."

"So, you agree—we have to go talk to old Tagget."

"Mr. Tagget."

"Whatever."

"Maybe not." He hadn't intended to tell Cam about the stock purchase, and he still didn't want to go into that much detail. "I think there may be a connection between your dad and the calves."

Even in the half-light, Kiel saw the boy's eyes open wide with excitement. "Really? What?"

"I'm sorry, Cam, but I'm going to have to keep that one to myself for now."

His young friend shrugged. "Fine."

Kiel had the idea that Cam was satisfied as long as they were making some kind of progress. "You can help, though, by answering a question without asking why I'm asking."

"Sure. What?"

"Has your dad brought anybody around—people that maybe looked like engineers?"

"I wouldn't know what an engineer looks like, other than that they might have their glasses taped up with a band aid."

"Right . . . stereotypes die hard. These would be men that would be talking technical stuff—you'd recognize that."

The boy thought about it. "Some men came a couple of months ago. They were with an oil company."

"An oil company?"

"Well, not exactly. I think this was a company that does fracking. That's where they extract oil from shale deposits that—"

"I know about fracking. There's a lot of that moving into Pennsylvania where I'm from."

"Anyway, everybody was excited for awhile because they all thought they were going to get rich, but it turns out that there's no deposits anywhere near here."

"The men I'm thinking about wouldn't have talked about oil. They would have been more interested in . . . oh, maybe how much air traffic goes over the area—small private planes that fly a lot lower than jets. Or maybe helicopters. They might have been interested in wind patterns and the layout of access roads. They might have been checking out visibility from the highway."

Cam seemed to be looking at him out of the corner of his eyes. "You're thinking that the flying things we saw are unmanned drones, aren't you?"

The kid is no dummy.

"Maybe."

"What would be the connection with my dad? Why would this make him want to buy Tagget's land?"

"That, I don't know. That's what I'm trying to find out."

"We need to find out more about the colony."

"You still think that's what it is? A colony of little crablets that hook up together to make flying beasts?"

He shrugged. "Sure. We saw them."

Indeed. Kiel had no doubt that this was the case. He would never forget lying against the canyon wall staring at the thousands of incorporated little beings, all studying him like a specimen under a glass slide.

Kiel stood up. His eyes had now adjusted to the dim light. The cavernous interior was a matrix of great, hewn beams, jammed with loose hay, and bags of fertilizer and feed. Cam led him off to the side where chest-high partitions created a small workshop. Inside, lying scattered on the floor, was a hodge-podge of metal bars, gears, belts, cans of nuts and bolts, and what Kiel took to be the dismantled gasoline engine from a lawnmower.

"I'm replacing the bearings in the drive gear—I have a ways to go still," Cam remarked as they gazed down at the metal menagerie.

"Not exactly an unmanned drone yet," Kiel agreed.

The boy toed a two-foot wheel that must have been scavenged from an ATV. "Seems kind of dumb now, compared with things that fly."

"Yes, but those things can't carry a person."

At least that we know of, he added to himself.

Chapter 8

"You got it?" Kiel asked, ready to catch the laptop, but Cam held it steady, propped between one knee and a large rock.

They'd promised Julie that they'd be careful with it. They had implied that they were going to use it to look up plant and animal types on the built-in Britannica encyclopedia. An implied lie, not a real one.

Kiel turned and scanned back along the canyon, making sure one last time that there were no arriving beasts on the wing, then turned back and lifted the Visual Probe. This was primarily a long pole saw handle hosting a lot of duct tape. Under the duct tape—prisoners forced into dangerous duty—were Cam's Bluetooth vid-cam and a powerful LED flashlight that they'd borrowed from Daniel (unbeknownst to him).

Kiel was originally just going to crawl part way into the hole to see what he could see, but gave in to his young friend's desire to go the contraption route, mostly because he hated to stifle creativity.

Reaching out, he flipped on the camera.

"Okay," Cam reported. "I've got an image."

Kiel flipped the switch on the flashlight and carefully maneuvered the electronic periscope into the black, frowning hole.

He worked his way around to the front of the hole so that he could insert the probe straight in. "See anything?" he asked.

He glanced over and saw that the boy was cupping his hands around the top of the display.

"No ... I think it's just too bright too see the screen in the sunlight."

Kiel could see the flashlight beam sweeping around inside as he slowly probed back and forth, but he couldn't make out any details other than that there was a lot of stone surface inside. "That should do it for now," he declared, pulling the pole back out. "Let's find a dark place to see what we've got."

Cam had recorded the feed, but it was nearing noon, and the sun washed the whole canyon. They picked their way off the rubble ramp, and after looking around and scratching their heads, Kiel finally took off his shirt and held it up as a screen, while underneath, Cam peered at the dim replayed image.

"Um, yeah," he reported. "I can make some of it out. It's blurry, and smeared with the motion. I need a better camera. It's just a bunch of rock—it looks like it's been carved out, though. There's sort of a room, and the walls look chiseled—not natural. The stones that fell off the cliff have also fallen inside, covering a lot of the floor. Wait ... towards the back ... hold on."

Cam tapped a couple of keys, waited, then tapped some more, obviously backing the sequence up to take another look. "Yeah! There's definitely a tunnel leading away at the back ... but I can't see inside it—the flashlight beam doesn't reach that far."

"That makes sense," Kiel said. "The beasts must be going somewhere inside there."

"Hey!" Cam exclaimed. "What's this?" He backed up again, looked, and backed up a second time. "There's something lying on the floor, just beyond where the loose stones have fallen."

"What is it?"

He backed up a third time. "I can't make it out. It's too smeared. It sort of looks like ... maybe a wallet—no, more like a notebook."

Kiel turned his makeshift shade screen back into an article of clothing. "That sounds like something we definitely want," he concluded, buttoning the shirt.

Cam powered down the computer and looked up at him. "I'll go in and get it."

"Like my brother's pajamas you will."

"Why not?"

"Cam, really. It's bad enough that we lied to your mom about where we were going with her laptop. Now you want me to go back and explain how I let her only son get chewed into little pieces by micro-zombies that band together so they can fly around and eat old bridges."

"You're making a scary story out of a molehill."

"You're scrambling a perfectly good metaphor."

"And you're scrambling our chances of catching my dad pooping on my mom."

Kiel stared at him.

"That didn't come out right."

"Look, kid. You're not going in there, and that's final."

"It's probably the same as Grandpa's. I've been in that one a hundred times."

"Your grandfather has a cave like this on his land?"

"Sure! Just like it . . . okay, it's a lot smaller I think, but still."

"Well, that's quite a coincidence."

"Not really. These hills are all limestone. There's other little caves all around—at least that's what Uncle Daniel says. He uses his for storage."

Kiel looked at him a moment and then shook his head. He was letting Cam get him sidetracked. "It doesn't matter how expert you are with these limestone caves, I'm not letting you go in. Look, I'll go. Your mom won't be as mad if I get chewed to little pieces."

"You won't fit."

"Come on! I'm not that fat."

When it came down to it, Kiel sort of wished he didn't fit. In fact, he didn't fit until he removed half a dozen rocks. Flashlight clenched like a club, he wiggled his way through the opening on his back, feet first. He winced as sharp corners poked him.

As the roof of the cave opening passed by an inch above his nose, he saw that this was also the height of the interior space. The cave was only as high as the opening. It was only because the pile of rocks fell away quickly inside that he didn't claw his way back out from claustrophobia.

Once he could face forward, he paused. He was sitting on the steep slope of fallen rocks, facing inwards. He was in a sort of ante-room, half filled by the fallen rubble. The walls were indeed carved, surely by miners at some time in the past. He could see the grooves where dynamite sticks had been inserted to carve out the space. Just as Cam had reported, there was a tunnel leading away into the interior. It curved to the right, and his beam only revealed the first thirty feet.

He made his way down off the stone pile. The ante-room was at least fifteen feet high, and the tunnel beyond, maybe ten feet. He could have easily strolled down along it, had he the nerve. Which he didn't.

He turned his attention to the reason he'd entered the cave. Lying on the ground was the object that Cam had seen. It was covered in dust, and almost invisible. The boy had sharp eyes. Kiel picked it up and carefully brushed it off. It was neither a wallet nor a notebook, but four sheets of paper that had been stapled together and folded twice.

Kiel jumped when he heard Cam yell something unintelligible outside. "What!" he yelled back.

Cam called out again—it sounded like a warning.

"Is it the beasts?" he asked, but there was no answer.

He jammed the papers into his pocket and started back up the rock pile. And then he heard it—the all-too-familiar burring roar. *Shit!* He was trapped. He could tell that it was already near. He swept the beam around the small room, but he knew that there was nowhere to hide, unless he wanted to sprint down the tunnel, and there was no way in hell he was going to do that.

The angry burring swelled until it filled the cave. Inexplicably, it remained like that, growing neither louder nor softer. It modulated back and forth, as though teasing him with an outstretched hand poised to slap. Suddenly, it seemed to explode inside the cave, and Kiel realized that it had entered. He also realized that he'd left the flashlight on, pointing aimlessly at the floor. He couldn't see the beast, but he could tell from the sound that it was heading for the tunnel. But then it stopped, the roaring burr blasting out a continuous wail from the inside bowels of the ridge. And then it came back. Kiel could feel each heartbeat thump inside his chest. The sound swelled until he thought he would be swallowed in it. He tried to stay completely frozen, struggling to resist raising the beam of light to see what the menace was doing. Finally he gave in, and moving just his wrist, he tilted the flashlight up. He nearly cried out when he saw that the flying syndicate of crablets hovered just inches from his face. Without warning, the beast backed off and sank. It was examining his hand and the flashlight. After a thousand pregnant seconds that probably amounted to five, the inspection was complete, and the thing flew off down the tunnel.

Kiel didn't breathe until the sound was just a distant echo. He then scrambled back up the pile of rocks so fast that he banged his head on the cave roof.

Back outside, he was blinded by the sunlight. "Cam!" he called, squinting and shielding his eyes with his hand.

"I'm here," the boy replied. He was sprawled among the rocks. He looked like he'd been shot and lay where he had randomly crumbled. But he gathered himself and sat up.

"Are you okay?" Kiel asked, feeling panic return.

"Sure. I'm fine. It didn't even see me, or if it did, it just ignored me."

"Whew," Kiel said, relieved. He sat down next to Cam. "I was worried. I heard it doing something out here before entering the cave."

"It was inspecting the opening. It seemed surprised. I think it noticed that you moved rocks to make the opening bigger."

"No kidding? That's interesting. It didn't bother you, though?"

"Not at all. I stayed completely still. I don't think it really sees you if you don't move."

Kiel turned off the flashlight and laid it in his lap. "You may be right. It turned around to investigate me. It may have sensed that something was different, like the changes to the opening. It was especially interested in my hand when I moved to shine the light at it. It's strange—it didn't seem to be bothered by the light, just the movement of my hand."

"Maybe it doesn't see with light."

"That sounds like a contradiction. I know what you mean, though—visible light. You're thinking maybe it might see with infrared?"

"Or ultraviolet, or even microwaves."

"You know about microwaves?"

The boy shrugged. "I know that the wavelength is shorter than regular radio. It's easier to transmit and receive with small devices. That's why cell phones don't need antennas."

Kiel chuckled. "And our crablets certainly are small devices. Are you sure Mr. Dickson can really teach you anything?"

"He's the one who explained that to us."

"Ah. So he is a smart man."

"He's knowledgeable," Cam suggested. "But he's also pretty smart, too."

"I see. And it was he who explained the difference?"

"No. That was Mrs. Craigle, our English teacher."

"Sounds like your parents' tax dollars are well spent." He got to his feet. "We should be heading back."

"What about the inner tunnel? That's where the thing went, right?"

"What about it?"

"That's where they *go*," he repeated as though Kiel didn't get it. "We have to check it out."

Kiel gave him a hard look. "You're kidding, right?"

"No! That's why we came in the first place."

"I thought we came to find out what shenanigans your dad is up to."

"Same thing."

"Is it?"

"It has to be. There's nothing else here—just a bunch of rock."

The kid had a point. "Maybe, but I think that's enough for one day. I need time to recover. I'm not young like you. Also, this cave is old. Maybe we can find out more about it."

He remembered the papers. "Whoa! Look what I've got."

He pulled the packet from his pocket. What he thought was dust, was actually very fine sand. The staple was rusty. It was also big, as though the manufacturer hadn't yet figured out how to make small ones. The left edges were ragged. "It looks like pages from a book." He scanned randomly. "It sounds like a geology text."

"Maybe somebody ripped them out of a library book," Cam suggested, leaning in to look.

"Now why would that idea come immediately to mind?"

"I don't know. It just seemed—" He looked at Kiel. "Hey! I never did that kind of thing!"

Kiel just shrugged, grinning, and read some more. "It sounds like a foreign language. Listen to this stuff: 'alluvial deposition of high-matrix wacke'; 'well-sorted arenite due to repeated filtering and sedimentation'; 'grains of clastic carbonate large enough to constitute calcerenite when not precipitated as linear crystals'." He shook the pages, as though he could re-order the words into some kind of sense. "Somebody actually understands this?"

"It's called jargon," Cam informed helpfully.

"Well, it's gibberish to me." He folded the pages and slipped them back into his pocket. "Let's go before they send the search party."

"But what about the—"

"Tomorrow—maybe."

When they came around the edge of the canyon, they found an old Ford pickup parked at the bottom of the slope. Kiel could see that somebody was sitting in the driver's seat.

"Uh-oh," Cam whispered. "It must be old Tagget."

"You said he wouldn't mind if we were here."

"Yeah. Well. Maybe we should go back. Maybe he hasn't seen us."

On cue, an old man dressed in overalls opened the door and slowly stepped out.

"We'll look pretty silly if he comes up and finds us hiding," Kiel said, and started down the slope. After a moment, Cam came trotting up behind him.

The man obviously had seen them. He stood, watching and waiting for them to come down.

"Just couldn't wait, could you?" he said when they got near.

Kiel couldn't get over the guys' ears—they were huge. Even from ten feet away, he could see hair sprouting out from where the sound is supposed to go in. The small, spare frame made the ears seem even bigger. Kiel thought of a monkey, and then felt ashamed.

"Are you Mister Tagget?" Kiel asked, extending his hand.

"I am," the old man replied, taking Kiel's hand in a very firm shake. Calluses covered every square inch of palm and fingers.

"I'm Kiel Martin, and this is my friend, Cameron."

Tagget eyed Cam. "You're Julie's boy," he declared. From the tone, Kiel would have guessed the man thought that they were trying to hide the fact.

"Yes, sir," Cam replied, tentatively.

Tagget didn't try to shake Cam's hand. He was just a child.

"We couldn't wait for what, Mr. Tagget?" Kiel asked.

"You tell me!" He didn't wait either. "Scoping the place out, that's what."

Kiel shook his head. "I don't understand. Scoping for what?"

The old man peered into Kiel's eyes. "You telling me you ain't workin' with Chipdown?"

"No. Who's Chipdown?"

"That's my dad," Cam whispered. "That's my last name."

"Ah! That would be Brandon."

"That's his name. He's this boy's father, and you ain't in association with him?"

It was an accusation, not really a question.

"Mr. Tagget, I met Brandon once, for about five minutes. I do know that he's trying to buy some property from you—all this in fact," he said, sweeping his arm around. "I assure you, sir, Cam and I have been trespassing for reasons completely unrelated to Brandon."

Tagget watched him a minute. "You talk like Brandon—like a lawyer."

"I am an engineer, sir. Currently unemployed and seeing the great U-S-of-A with this." He held up his thumb.

"Then what you doin' on my land?"

"Honestly?" He glanced at Cam. "We've been watching one hell of a strange beast."

Cam sucked in his breath, aghast that Kiel had given away their secret.

Tagget, though, showed recognition. He nodded slowly. "A bird of some sort."

"Of some sort."

"Flies like a big hummingbird, though."

"I think that would be it."

"I thought it was a toy helicopter at first. Never got close. It seemed to be heading up towards the old mine."

Kiel and Cam exchanged glances. "You know about the mine?" Kiel asked.

Tagget laughed. "You think I'm senile, young man? Now how could I live on this farm for seventy-eight years and not know about the old Fool's Mine? I was just a tike—half the size of Julie's boy here—when my daddy finally had had enough and chased the simpletons away."

"What were the . . . simpletons mining for?"

"Why gold! What else drives the sense right out of a man's head?"

"Gold? In Wisconsin?"

"You bet! We had a bona fide gold rush. Some fool found a wee little bit of the devil's bait in the stream and figured that it had washed down from the ridge. Convinced himself there was a load vein running through the middle. He tried to keep it secret, and my daddy let him have his fun, but nobody can keep that kind of secret long, and before you could shake a stick, the farm was just crawlin' with idiots."

"Did they ever find any?"

"Nah! Not an ounce. Pretty much the time the crowd of bat-brains arrived, the original poor fool had already figured out it was all for nothing. Spent his life savings, and all he got for it was a bunch of sand."

"Sand?"

"That's what did him in. He didn't get very far into the ridge before he found that the inside stuff—sandstone it is—was all soft. Wasn't even strong enough to dig into. Every time he blasted a stick—that's dynamite—a few tons of the soft stuff would just dissolve into a flood of sand that he had to haul out. By hand, too. Fine, white sand it was. He sold some of it. It made dandy potting fill and cat litter." At this he laughed. "But that didn't make a dent in the man's debts. Nope. He was hungry to get rich, and he ended up hungry for food."

"Interesting," Kiel said. "Sounds like the sort of story somebody writes a book about."

"Be my guest. You can have it. Make a might short book, though, without a whole lot of embellishments."

"I suspect that embellishments is maybe the primary talent for a writer."

Tagget paused and studied him a minute. "Don't get into any trouble," he cautioned, turning to climb back into his truck. "Don't get yourself hurt and have Chipdown suing me on top of his pestering about the land."

"Er," Kiel started. "So, you don't mind if Cam and I try to catch more sightings of the . . . bird?"

"Nah. Like I said, just don't make trouble for me. I'm old. If you do figure out what the darn thing is, I'd sure like to know."

"You bet, Mr. Tagget."

The old farmer started up the truck.

"Uh, just one more thing, if you don't mind," Kiel asked. "Speaking of Brandon, can you tell us why he wants to buy your land?"

Tagget leaned out through the open window. "No, I can't. Because I don't know. He won't say. In fact, it's lucky for me you already knew he was after me."

"Why is that?"

"He told me that if talked to anybody about this, the whole deal was off. To tell the truth, I'm not sure I'd mind if that happened. If the county wasn't on me about those goddamn taxes . . . well, that's another story." He wrestled the gearshift into first. "So long. You boys be careful, now."

Kiel and Cam stood and watched as the ancient truck bounced its way back from where it had come.

"Well, now we know," Kiel said.

"What?"

"We know what the beasts are after."

The boy looked at him, puzzled.

"Why, gold!" Kiel shouted. "Why, there's gold in them thar hills!"

Cam rolled his eyes. "Are you ever serious?"

"When I can't avoid it. I'll race you back."

He took off, but stopped and turned to find Cam standing with his fists on his hips watching him. Kiel walked back, but as soon as he reached the boy, Cam shouted and sprinted forward.

Chapter 9

Kiel tossed the garden tools in the shed and headed for the house, disgusted. Somehow the sweat sacrificed for vegetables at least seemed like a payment. You worked, and food appeared. People could eat this. He couldn't help feeling, though, that he'd wasted the last two hours of his life tending to Mrs. Bakke's recreational botany.

He'd never understood women's fascination with flowers. All that work just so you could admire a plant's colorful attempt to reproduce itself for a week or two. Flowers evolved to attract bees; did women become confused somewhere along the way and think that they're related to insects? The devotion was simply not commensurate with the effort involved. Turnips were grown in patches, corn in rows, but flowers were nestled in beds.

The work had indeed been payment, he reminded himself. He'd surely earned his breakfast, lunch, and dinner.

His slave master had turned hostess again and met him on the porch with a tall glass of lemonade. A few minutes later he realized that he'd just pontificated his complete philosophy about women and flowers. She just smiled serenely and said, "If it was up to men, the world would be one huge lawn, sprinkled here and there with trees and a hole every hundred yards around which they'd stand cursing."

"Sounds great. How do I get there?"

"You can't get there from here. Ever."

"Well, how about from over there?" he suggested, pointing randomly into the distance.

"From Tagget's farm? Ha! If it was up to him, he'd do away with the grass, trees, and golf holes, and plow it all up to plant. If you talk to him for more than five minutes, he'll explain that God created the earth for crops."

"Hey, speaking of Tagget, we ran into him this morning."

Kiel checked himself, wondering whether he'd just goofed with his loose tongue, but decided there was no harm. After all, it was inevitable that he'd eventually run into their neighbor.

"What's he complaining about now?"

"He thought at first that we were spying out his property for Brandon."

"Surprised he didn't shoot you."

Kiel looked at her.

"Oh, I'm just kidding," she said. "Old Tagget wouldn't hurt anybody. Not unless they tried to hurt one of his precious cows first."

"He was actually quite talkative, a regular library of information—a 'gold mine,' in fact."

She laughed. "Did he go on about Wisconsin's one and only gold rush?"

"He did indeed. It was interesting." He desisted telling her the full extent of his interest. "Greed for gold called to men, but all they found was sand. It sounds like a metaphor."

"That sand was the best thing that could happen to folks around here."

"How's that?"

"If they'd found gold instead of just sand, this whole place would be a sad, rundown ghost town by now. They would've tore up the earth, making an almighty mess of things, and then they would've skedaddled faster than a politician from an honest debate once the gold was gone. As it was, we got some mighty fine sand out of the deal."

"So Tagget explained. They sold some of it."

"Nice sand it was. Reminded me of the beaches of New Jersey—we took a vacation there when I was just a teenager."

"I've seen lots of sand since coming to Wisconsin."

"Not like this. Fine and smooth it was. Daniel and Julie spent half their childhood buried in it, in fact."

"That's a heck of a way of getting them out of your hair. I'm surprised the sheriff didn't hear about it."

She looked at him perplexed a moment, and then gave him a friendly swat. "Oh you! No, Daddy bought half a truckload and built a sandbox for the kids. They'd spend hours and hours in there. Kids go for sand like a fish goes for water. It's still there, around the side of the house. All grown over with grass now, though."

They both looked up when they heard an engine approaching. "That's odd," Mrs. Bakke remarked. "I wasn't expecting Daniel back from Rapon until after supper."

A minute later they saw that it was Brandon's Lexus gunning and fishtailing along the gravel lane. "That man's always in a hurry," she said. "Hurry to get here, and then even more hurry to leave."

Kiel and Mrs. Bakke sat on the porch and watched as the lawyer parked and stepped out, carrying a briefcase. "I get a welcome party?" he asked amiably.

"A history party, more like it," Mrs. Bakke replied. "Kiel ran into Tagget, and between that old farmer's picked brain and my youthful version, our young friend here is now a credible expert on The Great Wisconsin Gold Rush."

Brandon's eyes flashed and he gave Kiel a hard look. "Is Julie in?" he asked gruffly.

Mrs. Bakke seemed surprised at the sudden change in mood. "She's upstairs with the kids."

Without another word, Brandon strode past them and into the house.

A minute later they heard loud talking falling down through the open window above. The talking blossomed into yelling. "Don't sound like no simple love spat," Julie's mother remarked. "First sound of a slap, and I'm going up there with my rolling pin."

They heard no slaps, though, and after a while the argument went quiet, and then Brandon came out through the door with a face so hard, it would have been impervious to a slap. "Can I talk to you a minute?" he said to Kiel, who didn't think the question sounded much like a question. "Let's go for a walk," the lawyer suggested in a non-suggestive tone.

They walked along the gravel lane. Once they were out of earshot of the house, Brandon asked, "What were you doing at the old mine?"

Well, well, Kiel thought. *Cam was right after all.* And also, perhaps, his own suspicions about Tandem-dyne and drones. "Just poking around—taking a walk."

Brandon's hard edge had melted. He'd returned to his cool and collected lawyer mode. "Did you find anything . . . interesting?"

Kiel stopped, and Brandon turned to face him. "Look," Kiel said, "let's skip the games; I think we both know what we're talking about here."

Kiel wasn't at all sure what they were talking about. He had not the slightest clue what the beasts were, but he knew that when it came to dealing with lawyers, the important play was making them think you knew a whole lot more than you actually did . . . unless you were trying to make them think you knew a whole lot *less* than you actually did. The games could be mind-boggling, and he hated playing them.

Brandon was too good to fall that easily, however. "What exactly are we talking about?"

Let the games begin. "Come on," Kiel scoffed. "There's nothing else of interest in the old mine—the fool miners found that out seventy years ago, and we're not talking about sand for play-boxes."

The lawyer nodded, neither agreeing nor disagreeing; just listening.

Kiel jiggled the bait. "Engineers are always coming up with some new miracle. Technology marches on, eh?"

Brandon watched Kiel. It was the oppressor's game, and he could play as long as he wanted. "Julie's probably told you that I can take the kids if I want to," he said, opting out of the game.

Kiel put his hands in his pockets, trying to look casually confident, like he'd seen defense lawyers do on TV. "Isn't that a decision for the judge?"

Brandon's eyes narrowed in anger. "I see; so now you're going to teach me about the law? Listen, Mr. Amateur Lawyer, if you tell anybody—and I mean one soul—about the mine, Julie will be lucky to see those kids once a year on Christmas." He poked Kiel with his finger. "Got it?"

Kiel hated when guys did that. Instead of taking a swing, though, he replied, "It works both ways, you know."

Standing with his hands in his pockets didn't seem appropriate now. He removed them and folded his arms across his chest.

"What are you talking about?"

"Let's say I keep our little secret and you get what you want. Once Tagget signs the contract to sell the land, you give Julie custody of Cam and Nicki."

The lawyer eyed him, the eyes of a snake. He shrugged. "Sure."

That seemed too easy. "Maybe we should put that down in writing."

He shrugged again. "Why not? I'll draw them up."

That seemed a little like asking the alligator to carry the mouse across the river on its back, but it was better than nothing. At least for now.

Kiel decided to take one more shot at picking Brandon's brain. "Are you sure that our little cave secret is safe?"

"Why would I tell anybody?" Brandon retorted.

"No, not that the secret itself is safe. I mean, you know—it's not dangerous?"

He looked at Kiel as though trying to understand the real meaning behind the question. "It can't hurt anybody," he replied hesitantly. "Somebody could get hurt I guess if they fool around and cause a cave-in. That sandstone is not very stable."

"So I've heard."

So why the hell use a dangerous place for testing these drones? he wanted to shout.

But he didn't.

Kiel discovered the reason for Brandon's visit after the bully had left: he'd come by to deliver the court papers for the divorce. Julie came down and sat with Kiel and her mother on the porch. "It's for the best, my dear," Mrs. Bakke assured. "It could be worse, you know. He could be refusing a divorce instead of shoving it down your throat."

"I know that, Mom," she replied despondently. "I'm just so scared about the custody outcome." She buried her face in her hands. "Oh, I just wish I could make it all go away."

I can make it go away, Kiel thought. *I just have to keep my mouth shut.*

He wanted to gently lift her head with a finger under her chin and tell her the good news.

But he couldn't. Then it wouldn't happen.

ж ж ж

"He said that they couldn't hurt us," Kiel noted.

He knew that he was probably simply justifying his own curiosity.

"My Dad said that? About the drones?"

"Yes. Like I explained, we were playing a cat-and-mouse game. Neither of us would come out and call the spade a spade. We were calling it 'the things in the cave,' but not even that direct."

In truth, Kiel didn't remember exactly how they had referred to the drones. Ever since the conversation with Brandon, he'd been referring to the beasts as "drones," and Cam had picked up on it. It was at least a little more specific than just "the beasts."

"If they won't hurt us, then why are we bringing all this stuff?"

Cam was referring to the old fencing mask, bicycle helmet, and long-sleeved shirts that Kiel had lugged along in a green plastic garbage bag slung over his shoulder. "Better safe than sorry. Besides, there's a possibility that your father lied and would actually like to see me done in by them."

"You're joking, right?"

"Of course. I hope."

They came to the mouth of the canyon and Kiel dropped the garbage bag. It hadn't been heavy when he picked it up at the house, but gravity was insidiously persistent. They had tried to gather the things surreptitiously, but Mrs. Bakke had happened upon them as they were stuffing it all into the bag. Cam had simply said, "Go-kart," and his grandmother just grunted something about breaking his neck and carried on with her laundry.

Kiel pulled out the fencing mask and handed it to Cam. "I'd rather have the bike helmet," Cam suggested.

"No. Wear this."

"I can hardly see. The mesh is so fine."

"That's the whole point. Nothing sharp and stingy can get through."

"Your face will be exposed with just the helmet."

"I'm the adult. I get to disfigure myself with spinning drone blades if I want to."

"You're right. Besides, I'd say the blades probably couldn't make things any worse—" he noticed that Kiel was looking at him surprised "—I'd say that if I were that kind of person."

"Ho, ho. Very funny. Now hurry up. I'm sweating in this long-sleeve shirt."

The sweating had only begun, since Kiel decided that they needed to move a couple more rocks, which turned into a couple of dozen to open up the hole entrance. "In case we need to leave in a hurry?" Cam had asked, to which Kiel had replied that prudence was the mariner's guiding angel. As they moved the stones farther down the pile, Kiel saw that they were revealing fine white sand filling the cracks underneath, as though the drones had been doing additional excavations, and had only gotten this far before deciding to drop their load.

Inside, the mine's little atrium was quiet, and the enlarged entrance allowed sufficient light to see once their eyes adjusted. "Ready?" Kiel asked. He couldn't see the boy's expression behind the fencing mask, but the basket-head nodded wordlessly. "Keep your ears open for returning drones coming up from behind."

Kiel made sure his flashlight worked, and set off for the inner tunnel. Having talked with Brandon about the drones made all the difference. He didn't think he would have braved this otherwise.

The light from outside faded quickly as he made the turn to the right, and soon only the three-foot diameter spot of his flashlight revealed what lay ahead. Almost immediately, they came to a decision. The tunnel split. What seemed to be the main branch angled off to the left, and a smaller version continued around to the right. "Let's check this out first and see where it goes," Kiel suggested, pointing to the side branch.

It was clearly dug out later, almost as an afterthought. It was smaller, but more strikingly, the floor was not flush with the main tunnel. They had to step up a good foot. Also, whereas the tunnel they were leaving had a reasonably level floor and straight walls, this was almost perfectly round, as though a giant drill bit had been used to bore it out.

Within thirty feet they came to an enlarged area which comprised the end. It was a featureless empty sphere inside the ridge. The sides curved around above and below smoothly, showing no telltale grooves of dynamite use.

"I wonder why they dug this out?" Kiel mused, his words amplified hauntingly by the concave walls.

"Maybe this is a clue," Cam said from behind.

Kiel turned to find the boy inspecting the wall closely with his own light.

"See?" his companion said, pointing. "The tunnel is made of this smooth white stone." He rubbed his finger along the wall and held it up to show that it was coated with the fine, almost microscopic grains. "This is the same stuff we've seen from the beginning. But inside the room the stone is different."

Kiel saw what he meant. It was obvious once you knew what to look for. The inner chamber was still what Kiel assumed to be some sort of sandstone, but the texture was rough—the grains larger, and the color darker, much more varied.

"You think they came in here especially because of this other rock?" Cam asked.

"It would seem so. Maybe they thought this other kind of rock would be more likely to contain the gold lode."

Cam swept his light around the inner surface of the sphere. "They gave up without going very far."

"Maybe they found this rock too hard to dig through."

"Then they must not have wanted the gold that bad."

The kid had a point. He always seemed to.

They retraced their steps back to the main tunnel and proceeded on.

The tunnel quickly curved back to the right, and then came to a T, splitting off at right angles both to the left and right. "What do you think?" Kiel asked.

"Shh, listen!" Cam hissed, and pulled off his fencing mask. He turned his head slightly one way and then the other. "Hear that?"

Kiel listened. "My breathing, or yours?"

"No!" the boy insisted, annoyed. "Don't you hear it?"

"No. What?"

"The buzz." He pointed down the tunnel to the left.

Kiel shrugged and headed off that way. After a few steps, he turned and pointed to the mask that Cam still held in his hand. The boy scowled and slipped it back on, and they continued.

Fifty feet farther, Kiel could see another inner room opening up. He thought he saw motion. He stopped and turned around to look at the inscrutable inanimate mask he had forced his young friend to wear, and found no communication to guide him. Slowly, ever so quietly, he tip-toed on. The room opened up with each step, and Kiel's little beam of light caught more and more blurred flashes of motion. The buzz swelled to a near roar. At the entrance to the room he stopped and sensed Cam standing next to him. Both of them swung their beams around the deep inner cavity. They had found the lair. The room was crawling with drones. Some, walking, some flying, some sitting motionless, they filled the chamber.

Chapter 10

"Oh, wow!" Cam whispered next to Kiel. "There's, like, hundreds!"

Kiel wasn't sure about hundreds, but there were at least a few platoons. It was difficult to get a perspective in the confines of this inner chamber, but Kiel had the idea that the drones had gotten larger. Instead of flying rats, they seemed now more like loose-jointed cats -- cats with no mouths or eyes, and no calming purring.

At first he saw just random meandering, like ants scampering around after their protective rock has been removed. But he soon realized that this was simply the sampling effect of their flashlight beams. The whole picture wasn't obvious when observing only small areas at a time. As he swung his beam around and integrated it all in his mind, he saw that there was purpose to all the motion. Things were being carried one way, and other things another way. The room was a miniature Charlie Chaplin version of a frenetic factory. It dawned on him that the "things" that were being carried were themselves composed of tiny crablets, barely discernible from this distance. He wouldn't have recognized this if he hadn't seen them close up before. Indeed, the crablets seemed to have grown as well, from fleas to ticks.

One pattern of behavior among the frantic, complex operation caught his attention. A continual background drift moved continually to the left. At any moment, some fraction of the miniature crowd were all moving in the same direction—towards a watering hole at the far left end of the room. Once there, they waited their turn to hunker down in one spot before resuming their enigmatic task. He noticed that Cam's flashlight beam had settled there as well.

"What are they doing there?" the boy whispered.

Kiel had a hunch. "They're feeding."

"Feeding?" Cam hissed, alarmed at the thought.

"Metaphorically. Look above that spot," he directed, moving his beam up a little.

"What is it? It looks like ice—like a dribble of water that froze on the wall."

"I think it's their power feed—electricity. That dribble of ice might be metal, a conductor."

Suddenly Cam's light was shining right into his eyes. "Hey!" Kiel exclaimed, putting his hand up to block the searing beam.

"Sorry. So, you don't think that they're animals? You think they're some kind of machine?"

The boy's tone indicated that he wasn't surprised. Kiel hadn't talked to him about Tandem-dyne yet. "I do."

He remembered the smell of fresh laundry when he'd first stuck his head in the cave. It was probably ozone.

"I thought so too," Cam said. "It didn't make sense otherwise. Did you see this?"

Cam swung his beam to the other side. Kiel hadn't notice it, but there was something . . . bigger going on. At first Kiel thought that the drones were having a huddle, maybe forming a mosh pit. He soon realized that a lot of what he took for drones in the middle of the pile were actually parts of a . . . he didn't know what. He couldn't make sense of the shape, if it even had a definite shape. All he could tell was that its parts seemed to be made from similar materials as the drones themselves.

"Maybe we should leave," Cam suggested.

Kiel shared the sense of foreboding that was obvious in the boy's voice. He started to turn, not realizing that Cam was so close.

When he bumped him in the dark, he took a half step back in surprise, and gasped from a second surprise: the room was a few inches lower, and he stumbled, flailing his arms to keep from falling. He regained his balance, but sensed with horror that he'd stepped on something that had gone "crunch." He tilted his beam down, and was relieved to see that it was just a piece of green glass, a remnant of an ancient broken bottle long abandoned by a gold miner.

"Uh, Kiel," Cam warned, looking over his shoulder with wide eyes. "Don't move—"

It was too late. Kiel had already spun around, only to find himself face-to-face with a drone, illuminated by Cam's light. He cried out and leaned back a little. The drone eased forward, maintaining the same distance. Kiel froze. *If you don't move, they don't see you.* He noticed that a second drone had approached, hovering just behind and below the first. After a few chest-thumping heartbeats, the first drone rose slowly until it was level with Kiel's head, and the second eased in at the level of his belt. Then, synchronized, as though connected by a rod, they slowly sank downward, along his front. They backed off, swung around to the right and repeated.

"They're studying you," Cam whispered.

Kiel hoped they approved of what they were finding. Seconds later, the two drones backed off a little, floating a foot away. His fear eased, and that's when the trouble began. His fear had suppressed a sneeze, and now the dust he had kicked up when he'd stumbled induced a bedeviling tickle. He didn't want to sneeze. He tried to resurrect the fear, but his brainstem refused to cooperate. He sucked in one snort-full, and then another, and finally blew it all out explosively. He didn't even have time to cover his mouth.

The drones didn't like his sneeze either. They jerked back another foot, but then, before Kiel even had time to recover, the first drone drove straight in for his face. Kiel had just enough time to lift his hands before the attacker made contact. He felt a blow to the backside of his left hand, and then a searing pinch. He yelped and stumbled back into the tunnel, falling all over Cam. He scrambled, regaining his balance, and called out, "Run!" but he already heard the boy's pounding footsteps receding away, the spot from the boy's flashlight bobbing along the floor ahead of him.

Kiel didn't wait to see what the two nasty biters were doing, but sprinted off as well.

He didn't catch up to Cam until they burst into the atrium room, now blindingly bright with daylight. They stood panting a moment, watching the dark tunnel.

"What happened?" Cam asked.

"The goddamn thing bit me!" Kiel exclaimed, looking at the backside of his hand, where blood was oozing down onto his wrist. "Jesus!" He put it to his mouth, the warm, metallic taste of his life-juice amplifying the sense of trauma. He looked at his hand again, and now with the blood gone he saw that the wound was trivial, a nick that could have happened from the slip of a screwdriver.

They kept their eyes on the tunnel. "Do you think we should get out?" Cam asked.

Kiel was a little abashed at his own reaction. He was the adult, after all. "If you like," he replied, implying the lie that he was comfortable remaining. He let Cam climb up the rock pile first, and resisted pushing the boy from behind to speed up the process as he followed on his tail.

Once outside, standing at the base of the stone ramp in the bright summer sunshine, the ominous fear of the mysterious creatures inside the mine seemed far away and safely remote. Kiel knew that this wasn't logical; the drones could attack them as easily, or more so, outside, but danger in the dark takes on supernatural proportions.

"They didn't know what a sneeze is," Cam observed.

"I guess so," Kiel said, watching the dark mine entrance above the ramp. "They interpreted it as an aggressive act. I guess it just supports the idea that they're machines of some kind."

"All animals know what a sneeze is," Cam agreed. "That's why they need electricity for power. Where do you think it comes from?"

"Now that's a good question. If that dribble on the wall was indeed a conductor, it seems that they're bringing it down from somewhere above." He took a few steps down the canyon, but the hill above the rim remained hidden. "There's nothing up there, is there?"

Cam shrugged, a qualified "No."

"No power lines on the other side, out of view?"

The boy shook his head. "I don't think so."

Kiel had an image in his mind, though—the wreckage of a small airplane. He remembered that this was just something he'd let his imagination conjure from the glint he'd seen when they had first followed the drones. He had thought then that it must be a piece of glass or mirror, but now he wondered.

"I have an idea," he said. "I'm going to climb the ridge. You can wait for me if you want. It's going to be hard work getting up there."

ж ж ж

It was harder than he'd even guessed, but Cam kept up, even with significantly shorter legs. They'd left the canyon, and attacked the hill farther to the north. Kiel had done a fair amount of hiking around the Appalachians, but he now appreciated just what an advantage a maintained trail provided. Every step, it seemed, required him to drag his leg away from some clawing branch. He guessed that it would have been a lot easier if the hill had been populated with trees. The bushes were just the right height to constitute a sea of nearly impassable man-sized obstacles. For Cam it was even worse, since he didn't have Kiel's bulk and strength to push through the mini-jungle. But the boy was persistent, to the point of obstinacy. The degree of his efforts leaked out as frustrated grunts and whimpers, and once Kiel would have sworn the boy actually cursed.

Just shy of the top, Kiel stopped and Cam struggled through the last ten feet to pause next to him, panting. The glint he'd seen couldn't have been much higher, otherwise he wouldn't have seen it from the stone fence lying now tiny and clear so far below.

"Okay," he said, "the mine should be somewhere south of us. Let's keep about fifty feet apart and just head down along the top of the ridge in a straight line."

"What are we looking for? A windmill?"

Despite being nearly torn to shreds by hungry bushes, the kid still had a sense of humor. "I'm not exactly sure. Whatever it is, it'll be shiny."

They started off, and it soon became clear that their route would be anything but a straight line as they weaved around the bush obstacles. When they finally came upon their goal, though, it was totally obvious, if unfathomable.

"It looks like the wreckage of a plane," Cam observed.

"Yeah," Kiel agreed. "It does, sort of. I should have trusted my wild imagination."

Cam looked at him.

"Never mind. If it was a plane, it must have been piloted by elves."

The mass of silvery material was about the size of a car, but less than a foot thick, as though a huge foot had squashed it.

"What do you think it is?" Cam asked.

"To tell you the truth, it's not what I was expecting."

"What was that?"

"I thought we were going to find solar panels up here."

Cam stepped forward and leaned in to take a closer look.

"Be careful," Kiel warned. "We've both been bitten already."

"But, this isn't a drone that can . . . huh!"

"What?" Kiel asked, moving closer for a better look.

He could see what had surprised the boy, and he felt a shiver go up his spine. The metallic material that had looked like textured silver paint was in fact their old acquaintance. Locked together limbs-to-limbs were thousands upon thousands -- millions -- of tiny crablets. Kiel picked up a stick and gently poked one flat surface. The incorporated mass gave under the pressure, but then Kiel felt them push back, resuming their original shape. He didn't have the nerve to press harder. He tossed the stick aside and pulled Cam away. Whatever these things were, they were good at giving him the willies.

"Why do you think these aren't solar panels?" Cam asked.

"Because they're not . . . well . . ."

Kiel realized that he was making an assumption based on limited samples. He had assumed that any solar collecting device they'd find would be flat and shiny, like all the solar panels he'd seen. This was simply a result of the manufacturing process, however; the photo-electric transistor junctions were etched onto the same flat, smooth, and shiny silicon wafers as all other micro-electronic components.

"You're right," he admitted. "It could be a solar collector. It could be one huge milkshake maker, but it could also very well be a solar collector."

On the other hand. "It still doesn't make sense," he went on. "I remember reading that a good solar panel is only about twenty percent efficient. Even if these . . . things were, like, eighty percent efficient, that would mean that they'd be getting about four times as much power as the same size solar panel. And a typical panel is only about a hundred Watts. I don't think four hundred Watts is enough to keep all that activity going down there. And keep in mind that whatever they collect has to last through the night."

Cam was listening to the lecture, but he was also continuing to explore the perimeter of the strange object. "Look here!" he called.

Kiel walked around and Cam pointed to the same thin frozen water stream they'd seen snaking down the wall of the mine. This one seemed to melt right out of the side of the squashed truck thing, and plunge down into the ground. "It sure does indeed look like it's some kind of power collector," Kiel agreed, scratching his head. "I just don't see how they can get enough power . . ."

He thought of something. He stood up and peered around. Sure enough, through the bushes, maybe fifty feet away, he caught the glint of another squashed truck. He looked some more, and found another, and another.

Well, that solved that.

"Look at this!" Cam called.

He was pointing directly at the frozen water power feed. Kiel looked closely, then closer still. "Damn!" he exclaimed pulling back as though it had jumped up at him. Even the power feed line was made from inter-connected crablets. These, however, were packed so tightly together that it was not easy to see individual cells. It made sense. There would need to be a lot of surface contact to reduce the resistance.

As he watched the multi-cellular power feed line, a shadow crossed the hill, the gliding footprint from a small little puff of cumulus cloud. As the sunlight dimmed and then, seconds later, brightened again, the power line undulated, reacting to the change in load.

The hairs on the back of Kiel's neck stood to attention. This was definitely getting too weird. "Let's get out of here," he urged, starting back the way they'd come.

Instead of going north before heading down the hill, they angled straight down, cutting the corner. Progress was much faster with gravity as their ally. In fact, Kiel was letting his feet skip along autonomously in a quasi-controlled jog, and so tripped and fell on his face over what he took to be an extra large root. When he pushed himself up with his hands and rolled over, though, Cam was standing behind him staring transfixed at the ground.

Kiel dreaded looking, but curiosity and the burden of adult responsibility forced him. Sure enough, he'd caught his foot on something weird. It looked, in fact, very much like an extra large root, except that this one was made of metal . . . and moved. At least, Kiel thought it had moved. No, there it went again. It had inched ahead a tiny bit, as though being nudged along from somewhere down the line.

Kiel scrambled hastily to his feet. Cam was already squatting down, looking at it closely. "Let me guess," Kiel started.

"Yep," Cam confirmed. "The same segments."

Kiel scanned along it in each direction. He couldn't see very far, as it was quickly lost in the thick brush. He could tell, though, that one direction pointed towards the mine. He turned. In the other direction there was . . . nothing. Just the ridge slowly losing altitude as it passed Tagget's place and eventually merged with the flat farmland in the distance. Where was it headed? *Why* was it headed?

"We're out of here," Kiel declared, and started off again down the hill. He stopped and turned. Cam was still squatting next to the crablet root. The boy reached forward, and then screamed and jumped back, falling on his back. "Are you okay!" Kiel called, stumbling back up the hill.

Cam seemed embarrassed. His face was blushed.

"Did it shock you?" Kiel asked.

The boy shook his head. "It just wiggled a little, that's all."

"Took you by surprise, didn't it?"

He nodded, his blush deepening.

"That reaction was your body doing the right thing," Kiel explained. "You should be worried when you don't jump after touching something totally alien that moves."

Cam nodded, smiling now.

Kiel looked at him. "But you're not going to touch it again, right?"

He shook his head vigorously.

ж ж ж

They didn't talk as they came down off the ridge, since it took all their attention to navigate the tangled terrain. Once they were back in Tagget's field, though, Cam proclaimed that he knew what these strange conglomerates were.

"Okay," Kiel said, "shoot."

His young friend became serious, ready to present his doctoral thesis. "They're clanking replicators."

"Huh? I didn't hear any clanking."

"It's just a name. It's used to distinguish between big machines and molecular replicators, like nano-technology." He glanced at Kiel. "Big here is relative."

"Of course," Kiel confirmed agreeably. "I presume that our strange beasts are in the big machine category."

"Well, we can see them."

"You're talking about the crablets."

"Yeah. The crablets are the universal constructors in a Von Neumann cellular automata environment—"

"Whoa! Hold on, there. There's a little too much—as you say—jargon there. Let's put it in terms a simple engineer can understand."

"You never heard of a self-replicator?"

"Uh, probably. I don't remember where, though."

"You don't read science fiction, do you?"

"I read The Martian Chronicles when I was your age. Ray Bradbury."

"I know who Ray Bradbury is," Cam objected. "That's hardly science fiction. Bradbury himself called it fantasy."

"Huh. Too bad. I really liked it."

"I didn't say it wasn't good; just not really science fiction. Anyway, a self-replicator is a machine that can extract energy and material from its environment to reproduce itself. There's tons of stories about this. Some are designed as spaceships. So, they could be dangerous for, like, a whole galaxy if they get loose."

"I guess this presumes that these self-replicating spaceships also have FTL drives."

Cam gave him a skeptical look. "I thought you said you don't read science fiction? How do you know about faster-than-light drives?"

"I used to watch Battlestar Gallactica."

"Oh, right. Anyway, I think your crablets are clanking replicators."

"Right. What's their purpose?"

"A self-replicator doesn't necessarily *have* a purpose, other than to replicate itself."

"Sort of like DNA."

"Sure. That's not a new idea, you know."

"I didn't expect so."

"Not that it wasn't a good idea," Cam added quickly.

Kiel smiled. "No hurt feelings."

Cam looked at him a moment. "Are you patronizing me?"

"No! Of course not! Okay, just a wee little bit. But you have to admit, you said yourself that this stuff comes from science fiction stories."

"Von Neumann was *real*! He invented computers!"

"Sorry, sorry."

They walked along in silence a while. "So, where do you suppose they come from?" Kiel asked. "These crablets?"

Cam threw him what Kiel took to be a defiant look. "Probably from space."

Kiel nodded.

"You're definitely patronizing," Cam concluded.

ж ж ж

They came to the abandoned bridge and crossed back over. Kiel didn't remember it being so . . . unstable. In fact, he'd been impressed at how well it had held up over the decades. He stopped in the middle and jumped up and down. He had the definite sensation that the whole structure was bouncing with him. It felt springy.

On the other side, he walked a bit along the bank, but from the side, the bridge looked normal. Steeling himself, he crawled down into the hole where he'd spent the first night. Shining his flashlight along the bottom side of the bridge, he gasped.

"What do you see?" Cam called down.

"You wouldn't believe it! They've eaten it nearly all away!" He leaned forward, peering along underneath. "Christ! Almost the whole bridge is gone! No wonder it felt like a trampoline."

He crawled up and sat at the edge of the hole, marveling at how completely unaware one would be from above of the damage below. "Like metal termites," he muttered.

"Clanking termites?" Cam suggested.

Kiel chuckled. "Clanking replicator termites. We're living in an honest-to-goodness Ray Bradbury story, kid."

"Except that his stories were fantasies."

"Exactly," Kiel declared, gesturing grandly at the decayed bridge. "How else can you explain this?"

Chapter 11

Kiel was glad at first to see Julie waiting on the porch for them. He was looking forward to sitting with her again. But then he noticed the way she was standing, with her hands balled into little fists on her hips, her elbows out to the sides.

"Uh, oh," Cam warned, "Mom's on the rag."

Kiel looked at him. "Where did you hear that expression?"

He shrugged. "The guys at school."

"Do you know what it means?"

He shrugged again. "That she's mad."

"I mean, where the expression came from?"

"Uh-uh. Do you know?"

Sometimes you just have to lie. "Nope."

Julie didn't say anything until they were standing right in front of her. That in itself was not a good sign.

"Where have you two been?" she demanded.

Cam glanced at Kiel. "Well, we—"

"Gamma and I have an appointment," she admonished, cutting him off, "and now we're going to be late." She called over her shoulder, "Mom, they're here!"

Kiel wanted to run, run away as fast as his legs would carry him. He was in trouble for being with a child. He took a deep breath.

You're not in trouble for what you did with him, he urged to himself, *just that you're late.*

"Where are you going?" she asked Cam, who was moping off towards the barn.

"To work on the go-kart," he called back, annoyed, as if his mom was out of line, not him.

Kiel needed Julie to know, though, what they'd done—or, rather, not done. "I think we found the Tandem-dyne connection," he blurted.

She looked at him as though he'd just suddenly spoken in Italian. "Mom!" she called again. "Let's *go!*" To Kiel, she said, "Sorry, this is going to have to wait. I really don't want to be late. This guy probably charges by the hour—he's a lawyer. Listen, I need a favor from you. I need you to watch Nicki while we're gone. My car's in the garage, and Mom has to drive—the truck's a stick . . . what's the matter?"

Kiel was shaking his head, feeling the panic well up again, smothering him.

"You can't watch her?" she asked incredulously. "It's just for maybe an hour."

All he could do was shake his head. He couldn't find the words.

She growled under breath, not having time to argue with him. She stomped back inside, and he heard her calling Nicki.

Kiel gasped. He'd been holding his breath. He didn't want to be here when Julie came back. He walked around to the side of the house and just stood there. It seemed like he'd never escape. He could run, but he'd always be a prisoner to the accusations.

Julie came around the corner, dragging a protesting Nicki along towards Daniel and Peggy's small house. She glanced over at him standing forlornly by himself. The look spoke of consternation and maybe even suspicion.

Kiel wanted to melt into the grass. He wanted to move around to the back of the house, to get away from the disapproval. That would be too weird, though, to be so obvious about hiding from her. Instead, he sat on the grass, facing away from Daniel's house, pretending to contemplate the distant profile of Chippewa Ridge.

He heard Julie's hurried footsteps pass by behind him. It was the sound of his despair at ever having a normal life.

After the old pickup truck bounced away down the lane towards the highway, Kiel kicked some gravel around and then went to the barn to watch Cam. Amazingly, the pile of parts that had lain strewn around the floor a couple of days before had been assembled into a bona fide go-kart, the sparse frame suspended inside four large ATV wheels. Kiel commented on the miracle.

"Ah, I could put this thing together with my eyes closed," the boy said, lifting the front end and spinning a wheel to check the balance. "I must have taken it apart and put it back together a dozen times."

"Why?"

"Uncle Daniel won't let me ride it until he has a chance to check it out."

"And he's a busy guy," Kiel surmised. "So, why take it apart so many times?"

The boy shrugged. "It's therapy."

"Therapy? You're twelve; what kind of therapy would a twelve year-old need?"

Without looking up, Cam replied, "A broken home. And I'm thirteen, remember?"

"I see. You don't want to see your parents split up."

The tween put the homemade vehicle down and wiped his hands. "Actually, I don't mind them splitting up. I just don't want to have to live with my dad. I hate him."

"Oh, come on. You don't hate him."

"Oh, I do," he confirmed earnestly.

"Why?"

"What he does to Mom."

"He, er . . . does he—?"

"No. He doesn't hit her or anything like that. He's too smart for that. Mental and emotional abuse."

"I see. You read about that on the internet?"

Cam shrugged one shoulder, an admission.

ж ж ж

Kiel and Cam were in the house playing cards when Mrs. Bakke and Julie returned. Julie pulled Cam to her and knuckled the top of his head while he squirmed to get away. "Don't worry me like that," she admonished, but her tone was lighthearted. "Now, go get your sister. Gamma will have dinner ready soon."

She stood up and looked at Kiel. "Maybe we should talk?" she suggested, gesturing towards the front door.

Kiel's heart beat a foreboding rhythm. He was going to catch hell, and from a woman he had really wanted to please.

Once outside, Julie started off, strolling along the lane, and Kiel walked alongside. "What's going on?" she asked simply.

He didn't say anything at first, collecting his thoughts and feelings. She waited patiently.

"I'm a fugitive," he heard himself say.

It was strange. He hadn't intended to tell her. Right up until that second, he was going to continue the furtive path he'd set himself on months before. Maybe he was tired of the deception, or maybe he just trusted her. Whatever the reason, he was surprised to feel a release, as though a heavy, decayed part of him had been sliced away.

"From what?" she asked.

She thought he might mean figuratively. He still had a chance to backpedal.

"The law," he replied, refusing to take back the rotten part.

"I see," she said gently.

He had revealed that part of the truth, but now he found he couldn't go on. It was like taking a sharp knife and drawing it along his own throat. He wanted to just leave it at that. He wanted to just keep walking next to her in silence. They could walk and walk, and just share their company without the pain of putting problems to words.

"Can I know why?" she asked, inevitably.

He stopped and put his closed fist to his mouth, pressing his curled forefinger against his upper lip. Could he really do this? "I told you before that I was running from Maria, my girlfriend—ex-girlfriend."

"Yes. She's schizophrenic."

"Right. But a very wild sort of the disease."

"Sometimes she would really go crazy," Julie confirmed, remembering.

He took a deep breath. "I also told you that I couldn't take it anymore and so I left. Well, that was only part of the truth. The nightmare started after that."

Julie stood watching him. Her eyes were reassuring, promising not to judge until she'd heard the whole story.

"I didn't mention that she has a daughter. Her name is Bernice—they call her Bernie. She's five—"

"The same age as Nicki," Julie said. Kiel thought that her tone might have hardened ever so slightly.

"Yes, the same age as Nicki. Bernie and I were . . . close. We got along great. I think that I may have represented stability. Anyway, after I finally got up the nerve to tell Maria that I wanted to break up, she . . . well, she went nuts. At first she took it kind of normally—crying and trying to talk me into staying; the sort of things you would expect. I was relieved. But then the next morning at 5:30, she called to tell me that I had one last chance to 'do the right thing.' I told her that I had already made up my mind. At 3:00 that afternoon the police came to where I was working and arrested me."

Julie shook her head a little, perplexed. "For what?"

Kiel looked her in the eye. "Maria had accused me of molesting Bernie."

Julie gasped and put her hand to her mouth. "Oh my God! No! Kiel, did you . . ."

"No! Of course not! She totally fabricated it."

What Maria had told the police was indeed entirely fabricated, but that wasn't exactly the end of the story. "Actually—"

"But, they arrested you?" Julie objected, her brow furrowed in indignation. "Just on her accusation?"

She was on his side, for the time being at least. He couldn't bring himself to put the final piece out there. Maybe later, after this much had a chance to sink in.

He lifted his shoulders. "That's all it takes. You're supposed to be innocent until proven guilty, but when it comes to accusations like this, you're pretty much on your own."

She shook her head, refusing to accept it. "But if she was schizophrenic—I mean—"

"Why would they believe her? That's the question I posed to my lawyer. You see, I dug my own grave on this one. Maria and I had been together for a long time, we started dating when Bernie was just three. We had actually been high school sweethearts for a while—"

"I thought you grew up in Baltimore?"

"I lied. I spent my whole life in Altoona. Anyway, her illness developed slowly. I wanted to protect her, and so I . . . well I sort of did my best to keep it hidden. Nobody else except her mother and her doctor knew just how sick she was getting."

"But, still. Couldn't your lawyer have somehow gathered evidence?"

Kiel sighed. "Possibly. It was a gamble. You'd have to know Maria. She's beautiful and smart and very, very charming. When she's not nuts, she could charm the crown right off the Queen of England. I imagined her in the courtroom with the jury, and I just knew that my odds were going to be pitiful, no matter how good my lawyer."

"So you . . . ran?"

"I skipped bail. I packed a bag and took off."

"Which makes you look very guilty."

"Exactly."

Julie took a deep breath, absorbing the gut-full of information. "I see," she finally said. She reached out and took both his hands in hers. "Thank you, Kiel, for telling me the truth."

He tried to smile. "You're the only person in the world who knows."

She breathed again. "Well, your secret is safe . . . for now. I need to think about this, but I promise not to tell anyone before talking to you first."

He looked at her. "So . . . you believe me?"

She returned his gaze with equal gravity. "Maybe." She let go of his hands and crossed her arms across her chest. "Maybe." She grinned. "At least I understand why you didn't want to be left alone with Nicki."

He returned her smile and nodded.

Her face became troubled.

"What's wrong?" he asked.

She waved it off. "I was just remembering the blow-up with Brandon earlier today. I guess you and I are both dreading our day in court." She smirked, a self-directed sardonic smile. "The whole Tandem-dyne thing was something of a red herring."

Kiel stared at her. "What?"

"Oh, don't look so distraught," she reassured, misinterpreting his reaction. "How could we have known? He was just executing that transaction for his brother—some kind of tax maneuver."

"You believe him?"

"He's a lawyer. They're experts at half-truths, but they rarely outright lie."

"So, Brandon has no vested interest in Tandem-dyne?"

"His brother doesn't either. He apparently sold the stock a few months later. I would suggest some kind of insider-trading, but I wouldn't want to be accused of slander."

"Huh. I see."

She studied him. "Don't take it so hard. It probably wasn't worth anything to me anyway."

He took a breath and nodded. *What the hell was going on?* he wondered. If the crablet colony wasn't some surreptitious defense project, then what in God's name *was* it? Maybe it was time to confront Brandon directly. Kiel wished that he hadn't been so coy about it before.

He found Cam still working on the go-kart. The kid was disassembling it yet again, claiming that he had an idea how to rig up a speedometer. Kiel didn't query his young friend about what possible circumstances one might need to accurately know the speed of a go-kart. That would be like asking Nicki what possible reason could there be for spinning in a circle until she fell to the ground, dizzy. He asked Cam for his father's phone number. Minutes later, Kiel was standing in Mrs. Bakke's bedroom—where she'd suggested he'd have more privacy than the living room—listening to Brandon's phone ring. "Hello, Chipdown speaking," came the lawyer's voice.

"Brandon, Kiel here."

"Hold on."

Kiel heard him in the background explaining to somebody that he had to take this, but he'd be right back.

"What's up?" he continued after a few seconds of rustling and the sound of a door closing.

No use pussy-footing around. "I need to know what the hell's going on in the old mine."

There was a long pause. "You don't know, do you?"

Kiel could almost hear the gears in the lawyer's mind backing up. Maybe he could renege on his deal about not going after the kids after all.

"I know that there's a whole colony of really weird . . . things breeding there," Kiel whispered harshly. "Are you certain they're not dangerous?"

Again the long pause. "What the hell are you talking about?"

"Come on. I've *seen* them. They've practically eaten away all of the abandoned bridge. They're . . . *multiplying*."

A sigh. "Have you been taking drugs? Look, I'm coming down tomorrow—you can tell me all about the multiplying 'things' then."

"Now wait a second I want to—"

Kiel could tell that Brandon had hung up on the other end.

Kiel chewed his lip, debating. If Brandon wanted to play dumb, he decided, then it served him right if his secret was blown. And if he wasn't, well in that case they needed help out here—quickly.

He found a phone book in the night stand and looked up the county sheriff's office. After a couple of rings, a no-nonsense man answered, "Lanner."

"Er, I'd like to speak with the Sheriff," Kiel said.

"You're speaking with him. What's the problem?"

Kiel realized that this was not going to be easy. This man was going to think, like Brandon had accused, that he was on drugs. "It's about the old gold mine on Tagget's land."

A pause. Again, that pause. "What about it?"

"There's something very strange going on there—"

"How do you know that?" Lanner asked immediately.

"Well, I've been there. It wasn't easy—"

"Who am I talking with?"

"Er, I'm Kiel. Kiel Martin." Saying his alias to a sheriff caused his heart to migrate to his throat.

"Martin—don't know any Martins. You at Tagget's place?"

"Er, no. I'm staying with Mrs. Bakke. She—"

"You're at Bakke's place?" He sounded surprised.

"Uh, yeah."

"I see. You a friend of Julie?"

"Yes."

Well, I am, he thought.

"Tell you what," the sheriff said, "I'm heading right by there tomorrow morning. Why don't I stop by and you can tell me about it?"

Kiel looked at the alarm clock on the night stand. It was nearly suppertime already anyway. "Sure. That would be great." He remembered that Brandon was coming as well. "Uh, could you make it early?"

"As early as I can."

The line went dead. People in Wisconsin apparently saw no reason to hang on the line a second longer than necessary.

ж ж ж

Dinner that night was somber, or at least it started that way. Julie was worried about the pending divorce, and Cam was worried that his idea to help her by digging up some dirt on his father wasn't panning out—in fact, probably the opposite; Cam seemed to share Kiel's troubled concern about the latest discoveries they'd made that day in and out of the mine. Mrs. Bakke, although pretending otherwise, was worried about her family being so worried.

Only Nicki was immune to such worldly disquiet. Despite Julie's urgings to sit quietly while she ate, the little girl was convinced that, even more than eating, what everybody really wanted was a song. So she gave them one. A nonsensical simple tune that involved a parade of animals, each verse longer than the last as a new parade member joined the existing menagerie. She'd gotten as far as the large African mammals, and Cam was about ready to take discipline into his own hands, when the lights flickered. Nicki stopped and looked at her mom expectantly, as though she'd arranged this just to distract her.

"What the devil?" Mrs. Bakke muttered, pausing with a forkful of mashed potatoes half way to her mouth.

The lights flickered again. And again. And then went out.

Nicki whimpered in the darkness, but the lights came back on, the refrigerator compressor kicked into gear, and the microwave hummed a moment and then went back to sleep.

"I wish they'd give us some warning," Mrs. Bakke complained. "Now I'll have to go around and set all the clocks again—"

The house went dark.

And stayed dark this time.

Nicki started to cry.

"Oh honey, it's okay," Julie assured. "It's just the power company having problems."

"They have problems, all right," Mrs. Bakke declared, scraping her chair as she stood up in the darkness. "The problem is that they don't have the brains to keep the electricity flowing. It can't be all that hard."

The squeak of a kitchen drawer opening and utensils being jiggled about was followed by a sudden burst of light as she found the flashlight. "Everybody sit tight while I get some candles."

The bobbing spot of light wandered away out of the kitchen, leaving them in darkness. "A relay somewhere trips, and we're instantly transported back a hundred years," Kiel commented.

"A hundred years ago, there were still wolves roaming the forests around here," Cam said.

Out of the blackness came Nicki's tiny voice. "There's no wolves now, right Mom?"

"No, honey. No wolves."

"No wolves," Cam added, making his voice deep and menacing, "but maybe wild dogs! Big, hungry dogs!"

"Cam, you stop that right now," Julie ordered. To Nicki, she assured, "Your brother thinks it's funny to scare you, honey. No wild dogs, no wolves, no anything. Nothing has changed just because the lights have gone out."

Maybe no wolves, Kiel thought, *but what about crablet drones?*

Wavering, warm light returned in the form of a candle carried by Mrs. Bakke. "Not so bad," she observed, putting it down on the shelf, and lighting another. "It's elegant—dinner by candlelight."

"Yeah," Cam said, eyeing a forkful of string-beans, "cold dinner by candlelight."

"Hush, boy," his grandmother reprimanded. "If a miracle suddenly allowed pigs to fly, you'd just complain that their mess was spreading beyond the pigpen."

"Well, it would," he concurred.

"I said hush," she commanded.

They all resumed eating, and after a few minutes, Cam said quietly, "Pigs can't fly."

" 'course not," his grandmother agreed.

"They're not clanking replicators," he added off handedly, giving Kiel a sly look.

Kiel wished that he could feel as casually about them. He imagined what the hive of crawling, flying, twisting colony creatures were doing now that the darkness of their lair had expanded to include the whole countryside.

He shivered, and then tried not to imagine.

PART III

EXECUTION

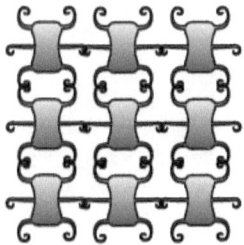

Blaine C. Readler

Chapter 12

Kiel woke to the sound of pounding. He snapped awake, and then lay back when he remembered where he was. It wasn't his house, and whoever was at the door wasn't his problem. He glanced at the alarm clock next to the bed, but it was dead—the electricity was still out. He'd heard a helicopter in the middle of the night, and had hoped that it was the power company searching out the problem. At times, it seemed to be close, as though maybe following the power lines.

The pounding downstairs continued until he heard the door open and then voices. He probably wouldn't go back to sleep now, even though it seemed still very early. He rolled over and looked at his watch on the nightstand. It was only 5:40! No wonder he still felt sleepy.

Mrs. Bakke called his name. She sounded anxious and this set his heart suddenly pounding. He had a vision of men in black FBI windbreakers surrounding the house. Who else would come for him? Nobody knew he was here. Didn't the FBI always strike very early, the element of surprise? He shouldn't have told Julie.

She called again. "Kiel, it's Sheriff Lanner!"

Not the FBI, but just as bad—the sheriff. Then he remembered that he'd called the day before. He'd asked Lanner to come early, but he hadn't meant before the sun was even up.

He pulled on his jeans and T-shirt, and slipped into his shoes, not bothering with the socks. Coming down the stairs, he found a tall, slightly pudgy man, half bald, with a stoop. Not exactly Kiel's impression of Wyatt Earp's legacy.

"Mr. Martin?" Lanner asked.

Kiel nodded, shaking the man's hand.

"Looks like I woke you up," Lanner observed with a hint of a grin.

Kiel shrugged. "I overslept," he replied, not sure if his joke was obvious.

"Sorry to bother you so early," he said to Mrs. Bakke. "I'm heading out to Tappiqua Lake for some fishing, and Mr. Martin's concern couldn't wait until tomorrow."

Kiel stared at the man. He'd never said that. It was the Sheriff's idea to stop by instead of talking on the phone.

"Kiel called you?" she asked, concerned. She looked at him.

"I'm sorry," he said to her, "I should have mentioned it." This was difficult. He really wanted to talk to the Sheriff alone. "It's, um, private." To Lanner, he said, "Can we maybe talk outside?"

"By all means," the Sheriff agreed, holding out his hand for Kiel to lead the way.

Kiel took them away from the house, and the Sheriff seemed content to get out of earshot before starting. "So, what's all this about the mine?" he finally asked when they had gone a good hundred feet.

Kiel hesitated. How to even begin? "It's going to sound nuts. Julie's husband thinks I'm on drugs."

"You talked to Brandon about it?" Lanner asked.

"Oh. You know him?"

"I know everybody here—those who belong, that is."

Kiel glanced at him, but the Sheriff's face showed none of the hostility the words might imply.

"So, what about the mine?" Lanner repeated.

"You haven't heard anything?" Kiel asked. "Rumors about strange . . . things?"

Lanner studied him a moment, looking for information behind his question. "Not a peep," he finally replied, putting his hands in the pockets of his jeans, which seemed to accentuate his stoop. "What sort of things you talking about?"

"Machines. At least, I think they're machines."

The Sheriff seemed troubled. "What do you mean? Like construction equipment?"

Kiel shook his head. "No. It's not like anything I've—or you've—seen before."

Now the Sheriff seemed confused. "Like what?"

Kiel found it difficult to go on. It really did sound nuts. "They're hard to describe."

"Well, are they bigger'n a breadbox?"

Kiel looked at the man. He was the Sheriff. His job was to uphold the law, but also to help the community, and Kiel had a growing suspicion the community was going to need help.

"Individually, they're smaller than a breadbox."

"What the hell does that mean?"

Kiel told him. Once he started, once he'd broken through the nut-barrier, the whole story flowed, from his initial discovery, hiding from the rain in the hole, to the previous day's discovery of the solar collectors and the creeping snake on the ridge. The only thing he held back was Cam's theory that the crablets were Von Neumann clanking replicators from outer space. He decided that this was a nut-bridge too far.

Throughout the whole narrative, Sheriff Lanner watched him impassively, as though listening to a long and inconsequential reenactment of a spousal argument. Kiel guessed that the sheriff heard more than his share of nutty stories.

When Kiel had finished, Lanner gazed off at the horizon a moment, clicking his tongue absently against the inside of this teeth. "Well, Mr. Martin," he finally concluded, "you were right—it does indeed sound nuts." He looked at Kiel, maybe contemplating whether he should restrain this stranger for his own safety. "What do you propose I do about these . . . 'incorporated crablets,' I think you called them?"

"Well, er, I guess the first step would be to go to the mine and have a look."

"I see." He continued to watch Kiel with cautious attention. "I tell you what," he finally said, taking his hands from his pocket and folding his arms across his chest, "I have to stop at Tagget's anyway to deliver some tax papers. You say he claims he's seen these flying machines as well. I'll get his side of the story. It's his land, after all."

"Um, sure. He may have only seen them once, and he didn't get a good look. In any case, I think we should go to the mine and—"

"I'll talk to Tagget," Lanner repeated. "We'll take it from there."

Kiel could tell that the man had made up his mind. "I'll go along, if you don't mind—"

"That won't be necessary," Lanner said bluntly. "I won't be coming back this way after Tagget's."

"I can walk. It's not far."

The Sheriff was already walking back to his car. There was no negotiating. "That's okay, Mr. Martin," he said without turning around. "I'll get back with you later."

He watched as the Sheriff drove away, the cloud of dust slowly settling back from where it had been disturbed.

ж ж ж

Kiel was digging fence post holes around a backyard flower garden when he saw Brandon's Lexus swaying along the lane like a small boat wallowing in heavy seas. It disappeared in front of the house, and he tossed the work gloves on the grass and started for the house. The lawyer stormed around the corner to meet him, and Kiel stopped when he realized that anger fueled the stride. Brandon, his eyes flashing, walked up to him, and gave him a hard push. Kiel was taken by surprise and stumbled backwards, tripped on a stone, and fell on his butt in the grass.

"What the fuck are you doing?" Brandon demanded.

Looking up at the furious man, Kiel took a moment to catch his breath. "I think I'm recovering from an assault. Isn't that a felony?"

"You goddamn ..." he muttered between clenched teeth, taking a step forward.

Kiel crab-walked away, afraid he was going to kick him. "What did I do?" he asked, getting to his feet, ready to run if needed.

"You called the Sheriff! What the hell did you do that for!"

Kiel had the idea that Brandon wasn't dumb enough to actually hit him, and a bit of courage returned. "Let's turn it around; why do you care? You certainly didn't seem interested on the phone yesterday."

"I *told* you I was coming by today to talk about it!"

"Yeah, and you hung up on me!"

"What's going on?" It was Julie, walking towards them from the house.

Brandon looked from her to Kiel. "Don't," he warned ominously.

"Don't what?" she asked. She looked at Kiel. "What is this?"

"He . . . I . . ." Kiel stammered and then just looked at her. He didn't know how Brandon was connected with the drones, but he didn't want to blow a chance at getting her custody of the kids. He sighed. "I can't tell you. I'm sorry."

"Secrets?" she challenged. "First the visit from Sheriff Lanner, and now you two are fighting. I want some answers."

Kiel's wits were returning. "Wait a second," he said, turning to Brandon. "How did you know I called Lanner?" To Julie, he asked, "Did you tell him?"

"I'm still waiting to find out what's going on," she replied.

Brandon was watching him. His nose was turned up ever so slightly in a defiant pose.

"You and the Sheriff are in cahoots!" Kiel blurted. "What the hell!"

"What the hell, indeed," Julie said. "If somebody doesn't tell me—"

Kiel had already set off at a trot towards the house.

"Where are you going?" Brandon and Julie called on top of each other.

"To Tagget's!" he yelled back. "Julie's right; it's time to get some answers."

"Hold on, goddamnit!" Brandon called. "I'll drive."

"I'm coming too!" Julie cried.

Kiel and Brandon turned together and shouted, "No!"

They glanced at each other and sprinted off for the Lexus.

ж ж ж

Kiel thought he might be getting sick from the motion. He grasped the handle above the passenger door with one hand and steadied himself on the seat with the other, but the Lexus jerked back and forth so wildly he felt like an ice cube in a margarita blender. Tagget hadn't maintained his lane at all, and it seemed that the ride might have been smoother if Brandon had just eased over into the plowed field.

They hadn't said much during the short ride from Mrs. Bakke's house. Brandon had cooled off, but seemed to be taking what might be his own lawyerly advice: don't offer more information than needed.

Tagget's farm turned out to exhibit about the same state of disrepair as his lane. The barn was bare, weathered wood, and dark, vertical gaps, like missing teeth, showed where planks used to exist. The house wasn't much better. Blue, tattered tarp covered one corner of the roof, and yellowing plastic was attached with duct tape across a broken window. A variety of inoperable vehicles—a rusting tractor with half-buried spring teeth of a harrow still attached, an abandoned bailer, and a selection of ancient cars on blocks—crowded the area around the house. A newer model sedan, out of place like a groom at a barn raising, was parked in front of them.

"That's Lanner's," Brandon indicated. "How long ago did he leave Bakke's?"

Kiel glanced at his watch. "Three hours, at least."

"Huh. He said he was going fishing."

"You think they went to the mine?"

"Dunno. Let's check it out."

Kiel followed Brandon through the weeds that once, long ago, had been a lawn. The front door was not only unlocked, but already open an inch. Brandon pushed it all the way. "Tagget!" he called. When there was no answer, he stepped inside and called again. To Kiel, he added, "Whew! The guy might as well live in his barn."

There was still no answer.

"I guess we should go to the mine," Brandon suggested.

Kiel looked at him. "Maybe it's time to talk about what's there—"

He saw something lying on the floor in the next room. It looked like a boot sticking out from around the corner. But the boot had a pant leg attached. He walked towards it, and as he did, more of the room came into view, and with it, the body of a man. "Holy shit!" he cried and then stopped short. "Oh my God!" he whispered, covering his mouth with both his hands.

"What the—" Brandon started, then, "Oh Lord!"

It was Tagget, but Kiel wouldn't have recognized him without the context of being in his house. There seemed to be more blood than a man could possibly contain in his body. Red goo was smeared at least five feet across the carpet. Tagget's shirt was soaked—a dark, wet mass, torn and exposing slashes of red pinkness. Kiel remembered reading that a clean kill usually results in little blood—once the heart stops, blood is no longer pushed out the wound. If so, Tagget must have died a long and agonizing death.

"His throat," Brandon stated, pointing.

Kiel saw what he meant. This was obviously what had ultimately killed the old farmer. The deepest pool of blood had spilled from a gash across the man's jugular.

"Who in God's name would have done this?" Brandon said, staring at the horror.

"Or, do you mean what?"

The lawyer looked at him, puzzled. "What do you mean?"

"What do *you* mean? Don't you think those ... things in the mine are capable of something like this? What else could do this?"

"What in good God's name are you babbling about?"

Kiel heard a whimper and spun around. Cam stood there, frozen in terror. His hair was matted to his forehead, and he was flushed and breathing heavily.

"How did you get here?" Kiel asked, stepping between the boy and the horror that used to be Tagget.

Cam looked at him as though he didn't see him, as though he was sleepwalking. "I—I ran."

"Come on," Kiel urged, herding the boy back out the front door. "It's okay."

"It's o-*kay*?" Cam demanded as Kiel practically pushed him outside. "Tagget is *dead*!"

"I know," Kiel replied, trying his best to sound calm. "But it's okay." He didn't know what else to add.

"Adults always say that!" Cam insisted, almost hysterical. "Everything's 'okay,' when it's *not*! Mr. Tagget is *dead*!"

"You're right," Kiel agreed, taking a deep breath. "It's definitely not okay. I guess I meant that you shouldn't be afraid."

"Oh, really? The drones did that, didn't they?"

"I don't know. It's up to the Sheriff now to figure that out."

"You know they did, and they could be anywhere around here."

Cam scanned the skies, looking for telltale glints.

Kiel wanted to dampen the panic, so he resisted, but he felt the hairs rise on his arms at the thought.

He heard Brandon calling him. It sounded like it came from behind the house. "Stay here," he said and started around the side.

Cam followed. "You think it's safer here than any place else?"

Kiel didn't answer. He wasn't up to arguing logic that made sense.

When he rounded the far corner, he saw immediately that Brandon had found further bad news. Very bad news. Sheriff Lanner lay sprawled in the dirt.

"Stay here!" Kiel commanded, and this time the boy seemed willing to comply.

At first, Kiel thought that the Sheriff wasn't even wounded, but when he came closer, he saw that his neck too had been slashed, and a little pool of blood had formed next to the man's crooked arm, as though he'd been trying to contain it.

"No struggle," Brandon commented woodenly. "Just the throat."

Tagget had been practically torn to shreds before being killed, but Lanner had been murdered as though by the efficient hands of a practiced professional.

"He put up a fight, though," Brandon observed, indicating with his toe at spent shell casings. "There," he further directed, pointing with his finger at a revolver lying a few feet away.

Kiel had to hand it to the lawyer—he could keep his cool under pressure.

He noticed something. "Look at Lanner's head—the scalp," he said. There was a red streak above the man's ear.

Brandon squatted down, careful to avoid contact with anything. "He's been grazed by a bullet."

"You sure?"

"No. Of course not. But that's what it looks like."

Kiel's mind seemed to lock up from the conflicting information. The drones wouldn't have shot a gun—would they? If it wasn't drones, then who?

"What's this?" Brandon said, peering at the ground next to the fallen sheriff.

Kiel saw it. It looked like a little wad of aluminum foil. "There's another," he said pointing a short distance away. He reached down and picked it up.

"Hey!" Brandon objected. "Don't touch anything!"

Kiel ignored him. Protocol could wait. His hunch was correct. He carried it back to Cam who stood holding himself with his arms wrapped around his sides, as if chilled despite the summer heat. He opened his palm and showed the boy. The kid's eyes were keener than his.

"Crablets," Cam concurred. His voice was a little shaky, like he really was cold. He looked closer. "They're damaged. Looks like they've been squashed."

That did it.

Kiel strode back to Brandon, who had stood up, and grabbed the man's shirt in his fist. "What the hell is going on?"

The lawyer was stronger than his dapper demeanor might imply as he knocked Kiel's hand away. "How should I know? Do you think I had something to do with this?"

"Not you directly, but your drones sure as hell were here."

Brandon stared at him. The lawyer could have been looking at something inanimate, something unwelcomed that had fallen onto his porch. "This is the same nonsense you told Lanner? Strange machines living in the mine?"

"So, Lanner did tell you."

"So what? It's nonsense! You're nuts! He was just warning me that I might want to keep an eye on you. You might be dangerous."

That could be, Kiel thought. But somehow it didn't sound right. He was sure the Sheriff was somehow in on something with Brandon. He hadn't wanted to talk until they'd gotten away from the house, and then he'd been all ears until he decided that Kiel was talking nonsense. Whatever it was, it had to do with the mine. That's what had caught Lanner's interest.

Also, Brandon and Kiel were supposedly sharing a secret about the mine, one so important to Brandon that he was willing to sign over Cam and Nicki to Julie. He remembered how it had all begun. Daniel had told him that Brandon was trying to buy land from Tagget.

"Whatever you're up to, Brandon," Kiel said, "I'd say the game's done. Tagget's dead, and you never got to buy the mine."

He didn't reply. He just stared at the corpse.

"A county sheriff has been murdered," Kiel went on. "Seems to me like the state's Attorney General is going to have to pick this one up. There's going to be an investigation. If any out-of-state links turn up, the FBI will be brought in. I'll be a key witness—you had some secret deal brewing, and now one party is dead. I think you should come clean with me. What in God's name is going on here?"

It was a bluff. At his first opportunity, Kiel knew he was going to get as fast and far away as he could manage. Julie knew everything, and he'd be crazy to assume she'd be silent in the face of murder investigations.

The bluff seemed to have worked, though. Brandon looked like a broken man. He sat on the ground and held his head in his hands. "Sand for fracking," he said.

At first, Kiel thought he'd used a euphemism for the ultimate expletive. "Fracking? Like extracting oil from shale?"

Brandon nodded without looking up.

"They use sand?"

The defeated lawyer took a deep breath and lifted his head. "They use sand for fracking," he repeated. "Not just any sand. It has to be very fine, and the grains must be spherical."

The sandstone in the mine dissolved into perfect, white beach-sand. Mrs. Bakke had used it as a sandbox for Julie and Daniel. Cam had said that men from an oil company had been there—they probably took samples from the sandbox. "You were going to buy the mine and then sell *sand* to an oil company?"

Brandon raised one eyebrow, and his condescending sneer eased back. "That *sand* is worth millions."

There was deep irony here. The very sand that had driven the gold miners away a century ago was perhaps worth more than whatever gold they'd expected to find. It was indeed a gold mine, but the gold required the Midas touch of advanced oil extraction technology to be transformed.

"Nobody knows about this?" Kiel asked.

"Now there are two of us," Brandon replied.

"Then who killed Tagget and Lanner?"

"The drones," Cam said from thirty feet away. He was pointing across the back yard towards a utility pole. "They need power."

Chapter 13

Kiel followed where Cam was pointing and saw what he was talking about: what appeared to be a dark snake of frozen water spiraled up the pole. "This is where it was headed," he said, taking a few tentative steps towards the pole.

"What is it?" Brandon asked, walking on ahead to get a better look. He stopped at a deep irrigation ditch a dozen yards from the pole.

"We found it yesterday," Kiel explained. "It comes from the mine. It was heading down the ridge, moving along at only an inch a minute, but who knows how close it had already come by then."

"Who made it?"

"The drones."

Brandon looked at him, annoyed. "I've been in the mine. There's nothing but rock and sand."

"Really?" Kiel said, surprised. "When?"

"I don't know—maybe a month ago."

"That would have been plenty of time. They ate most of the bridge away in just a few days."

Brandon threw him an irritated glance. Two murdered men was overwhelming enough, the guy obviously had no patience for what he thought was imagined nonsense.

Kiel realized that a buzzing sound had been growing in volume just as he heard Cam cry out. He spun to find a drone circling above the boy, who flailed madly. The machine creature deftly avoided his swatting hands. Then Kiel saw a second one appear around the corner of the house. The first one was obviously just keeping Cam occupied until its backup arrived.

"Hold on!" Kiel yelled, sprinting towards them.

As he ran, he grabbed a three-foot length of two-by-four. He'd fought off enough bullies in Altoona to know how to come prepared for a fight. The second drone had arrived, hovering a few feet away, while the first one dove in. It extended a taloned foot and grabbed Cam by the hair.

Kiel was upon them now, though. Holding the piece of lumber like a baseball bat, he swung at the one above Cam. He didn't use all his force, since he was afraid he might graze the boy, so the two-by-four smacked into the drone feebly. Even so, the board penetrated the machine beast, bending and distorting it so that it flopped about, unable to maintain attitude. Kiel was surprised and pleased at how easy that had gone.

His satisfaction was short-lived. The warped drone morphed before his eyes so that within seconds, it was as though Kiel had never struck it. In his mind's eye, he could see the crablets reconnecting, grasping hand-holds that had been parted, re-forming what had been deformed.

Something bit the back of his neck. It hurt! *The other drone!* Kiel ignored it—deal with one at a time. He cocked the makeshift club and yelled to Cam to duck. The boy jerked his head down against the strain and obvious pain of hair ripping out by the roots, and Kiel swung, this time with all his force. He felt the impact and heard Cam cry out as his head was jerked upwards. This time, the drone didn't just deform, but broke into two complete parts. One piece, a mangled mass of crumpled metal, fell to the ground. The other hung limply along the side of Cam's head.

Time to deal with the other one. He swung around. Where was it? He still heard the burring of its wings. He looked down. It hovered above the piece that had fallen. As he watched, the mangled remnant extended a hook, which the second drone grabbed to lift it up and away and back around the corner of the house.

The other half still dangled from Cam's hair. The boy was cautiously feeling, trying to understand what was there. Tossing his club, Kiel reached out and grabbed it. It squirmed in his grasp, and he had an overwhelming urge to let go. He hung on, though, and using his other hand to hold Cam's head, gently pulled it out of the boy's hair. It bit his palm, and he threw it forcefully to the dirt and stomped on it. He retrieved the two-by-four and beat the living hell out of the flattened vestige. When he finally gave up, letting the club fall to the ground, the piece of drone was nothing more than tatters and shreds of dirty metal.

But then, horrified by its refusal to die like any living creature graciously would, Kiel watched as his victim dissolved. It seemed to melt, but he knew what he was seeing, and he could tell that the melting material was actually hundreds upon hundreds of individual crablets giving up their incorporated cooperation to fend for themselves and scurry away into the dirt. Within seconds, all that was left was a faint speckling of metal. He squatted to peer more closely, and saw that some few dozen had actually succumbed. His best effort to kill the machine had destroyed a tiny fraction of one percent of the whole.

"Holy Christ!"

It was Brandon, standing next to him.

"What in God's name *were* those things?"

Kiel glanced at him. "Hard to ignore the reality once you've seen them, isn't it."

He examined Cam's head, but it looked fine. "You okay?" he asked.

The boy nodded in short, jerky shakes. He seemed almost in shock.

"Those were the drones you've been talking about?" Brandon asked.

"Those were the drones that I tried to describe, but you refused to listen," he replied, probing the back of his own neck. He felt the welt of a wound, and his hand came away bloody.

Cam's father stood watching the house, obviously worried they might return.

"Your son seems to be okay," Kiel declared.

Brandon nodded. "Uh-huh, good." he muttered, not catching the sarcasm. He didn't even look at Cam.

Kiel's heart was easing back to a mere pounding thump. Things were beginning to make sense. Brandon was in a rush to get a divorce so that he wouldn't have to split the wealth of the mine—so much so that he was willing to forfeit his run for Senator. He chose money over power. People in the area knew that the mine had once been closed because of sand, but Brandon was hoping that they no longer remembered the fantastic quality of that sand, and wouldn't make the fracking connection should they hear about the oil company's needs. He had to keep people's attention off the mine at any cost.

Kiel now also knew the reason for the power outage at the Bakke house. At least, it seemed obvious.

"Keep an eye out for those drones," he instructed and walked over to the utility pole.

He hadn't majored in electrical power distribution, but he had a general idea of the technology. The substation was probably off to the west, and the three lines coming in from that direction would be two phases at five or maybe ten kilovolts, plus a ground lead. The transformer box on the pole would step down one of the phases to 120 and 240 Volts for Tagget's farm. The same three lines continued on to the east, towards Mrs. Bakke's house. When tapping in to the power, the colony had apparently accidentally broken the connection downstream, killing the power for Mrs. Bakke.

He peered up, trying to see where the metal snake connected. It couldn't be to the high-voltage lines, otherwise at ten or even five kilovolts, it would short to Earth—the machine snake lay, after all, right in the dirt. It had to be tapping in on Tagget's side of the step-down transformer. Yes, he saw it—the snake arched from the pole around the transformer box to one phase of Tagget's feed. That made sense, since the transformer box casing was probably grounded.

"The solar collectors weren't enough?"

It was Cam. He'd come over to stand next to Kiel, maybe feeling safer there than with his own father.

"I guess not. They need more power as the colony grows."

"They'll continue replicating as long as they have enough to sustain them."

Kiel looked at the boy. His serious face was fixed with determination, as if thoughtful analysis was their only shield and weapon against these increasingly hostile intruders. He seemed mature well beyond his thirteen years. Kiel felt a little sorry for the kid. He'd have the rest of his life for that.

Kiel heard more footsteps, and saw that Brandon was coming over to join them. His eyes darted here and there, uncharacteristic for the normally self-assured lawyer. The man seemed to handle human death with equanimity, but was terrorized by the inexplicable. "What do you think?" he asked.

"I think that you were supposed to be watching in case they returned."

Kiel had the idea that Brandon didn't like being alone. The best defense against a shark is companions who are slow swimmers.

"I also think that we need to kill their power feed," Kiel added.

Brandon gazed up at the pole, and then off in the distance towards the ridge. "You think they've strung a line all the way to the mine?"

"I know they have."

"Let's just get out of here," Brandon urged. "This is one for the police."

"Now that Tagget's dead, it's okay to just walk away from the whole thing?" Kiel prodded.

Brandon shrugged. "Sure. What the hell. Let the authorities deal with it."

"They've killed the county authority, remember?"

"The State Police, then," he replied, getting agitated, "or the Army for all I care."

"We're fighting a geometric progression," Cam said quietly.

"I'm not fighting anything," his father retorted. "I'm leaving, and you two can come along or stay."

He started back towards the house.

"Brandon!" Kiel called.

The man stopped and turned around, his face a stone mask.

"I think you should hear this . . . from your son."

He stared at Kiel a moment, and then glancing quickly at Cam, he came back. "I'm listening."

Cam gulped. He was still his father's son. "Replication can proceed as a geometric progression—that means that the first cycle two can make four, and then the second cycle four can make eight, and—"

"I know what a geometric progression is," Brandon cut in.

"Right. Anyway, the longer they're allowed to replicate, the quicker the quantity becomes too big to deal with at a certain level."

"Obviously. So what?"

"So, we need to kill their power like Kiel said. If they're limited to just the solar collectors, the size of the colony is contained—they need a certain amount just to maintain activity, none left over to make more of themselves. But as long as they have access to this power line, they'll continue growing at a geometric progression. Eventually they'll need even more power—"

"Yeah, yeah," his father interrupted dismissively, gesturing with his hand that the boy was overdoing it. To Kiel, he said, "What do you propose?"

Kiel gazed back up at the pole and then down to where the drone snake exited to head off towards the ridge. "Well, the easiest would be to just cut their own feed—Tagget might have an axe."

"Fine. Let's get it done—"

"But I think that would be a mistake," Kiel finished.

"Why?"

"Cam?" Kiel offered. He wanted to include him, keep him engaged.

The boy studied the utility pole, taking the question seriously. "They'd just repair the damage. We know that they can reconfigure easily."

"Good point. So, what other options do we have?"

Cam looked at him. "You're patronizing me again, Kiel."

He smiled. "Perhaps. Think of it as a challenge, then."

"We don't have time for games—" Brandon started impatiently, but Kiel cut him off with an upraised hand.

Cam chewed on his lower lip. "It would be better to cut the power at the source."

"Maybe by cutting the main high-voltage lines?" Kiel offered.

Cam glanced at him. "You obviously have something better."

"Okay, here's my idea. I think you're right, Cam. Like you said, if we try to break the snake—their feed—they'll just repair it, probably within a minute or two. If we cut the main high-voltage lines, that should stop them for a while, but they might figure out how to tap into the downed lines. The power is still there if they can get at it."

"Unless it blows a fuse," Cam suggested.

"Exactly. I suspect that just letting a five or ten kilovolt line touch the ground would trip the circuit breaking mechanism back at the substation, but why take any chances?"

Cam looked at the top of the pole, then back at him with alarm. "You're going to short them out?"

"It's the safest approach."

"I think my mom might have something to say about that."

He grinned. "The safest approach for the rest of Wisconsin, not for me. That seems to be a common tradeoff in war."

"What war?" Brandon challenged irritably. He'd been pacing, and stopped, hands on hips.

Kiel gestured towards the house. "We have two casualties already, and one of them was armed. Do you know what these drones are, or where they came from? If they weren't dangerous, I don't think you'd be in such a hurry to leave."

That seemed to put a lid on the belligerent man. Kiel found Tagget's tool shed—one dilapidated shack among several. It was dark inside, and the light didn't work. He guessed that the colony had cut the old farmer's power as well. After a minute, his eyes adjusted to the sunlight filtering through the cracks between the wall planks. The shed was an unnavigable mass of rusty rakes, spades, shovels, and wooden bins of machine tools. He even found a horse whip buried deeply. He couldn't find exactly what he wanted, so he built his own. Using bailing twine, he strapped a four-foot iron pry-bar along the tines of the rake. A yard or so of wooden rake handle should provide enough insulation for ten kilovolts. At least, he hoped so.

The utility pole had a built-in ladder—protruding L-shaped hand and footholds for the linemen servicing the equipment—but the lowest rung was ten feet from the ground, presumably to prevent the odd curious youngster from experimenting with electrocution. Kiel found a stepladder and leaned it against the pole.

"You really are crazy," Brandon declared, picking up his rake construction.

"Maybe," Kiel replied, taking it from him. "They say the truly insane don't know it, so I might well be."

As soon as he started up the stepladder, Kiel realized he couldn't climb up the pole with one hand. He shaped a piece of baling wire into a hook, and tied it to the rake, and then inserted it over his belt. The weight of the combined rake and pry-bar tugged at his pants, trying to pull them down, and his contraption swung drunkenly from side to side, trying to twist him off the pole. But slowly, step by step, he worked his way until he was high enough to see over Tagget's roof, and Brandon and Cam were just two little foreshortened faces peering up at him.

"You look kind of silly!" Cam called up. "Like a giant dragonfly has landed on you, and you're trying to escape from it."

"It's going to be sorry when it discovers what ten kilovolts feels like," he replied, stopping. The step-down transformer box was now next to him, and he could hear the hum of the high-tension lines just a few feet above. From far below, he heard Cam confirm for his father that ten kilovolts meant ten thousand Volts. The lawyer whistled.

Beads of sweat rolled into Kiel's eyes, and he shook his head to knock them out of the way. His palms were wet too, which sort of worked against someone trying to avoid electrical contact. A lineman incurs limited danger, since the ground—his nemesis when communing with ten thousand Volts—is far away. The colony snake, though, provided a substantial path to ground, and presented Kiel with a very real danger of killing himself. He should have had Brandon break the snake with an axe just long enough for him to finish his task. Too late now. He'd have to count on the rake handle being a good insulator.

He reached behind and managed to snag the giant dragonfly, but immediately realized that he had another problem. Linemen use belts to hold them to the pole. Kiel needed two hands to work his unwieldy tool, and a third—and preferably a fourth as well—to hang on.

Shit.

He tried managing each task with just one hand, but almost fell when he momentarily lost his grip. Panting and hugging the pole, he contemplated his options. He didn't have many. After carefully jamming his T-shaped tool into a crook between the transformer box and the pole, he took off his belt, wrapped it around his left thigh, and then attached it to one of the pole's ladder rungs. It wasn't exactly a lineman's setup, but it at least provided a degree of attachment to something other than air.

Above him were three lines arriving from some invisible point off in the distance, and then heading away again to an unseen destination in the opposite direction. The outside ones, on both his left and right, were the ten kilovolt hot feeds. The line directly over his head would be the neutral, presumably tied to ground somewhere. Carefully, carefully, trying to keep his center of gravity as stable as possible, he eased the pry-bar up between the neutral and hot line to his left, keeping the bar parallel with the lines. He stopped. Maybe this wasn't the best idea. Once above the lines, he had planned on turning the bar ninety degrees and bringing it down, shorting the hot lead to the neutral. He realized, however, that this left no room for experimentation. If something didn't go right—like he could feel ten thousand volts seeping through his rake handle—gravity could pull the bar down, making contact whether he wanted it or not.

Carefully, carefully, he eased the bar back down. He rotated it so that it was perpendicular to the lines, and eased it back up. He stopped when he was six inches from the hot line. Now he had another problem. The neutral line was above the other two by a good foot. He could think of no alternative, so he continued easing the pole upwards. Three inches, two inches, he'd made contact. He thought he felt a tickle along his arms, but he decided that it was just his imagination. Continuing to raise the rake handle meant that he had to let it move to the side as the bar tilted up. The sweat ran freely into his eyes and he blinked and shook his head, but his vision remained blurred.

Oh, to hell with it, he decided, and he jammed the handle out and up, and the world exploded. A blinding flash nearly knocked him headlong off the pole, and he choked on ozone so thick, he thought it was eating away the lining of his nose.

He found himself hugging the pole, his sight slowly returning. Where was his makeshift shorting bar tool? He looked down, but it wasn't to be seen, just the awestruck faces of Cam and Brandon. Then he noticed the rake handle dangling off to the side. He wiped his eyes on his sleeve and looked up. The pry-bar and rake handle dangled from the two power lines. The arc had welded the bar to the lines.

Yikes!

He'd done it! Or, at least half of it. He wasn't sure if the circuit breaking mechanism back at the substation would disconnect both hot feeds when one shorted, but he sure as hell wasn't going to reach up to find out. He listened, and heard a hum. Apparently the other feed was still hot. He needed his tool back.

That was odd. The load on the other hot feed line must have increased—a lot! The humming was getting loader.

"Kiel!" Cam shouted from below. "They're back!"

Chapter 14

Kiel twisted around. Two of the drones were coming in from the direction of the ridge. They were maybe two hundred yards away, heading straight for him. He guessed that they were coming to investigate the loss of power. If so, it probably meant that they had no long-distance communication. Otherwise, reinforcements would have arrived long ago.

"Run to the tool shed!" he yelled down to Cam, grabbing the rake handle and giving it a yank. "Close the door, and find something to defend yourself!"

The pry bar was welded securely fast. He yanked harder, almost pulling himself off his perch.

"What about *you*!" Cam called up.

"I'll be okay!" A lie. "Just *go*!"

Brandon had already started for the shed. He glanced at the approaching drones, and then at his son. He returned, grabbed the boy by his arm, and dragged him off to the shed. Cam yelled and kicked the whole way.

Kiel gave the rake handle another yank, and felt the twine binding the rake handle to the pry bar giving way. He glanced at the drones. They had gained altitude. They were coming in level with his head.

He reached up. What he was about to do scared the dickens out of him. But so did the drones. He couldn't quite reach the pry-bar. He stepped up to the next protruding rung, but his belt went taught, preventing him from going farther. Straining, he managed to grasp the middle of the bar. He was alive; the hot line was truly dead. He gave the bar a tug, and then a harder tug. One end—the side welded to the hot line—came free, but he fell back at the sudden slack, and his foot slipped off its rung. His belt slid up his thigh all the way, giving him one tremendous wedgie and causing pain in his groin that was hard to believe. Gasping, he grasped the bar with both hands and hauled himself upwards. Suddenly he fell again with a jolt—the bar had come lose at the neutral end as well. He cried out in fear. Neither hand now held anything solid, and his groin felt as though a sword had been jammed up his crotch. He wrapped his arms around the pole and found rungs for his hands to grasp. No time to gather his wits. The rake and pry-pole lay dangling across his shoulder. He worked his feet onto rungs, and holding on with one hand, grabbed the rake handle. He had stretched the twine bindings, and the pole flopped around loosely on the rake tines.

He knew the drones were close. The burring was a roar, like a lawnmower next to his head. He lifted the rake handle, the pry-bar swinging back and forth, ready to slip out of its slack twine binding completely given the slightest opportunity. Suddenly his head jerked back as a hot pain burned his scalp. *Goddamn!* One of the drones had grabbed his hair, just like they'd done to Cam. He had no hands left to reach up. The bastard pulled back with a steady, inexorable force, seeming intent to yank him off his perch.

Fear screamed at him to drop the rake and pry-bar and extract the machine devil, but he was so close to completing the task. The ferocity of their attack was a measure of the value of the power line, and in turn the imperative that he deprive them of it. His head was pulled back so far, it was hard to see what he was doing, but he prayed that if he just blindly probed up and down with his tool he would eventually connect the two power lines.

The second drone swam into view above him. It seemed to be trying to get into the busy space of wires and insulator supports in order to intercept his probing hand. Kiel guessed that it must be having difficulty, judging by the searching, almost drunken maneuvers as it swooped back and forth above him. This seemed uncharacteristic of the precise performance he'd witnessed, but Kiel was glad for it. If he could just get the damn pry-bar to connect. He could tell by feel that it was swinging and twisting about inside the loose binding. As far as he knew, it might be nowhere near the two power lines.

And then all of a sudden he was again blinded by a glorious electrical explosion. Once more the shock nearly knocked him from the pole, but now the terror was equally balanced by jubilation. As a bonus, his head was free; the first drone had relinquished its clawing hold.

He hugged the pole with both arms, waiting for his sight to return, waiting for the drones' next move. His ears hummed from the explosion, but he could tell that the burr of their wings had departed.

Where the hell were they? Anticipation of a surprise attack was almost worse than fighting them off.

Once again he saw the rake handle dangling before him. He glanced up, and did a double-take. One end of the pry-bar had blossomed into a shapeless mass of spongy metal. As he watched in wonder, it decayed before his eyes. Tiny flakes of metal sloughed off and fell, swirling and twirling like snow to the ground far below. And then it came to him what he was looking at, and he gasped at the unexpected surprise. It was the second drone. In its probing attempt to get at him, it had apparently strayed between the pry-bar and the live line. The electrical arc and massive surge of current had fused it in place.

And it appeared to be dead, or more accurately, enough of the myriad of component crablets had been destroyed to cease incorporated operation as a drone.

In fact, Kiel guessed that most—maybe all—of the crablets were destroyed. He could imagine them abandoning their unified host of their own volition, but the flakes he saw falling looked lifeless, so much frizzled metal.

The disintegration slowed, the snow storm tapering to a light flurry. Revealed beneath was the core of crablets that had born the full surge of current, melted and fused together into a smooth, continuous mass of new-formed metal.

This thousand-fold horde of tiny cloned machines had found their ultimate incorporated nirvana.

"Kiel, are you okay?"

It was Cam, calling from far below. He realized that the boy had been calling to him for a while.

"Yeah!" he yelled back, unwrapping his arms and starting the long climb down. "How about you? What happened to the other drone?"

"One flew off. But there were two. Where's the other one?"

"Its days as a drone are over forever. It got caught in a giant bug zapper."

Once down from the pole, Kiel glanced around to make sure no colony representatives had returned, and then examined the scattered snowfall. He squatted down, wetted his finger with his tongue, and picked up a flake up with it. The crablet lay limp on the tip of his finger. He'd expected to find just a flake of fused metal, but it was an intact crablet. Its tiny legs, almost too small to see, wiggled around when he jiggled his finger.

"You've knocked out the power lines?" Brandon asked.

Kiel nodded, standing up.

"You're a hero, now let's get the hell out of here before any of those killer hummingbirds come back."

"Okay," Kiel agreed. "Let's go."

He suddenly imagined a whole flock of drones descending on the Bakke farm. He sprinted off, around the house towards Brandon's car. He came around the front corner and froze. He heard the footsteps of Brandon and Cam come up behind him, and he held out his hand to stop them without turning around.

"What is it now—" Brandon started, but then saw for himself.

Three—no, four drones hovered and buzzed about Brandon's Lexus, like bees intent on an unexpected windfall of a giant untapped flower. Kiel saw one of the drones ease down towards the rear fender and . . . melt into the car. It left a gaping hole behind. He realized that it hadn't melted into the car, but had merely crawled into a hole that had already been bored.

"What the hell are they doing!" Brandon yelled, oblivious to the fact that he was revealing his presence. He sprinted forward, towards his motive pride and joy. The three remaining drones obviously saw him as they ceased their probing investigation to hover a few feet above the car. Two drones came forward towards the human interloper, while the third maintained a defensive position above the curious mound of metal windfall, their version of flower nectar.

As the man and the machines met, flailing arms and deftly darting drones made a dizzying dance to watch. The jazz ballet didn't last long. Suddenly, one of the drones had Brandon by the hair, exactly as they'd done to first Cam and then Kiel. Pulling with concerted effort, the attacker forced the man's head up and back. Brandon resisted, but was unable to endure the strain. He reached up, trying to grab his tormentor. Blind to what was directly in front of him, Brandon didn't see the other drone come in low from the front.

In a flash of understanding, Kiel knew how Tagget and Lanner had been killed. Shouting, he sprang forward, not sure if he had time to save the life of Cam's father. The colony had worked out the method on Tagget, cruelly stabbing and cutting as they explored the weak points of the human anatomy. By the time Lanner arrived, they'd gotten it down: pull back the head, exposing the jugular for a quick slash.

Kiel saw that he would never make it in time. In his struggling, Brandon stumbled and inadvertently avoided the first killing slash, but the drone recovered and approached for the kill.

And then the world exploded.

The concussion that smacked Kiel felt like hitting the water when he belly-flopped as a kid. He was lying on the ground, gasping for air, but breathing only vacuum. The shock had stunned his diaphragm muscles, knocking the wind out of him. He lay there, panicked, terrified that he was going to die of suffocation, when suddenly his lungs relented and he wheezed in bucketfuls of wonderful air.

He was smelling scorched dirt and metal, and ... gasoline. After a few seconds, he rolled over and pushed himself up. Where Brandon's Lexus had stood was a blazing wreck of twisted metal.

"Kiel!" someone yelled. It was Cam. But the boy raced past him.

The gas tank had exploded, but why?

He remembered Brandon. The man had been closer to the explosion. Cam was kneeling in front of something crumpled, covered in ragged, torn clothes.

Kiel stood up and staggered forward, dizzy and stumbling. Cam had his hands on his father's chest, calling out to him, but the body just lay there, inert. Kiel knelt beside the boy and gently pulled him away, then turned his attention to the stricken man. Blood trickled from his nose, but not his ears. That must be a good sign. He laid his head against the man's chest, but could hear no heartbeat. He was about to attempt artificial respiration, even though he'd only seen it done on television, when Brandon groaned and then coughed.

"Try not to move," Kiel urged, not sure exactly why, but that's what people always said. "Just lay there until we get some help."

Brandon tried to say something, but only coughed, then waved Kiel back and lifted himself up unto his elbows to look. "Son-of-a-bitch!" he cried, and then rolled over and gave himself up to an extended fit of coughing.

"They're leaving," Cam observed, wonderingly.

Kiel looked towards where the boy was pointing. The early afternoon sun glinted off two receding drones, heading back to the mine. Movement caught his eye. Cam noticed the motion on the ground as well and took a step towards it before Kiel caught his arm. "Wait."

It looked like a reverse-motion video clip of snow melting. Within a swath perhaps five feet wide by thirty feet long, small patches of silvery-white emerged from the dirt. As each palm-sized section stabilized, it slid slowly along until it met another, and they merged. Kiel noticed that the swath lay radially away from the burning car, and the motion of each patch was backing away from the car.

"It's a drone, isn't?" Cam whispered.

"Or what remains of one," Kiel replied. "It must have been inside the car when it blew."

"What's it doing?"

Kiel had the sense that the boy knew, but was hoping he was wrong. "Pulling itself together, I guess."

"There never really is a drone," Cam stated.

Kiel looked at him. He wasn't sure what he was saying.

"I mean," Cam explained, "we call it a drone, but it's just the job that a collection of crablets decide to do for awhile."

"Sort of like men forming a baseball team."

"Or an army."

"Right. Or an army."

Brandon's coughing was easing, and he sat up and saw the migration. "What the hell—"

Conglomerated patches of crablets were large enough now that they could rise up, like a field of gophers emerging from their holes. One after another, they extended up and over, elongating into silver earthworms that wriggled their way towards a common, swarming mass whose structural complexity seemed just beyond Kiel's ability to comprehend.

"Christ! Stomp on it, already!" Brandon urged hoarsely, struggling to his feet and seeming intent to take on the task himself if they wouldn't.

"It won't matter," Kiel warned.

"Why, for Christ's sake?"

"Like Cam said, there's no 'it.' There's just a brigade of tiny cooperating machines. You might destroy a dozen, or even a hundred, but it won't much matter to the collective. I think Lanner shot one of the drones before they got him. There were a few scattered dead crablets on the ground. That was the extent of the damage. Remember the bullet that grazed the side of his head? Lanner tried to shoot the drone that had him by the hair."

Kiel hadn't made the connection until just now, but he could see it clearly in his mind, and it was a vision he wished he hadn't summoned.

All the wriggling crablet worms had arrived at the mosh pit, and the mass of swarming complexity morphed into the vague shape of a drone. The form softened and reformed, and then softened and reformed again, this time in the definitive familiar double-wing drone shape. It seemed to pause, as though catching its breath, then the wing-ears blurred into motion and it rose into the air. Kiel reflexively flinched, but the newborn drone headed off straight after its companions towards the mine.

"It's smaller," Cam observed.

Kiel saw that he was right. "The explosion must have killed a good portion of the crablets. That's why it took a couple of tries to get the drone-function worked out. Almost everybody needed reassignment."

"You sound like an expert on these mechanical piranhas," Brandon complained, wiping his face with his shirttail.

Kiel shook his head. "Just guessing—taking an engineering perspective, I guess."

Brandon ran his fingers through his hair and glanced around, then peered off towards the last diminutive drone, almost invisible now in the distance. "Why are they leaving?"

"If you're asking me to take another engineering guess, I'd say that they have no other reason to be here."

"They're just going to let us walk away?"

"I don't think that they were after us particularly. We just got in their way. They'd probably leave us alone if we avoided them. Sort of like bees."

Kiel didn't voice the rest of his thought, but Cam picked up on it anyway. "If the colony continues to grow, though, it will be harder to stay out of their way."

And eventually impossible, Kiel thought. "That's why we have to keep them from getting more power."

"So you're going to go out of your way to get in their way," Brandon concluded with sarcasm.

Kiel noted that the man had said "you," not "we."

Brandon turned to the burning relic of his Lexus. "Fuck! Why did they blow up my car?"

Kiel shrugged. "It's pretty obvious that it was an accident."

"How do you know?"

"Well, they were about two seconds away from killing you. If it wasn't an accident, I'd think they'd wait until they'd finished you off first. As it was, they shot themselves in the foot—if they actually had feet."

"But why? How?"

Kiel shrugged again. "Maybe they were just exploring. Maybe they'd never seen a car before. To them it probably seemed like a goldmine—their version. All they see is a couple of tons of metal. They obviously made the mistake of boring through the gas tank. Metal-on-metal. They must have made a spark."

Brandon just sighed, obviously deeply grieving his loss.

Kiel's explanation didn't make complete sense, but he decided not to voice his doubts. He was bothered that the colony drones had left. The metal was still there to protect, after all. In fact, if anything, it was even easier to access now that all the plastic and cloth had been burned away. And what about all of Tagget's other rusting hulks lying around? Why weren't they just feeding on those?

"Well, I vote for just staying the hell out of their way," Brandon finally groused.

"Sure; as much as we can manage."

The drones were gone. For now, they were safe.

Kiel had a thought, though. They'd disrupted the colony's main power source. It seemed likely that drones would be sent out looking for other sources, searching farther afield.

"Come on!" he yelled, taking off at a jog.

"Where are you going?" Brandon called to him irritably.

"Back to the house!"

"What's the rush?"

He didn't want to scare Cam. "We need to regroup—figure out where we go from here."

In fact, Kiel was racing to get there before drone scouts arrived and decided to clean house, and they wouldn't be taking directions from Mrs. Bakke.

Chapter 15

"They learn and then adapt to each new environment," Cam expounded. It had taken him all of five minutes to recover from the shock of The Battle for Tagget's Farm, and the bookworm's mind was doing cartwheels.

Kiel was consumed by worry about what they'd find back at the Bakke place, and was giving the boy just enough attention so he wouldn't feel slighted. Kiel wanted to sprint ahead, but he daren't leave the other two behind, and Brandon was moving slow, limping from a bruised thigh where a piece of Lexus shrapnel had apparently slammed into him. The half mile through the fields seemed endless.

"The crablets are the basic unit," Cam continued unabated. "They would have the ability to replicate themselves, and when there was enough of them, they could group together for phase two functions. It's possible that just one crablet somehow came to Earth."

"What the hell is he talking about?" Brandon asked Kiel, who wished that fathers wouldn't talk about their sons in the third-person when they were walking right next to them.

"Cam has a theory," Kiel replied. "It's based on Von Neumann's theory of self-replicating automata. The crablets comprise the basic automata cell."

He wasn't sure he'd repeated it correctly, and he wasn't sure he even bought Cam's theory, but he did enjoy giving the boy's father an intellectual poke.

Cam seemed impatient to continue, addressing Kiel, since he knew from long experience that his father could care less. "You see, each crablet has just enough intelligence—programming, I guess—to perform basic replication and maybe just a couple of phase two operations. The drone is probably a basic phase two. It might be sort of a common denominator—a form that works on any world that has air."

"Where the hell does he get these ideas?" Brandon complained.

"You can ask him," Kiel replied mildly. "He's right here. Cam?"

Kiel realized that he'd probably put the boy on the spot.

"Books," Cam replied with little enthusiasm.

"Science books?" his father challenged. "Is this what that science teacher—Dickson—teaches you?"

"No, Dad. I read—you know—science fiction."

"Oh, yeah," Brandon agreed, mocking him. "Science fiction. You're working on your lucrative Star Wars career."

"Not Star Wars—that's for little kids. I mean stuff like Larry Niven . . . just forget it."

Kiel was growing to despise the man. He felt bad that he'd pushed Cam into the trap. "Who do you think made the first crablet—the one that seeded the Earth?" Kiel asked in an attempt to draw the boy back out.

Cam didn't answer at first, gun-shy from his father's ridicule. Kiel was expecting Cam to accuse him—rightly—of patronizing him, but he responded. "The first crablet could be sent in advance of the designers, or it might just be a random one floating around that happened to fall on the Earth. The designers could be really far away—the other side of the galaxy—or they might even be long gone, extinct. This crablet could be many generations away from the original one. Sort of like gypsy moths. The first one escaped from a lab in Massachusetts in the eighteen-hundreds.

"Or maybe more like the killer bees," Kiel offered.

"Except that killer bees aren't really deadly at all."

"Right. So the colony isn't like killer bees."

"And killer bees don't learn as they go," Cam added.

"Huh. You think the crablets do?"

"Maybe not individual crablets, but more like the colony as a whole."

"You really think so?"

"They learned the best way to kill people."

Kiel hadn't talked about that. The kid was sharp, alright.

"Can we maybe quit with the slashed throat talk?" Brandon protested. "In fact, can we just shut up for awhile? I've got a headache."

Kiel decided that he did indeed despise the man.

ж ж ж

When they arrived at Mrs. Bakke's house, the elderly farm woman took one look at Brandon and declared that he needed a hospital. Julie came down from upstairs, gasped at her barely recognizable husband, and helped Kiel get him up the stairs so that he could collapse on Julie's bed.

When Kiel returned downstairs, Mrs. Bakke reported with furrowed brow that the phone line was dead—first the power, and now the phone. Daniel was due back any minute, and he could take Brandon to the hospital in Oshkosh.

Kiel's first chilling thought was that the colony had cut the phone lines in retaliation. Reason soon deduced that the consequence of shorting the power line was perhaps much greater than simply bringing that feed down. He'd always thought that the telephone system was backed up by batteries, but maybe not.

He sat at the kitchen table with Cam and started to explain to Mrs. Bakke all that had happened, but Julie came down a few minutes later, so he started over. As he progressed from discovering the crablets the night he had arrived to following the drones to the mine, and finally the terrorized last couple of hours, Mrs. Bakke seemed skeptical, but Julie's pretty face progressed from concern through anger to horror when he described finding Tagget and Sheriff Lanner.

"I should have told you earlier," Kiel concluded, guessing the reason for the anger phase, "but it all seemed too fantastic and . . . well, kind of innocent. The drones are no bigger than a flying rat at first. Then too . . ." He looked at Cam, but the boy just sat staring as though bored—probably dead tired, combined with lingering shock. "Well, here's the thing: Cam and I thought that we could find something to help you, Julie . . . with, you know . . ."

She shook her head. "No, I don't know. What?"

"The, er, divorce."

So then he had to back up and explain how their initial idea versus the reality of Brandon's maneuverings for economic gain had converged.

Kiel was interrupted by the sound of Daniel's pickup pulling up out front. He came in and announced that power was down all over the area, and Kiel had to summarize everything all over again. Daniel listened patiently, but his tight mouth and silence implied that he shared his mother's doubts. When Kiel finished, Daniel asked Cam, "You saw Tagget and Lanner?"

His nephew nodded solemnly.

"They really dead?"

Cam sighed. "Yeah, really dead."

Daniel nodded and sat thinking a moment. "We've got murdered men," he finally concluded. "We have to get some kind of authority in here. Hell, with the Sheriff dead, who would that be?" he wondered, looking at Julie.

"State Police?" she ventured.

He nodded. "Probably. We should also get word to Donny." To Kiel, he explained, "Donny's Lanner's Deputy Sheriff." Then to his mother, he asked, "The phone upstairs is out too?"

"Don't know—I'll check."

"How about your cell?" he asked Julie.

"It says, 'no service,' so I guess not."

The farmer stood up. "I'll check with Peg, and if our phone's out, I'll go see if I can find one that's working. Otherwise, I'll try to track down Donny."

"How about Brandon?" Julie asked. "We should get him to a hospital."

Her brother looked at her a moment. "Any broken bones? Spitting up blood? Lapsing into unconsciousness?"

"No, but he seems awfully—"

"Then he can wait. Dead men take priority."

"You want me to go along?" Kiel asked.

Daniel studied him a couple of seconds. "Seems like you'll need to guard the place. After all, you're the expert on these . . . what do you call them? Drones?"

The sarcasm was obvious, but Kiel let it go. He just nodded agreement.

Daniel, the authority of the farm, his domain, grabbed his cap and left. The rumble of his pickup faded in the distance. The sound was replaced by silence. For this, Kiel was glad.

ж ж ж

Kiel decided that, sarcasm or not, Daniel was right. He wondered how to go about guarding against killer cat-sized drones. One obvious step would be to board up the windows. Based on Mrs. Bakke's skepticism, he was reluctant to suggest hammering dozens of nails into her window casings and advertise to the world a conviction that a terrible danger lurked—a danger, by the way, mysterious and unknown to everybody else.

It did seem kind of nuts when viewed from a little distance. On the other hand, so did tales of killer Australian jellyfish no bigger than your hand, until you saw the horrendous consequences of an encounter.

He settled for gathering together battle axes. These consisted of a baseball bat from Daniel's teenage years, a pick handle minus the business end that Cam found, and a short pitch fork from Mrs. Bakke's tool shed. He knew he couldn't kill a drone with these, but splitting them in half tended to slow them down, as they then had to find each other and re-incorporate. The pitch fork seemed even better, since if swiped squarely by it, might mince the colony warrior into multiple slices. This weapon was still in the experimental stage, however, and would have to be pressed into service with no field trials.

Kiel was at a loss as to what he could do next without drawing the evil eye from Mrs. Bakke. Maybe they didn't have to actually nail boards across the windows, he mused. He and Cam could find some heavy boards that they would just lean against the windows on the outside. The drones could cut and slash with wicked effectiveness, but they hadn't demonstrated much heft. Perhaps a loose one-inch board would prove an effective shield.

He was outside surveying the access to the first floor windows when Julie found him. "Looks like you've found your calling," she said, standing next to him and gazing as well at the space below the windows.

"Er, you know what I'm doing?" he asked, guessing that she must have talked with Cam.

She raised one eyebrow and gestured towards the flower beds along the side of the house. "Once Mom started you weeding, you can't seem to stop. Don't try to weed Peg's flowers, though; she'll take it as a personal insult."

The flower beds indeed had his attention. To get the boards close enough, they would have to risk doing some flower damage. "Actually," he replied, "I was thinking about how to deal with another type of unwanted intruder."

"Ah," she said, understanding. "The drones."

He looked at her sweet face. He hated what she was probably thinking. "Do you think I'm nuts?"

She took some time answering. She pursed her lips and gathered her brows; she wanted to be honest. "I don't think that you're making any of this up, if that's what you mean. Brandon is babbling on about clandestine military drones, but I'm not sure he's in a state to be credible, and I wouldn't believe anything he says anyway. Cam, though, insists that what you described did happen. And I believe my son implicitly."

"You do have to wonder how Brandon produced a kid so forthright."

Kiel felt himself blushing. He realized that this could imply that Brandon was not the father.

If Julie saw his embarrassment, she didn't acknowledge it. "Speaking of the complete truth," she went on, "Cam told me some details that you left out."

He waited. He'd managed to place her son in more than one dangerous situation.

"Apparently you are quite the hero."

He shook his head, not understanding.

"Cam told me that bringing down the power lines wasn't the easy knock-off you described. He said you risked your life. In fact, for a while he was sure you were a goner. According to him, you worked miracles up there."

Kiel could feel the blush deepening. "Okay, so the kid exaggerates sometimes. Despite what Cam thinks, though, I have the feeling your mom and Daniel are not at all happy that I've single-handedly killed both your main power feed and your phones."

She thought about this, how to respond. "They tend to be practical to a fault sometimes—my friends used to say hardheaded. They get that from my grandfather. He expanded the farm and built this house. Here's an example: while the rest of the country was wringing their hands over the Soviet's coup d'état with Sputnik, Grandpa declared that it was just a propaganda stunt. He said that being first was symbolic. Sputnik was only a little ball that beeped. Our own Vanguard program would make orbit any day, and it was real science."

"He was both right and wrong," Kiel observed. "Sputnik was mostly symbolic, but it was a symbol that affected Americans deeply. In that sense, it was a huge success."

"That's my point. Grandpa recognized it for what it was, but missed the emotional impact. The concept was foreign to him."

She paused and looked at him. "Daniel and Mom like you, Kiel, but they don't understand what's going on. In their practical world, if they don't understand something, they can't believe it. You could say their juries are out, waiting more evidence." Looking at him, she raised an eyebrow. "Now that's a sardonic grin if I ever saw one."

He chuckled. "I was just thinking that I lose both ways. If we never see another drone, then your family thinks I'm slightly askew, and if we do see one . . . "

"We all lose?" she offered.

"Maybe I should try to be practical and just say that the jury's still out on the consequence."

Julie folded her arms across her chest and contemplated the flowers. "Kiel," she said after a few seconds, "I've been thinking about the cockamamie idea that you could find something in the mine that might help me against Brandon."

Kiel held his breath, waiting her reprimand.

"I know you didn't understand the danger at first, that you would never knowingly put Cam in a dangerous situation. Anyway," she said, unfolding her arms and taking him by his shoulders, "that was very sweet of you to try." She leaned over on tip-toe and kissed him on the forehead.

As a joyous tingle ran down and then back up his spine, he decided to delay explanation that the whole thing was actually Cam's idea.

His sensual pleasure was interrupted by the sound of Daniel's truck returning. They walked together around the house to meet him.

"Looks like you managed to black out at least half the county," Daniel remarked darkly. "All up and down the highway, folks have no power or phones. I'd say you're lucky the police have two murders to distract them. You still might catch hell. Heck, they could throw you in jail."

"But if I hadn't killed the power, the colony would, er, grow."

Julie's brother was looking at him reprovingly. "Anyway, I managed to leave a message with Donny's wife. She expects him home any minute."

"What about Brandon?" Julie asked.

"In good time. After we talk to Donny, I'll take him to Oshkosh."

He seemed to consider something. Mrs. Bakke came out, wiping her hands on a towel, and he asked her, "Anybody come by asking for help?"

His mother shook her head. "You see anybody?" she asked Julie, who also shook her head. "Why do you ask?"

Daniel stared back towards the highway. "That's odd. There's a car on the side of the road, abandoned. I figured they maybe ran out of gas and came in to call for help. The plates are from Alabama."

"Maybe they already got a ride," Kiel offered.

"Could be," Daniel agreed. "It wasn't there, though, when I drove out."

Cars parked along highways were a common sight. Any other time, Kiel wouldn't have given it a second thought, but this wasn't any other time. Two men lay dead half a mile away, and Brandon and Cam had come close to following in their misfortune. "Maybe we should check it out," Kiel suggested.

Daniel nodded, climbed back into his truck, and waited for Kiel, who came around the front, but then paused. Gesturing that he'd be right back, he sprinted up onto the porch and grabbed the baseball bat.

"You afraid of folks from Alabama?" Daniel asked as Kiel climbed in the passenger side.

It took Kiel a moment to realize he was talking about the bat. "Yes," he replied. He'd let it be up to Daniel to decide if he was joking.

When they reached the highway, Kiel saw that the Ford Focus was parked in a turn-out area next to the Bakke's lane; no wonder Daniel assumed they'd walked in to get help. More curiously, the passenger door was wide open. Who would walk away from their car leaving it wide open?

Daniel stopped the pickup at the end of the lane and they got out and walked over to the abandoned car. Kiel saw a woman's purse lying on the passenger floor. On the backseat were a man's jacket and an umbrella. Why in the world would the woman leave her purse? Kiel was tempted to look for some identification inside, but mostly he was just curious whether she'd left her wallet. He couldn't bring himself to touch it, though; not without the Sheriff's deputy standing next to him.

He stepped back to see what Daniel thought, and only then noticed that the gas cap cover was missing. He found it lying on the ground, and it was mangled. He picked it up. The metal disk was bent, scratched, and gouged. He could tell that the cover had been ripped out of its hinges, and the gas cap itself was also missing.

"Look at this," he said, turning to where Daniel was searching through the weeds along the bank.

The farmer didn't answer. He was staring down at something on the ground. His mouth fixed tighter than ever, he stooped forward, then immediately jumped back, shouting, "Damn! Shit!"

Kiel scrambled over through the high weeds. Lying on her side, curled up as though taking an afternoon nap, was an elderly woman. Her yellow blouse was splattered with blood, and Kiel saw that the base of the weeds under her head was dark, as though a quart of oil had poured from her open mouth. He didn't look closer; he knew he would find that her throat had been slashed.

Daniel stood staring in horror. Kiel glanced around. If the woman had been driving, she wouldn't have crawled over to exit through the passenger's side, leaving that door open. Also, there was the man's jacket on the backseat. He imagined the scene; the husband would have tried to chase them away from his car, keeping his wife behind him. Kiel walked back to the rear of the Focus where the drones had pulled off the gas cap cover. He peered around, and found what he was hoping not to find: tan cotton cloth in the weeds twenty feet away. He walked over, dreading what he'd find, and found it. "Here's her husband!" he called to Daniel.

After a moment, the practical man came over, his eyes burning with anger that anybody or anything could do such a thing. They stood looking at the dead man together. The husband lay on his back, his wound all too visible. Daniel retched once, then turned away to puke. A little part of Kiel's brain wondered that a farmer who butchered animals regularly would be so affected.

Then he noticed that the old man was bald. His cap lay a few feet away. Stepping gingerly around, Kiel squatted down and studied the top of the victim's hairless head. Sure enough, clearly visible were half a dozen puncture marks where the drone had grasped. A head of hair made a convenient handle, but the drones were capable of improvising when necessary.

He realized that he had been hearing a lawnmower, and it was getting nearer. It was a sound that froze his heart. He stood up, grabbed Daniel's arm and pointed at three silver predators cruising towards them along the lane.

"Time to meet the colony," he warned.

Julie's brother uttered a word that Kiel wouldn't have guessed he knew.

Chapter 16

"What do we do?" Daniel said as the drones came closer.

Kiel had left the bat in Daniel's pickup. The marauding colony emissaries were close enough to intercept him if he tried to get it. In fact, they seemed to be flying straight for the truck. He glanced around. There was no cover whatsoever, except . . . "Get in the car," he directed, running around to the driver's side.

"Are the keys in it?" Daniel asked, staring in fascination at the otherworldly creatures.

"It doesn't matter! Just get IN!"

Daniel finally shook himself from his trance and climbed in the passenger side.

"The door!" Kiel cried.

"Huh? Oh, yeah," Daniel muttered, reaching out to close it.

The keys were gone; the dead man must have taken them . . . and the driver-side window was open a few inches. Kiel reached back, grabbed the old man's jacket, and stuffed it into the window opening.

"Look!" Daniel yelled, pointing.

Like ducks in formation, half a dozen more drones were approaching along the lane. These were different, though. The undersides sagged, as though each one was pregnant and ready to give birth.

"Hey!" Daniel cried again. "What the hell are they doing?"

What they were doing was attacking his gas-cap cover, just like they'd done to the dead couple's car. Two of them worked together at it. While one hacked away at the cover, the other hovered above, stabilizing his partner.

"They're stealing your gas," Kiel answered.

He'd had an inkling when he'd seen the gas cap missing on the car, but didn't have time to process the information. They had been after the gas in Brandon's car as well, but hadn't yet figured out how to get at it.

"Why, for God's sake?"

"I guess it's my fault. They're making up for the lost electrical power."

"But . . . gas?"

"Why not? The energy in a gallon of gas could light a sixty-Watt bulb for a month. Compared to what they had to fall back on with their solar collectors, a car is a windfall."

"What the hell are you talking about?"

"It doesn't matter; they want your gas."

With a loud bang, the double-decker drone pulled the gas cover off. Seconds later, they'd removed the gas cap as well. They understood the concept of twisting.

By now, the large-bellied crew had arrived and hovered in a close queue, the congregation waiting their turn for the Eucharist. The drone that had torn off the gas-cap cover morphed, and a tentacle extruded and slithered down the revealed cavity in the truck. One by one, each transport drone moved in to receive its share of proffered gasoline. When full, it lumbered away, back along the lane, seeming to struggle to stay aloft.

Daniel whispered that bad word again, and then again.

The third of the original three drones had been keeping watch ten feet away, but as the loading began, it turned its attention outward. The drones had no eyes that Kiel could discern, but he had the distinct sense that it looked directly at them. Without hesitating, it glided over.

Kiel echoed Daniel's bad word.

The scout drone stopped, hovering just over the car's hood. It settled down and sat on the metal surface.

"Don't move," Kiel whispered.

"You think I can?" Daniel replied.

The drone's ear-wings whirled back into blurred motion and it rose, up and up, until Kiel couldn't see it above the car. The burring sound continued unabated, though, and suddenly the mechanical beast was right next to his head and he yelped involuntarily and jerked away. Another sound joined that of its wings—a machine gun staccato thump as the jacket he had stuffed in the window crack jerked in rhythm. Before Kiel could react, the attacker figured out that the plug was not something solid, and with one deft pull, jerked it out and dropped it to the ground. An instant later, it hovered at the window again, confronting Kiel, three millimeters of glass away.

"What does it want?" Daniel hissed.

"Maybe it's just curious," Kiel offered, more from hope than reason.

If it was curious, watching through a window wasn't sufficient. Following the example of its gas-sucking brother, it slowly extruded a tentacle. Kiel watched in a trance fascination as the main body shrank proportionally. This close, he could actually see the individual crablets reorganizing, flowing into new positions. This tentacle was no siphon tube, however; the tip terminated in a three-talon claw, one sharp sickle opposing the other two.

"That doesn't look good," Daniel observed.

"Find something to block the crack," Kiel implored, glancing around, but unwilling to take his eyes off the menace for more than a second.

Too late. The clawed tentacle slithered through the crack. Instinctively, Kiel reached out to intercept it and a moment later felt intense pain as the claw gripped his forearm. Yelling hysterically, as much from surprised alarm as pain, he jerked his arm back. The talons held fast, and the tentacle drew taught until the drone was pulled tight against the window. Despite the pain and hysteria, he saw that the wings had turned into grasping paws, clinging to the top of the open window.

The horror had only begun, though. Crablets flowed to new configurations, and the entire inanimate beast began oozing through the opening.

"Oh Christ!" Kiel screamed, yanking at the gripping arm despite the searing pain.

Daniel was yelling at him, shoving something next to his head. He reached up with his free hand and grasped it. It was the umbrella, soft and cushioned inside its wrappings of cloth. It was the only weapon he had. He beat at the tentacle clumsily with his left hand in the restricted space. Each strike stabbed his right arm, as though he was using the umbrella to drive nails into his flesh. In fury and hysterical frustration, he gave one hard blow, feeling the talons sink even more deeply. Something gave. The taloned claw still gripped tightly, but his right arm had swung back, into Daniel's face. The tentacle had broken in half. One end waved back and forth frantically in front of him, searching. The other half hung limply from his arm, but the broken tip slowly curled up, like a cobra emerging from its basket. Each broken end was covered in silver fuzz that Kiel realized was hundreds of crablets reaching out near-invisible appendages that had seconds before been anchored with a partner.

He couldn't let the two ends find each other. He waved the umbrella up and down between the searching stubs, knocking first one, and then the other aside as the severed appendage sought inexorably to re-incorporate. The embedded talons clung fast with nearly unbearable pain. Meanwhile, the main body of the drone continued its ooze through the window opening.

Suddenly a young man's face appeared, serious and confused.

"Donny!" Daniel called. "Kill it!"

"What *is* it?" the Sheriff's Deputy called back, peering at the spreading blob of silver.

"Later! Just kill it—now!"

The deputy took a couple of steps closer, studying the situation. "How?"

"Shoot it, goddamn it!" Daniel screamed.

Donny took his pistol from its holster and pointed it at the unformed drone that now filled most of the opening. Deciding that he might also hit the men inside, he rotated the gun to the side, aiming parallel with the window. Kiel had taken his attention off the severed appendage ends, and they now made contact. A thousand near-invisible little legs groped to find their best partner as the limb began its re-incorporation.

A concussion rattled Kiel's head as Donny pulled the trigger. His vision seemed to swim, and then settled. When an animal is shot through the middle, it either falls dead, or flails around in torment. The drone just froze. The momentum of the bullet had pushed it forward a few inches, but otherwise, it remained motionless. Even the crablets reconnecting the wound seemed to halt in stunned surprise.

"What now?" Donny called.

Neither Kiel nor Daniel answered. They weren't sure themselves.

Whatever the monster's actual state, Kiel had had enough of it so close to him. Using his free left hand, he pushed at the center of it with the umbrella. It was like poking stiff dough. With little resistance, it slid away, back through the window and then dropped as Donny jumped back. It dangled for a moment, hanging by the partially repaired appendage, and then the wound gave way, and it fell to the ground with a plop. A sprinkling of crablets fell to his lap like dandruff, while the portion of the tentacle still grasping his forearm curled up as an earthworm does when feeling the tip of the fishhook.

Kiel was left with a thousand-segmented claw dug into his arm. And it hurt like hell.

Daniel was leaning back, straining to reach into his pocket. He extracted a pocketknife, opened it, and held it out to Kiel.

He shook his head. "You do it," and clenched his eyes shut against the coming pain.

The pain came as Daniel grasped his arm firmly and worked at the talons. After an interminable minute or two, the farmer sighed with satisfaction as Kiel felt the weight of the appendage fall away. Kiel opened his eyes to find Daniel delicately picking the last talon from his flesh. His caregiver grasped the exposed portion between knife-edge and thumb, but as he slowly pulled it out, the inch-long talon melted, dissolving into a small army of crablets that all simultaneously abandoned their collective claw-role to skitter away down off Kiel's arm, dropping en mass onto the car seat and away. The remains of the severed tentacle was melting and scattering as well. Before their eyes, it sagged around the console, spread, and seemed to evaporate as the myriad of crablets found refuge in the carpet and through cracks around the plastic panels.

Kiel's arm looked like a bloody mess, but that was mostly just smeared blood. All three puncture-wounds hurt, but the last one—the one Daniel had just cleared—still stabbed with little shooting twitches. Kiel looked closely, and was horrified to see that crablets still infected the wound, swimming and clawing amidst the oozing blood.

"Give me the knife," he muttered through clenched teeth. Clumsy with his left hand, he worked at the wound. The pain made him wince and gasp as he prodded and pressed the blood to flow freely, but the horror of leaving even one alien micro-machine was beyond pain.

Finally, he could neither see nor feel any foreign invader in his puncture wound. A half-dozen or so struggled ineffectually in their bath of thickening blood smeared across his arm. Daniel handed him a handkerchief, and he wiped the blood and crablets away.

Through the window, they saw Donny's lower back and butt poised high, as though the deputy was ready to dash off on a sprint right into the car door. The deputy stood up. "What the hell was that?" he asked through the now-empty window opening.

"It'll take a half-hour to explain, and you won't believe it anyway," Kiel replied, still peering at the wounds. He really didn't want any left inside.

"I thought it might be a possum," Donny remarked, opening the driver's door, "but it crawled right up inside the car—what the heck happened to you?" He was looking at the smeared blood on Kiel's arm.

"Did you say it crawled inside the car?" Kiel asked, ignoring the deputy's own question.

"Yeah. After if fell out of the window, it crawled under the car, and . . . just sort of disappeared into the undercarriage."

"Shit!" Kiel urged to Daniel. "We better get out of here."

He practically launched himself from the car and stood next to Donny, trim and neat in his uniform, red hair puffing out around the edge of his deputy's cap. All the other drones were gone. Kiel thought he caught a glimpse of silver far off, disappearing with their stolen fuel towards the abandoned mine.

"Karen said you left word that the Sheriff ran into some trouble at Tagget's place," the young man remarked to Daniel who eased out his side at a more leisurely pace. Kiel noticed that he held his pocketknife open and ready, though.

Daniel stood up and looked at the deputy. "Is that all Karen told you? That the Sheriff ran into some trouble?"

The young man shrugged. "She texted me. I'm lucky I made out that much with all her abbreviations."

Daniel glanced at Kiel. "Donny, Sheriff Lanner is dead."

The green eyes went round in shocked alarm. "Dead? *Dead!*"

Daniel nodded. "Sorry, son."

"I . . . how . . . why?"

"He's at Tagget's. The old man is dead too. That's not all—there's an old couple lying here in weeds dead as well."

Sputtering incomprehensible oaths, the deputy marched over to where Daniel pointed out the hapless travelers. "Don't touch anything!" Donny commanded, staring at the corpses. "I have to . . . I have to contact—"

"State Police, maybe?" Daniel suggested.

Donny threw him a wild, panicked glance. "Yeah. State Police. Maybe the Magistrate. Oh God, oh God—you sure the Sheriff's dead?"

"I didn't take his pulse, but I don't think there was any blood left in him. They got his jugular."

The young man's eyes grew hard. "Who?"

Daniel glanced at Kiel again. "It's a doozy of a story. Why don't we go back to Mom's and we'll explain everything."

Donny shook his head slowly, and then vigorously. "I have to see about the Sheriff. Where is he at Tagget's?"

"He's around back, but you really don't want to go there alone."

The deputy gave him a suspicious sidelong look. "Because *they're* still there?"

Daniel nodded. "Could be," he replied, letting the "who" go undefined.

The young man stood, his eyes flicking this way and that, as though answers might pop up from any direction. "I need you—both of you—to come with me."

Daniel shook his head. "Sorry, son. I can't leave the farm. In fact, we need to get back ASAP."

Donny's eyes turned hard. "Daniel, you gotta do what I say—I'm the Sheriff now."

"No, Donny. My family comes first. Sorry."

Daniel walked off towards his truck. Kiel glanced at the distraught young man and then followed.

Without another word, Donny ran to his car.

Daniel looked over. "No, Donny! I'm warning you, you don't want to go—"

The deputy wasn't listening, though. He slammed the car door, and seconds later, the tires spit gravel and squealed as they contacted the pavement and sped off down the highway.

"The young fool," Daniel muttered, studying the cavity in his pickup where the drones had ripped out the gas-cap cover. "Can't fault him, though," he added, climbing into the driver's side. "It's the first time he's had to deal with dead folk. The Sheriff, no less."

Kiel got in on the passenger side. "How much gas do you think they left?" he asked as Daniel turned the key and started the engine.

"Dunno. I've got a tank back at the house, though. Would be nice if we could at least get that far."

ж ж ж

They got almost that far. The truck balked and jerked to a stop within sight of the houses. They walked the rest of the way, and Kiel was careful this time to grab the baseball bat. As Daniel stopped by his own house and then went to the shed to get a gas can, Kiel waited near the front porch. The front door flew open, and Cam came running out. "What did you find?" he gushed. "Where's Uncle Daniel's truck?" he asked glancing around, perplexed.

Kiel looked the boy in the eye. "It's not good, Cam. The drones are getting more aggressive."

The young face seemed to brighten, as though gratified with having expectations met. "What happened?"

"They attacked your uncle and me."

No need to talk about more dead people yet.

Cam looked at his arm. "They got you?" he asked, concerned now.

"Almost. Luckily the Sheriff's deputy came along and shot it."

Cam waited expectantly.

Kiel shook his head. "It seemed to be stunned for a while, having a bullet plow through the middle. Other than the crablets that were directly in the bullet's path, though, I doubt it did any damage."

He shook his head again, thinking about it. "You can't kill something that's not alive. It seems that the best that you can do is temporarily knock them out of commission until all the thousands of crablets have time to find each other again."

The front door burst open again, and Nicki ran out and down the porch stairs, but the little girl stopped short when she saw Kiel. "You're an indy roper," she declared, "and Daddy says you should have kept your nose in your own business."

Kiel grinned. "I think you mean interloper," he corrected as Julie came through the door looking harried.

"I'm so sorry," she said to Kiel. "Kids are worse than parrots." To her daughter, she directed, "Inside, young lady—now!"

Nicki pouted and ambled slowly up the porch stairs, but then loitered in front of the screen door, hoping her mom would get distracted.

"Speaking of Brandon," Kiel said, "how's he doing?"

"Sleeping," Julie answered, "his best mood . . . you're hurt!"

He glanced at his arm. "It looks worse than it is," he assured, even though it really did hurt like hell.

"Come on," she ordered perfunctorily, "we need to clean that up."

Obliging seemed easier than protesting, so he followed her into the kitchen.

She took a bottle of hydrogen peroxide from the cupboard, and he winced as she dabbed some on his puncture wounds.

"Hold still," she ordered. "You're worse than the kids."

"It's what I do when someone causes me intense pain."

"What happened to 'it looks worse than it is'?"

"Addled ramblings of a fevered mind, I guess."

"Did a drone do this?" she asked, concentrating closely on her ministrations. Kiel had the idea that she might be embarrassed to talk about them as though they were real.

"Yes. It grabbed me with a claw."

She glanced at him.

". . . a claw that it formed in a matter of seconds."

She stared at him a moment. She blinked, sighed, and then unrolled a length of bandage.

"You don't believe it, do you?" he asked quietly. "I mean how fantastically alien these things are."

She didn't say anything. No answer was better than a challenge to veracity.

As she wrapped the bandage around his arm, he thought of ways to convince her. Daniel, of course. She'd have to believe him.

His problem was solved when Cam came rushing in all wild-eyed. "They're here!" he shouted. "They're here!"

"Calm down, dear," Julie admonished, holding him by his shoulders. "Who's here?"

"The drones! They're here!"

Through the window, Kiel saw Daniel running towards the house. One drone followed closely, flying just above his head. A second one was making a wide arc around to the side, maneuvering to get in front of him, where it could get at his jugular.

Chapter 17

Kiel grabbed the only thing lying at hand on the table and ran for the door. Daniel was half way to the house, and had another fifty yards to go. Debating just a moment, Kiel sprinted off towards him. The drone that had swung around to get in front was almost in position, but seemed to hesitate at his approach. The first one, though, decided it was time and deftly grabbed a talon-full of hair and lifted. Gasping and chocking, Daniel came to a halt as Kiel finally reached him.

"Here!" Kiel shouted, handing him the banana that he'd grabbed from the table, then lifted his own arms to fend off the second drone as it turned to harry him. Kiel's hands made several contacts as he waved them over his down-turned head, each time tensing for the bite of a needle-sharp talon. He soon realized that he'd made no contact in some seconds, and the dreadful burr of the drone's wings had diminished.

He looked up to find that it had returned to its original deadly task. Daniel held the banana in one hand like a midget sword, and batted ineffectually at the drone tugging his hair with the other. Kiel watched in horror as the second drone swooped in for the killing slice. His head upturned, Daniel could barely see the attacker coming in level, and he held up the banana as though it might possess magical powers of repulsion. In fact, the banana saved his life. As the drone struck, the fruit was pushed back against Daniel's throat in a shower of splattering white goo. This confused the drone for a moment, and it paused.

Just then Cam ran up shouting. He held out the baseball bat, and Kiel grabbed it. He cocked it behind his shoulder, and stepped forward. It was time once again to play drone-ball. If he missed, he would probably crush Daniel's skull, but he didn't. The bat connected squarely with the multi-thousand crablets all intent on killing. To Kiel, it felt like he'd struck a firm pumpkin. The next instant, the deformed drone was flopping around on the ground. Kiel cocked the bat for another strike, but the first drone let go of Daniel's hair and eased down to aid its twin.

"Get back!" Kiel shouted to Daniel, and swung anyway. He wasn't as lucky this time, and he only grazed the first drone. It was enough to knock it out of the air, though, and it tumbled to the dirt.

Kiel had the routine down now, or thought he did. He stepped forward to pound the floundering drone until the crablets unincorporated, but as he lifted the bat for the first strike, he saw the alien mercenary change shape. It flattened, but at the same time, seemed to thicken along the edges. Kiel saw this all in an instant as he brought the bat down. The last thing he noticed was that the center of the flattened beast disappeared, and he had one brief image of striking the bat's tip in the middle of a donut.

The next instant, he was holding a bat with a drone wrapped around the end. But it didn't stay at the end. Like a giant metallic slug, the transformed drone reached along the bat towards Kiel's hands. As it stretched towards him, the extending tentacle spiraled around the bat so that he couldn't shake it off.

With a hysterical shout, Kiel dropped the bat and jumped back. He shivered with horrid fear at the unexpected reversal. The other drone was already reforming its normal flying configuration.

"Come on!" Daniel shouted as he picked Cam up, tossed him over his shoulder like a sack of feed, and trotted towards the house.

Kiel needed no prodding.

Once on the porch, Daniel slung Cam down, shoved the boy through the door, and held it for Kiel to dash through. As he tumbled into Julie, nearly knocking her over, Kiel heard Daniel slam the door behind him.

"What *are* those things!" Julie shouted, her eyes betraying the same fear with which Kiel was becoming far too familiar.

"They're *them*," he answered, going to the window.

"They're . . . *terrible!*"

"That they are," he muttered, peering out. He didn't see anything moving.

"I was filling a can with gas from the tank when they caught me by surprise," Daniel explained.

"You tried to stop them from stealing it," Kiel said. It wasn't a question.

"It's the last of the gas," he said in defense. "Without it, we're . . ."

"Stuck here," Kiel finished for him.

"I was going to say trapped."

Bang!

Kiel jumped back with a yell as something slammed into the window inches from his face. Outside, a drone rose from the ground where it must have fallen. Julie gathered Cam and Nicki to her as the malevolent predator paused, studying the situation, and then eased forward towards them. Nicki screamed shrilly, and this seemed to give the monster a moment's pause, but after a few seconds, it continued its approach. When it came to the window, it paused again. Kiel held his breath. The mechanical beast reached out a dozen extruded earthworm tentacles to probe the smooth surface, at the same time titling the whirring wings back out of the way. Then the many wiggling tentacles spread out, like the rays from the sun, and the body of the drone settled in, making firm contact. The smooth, flattened surface seemed to swirl and dance, what Kiel knew to be thousands of crablets jockeying to find new positions. Nicki's scream notched up an octave and then muffled as Julie planted a hand over her child's mouth.

Kiel glanced around and picked up a large barrel flashlight that Mrs. Bakke kept next to the door. The question was whether to strike now, or wait until it broke through the window. He raised the flashlight, ready. Motion caught his eye—it was Daniel heading for the door. "*Where are you going!*" Kiel yelled.

"I've gotta' get it off the window," he replied, turning the doorknob to peer cautiously through the crack.

"You're crazy!" Kiel cried. "They almost killed you!"

"It'll break through," he explained, opening the door more.

Kiel wasn't sure if he should hit the glass-plastered drone, or Daniel.

Their attacker either heard the door open or saw it, for it pulled away from the window, took a moment to reconfigure itself, and then buzzed up and away, towards the front door.

"It's coming!" Kiel yelled, and Daniel quickly slammed the door shut and put his ear against it.

After a moment, Kiel asked, "Do you hear it?"

He shook his head.

Kiel was expecting the window to be smeared with slimy goo, but he realized that this was just conditioning from living among the living. There was nothing slimy about these mechanical beasts; whatever mechanism they used for movement, it didn't involve lubrication.

In fact, if anything, the window was cleaner where the drone had made contact. And through the newly cleaned portal, he saw other drones, a veritable platoon of them. His heart caught in his throat until he saw that they were not approaching. A dozen pregnant, gasoline-laden transports lumbered away, escorted by a handful of regular drones.

"They're leaving," Kiel announced. "I guess they'll be back, though."

"Why?" Julie asked.

"They can't be carrying more than ten gallons. How much do you think was in your tank?" he asked Daniel.

"That was probably it. I was waiting for the price to drop to put in another order."

"Maybe it's for the best," Kiel observed. "They would have taken it all anyway, and that would have just accelerated their proliferation."

"They're proliferating?" Julie asked, her question ending in a little squeak.

"Er, that's Cam's theory."

The boy looked at him with a critical eye from under his mom's protective arm. "I don't think it's a theory anymore."

"Well," Daniel said turning the doorknob, "I better see if they've done any damage."

He opened the door a few inches to peer out, but immediately jerked his head back as a talon-armed tentacle slithered in and grabbed him by the ear. Nicki's renewed scream drowned whatever response the man may have made as he shoved the door shut on the appendage. The claw held fast to his ear. The limb had no blood flow to squeeze off, no muscles or tendons to damage. It could hang on, despite what Daniel did to the rest of its corporeal structure.

It was a first step, though. He opened the door and instantly slammed it shut again, putting his weight into it. Kiel could see the edge of the door indenting the silver surface. Daniel repeated the attack, and this time the arm broke off, the severed end first falling limply at his side, but then curling just as Kiel's attacker had done in the car.

Julie had muffled Nicki with her hand again, and now Kiel could hear Daniel cursing as he probed the grasping assailant with his hand, trying to understand how it was holding him.

The severed end was not passively searching to reconnect as before, however. As Kiel watched, three curved fingers slowly protruded. He realized that it was creating a claw at both ends.

"Shit!" he cried, running to Daniel, red with blood that ran down his cheek and neck. There was no time to think, let alone develop some strategy. All he could do was reach out and grab the end of the morphing appendage. He squeezed it tightly in both hands as the extending fingers solidified into solid, sharp talons, opening and closing hungrily just above his clenched fists.

He had no hands left; all he could do was hold on tight to the alien tiger he now had by the tail. The barrel flashlight lay at his feet where he'd dropped it.

He had an idea.

"Cam!" he called.

The boy started forward, but Julie caught him and pulled him back.

"Find a hammer!" Kiel directed.

The boy tore away from his mother and ran off.

"But don't go outside!" Kiel called after him.

The alien snake was not about to oblige by waiting for Kiel to make the next move. It twisted and contorted, trying to break Kiel's grasp. The creature's movements were odd; the strength that it demonstrated when making large, sweeping movements seemed almost feeble, but once it settled into a stable position, small, incremental changes were iron-firm, impossible for Kiel to resist. He could imagine the crablets only loosely connected when performing major reconfigurations, but then locking arms tightly when done.

Suddenly Mrs. Bakke was next to him. She had been upstairs, but must have heard all the ruckus. She was holding a small tack hammer out to him. "Cam said you needed this," she explained, eyeing the silver snake with astonishment.

"You don't have a bigger one?" he asked, grunting as he struggled to keep the claw away from his face.

"Out in the shed. You want me to go get it?"

"*No!* Don't go outside. This one will do. Just stand there and hold it. Give it to me when I'm ready."

Calculating his moves carefully, he leaned down and let go with one hand to snatch the flashlight. The claw was tilting inexorably towards his eyes as he slapped the flashlight sideways into its jaws. His gamble paid off as the talons snapped closed around the metal canister.

He might only have seconds, though, before the unliving beast realized it wasn't grasping human flesh.

"Now!" he called, and Mrs. Bakke thrust the hammer towards him, handle first. He grabbed it while simultaneously pushing with his other hand towards the wall. The tentacle twisted and fought, perhaps understanding what he was doing. Holding the clawed end in place against the wall proved impossible, but he hammered away anyway at any portion of the squirming tentacle he thought he might hit. With the diminutive head of the tack hammer, it was like trying to thread a needle while wearing mittens. It didn't help that his missed blows were sinking into the gypsum drywall, threatening to trap the head of his hammer.

Finally, by pure chance, he managed to strike a direct blow to the silver snake's body. Instantly he felt its strength weaken, but quickly return. One more; if he could land just one more. He did. This time he took advantage of the weakened spot, and jerked the end so that the tentacle was forced to bend sharply at the compromised point. This gave him a better target, and he lay in three more solid whacks at the bend.

That was the turning point. The attacker lost all ability to move the joint, and Kiel could hammer away at will. Before long, the beast decided to cut its losses, and disassociated all around the area he'd been beating. A foot-long section dissolved into a rain of pebble-sized pieces that fell to the floor.

Kiel expected that his end would be much easier to handle now, but he was underestimating the capabilities of hordes of interconnected autonomous creatures. When it set its mind to it—or rather, when the thousands of crablets set what served as their minds—the collective could tighten their mutual grip and become an essentially solid structure. Kiel still held the talon claw in his left hand, and in a series of incremental moves, the foot-long tail wrapped itself in a spiral around his forearm. It felt like he'd gotten caught in a giant metal Chinese finger trap.

The claw had finally dropped the flashlight, and waited hungrily again to dig into something human. Holding his arm out to keep the talons isolated, he glanced around. Nicki's face was buried in her mother's thigh, and Cam looked on intensely from under her strong, protective arm. Julie herself was horrified, aghast at something so vicious and alien.

Mrs. Bakke just looked angry. It was her house, by damn, and this thing was intruding.

Or maybe she was just mad that he'd pounded holes in her wall.

Daniel was in trouble. His attacking claw still hung on to his bloody ear, and its tail remnant had encircled his right wrist once, and was now trying to get a final loop around his neck as he struggled against the choking maneuver with his left hand.

Kiel had his own claw to deal with first. He lay his arm down on the carpet. He had intended on beating away at the spiral wrap trapping his arm, but decided to put the claw out of action first. With his little tack hammer, he carefully tapped at each talon in turn. The crablets recognized that they were defeated. Instead of risking additional individual injury, they abandoned their posts in concert. One second, a spiral grasp held Kiel firmly, and the next, his arm tickled as thousands of tiny flies skittered away. His hand that had been gripping the base of the claw was suddenly full of micro-wiggling sand.

A silver sheet of crablets moved slowly in a wave towards the door. Connected together, they could orchestrate large, sweeping movements, but separated, they moved only as fast as microscopic legs could scurry. Kiel gave a few taps with the hammer among the fleeing crowd for good measure, but Daniel waited rescue.

Julie's brother had fallen to his knees in his struggle, and the tail of the severed tentacle had gained a coil around his neck with his left hand caught inside, rendering both hands immobile.

Kiel knelt next to him. "We'll have you out in a minute, buddy" Kiel assured.

"I don't know if I have a minute," Daniel gasped.

This entanglement was more problematic than Kiel's own had been. With the entire tentacle wrapped tightly around Daniel, there was no solid surface against which to land hammer blows. And there was no time for experiments.

Foregoing explanations, he tore off past Julie and the kids, through the kitchen, and out the back door, remembering to slam it shut behind him. He heard the burr of drone wings, but didn't even risk the time to glance around, sprinting instead for the tool shed with his head down. Inside it was dark, and he could barely see. He floundered around, knocking rakes, shovels, and pole saws clattering to the ground in his frantic search. If large bolt cutters were inside, they remained hidden. Instead, he grabbed a pair of long-handled bypass loppers used for cutting brush, and dashed back outside.

A drone hovered at eye-level between him and the house. Ah hell. Gripping the garden tool in both hands, he ran for it shouting a cry that a spear-brandishing ancestor might have screamed charging an enemy tribe. Kiel saw two claw-equipped tentacles dangling below the drone, waiting, like an eagle ready for the prey to rush conveniently into its grasp. Kiel ran straight for the drone, and at the very last minute darted to the left, swinging the lopper at the same time.

He hadn't had time to think this through, and realized too late that this tactic had its drawbacks as he felt a weight tug firmly on the lopper, swinging him back around so that he once again faced the drone. Whether by chance or by intention, the tentacles had gotten tangled around the blade-end of the tool. The burr of the drone's wings rose an octave as it struggled to hold its own.

Kiel twisted the tool back and forth, but the tentacles were securely wrapped. This gave him an idea, though. He rotated the lopper handles as far as he could counterclockwise, watching the tentacles take another wrap around the opposite end. He then uncrossed his wrists, grabbed the handles and gave another turn. And another. And another. It was like turning the wheel on a submarine hatch. The tentacles wrapped until there were no more left to wrap and he was now turning the drone itself upside down. The collective alien brain cried uncle, detached its appendages, and flew off. The wrapped tentacles, finding themselves abandoned, called retreat, dissolved, and fell from the tool in a shower of silver hail.

Into the house, through the kitchen, and to the front door. He'd been gone more than a minute, and Daniel's face was turning blue. Julie was on her knees tugging futilely at the choking snake.

"Back!" Kiel commanded. He spread the lopper handles wide, and pressed the open blades against the coil that was choking the farmer. The short scissor-like blades failed to get a purchase, and they slid back off the tentacle, leaving a visible gauge of damaged crablets, but otherwise having no effect.

The crushing appendage was barely an inch in diameter; the garden tool should be able to manage that. "This is going to hurt," he warned as he tried again, pushing the tool in with enough force to press Daniel up against the wall. This time, he felt the blades grab and cut confidently through the matrix of crablets. An instant later, a silver waterfall flowed down off of Daniel and under the door as he gasped deep, ragged breaths, washing away the blue pall of asphyxiation.

Daniel lay panting on the floor. His ear looked like the ragged and bloody end of a favorite chew-toy, and his neck was bruised and nicked where the lopper had cut him. "Thanks," he gasped, getting to his knees. "I really hate those things."

Chapter 18

Daniel sat with his back against the door as Julie dabbed his torn ear with a wet cloth. Kiel sat against the wall not far away. He was exhausted. Mrs. Bakke had gone off to make some tea. The thought of a hot cup of tea with cookies was a glimpse into heaven. He had a hard time remembering waking up that morning. It seemed like a different life when Sherriff Lanner was still alive, pounding on the door.

"Enough," Daniel protested. "I need to just rest a minute."

Julie reluctantly stopped, and then sat with her back to the wall between the two men. Cam and Nicki took this as an invitation and came over, Cam to her left, and Nicki next to Kiel.

Nobody said anything. Their brains were catching up with everything their bodies had been through.

"What was all the shouting about?"

It was Brandon, bracing himself against the wall at the bottom of the stairs. Now that Julie had cleaned up her estranged husband, Kiel could see that the once-handsome man's eyelashes and most of his eyebrows had burned away. He looked like Henry of comic strip fame, minus the shorts.

The charred man eyed them sitting in a row. "Well, doesn't this make a fine family photo? Uncle, mom, kids, and . . ." He stared at Kiel ominously.

Nicki was squeezed in next to Julie, and her hand rested casually on Kiel's thigh. Feeling his face blushing, he scrambled to his feet, and then put his hand to the wall to steady against the dizziness that followed.

"Devil birds," Daniel said in explanation.

Brandon looked again at Kiel with lifted brow where his eyebrow would have been. "The same drone things?"

Kiel nodded.

"They're here?" he asked warily, letting one layer of confident cool temporarily slip.

"They're here," Kiel confirmed with a sigh.

"All the way from Tagget's?"

"All the way from the mine."

Brandon didn't say anything. Kiel realized that he had never believed them about the mine.

"Why are they here?"

"They're after gas," Kiel replied. "They took it all."

"Gas?" The lawyer looked at him. By profession he was trained to analyze all angles. His mouth turned into a self-satisfied smile. "Way to go, brainy-boy!" he exclaimed. "You had to go and cut off their power. Looks like you owe me a new car."

"He had to do it!" Cam challenged, standing up.

Brandon looked from his son to Kiel. "What's this? The Mod Squad? The grade school science-fiction club on a field day?"

Kiel wanted to ask him when exactly *he* had become the expert on the colony, but that ominous look still smoldered in his brain.

"As long as they had unlimited power, they would have continued replicating geometrically," Cam continued.

His father gave him a tired look. "You still stuck on that nonsense?" He wobbled his hands in the air, as though they should all be terrified with what he was about to say. "Soon the whole world will be thick with flying machines blowing up cars," he intoned dramatically.

"They blew up your car by mistake," Cam corrected.

"They don't blow up cars," Kiel finally found the courage to say, "they kill people. And your sarcasm could turn out to be a joke on you—a morbid joke."

Brandon peered at him through calculating eyes. "Cut me a break. It has to be some sort of secret military project. They'll come through soon, clean everything up, and buy us off with affidavits promising that we won't talk to the press."

"Fine," Kiel said, pointing towards the door. "In that case, why don't you go out and flag down the patrol?"

The look Brandon gave him was pure hate. He ignored Kiel's challenge. "What makes you think it's not military?"

"They're evolving," Cam answered for him.

His father sighed, as though patience with his child was wearing thin. "Well?" he repeated, looking at Kiel and ignoring his son.

Kiel turned to Cam. "What do you mean?" he asked the boy.

"They're learning as they go. At first, the whole thing probably started with just one crablet. All it knew was how to make more crablets, and that they could then come together to make a phase two version—the original flying drone we saw near the bridge. That's the universal version. It could operate on any world with some atmosphere. Each colony has to learn and adapt to the environment it finds itself in."

He stopped, maybe thinking that he'd gone on too long. His father was picking at a hangnail.

"You think they're demonstrating learned intelligence?" Kiel asked, encouraging the boy.

"Sure!" Cam exclaimed, as though you'd have to be blind or an idiot not to see. "At first they almost completely ignored us—people, that is. We were just one part of this strange world they were trying to figure out. As time went on, they learned that we could get in their way, and they figured out the best ways to . . ." He nodded. "You know, kill us. And then there's the window."

Kiel shrugged. "What about it?"

"It was obvious that the drone had never seen one before. They haven't figured out yet how fragile the glass is. They don't yet know that they could easily smash a window."

Nicki whimpered and buried her face in her mom's thigh again.

"I think that's enough, honey," Julie admonished. "You're scaring your sister."

Kiel looked around the room. Mrs. Bakke stood waiting patiently with a dish of cookies. To Julie he said, "Why don't you take Nicki to the kitchen for milk and cookies?"

He waited until they'd left. "Cam's right," he declared quietly. "It sounds scary, because it is. They're getting more aggressive. They probably killed Tagget and the Sheriff because they tried to stop them. Same thing maybe with the couple out on the highway—"

"What couple?" Brandon asked.

Daniel answered. "They killed some old folks that were just passing through. Took their gas."

This seemed to sober the lawyer, and he listened without protest.

"So," Kiel continued, "they started off just attacking when we directly got in their way. You were trying to stop them from investigating your car," he said to Brandon. To Daniel he asked, "What did you do to instigate them?"

He shook his head. "Nothing. They didn't even give me a chance. They came after me as soon as they saw me."

"There you go," Kiel proclaimed. "Then they continued to harass us, even after they'd gotten their gas."

"They now recognize us as the dominant species," Cam added, "their enemy."

Brandon rolled his eyes at this. He apparently could remain intimidated only so long.

His son didn't see this, and he continued. "The individual crablets are the phase-ones. The phase-twos are the drones, and they're now evolving from the original universal form—tentacles with claws and sacks to carry gas. They probably copied the claws from birds, and got the idea for carrying gas from the gas tanks in the cars."

"What do you think is next?" Kiel asked him. "A phase three?"

Cam shrugged. "Sure. Why not? The next phase would take more time. They'd need to find out how to fit it into their new environment. Plus, it would require a whole lot more crablets. I'll bet they've been using the gas to work on it."

All of this brought an image back to Kiel. Drones clustering together, just as crablets do to create the drones. "Cam, you remember that huddle of drones in the mine—the mosh pit?"

Cam thought about it. "You mean that pile of them on the opposite side from their power feed?"

"Yeah. Do you think that was . . . ?"

The boy's eyes lit up. "Yeah! They were already experimenting with a phase three, still working out a good form for the Earth. They weren't ready to bring it out yet."

"Well if the size of the pile was any indication, it looks like it's going to be a real monster."

The room was silent. Kiel realized that the level of his voice had risen. The whole idea was not to frighten Nicki.

"And maybe a lot smarter," Cam added quietly.

After another minute of silence, Kiel said, "So, what'll we do now?"

"The phones are still out?" Brandon asked.

"Land and cell both," Daniel replied.

"And no gas left? None at all?"

"Maybe some in the tractor. Not enough to bother with, though. And that's only if they haven't already gotten to it."

"Then I say one of us walks out to the highway and flags down a passing car."

"Are you volunteering?" Kiel asked.

Brandon stared at him. "I was nearly blown up," he finally pointed out. "I can barely walk."

In answer, Kiel pointed to his own bandaged arm, and then to Daniel's shredded ear. "None of us are in great shape," he concluded. "In any case, it doesn't matter. It would be suicide."

"Well, what do you propose?"

Kiel lifted his shoulders in a long shrug. "Hunker down. Protect ourselves the best we can."

"That's your proposal? Just hide?"

Kiel had the idea the lawyer was playing him, trying to trip him into saying something he'd regret later.

He glanced at Daniel who was watching, tired and patient. "Sure," Kiel confirmed. "For now. We need time to think about it, understand more about them, come up with a viable strategy."

"Fine sounding logic," Brandon said, boring a hole into Kiel's head with his eyes. "But doesn't it all boil down to just a single word: 'cowardice'?"

Kiel knew that Brandon the lawyer was trying to manipulate him into reacting emotionally. But knowing didn't prevent it. "I told you! It would be suicide!"

Brandon looked at Daniel and shrugged. A gesture that said, *what did we expect?*

"What am I?" Kiel objected, raising his voice. "The sacrificial lamb? I should go because I have no family?"

Brandon nodded, pretending that this was a novel new point. "Okay, we can run with that. You go because you have no family."

Kiel was pacing now, fuming. "Oh, and you do? It looks to me like you're in the same boat. You don't even live with your family!"

Brandon had won. He'd gotten him to say something that he already regretted.

But the practiced lawyer hadn't even presented his best evidence yet.

"Not exactly the same boat," Brandon objected. His tone portended trouble, and Kiel went cold remembering the ominous look he'd given him before. "I, for example, am not wanted by the FBI."

Daniel's tired eyes turned to Kiel with alarm.

Kiel went from cold to burning hot in two seconds. "It's true. But I haven't been keeping it a secret. I've already told Julie."

Thank God I did, he thought.

Brandon's hairless face went from surprise to concern. It meant that Julie probably hadn't told him, and he didn't like that. "Ah, but did you tell her why?"

"I told her the truth; that my schizophrenic ex-girlfriend falsely accused me of . . ." It was so difficult to say the words.

"Of what, Mr. Martin? Or would you rather use your real name, Bilinski?

Kiel turned to Daniel. "She fabricated an accusation of child molestation—her daughter."

Julie's brother nodded slowly, indicating only that he heard.

"How about the rest?" Brandon pressed.

Damn! He should have guessed that a lawyer would somehow gain access to police files.

Kiel just stared at him. His brain had frozen up.

"On February sixth of this year," the lawyer expounded, "Mr. Kiel Bilinski—aka Kiel Martin—was found half dressed with five year-old Bernice Stintson who was one hundred percent, stark naked. Further, little Bernice was running from Mr. Bilinski's residence in the dark, screaming. There was three inches of snow on the ground."

Kiel shook his head. His mouth felt like it had been injected with a dozen novocaine needles.

"Are you saying that this is not true?" Brandon challenged.

"No," Kiel managed to utter. He took a deep breath, feeling the pulse thump in his temples. "I'm saying that it's not what it sounds like."

A little cry—a whimper—caught their attention. It was Julie, standing with her hand to her mouth in the doorway to the kitchen. She'd been listening. Her face tight with anger, she turned and disappeared back into the kitchen.

"Apparently you didn't tell her the whole story," Brandon observed, self-satisfied.

"We haven't *heard* the whole story yet," Kiel rebutted, getting up to go to her. Daniel caught his arm though, shaking his head. His grip was firm. The gesture was not just a suggestion.

They all jumped when the front door burst open.

It was Peggy. She glanced around. "Nobody told me there was a party," she protested playfully.

"I thought I told you to stay in the bathroom!" Daniel scolded.

"Don't be silly. You think I'm going to sit around on a toilet for hours while everybody else is part-y-ing?"

She did a little disco dance as she said this, waving her bent arms above her head, first on one side and then the other. The fat rolls around her stomach jiggled in double-time with her beat.

"You could have been killed!" Daniel warned, running to the door. He glanced around, listening, and then closed it.

"By a duck?"

Her husband studied her. "What are you talking about?"

"A duck—a bird that swims in water and eats frogs."

"Peg, come on. What duck?"

She glanced at Kiel and Brandon and rolled her eyes. "Honey," she said to her husband, "you've been working too much. Your 'dangerous drone' came to the back porch. Mitsy tried to catch the poor, confused thing, but luckily it was able to get away." To Kiel she explained, "Mitsy's our cat."

"You got a good look at it?" Daniel asked.

"Enough to see that it was a duck," she replied.

"You saw a bill and feathered wings and webbed feet?"

"I know a duck when I see one," she insisted.

"What did it sound like when it flew away?"

"Like a duck. It was obviously frazzled by Mitsy—you'd be agitated too."

"Agitated as in wings beating so fast that it sounded like a lawnmower?"

She shrugged. "I guess. Did you hear it?"

"We've heard it, Peg. More than we'd like. Believe me, it wasn't a duck, and you're the one that's lucky to have gotten away." He pulled away the cloth he was holding to show her his ear, and she just stared, white-faced.

To Kiel, he added, "The cat was probably unfamiliar—not big enough to pose the same threat as a person."

Daniel glanced out the window. "It's going to be dark in another hour or so. We need to get ready."

The drones seemed to have left for the time being. Keeping a constant ear cocked, Kiel carried old weathered boards from a pile behind the tool shed while Daniel nailed them to the basement and first floor window frames. Mrs. Bakke handed Daniel the nails as he worked his way around the house. Kiel silently prayed that the drones didn't learn how to pull nails out with fabricated hammer claws.

The sun had set by the time they finished all the first floor windows. Daniel peered up at the second story and sighed. "I'm afraid nobody'll be sleeping in beds tonight."

Inside, it was already getting dark, and in the gathering gloom, they carried mattresses and bedding down from upstairs. Then, working with an LED forehead light, Daniel took off a closet door and nailed it over the opening at the top of the stairs. Kiel tried to help, but in the confined space, only managed to knock over a vase, soaking the carpet.

They all sat down to a crowded candle-lit dinner of canned meat and boiled potatoes that Mrs. Bakke had warmed with a propane torch. Hardly anybody spoke. Nicki was obviously terrified by all the seriously drastic preparations, and although Cam tried to look stoic, Kiel could tell that the boy was frightened as well.

Hell, who wasn't?

After they'd pushed aside the sofas in the living room and laid out the mattresses and blankets, there was barely room to walk. With eight of them crammed into the first floor, it was impossible to avoid contact with Julie, but she refused to meet Kiel's eyes. Among the waltzing light of multiple flashlights, people began to stake out bedding territory.

"Maybe I should sleep in the laundry room," Kiel offered.

He didn't want to, and knew that he was making a passive-aggressive play spawned from self-pity. Nobody stepped forward to play along, though. With tired nods of approval, he was handed blankets and a couple of sofa cushions and sent off to find what comfort he could on the linoleum floor next to the washing machine and dryer.

He was so exhausted he needed no physical comfort to find sleep. And he would have fallen asleep immediately, except that the hairs on the back of his neck stood up straight when he heard a buzzing sound. It took only a moment to realize that it was inside the little laundry room, and obviously not a drone.

He found the little flashlight Mrs. Bakke had given him and saw that the intruder was a fly, zipping around in the darkness. He watched its meanderings as it flicked in and out of the narrow beam, wondering what it was searching for in the laundry room where the only food was the oil on his own skin that had collected since his last shower . . . when? Over two days ago. He consoled himself with the thought that at least everybody was in the same unwashed boat.

By pointing the beam at the wall, he was able to fill the little room with a soft, diffused illumination. Now he could watch the fly execute the entirety of its unpredictable pattern. Watching the apparent randomness, Kiel detected purpose; the erratic insect would make a difficult target for a predator, yet it managed to cover the entire interior space in its search. It was an organic, living type of behavior, and it contrasted with the drones, which navigated in direct, linear movements. You could almost envision the geometrically precise flight plan residing in their collective intelligence. But were they really intelligent? Perhaps a better analogy would be a collective program.

Curiously, the fly periodically deviated from its zig-zag meanderings, occasionally swinging wide towards the center of the room before resuming the drunken wandering. Kiel watched closely, and realized that the little insect was encountering a draft from the dryer vent. He could hear a slight sigh of wind outside each time the fly was pushed off course. The breeze was somehow finding its way back through the vent.

And here Kiel found common ground between the inanimate drones and the living little fly. As he had struggled at the top of the power utility pole, he'd watched a drone in a similar situation, being pushed aside, forced away from its intended direction. The attacking drone had difficulty getting to him. In the chaos of the moment, he'd assumed that it was the obstacles it encountered while maneuvering among the superstructure. But he saw it differently now. As he had perched there at the top of the pole, he was just a few feet from a massive amount of voltage—voltage and current that created an electro-magnetic field. This was what had pushed the drone around, if not directly, then perhaps by confusing its sense of orientation. The powerful electric field had acted as an invisible wind to the metal beast.

These thoughts were derailed when he realized that the buzz of the fly had grown in volume. Not only that, but a different timber was swelling as well. Instinctively he flicked off the flashlight, concealing his presence. He lay in the darkness, willing the new sound to be just some fluke of the wind in the exhaust vent.

His hope was shattered by the sound of a window shattering upstairs. This was followed by a second crash and tinkle. And then a third.

Suddenly the sound of flying lawnmowers was directly overhead.

Chapter 19

The living room was mad chaos when he stumbled out, blinding others with his flashlight just as they were blinding him. Daniel's voice boomed over the jabber and Nicki's crying, "Everybody, turn off your light!" Beams went dark one by one until the only light was Daniel's that he held on himself so they could see him. "Okay. Kiel, you here? Turn yours on, but keep it pointed at the floor."

He did as instructed. A third light came on, and Kiel could tell that it was Brandon, refusing to be the odd man out. Upstairs, the burring had subsided by some degrees, and Kiel surmised that there was just one drone still in flight, which meant that at least two others had landed. This was more ominous than if they were still airborne.

"Brandon," Daniel directed, "get the kids and my mom together in the middle of the room. I want them huddled together under all the blankets—Julie too."

"I don't understand why I—" Brandon started.

"*Shut up!* Just do it. Kiel, do you still have your bat?"

Kiel held it up in answer. The blunt weapon had been at his side ever since the attack on the highway.

"Good. Walk around and check all the windows."

Either Daniel had been thinking this through, ready for the nighttime raid, or he was the most efficient and level-headed man Kiel had ever met.

Daniel rooted around in a closet as Kiel quickly made the first-floor circuit, and then headed for the basement. He stood at the top of the basement stairs, bat in hand, sweeping the blackness below with his tiny light. It took all his nerve to descend step-by-tentative-step down the stairway. The basement was dank and creepy. The dirt floor was constantly damp and nurtured a musty mold odor. Ancient cardboard boxes full of Mr. Bakke's collected junk guarded over rows of Mrs. Bakke's canning jars. All was quiet. Down here, he couldn't even hear the lone airborne drone two flights up. He flashed his light quickly along the four windows, and headed back up. His feet found an up-tempo rhythm as he ascended, and his back crawled with an irrational fear that it was about to be pierced with a metal talon.

When he arrived back in the living room he found Daniel loading shells in a pump-action shotgun. "That should do a number on them," Kiel commented quietly.

Daniel shook his head. "It's just rock salt. Dad kept the gun in the closet next to the door for the deer that came into Mom's garden at night. The real shells are upstairs where the kids can't get at them."

He looked frustrated—probably kicking himself for forgetting to get them before blocking off the stairs.

"Still," Kiel said, "it's got to be better than a baseball bat."

Daniel grunted in halfhearted agreement. "Maybe at real close range."

Suddenly a new, meatier buzz joined the familiar droning lawnmower, and an instant later erupted into a full-throated rattling roar at the top of the stairs, causing Nicki to scream, and them all to jump and gasp.

Silently Daniel hefted the shotgun and headed for the stairs. The racket sounded like a chainsaw, and Kiel guessed that a drone was playing exactly that part, perhaps whipping a newly formed saw-toothed appendage around at blinding speed. Hell, it might have created jagged teeth around its entire perimeter and then spun, turning its entire body into a mobile flying circular saw.

Kiel followed Daniel up, noting that Brandon seemed content enough now to make sure the women and children stayed covered. "What'll we do?" Kiel asked above the din. No need to whisper now.

"Wait," Daniel replied. He held the shotgun loosely, the barrel lying in his crooked arm.

"Until they come through?"

He shrugged. "Nothing we can do from this side."

"You have a *shotgun*!"

Daniel snorted. "The rock salt would barely penetrate the door."

The blaring staccato rattle of the alien chainsaw just a couple of feet away was unnerving. The sound of wood being chewed and spit out in a shower of sawdust was the very embodiment of rapacious evil intent. Kiel had never played the role of stalked prey, had never even imagined it. The predator diligently working to get at them wanted just one thing: to kill them all—man, woman, and child.

He couldn't stand it. He wasn't Daniel, so cool and patient. They had to do something, anything. Just minutes ago, before he was interrupted by their arrival, he'd been on a track. The drones seemed to be sensitive to electromagnetic fields. It was worth a try.

He pounded off down the stairs. Daniel didn't ask where he was off to, probably just satisfied to have him out of his way. Brandon called to him as he stumbled into the jumble of cushions and blankets in the dark living room, but he ignored him. "Julie! Where are you?"

Her head popped up from between the blankets. "I'm here," she replied, holding her open hand in front of her face to shield against his light.

"Sorry," he said, lowering the little flashlight. "Do you have that taser—that stun gun?"

"It's in my purse . . . uh-oh, up in my bedroom. No, wait. I think I brought it down when I got aspirin for Daniel."

"What does it look like?" he asked. The purse could be buried anywhere in the blanket rubble.

"It's black and textured—there it is! Hanging by the door."

He ran over and grabbed it off the coat rack. Holding the light in his teeth, he rooted around for the stun device, but then just dumped all the contents onto the floor. He didn't see anything that looked like a weapon capable of flooring a 250-pound man. "It's not here!" he called, exasperated.

"I can see it," she replied. "It's pink."

He held up what he'd thought was an old incandescent flashlight, but now he saw the two metal contacts at the end. He found the safety switch and turned it on. "Thanks!" he called, sprinting back up the stairs.

The drone had nearly completed its circular cut. Another couple of inches and it would be through. Daniel stood with the gun barrel pointed at the center, ready.

"I have an idea!" Kiel shouted above the buzzing saw.

Daniel glanced at the pink plastic box. "That's Julie's stun gun?" He shook his head skeptically. "They don't really pack a punch. They work by disrupting the nervous system. I don't think these devils have nervous systems."

"I know. It can't hurt to try."

He shook his head again, but pointed the barrel away. "I wouldn't count on that."

Kiel held the box close to the blur of the blade poking through the door and pressed the firing button. A little arc of blue fire danced between the contacts and he moved it forward until the electric arc licked the drone's spinning toothed appendage. Instantly the blade disappeared and the buzzing racket fell silent.

"Ha!" Kiel shouted triumphantly.

He looked at Daniel who grinned and said, "Well, I'll be."

The reprieve lasted only a moment, though. An instant later, the buzz saw returned, working quickly to finish the last inch of wood.

Daniel held the stun device against the protruding blade again, but this time the drone just pulled back a little, as it had done when Daniel had harassed it with the gun barrel. It obviously felt the electric arc, but wasn't hurt by it.

Suddenly the newly carved door tilted forward, and Kiel pulled his hand back as the circular piece of wood fell clattering to the floor. The drone hung there directly in front of him, just beyond the opening. It was morphing; it had attached itself to the other side of the door while it worked, and now retracted the cutting blade and took to the air again with re-formed ear-wings.

Mental inertia impelled Kiel. In his head, the little plastic box he held was still a weapon. Alone, a person is apt to run away when faced with danger, but a group instinct can drive the same person to greater risks when everybody's safety is at stake. Perhaps it's just hubris mistaken for bravery.

Self-confidence or self-sacrifice, Kiel didn't think, he just acted. He pressed the firing button and shoved the stun device through the hole. The drones, however, were becoming familiar with the direct assaults these humans seemed to prefer. A tentacle that it must have been morphing out of view, reached around and adroitly grabbed his wrist. Another tentacle, this one with knife-sharp talons reached up in preparation to strike for his neck. Something slammed him from the side, and the next instant the explosion of Daniel's shotgun compounded the disorientation so that he found himself crumpled on the floor. The drone still gripped his wrist, and the tentacle wriggled around on his stomach and chest, but there was no drone attached. Daniel's point-blank shot had severed the appendage.

Once again, Kiel found himself attached to a disembodied drone tentacle, but this time he was gripped by encircling fingers rather than sharp talons. This limb was intended to just hold him while the other struck with killing talons. And once separated from the body proper, a severed component doggedly carried on its portion of the mission, no matter how relevant in its new, isolated role. At least, for a while; experience taught that the isolated mini-colony of crablets soon formulated a new attack.

Kiel didn't wait to find out what that might be. With his left hand, he worked at the silver fingers. He wasn't able to unwrap them, but he found that he could work them one-by-one off his hand. He still held Julie's stun device, and he supposed that this confused the crablets—perhaps they considered the plastic box part of him, a part as important to grip as the soft flesh of his wrist and hand.

In the meantime, the severed end of the tentacle was finding a new mission. He'd been batting the wriggling snake-end out of the way as he worked at his wrist, but suddenly a sharp pain stabbed his shoulder. He punched at the metal python, and the pain seared as the end of the tentacle broke free, the tip red with his blood. The crablets had formed a wicked hook. They were learning just how vulnerable the soft flesh of animals was.

He managed to grab the flailing tentacle near the hook, and held it against the wall while he positioned his foot against it, then went back to working at the gripping silver fingers.

Kiel wondered why Daniel wasn't helping him. He glanced up and saw the farmer lift the shotgun and aim towards the hole where a half dozen drone tentacles were reaching through to anchor themselves against the edge. The shotgun jerked, and another blast filled the hallway. A second later, several wriggling finger-size drone snakes fell around him along with a little shower of dust that his tongue told him was salt, the remnants of the substitute shot.

Whether by coincidence or themselves affected by the trauma of the blast, the last of the gripping fingers slipped from his hand to take up new positions around the stun box, and he shook it off. He pushed with his foot and rolled away before the tentacle could get the hook back into him.

"Watch it doesn't get you!" Kiel called, but when he looked he saw that Daniel had already pumped the gun. He aimed at the floor, and pulled the trigger. Kiel felt the thump of concussion against the floorboards as the shotgun blast exploded yet again.

Kiel sprang to his feet behind Daniel. Beyond the hole was blackness; their flashlights lay on the floor where they'd dropped them, and the diffuse, reflected light didn't reach through the carved opening. He picked up one of the lights, wondering whether he really wanted to see what lay beyond. Chiding himself for being a sissy, he held it up and pointed the beam through. He could see two or three drones moving about in the hallway, their purpose a mystery. Suddenly one appeared seemingly out of nowhere directly beyond the hole. Daniel was ready, and fired another blast of rock salt. The collective colony crablets had taken note of this new weapon, however. As if reading Daniel's mind to know precisely when he'd pull the trigger, the drone stretched into an arc, as though made of warm taffy that someone had stretched with a tug. The volley of salt ripped harmlessly through the air inside. The evasive maneuver was similar to that taken when Kiel had last used the baseball bat outside.

Kiel felt his stomach drop away as he grasped that neither clubs nor guns were apparently going to be effective against this persistent killer.

But then the colony proved the alien nature of its logic. It retreated. The howling buzz of multiple drones in flight moved away down the hall and then faded. They had exited through the windows they'd broken and flew away into the night.

"What do you think?" Kiel asked quietly, afraid to jinx their luck by putting his hope to words.

"I think we need to patch up the hole," his ever-reasonable brother in arms replied. Daniel handed him the shotgun and went off to gather tools and material.

Kiel held the gun balanced in one hand and shone the flashlight through the hole with the other, sweeping the beam up and around the shadowed corners. He tried to ignore the pain in his shoulder since it was a reminder of the heartless viciousness of their enemy. He was obsessed with the worry that a lone drone had remained behind, hidden somewhere to reach out a taloned tentacle towards the unwary. He realized that his lower back felt wet, and wondered whether the wound in his shoulder was worse than he'd thought. Blood would be sticky, though. He concluded that it was simply water from the Mrs. Bakke's vase that had soaked the carpet.

Something tapped his foot and he jumped and cried out. It was the severed tentacle, or at least what was left of it. Daniel's shot had cut it in two, and one end still sported the sharp hook, while the other continued to grip the stun box tenaciously. But most of the rest of the limb had more or less dissolved. Except for the remnant tooled ends, most of the tentacle was smeared Cream of Wheat. Kiel would have guessed that the rock salt would blast only a narrow profile at this close range. In fact, the chewed carpet where the lightweight shot had impacted was barely two inches across. Maybe the horde of crablets had simply died of shock.

A blue flicker caught his eye. One of the tentacled fingers that gripped the stun box covered the firing button and occasionally made contact, discharging the device. Expired crablets squirmed and flowed where the electrical arc happened to sweep, as the last few inches of remaining limb writhed about purposelessly. Kiel found this ironic—that active, connected, intact and dangerous crablets seemed to be immune to the stun energy, but were battered about when expired. At least he had the satisfaction of the further irony that the crablets refusing to give up their grip were causing macabre humiliation to their dead brethren.

His thoughts on the relevance of humiliation to mindless machines were interrupted when the lights suddenly came back on. Shouts of relief issued from below as Daniel trotted up the stairs carrying the hammer, nails, and the round top of the table that had stood next to the front door. Kiel held the expensive patch in place while Daniel hammered a couple of nails, but then stood back to give him room to work.

Figuring that there was nothing further he could do to help, Kiel joined the lively crowd in the living room. From childhood he knew that monsters that flourish in darkness are banished in the light. Nicki bounced on the sofa cushions, and Julie and her mom grinned broadly and given half a chance probably would have joined the little girl.

The lights flickered and went dark for a second before returning, but it was enough to douse the party. It was a reminder that light was ethereal, a false security. Brandon raised his hand to get attention, and in the renewed silence, they all heard it—the dreaded sound of distant buzzing.

And then the lights went off. And stayed off.

In the darkness, Nicki whimpered softly.

"I don't think it's a drone," Cam's voice said. "It's too deep."

Kiel realized that the boy was right. The sound was more of a ground-thumping rumble. "It's a helicopter!" he cried, recognizing the unmistakable thwap-thwap of chopper blades.

"Maybe it's the power company," Mrs. Bakke offered. "I'd give anything for that little transistor radio Papa used to carry around."

A flashlight came on, and spun around the room blinding everybody in turn. It came from the direction of Brandon. "They've come to investigate the outage," the lawyer declared confidently. "Somebody should go out and get their attention with a light."

"By 'somebody,' I presume you don't mean yourself," Kiel commented, but Brandon ignored him.

"I don't know," Cam said doubtfully.

The thump-thump of Daniel's feet on the stairs was followed by his voice. "You hear that? Sounds like a helicopter."

"The power company has sent a crew," Brandon explained, promoting the conjecture into a fact.

"Hold on," Kiel interjected. "Cam, what are you thinking?"

After a moment of hesitation, the boy replied, "I just don't think it's a good idea to go outside and draw attention."

"Horse feathers," his father dismissed. "Who's got the brightest light?"

"I don't think it matters," Daniel said.

"Why?"

"It's leaving."

Daniel was right. The sound of thumping blades faded into the distance.

"Well, if it comes back," Brandon asserted, "we need to go outside with flashlights."

Quietly, almost to himself, Cam said two words. Kiel wasn't sure he'd caught it, but it sounded like the boy had said, "Phase three."

Chapter 20

Once again surrounded by smothering darkness, the six adults and two children retreated to the make-believe safety of cushions and covers. Kiel couldn't bring himself to self-banishment in the laundry room, and dragged his bedding into the living room and made camp off to one side right under a window. Soon, the sound of deep, steady breathing and the occasional rattle of snores gave evidence of people asleep. Perhaps they were comforted by the thought that men of authority, even if just utility workers, were on the scene. Kiel wished he could convince himself that the sound they'd heard was indeed a helicopter.

Nobody had suggested posting a guard, probably because everybody was too tired to take a turn. Kiel figured that it didn't matter; the drones made such a racket, they'd have to be comatose to sleep through an attack.

He lay under the boarded-up window listening to his heart keep a syncopated rhythm with the sound of slumbering breathing. This was the first chance he'd had to digest the day's adventures, and the events of the previous twelve hours seemed to tumble around and around in his head, like laundry in a dryer; he'd glimpse an image from one trauma—Sheriff Lanner lying dead on the ground—only to have it tumble away to be replaced by the next—the severed drone tentacle hanging on to Daniel's bloody ear. Around and around, until he was watching the same disturbing views over and over.

How could they sleep?

There was one thing that worried him: if the utility crews did somehow restore the power, it would simply remove the hard-won roadblock that they'd forced upon the colony.

He smiled in the darkness. There was one tiny advantage to the pickle-pit they'd fallen into: he'd forgotten about his own burden for awhile.

The smile melted. No, quite the opposite. Brandon had dug up the shallow grave and held up the hateful cadaver for Julie to view. Bad metaphor, there. It was that kind of thinking that gave credence to the crime.

He was so tired; more tired than he could remember. Why couldn't he shut off his mind and go to sleep?

ж ж ж

Kiel slept. He knew this because he woke up. There'd been a sound. He didn't know how he knew this, but he did. The last time this had happened was when he'd met the colony while seeking refuge in a hole. Were they back? Would waking to their sound again be the other bookend, marking the opposite end of his time with them? Marking the end of his time with everything?

The rustling of a blanket and the soft sound of bare feet padding off towards the bathroom was his reprieve. The boarded windows kept the room in pitch blackness, but he had the sense that the night visitor was Cam. Kiel lay waiting for the sound of the boy returning to his bed, but soon dozed off again.

When he woke the second time, it was to lights flashing about and shouts of confusion. Among the hysterical questions and terse replies, Kiel gathered that Cam had slipped out and crossed over to Daniel and Peg's house to retrieve a manual, crank-powered radio. Tanya, their daughter, had bought it, and everybody but Cam had forgotten about it stashed away in her closet. Julie seemed on the verge of tears at the thought of Cam outside alone, but her distraught reprimands were soon outranked by everybody else's intense interest in the news to be had.

Cam held a light on the compact device while Daniel experimentally turned the handle. When nothing immediately happened, Brandon grabbed the radio, saying, "Here, let me try." He spun the handle madly until the whining of the internal generator sounded like the turbines of a 737 powering for takeoff.

Cam reached forward and pointed. "It's set to battery power," he called above the bleating sound of wasted energy.

His father turned the selector switch, mumbling something about the stupid design, and now when he spun the crank, the dial lit up, and a static hiss issued from the speaker. Almost any movement of the crank handle kept the radio alive.

While Brandon slowly cranked, Daniel searched across the FM band, but the few stations he found seemed to be playing pre-programmed music—no surprise for the dead of night. He switched to the AM band, and soon found what they wanted. An Oshkosh station was broadcasting an all-night talk show, and every other call was about the big blackout. Over the course of twenty minutes huddled around the little glowing link to the world, they found that, while the utility company had been able to track down the trouble to one rural substation, their men had not been able to get to it. Two different crews had been sent out, but neither had reported back, despite repeated attempts to contact them.

At this, Kiel glanced at Daniel, who just shook his head.

The talk show host managed to get a spokesman from the Governor's office on the line, and the official statement from Madison was that if power was not restored by morning, or if the utility company executives still couldn't provide concrete reasons for the outage, the Governor was considering calling in the National Guard.

Finally a caller came on who identified herself as the wife of a utility company employee. Even though half the county was blacked out, she said that her husband insisted that a couple of hours ago power was again being drawn by the downed link. This was not supposed to be possible. This information was, predictably, followed by a flood of callers bent on airing their favorite theory about Iranian terrorists or space aliens. After ten minutes of an extraordinary variety of fantastic imaginings, Daniel waved disgustedly for Brandon to stop cranking.

"Danny!" Peggy objected. "Why'd you turn it off?"

"It's just nonsense. What do you expect from people that stay up all night calling radio stations?"

Kiel laughed.

"What's so funny?" Brandon asked.

"For once the fringe crowd's not so far off the mark."

The lawyer snorted. "It's not like they actually have a clue about what's going on. In fact, *we* don't even have a clue."

"You haven't been listening."

"What's that supposed to mean?"

"Cam had a theory from the beginning that's held up quite well."

"You mean that crap about geometrically expanding replicators?"

"That crap tried to kill you. Cam, any more thoughts on the subject?"

The boy was silent, and Kiel realized that he was once again putting him on the spot with his father. "Maybe we should try to get some—"

"They might have started off harmless," Cam said at the same time, and then went quiet again.

"Harmless?" Kiel probed.

"Sure. The crablets could be millions of years old—not any particular crablet, but the lineage. Over that much time they might have evolved, just like us through natural selection. Whoever made them might have used them as a tool, like we use computers. It would have been useful for them to be able to replicate themselves. Maybe some accidentally escaped, or were left behind. And then, well natural selection would have evolved them. The ones that were best at surviving continued to replicate."

"Made by aliens," Brandon mocked. "From another galaxy."

"Doesn't have to be a different galaxy," his son muttered, but quietly, showing obvious deference to this man, his father.

"Brandon," Kiel said.

"What?"

"You're an asshole," Kiel declared, getting up and heading off to his outpost under the window.

"Better than a pedophile," the lawyer sneered.

Kiel knew he couldn't win any poking matches with this shameful target pinned to his back. He'd have to just suck it up and bite his tongue around the bastard Brandon.

Dawn would arrive in an hour or so, but Kiel thought he might sleep some more. He lay listening to the others settling back in as well, and after a few minutes, Cam's voice came quietly into the silence of the late night, "Aunt Peg, I forgot to tell you . . . Mitsy's dead. I'm sorry."

After a while there was just the soft sobbing of Peggy mourning her cat until Kiel heard the rustling of blankets again and footsteps in his direction. A subtle waft of Julie's perfume announced the visitor. "Kiel?" she whispered.

He felt a hand brush his shoulder. He sat up. "I'm here," he whispered back ever so quietly.

He guessed that she was positioning herself cross-legged in front of him. Her hand lightly grasped his upper arm, finding orientation. "Listen," she started, so softly he had to lean forward to understand, "I—I just wanted to thank you."

"For what?"

"Sticking up for Cam again. You do wonders for his confidence."

"He has a lot to be confident about. I'm not patronizing him. I really think he's got these monsters figured out."

"Well, I just wanted you to know that I appreciate it. His father's a real son-of-a-bitch, and it just kills me when he treats Cam so badly."

Kiel didn't know what to say. He agreed, but it would be unseemly to lead the cheer.

"Listen . . ." she started, even more quietly, leaning in so close that her breath brushed his face. "About what Brandon said, that story about the naked little girl—"

"Bernice—Maria's daughter."

"Yes."

"You want to know if it's true," he suggested, feeling the familiar cold dread freezing his blood.

"I want to know your side of the story."

Kiel was silent a moment. He wasn't used to having someone listen to his story—the whole truth. "First of all," he began, "the charges were dropped."

"I'm confused," she said. "Isn't this the incident that you're, um, running from?"

He sighed. "No. This happened a few months before Maria decided to stick it to me. But it's pretty obvious that this gave her the idea."

"So, what happened?"

"We'd just had a fresh fall of snow, and the three of us made a snowman in my front yard. We had a great time. I knew that Maria was struggling that day—I could tell even though nobody else probably noticed. But for a half hour she seemed to have escaped—was actually happy. It came to a head later when I made hot chocolate for us and added those little marshmallows. Well, somehow Maria was suddenly convinced that they were pieces of bone—"

"Bone? Like animal bones?"

"I know; it sounds nuts. Not only that, but she thought that they were her *own* bones. How I could have gotten them from her is beyond logic, but reason isn't part of this game. The whole time I was trying to calm her down—to show her that they were just soft marshmallows—Bernie was humming a little tune. I'd noticed her doing this sometimes, and I think it was her way of disassociating. Even though she's only five, she knows when something doesn't make sense, and I think she was getting used to tuning out when her mom had episodes."

"That poor little girl. It must be horrible for her."

"Up until this last year Maria wasn't too bad. Plus her mom—Bernie's grandmother—was there a lot to balance things. In fact, when I couldn't calm Maria down that night, I called her mom, and she came over. We agreed that it would be best if she took Maria to her house, and I'd bring Bernie along later after she'd had a chance to check out Maria's meds situation."

"She was on medication?"

"Oh yeah. At least she was supposed to be. It was about this time that she started skipping it for periods. After they left, Bernie seemed reserved. She was playing by herself. To anybody else, she would have looked perfectly normal, but I knew that she had withdrawn. I hated to see her like that, so I suggested we play a game, one we'd played before and I knew she enjoyed."

He couldn't see Julie's face, but he sensed that she was holding her breath, waiting for the denouement. "It was hide-and-seek, but with a twist. Bernie has a great imagination, and I like to challenge it. So, before she runs off and hides, she has to think of a character to play, and the hiding place must fit that character. Then I not only have to find her, but also guess what her character is. One time she played the Queen of England—can you guess where she hid?"

"I don't know . . . wait, don't tell me—"

"Yes. She hid in the bathroom, sitting on the toilet—"

"Oh, no—the 'throne'! That's ingenuous for a five-year-old."

"Like I said. Anyway, I hid my face and heard her moving around, and then everything was quiet, so I started looking for her. I looked everywhere. She really had me this time. I looked and looked, and then started to get worried. I looked everywhere twice and started calling for her. When I couldn't think of anyplace else, I finally went outside. And that's when I found her clothes."

"Her clothes? The ones she was wearing?"

"Or not wearing, now. There's a little porch in the back, and her clothes were scattered around on the floor. I called for her, and heard a little whimper. It came from outside."

"Oh no!"

"Oh yes. She was in the backyard. Julie, she was squatting in the snow, buck-naked. She was shivering and nearly blue with cold. I called to her, but she said that I had to guess who she was first. I could hardly understand her from her teeth chattering. I started towards her, telling her that I'd guess once we got back inside, but she insisted. She got up and ran when I got to her, yelling that I had to guess first. Even though she was half froze-to-death, I had a heck of a time trying to catch her."

"And that's when the police showed up?"

"Yeah. Maria had gotten pretty loud by the time her mom had arrived, and one of the neighbors had put in the call."

Kiel waited, but Julie was silent. He couldn't even distinguish her breathing from that of the sleeping family.

"Maria's mom eventually helped clear things up," he continued. "She knew about the hide-and-seek game we played, and the fact that the police found Bernie's clothes in the unheated porch would have been difficult to explain otherwise."

"Plus, I imagine they talked to Bernie herself."

"I wasn't there for that, of course. The whole incident was supposed to be expunged from the police records, but I found out the hard way that information isn't so easy to erase."

"It came up again in the deposition after Maria accused you," Julie said, remembering.

"Falsely."

"Of course."

Kiel couldn't tell to what degree, if any, she was being sarcastic.

"What was she supposed to be?" Julie asked.

"You mean, what do I think Maria should have done?"

"No—Bernie. What character was she playing?"

"Ah, that's actually very interesting. She was supposed to be a snowman."

"Oh my! I see. You'd built one earlier. Do you think there's a connection?"

"I'm sure of it. Later, I asked Bernie why she chose that, and she told me that snowmen made happiness."

"Oh Lord. I know where you're going. Her mother had been happy and normal making the snowman. Bernie just wanted to go back to that place. Kiel, that little girl may need help."

"I know. Unfortunately, it's not going to come from me, though. So . . . do you believe me?"

Silence. "Kiel, how can I?" she finally replied.

His heart caught in his throat. He hadn't wanted to be disappointed, had prepared himself for the worst, but it still stung when it came.

"I mean," she went on, "how can I know what to believe? I would be lying to pretend otherwise. I . . . I don't really know you. You should have told me the whole story from the start."

"The 'story'?"

"You know what I mean. Brandon said that the police found you half-naked."

She was challenging him? Picking apart his 'story'? He wished that he could see her face. "Maria had spilt chocolate milk down the front of me in her frenzy. I took off my shirt, and put on just a T-shirt. I was wearing that when the police came. The front of my jeans were still wet."

"I see," she said.

Kiel wondered if she really did.

He heard her sigh. "I'm going to try to get some sleep," she said. "Listen, thanks again for helping Cam."

He heard her make her way back to her cushions and blankets. "I need you to believe me," he said. His whisper was much too soft for her to hear.

ж ж ж

Kiel's eyes snapped open to the early dawn light filtering through the cracks in their boarded up windows. The soft light set detail to the room in shades of gray. The sound of the helicopter had woken him. He sat up, and saw the dim shapes of others rising from their bedding as well.

"They're back!" Brandon cried, his voice rough with the phlegm of sleep. "We can finally end this miserable nightmare," he added as he stumbled among the bodies and blankets towards the front door.

"Don't open it!" Kiel warned. "We don't know that it's the utility company."

"Utility company, National Guard—hell, I don't care if it's Doctors Without Borders; I just want a ride out of this hellhole."

"No!" Kiel cried. "I mean it might be the colony—"

It was too late. Brandon had already opened the door and stepped out onto the porch. The chatter of the flying machine came through louder. This close, it sounded more like a small turbo-prop than the thwap-thwap of helicopter blades. The lawyer glanced around, and then froze, eyes staring mesmerized.

Kiel ran for the door. Standing on the porch in his bare feet, he saw it. Flying a hundred feet up, the beast was the size of an SUV and making straight for them. The dawn horizon provided backlight so that the elongated body and swept-back legs were in silhouette. Even without the benefit of viewing in three dimensions, Kiel could see that this was not just a giant scaled-up version of the drones. For one thing, rather than whirling helicopter rabbit ears, the blur of beating wings extended to each side. Kiel thought that this must be how a wasp would appear to an ant.

Cam joined them as the monster closed the last hundred yards. "Phase Three," he proclaimed.

He could have been describing Hitler's blitzkrieg rolling across the Polish border.

Blaine C. Readler

PART IV

DEFEAT

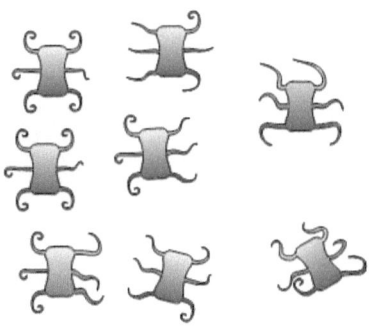

Blaine C. Readler

Chapter 21

Brandon uttered a word that perfectly expressed what Kiel was thinking and dashed back inside. Kiel grabbed Cam by the shoulder and ushered him through, shoving his fist against the door that Brandon had swung closed in their face.

"It's not rescue, is it?" Julie asked faintly, holding Nicki tightly against her.

Peggy sat up, rubbing her eyes. "What's all the ruckus? I'm trying to sleep!"

"They're back?" Daniel asked, picking up the shotgun.

"The Big Daddy," Kiel answered, peeking out one last time before closing the door. "Cam's Phase Three."

"Should we get under the blankets again?" Julie asked.

Her brother looked at her a moment as the throb of the approaching colony warrior swelled to a buzzing roar. "Won't matter," he replied, raising his voice above the howling maelstrom.

They stood transfixed as the threatening wail of giant wings seemed to pause just beyond the north wall. The boarded-up windows prevented a defining view, but they could see motion through the cracks, and a cloud seemed to block the pale dawn light. The sound of massiveness in flight modulated, and moved to the left, towards the front porch. A moment later, a dull thump was followed immediately by a crash and groan of wood twisting torturously as Kiel's feet simultaneously felt the concussion jar the very foundations of the house.

"What the hell!" Daniel cried above Nicki's scream. The farmer hefted his shotgun and made for the front door. Kiel thought of the salt shot and imagined pebbles thrown against the side of an elephant.

He went to one of the north windows where the monster had paused upon arrival. Despite a terror that clutched at his gut, survival insisted he keep an eye on the attacker's location. Pressing his face against the glass of the window, and peering through the crack between two boards, he saw just the yard bordered by Mrs. Bakke's azaleas beneath the old maple tree. The groan and screech of nails torn from wood continued to his left near the front of the house.

Suddenly a mighty crash shook the house and other voices joined Nicki's screams. An instant later, Kiel saw motion. A dark curtain covered his view, and then a claw the size of his head with T-rex talons that were opened wide for a killing grasp reached towards him. Kiel fell back with a shout as one of the boards covering the window flew away. Through the opened slot he saw just silvery textured movement—the beast was pressed up against the house. A single talon wrapped around the edge of the next board, and with one sharp squeak and thump, it too flew away, revealing more of their attacker. A rounded breast covered in interconnected ringlets appeared exactly like a dragon dressed in protective mail armor.

A blast exploded from behind him and the window dissolved in a shower of broken glass. A second blast from Daniel's shotgun shredded the edge of the curtain. The effect of the salt barrage on the monster was impossible to tell. Kiel finally recovered from shock enough to scamper away backwards, but immediately rammed into the back of the sofa. The third and final board covering the window flew away, and the giant claw came through, talons folded together. Once safely through the frame of the window, the talons opened wide and Kiel was staring into the gaping grasp of a claw able to tear his head from his shoulders as easily as a robin might pluck a worm from the grass. Poised in time, balanced between a living consciousness curious to see a monster, and obliteration by talon-skewering, Kiel's hyper-heightened mind registered minute details. He noticed that the regular pattern of interconnected ringlets was disrupted at the base of one talon. Over a span measured in micro-seconds, he realized that he was looking at one of fingerling trout from the aquarium squashed flat and plastered to the monster's paw, just as he was about to be.

But even as the killing talons loomed above, intent on rending flesh from bone, the shotgun barrel thrust forward and Kiel was deafened as Daniel gave the beast a claw-full of stinging salt instead.

This time the beast's reaction was immediate and violent. The claw swung forcefully downward, crashing against the bottom of the window, shattering the frame and the wall below. Simultaneously, a shower of crumbled drywall and splintered wood burst forth from above, and the tips of grasping talons appeared in the wall just below the ceiling as dawn light poured through the newly excavated window.

And then, having proved it could easily smash through this flimsy shell that provided humans with false security, the alien monster surprised them all. After a few thrashing struggles, where the claws pushed, pulled, and stabbed randomly about, enlarging the damage further so that Kiel was sure he would be impaled in the frenzy, the appendages disappeared, and they saw the massive taloned wasp rise, hover a moment, and then turn and fly away even faster than it had arrived.

The roar of beating wings faded, leaving just the whimpers of terrified victims and the fall of a few last pieces of debris hanging precariously from the broken ceiling.

Kiel got slowly to his feet, amazed and gratified that he wasn't leaking quantities of blood. The light of the blossoming day filled the room through the gaping holes. Mrs. Bakke, the hard-headed stoic, sobbed softly as she knelt before the destruction to the house that had been her home for forty-five years.

"Why did it leave?" Kiel wondered out loud.

"It must have sensitive palms," Daniel replied, putting his foot to the crushed wall below the window to test its stability. "That salt shot couldn't have done much damage."

"It looked like a giant humming bird," Cam mused, gazing with awe at the hole the monster had ripped in the wall below the ceiling.

"I was thinking a wasp," Kiel answered. A humming bird seemed too cute. "In any case, it sure didn't look like the previous drones."

"It's imitating the life it sees around it," Cam said, glancing at his dad, who sat dazed against the opposite wall. Satisfied that he wouldn't be ridiculed, he went on. "After all, life on each planet has spent millions—billions—of years evolving to fit and form the environment. It would be kind of stupid if it *didn't*."

"And you don't think that it's stupid?"

Cam shrugged. "It was at first, when it was just individual crablets. The more that collect together, though—the bigger the beast—the more collective reasoning that it has."

"It knew enough to pull off the boards."

"Exactly. I'm not sure even a chimp would know to do that if it didn't watch it being nailed on."

"Don't you two ever shut up?" Brandon complained, holding his head in his hands. "This isn't a science-fiction movie. We could be *killed*."

"Thanks, Brandon," Julie admonished, caressing Nicki's back as the little girl tried to bury her face completely in her mom's waist.

Mrs. Bakke sat in a chair with one foot propped up on the sofa. Her eyes were red from crying, and her face pinched. Kiel assumed that this was simply grief over the damaged house, but then he noticed that her ankle looked bruised. It seemed to swell even as he watched. She saw him looking at her. "Twisted it when I stepped on the edge of one of the damned cushions," she explained. "I'm my own worst enemy."

"Can I get some . . . ice, maybe?"

He realized his mistake immediately.

"Unless the power ever comes back on," she replied, "we won't see ice until December."

Daniel was rooting around among the blankets. He picked up the radio and handed it to Kiel. "See what you can find," he said, making for the stairs.

Kiel cranked, while Cam tuned. The world apparently still didn't know about the invasion. As far as the rest of Wisconsin was concerned, the utility company was simply inconveniencing a lot of people through incompetence. The Governor was demanding explanations, and the power company executives had promised to have answers by 7:00 AM. The only information they'd revealed so far was that they were still having trouble getting word back from the field crews. The Governor in turn suggested that they go out themselves and have a look, otherwise he was ready to call out the National Guard.

Daniel was making a lot of pounding racket at the top of the stairs, and following the sound of splintering wood, he returned carrying two boxes of shotgun shells.

Brandon gazed up the stairs at the light now showing from above where Daniel had broken through. "Are you going to board that back up?" he demanded.

"Don't be an ass," was Daniel's response.

Kiel gave him the radio update, and the farmer nodded, having made a decision. "We have to move to the cave."

Kiel stared at him, wondering if he'd lost his mind.

"I don't think he means the colony's cave," Cam offered, guessing at his confusion.

He remembered: Cam had said something about his grandfather having a cave on his land as well. "How far is it?"

"At the edge of the property against the hills. Four fields—fifteen minutes walking."

"We'll be running, not walking. But, how is the cave any safer than here?"

Daniel raised an eyebrow. "Solid limestone versus drywall?"

"I mean the entrance. What's to keep them from just coming in after us?"

The farmer held up the shotgun in answer. "I'll have only one direction to defend."

"How about the milkhouse?" Julie asked.

"It's not big enough for more than two people, and you'd suffocate within an hour," her brother countered. To Kiel, he explained, "Before electricity, famers kept fresh cow-milk in cool places—usually small buildings with thick cement walls. Our grandfather converted his into a bomb shelter during the cold war scares of the fifties. It would withstand the worst these aliens things could throw at us, but it's just too small."

Kiel shrugged. "Then let's get skedaddling! What should we take? Water, food, baseball bats?"

Daniel divvied out the collection of supplies, reminding everybody that they had to fit whatever they gathered into one grocery bag. When he told Brandon to find containers for water, the lawyer replied, "It's stupid to leave the house. The authorities will be looking for us here."

"What authorities?" Daniel replied. "Tagget's dead, remember? I don't think Donny's going to save us."

"You heard it—the Governor's calling out the National Guard."

"Don't be naive. He's just trying to bully the utility executives, or more likely making a show for his constituents that he's taking the outage seriously. The state has to bear the cost of a National Guard deployment when the governor makes the call. If I know this guy, he'll wait until the President offers to help."

"He's not going to wait, you idiot! There's people getting *killed* here!"

Daniel raised his voice to meet the belligerent level. "Nobody knows that! Look, stay here and get creamed—it's no skin off my nose. But I'm not wasting any more time with you."

And with that, Daniel turned his back on Brandon and proceeded with the supply gathering. Kiel went down to the basement to collect cans of food, and when he returned, Brandon was talking with Julie, who looked pained. "I'm their father," he reminded her.

She shook her head, as though gathering willpower to resist dessert. "I think Daniel's right—the cave will be safer."

Brandon stared at her a moment, and then said, "Okay, let them go with your mom, and you can stay here."

Her pained indecision gave way to anger. "If you agree that the cave is safer, why would you want me to stay here? If not, then you're pushing your kids into danger. What kind of man are you?"

"I'm your husband."

"You *were* my husband. As far as I'm concerned, that ended when you filed the divorce papers."

His further pleas were interrupted by Daniel. "Time to go! Kiel, Peg, Julie—make sure you each carry a bat or club. Mom—stay close to the kids. If the . . . thing comes back before we get there, listen closely to what I say, and then *do it!* Got it?"

Everybody nodded, glum and subdued at the prospect of what they were about to attempt.

Brandon grasped Julie's arm, but she peeled away his fingers with her free hand.

Daniel couldn't open the front door. The porch roof had apparently collapsed. They exited out the back. Kiel brought up the rear, carrying two gallons of water in one hand, and his trusty bat in the other. He gave one last look back, and saw Brandon standing all alone in the semi-darkness. The lawyer just stared at him. He could have been a ghost, trapped in the old house by invisible chains fabricated from a destiny of his own making. Kiel had no free hand to wave, so he just turned and walked out.

Outside, Daniel surveyed the horizon to the north while everybody else glanced nervously around, trying to see in every direction at once. The sun had climbed above the low hills off to the east, presumably where the cave lay. They'd be going with the morning sun in their eyes. Kiel remembered the attack helicopters in *Apocalypse Now* using this to their advantage. No Wagner soundtrack here, though; just the low groan of Peggy's angina and Mrs. Bakke's muttered curses over her sprained ankle—both already struggling even though they hadn't set out yet.

Daniel stared off to the north, brows furrowed in thought, and then seemed to come to a decision. "We'll make for the barn first. Everybody GO! Double time!"

This was only slightly out of the way. It made sense to take cover anywhere they could. Double time, though, meant double the hobble of Mrs. Bakke's pained limp, so they shuffled slowly along across the hundred yards—so many tempting monster appetizers. Although Mrs. Bakke set the pace, Kiel noticed that Peg wasn't exactly striding along at ease.

The slow pace gave Kiel time to look around, and that's when he discovered what Daniel must have intuited when he had urged them off to the barn. Kiel sidled up to their leader and nodded his head towards Tagget's farm where two mini tornadoes seemed to hover just above the tree line. Daniel glanced over, fixed his eyes a moment, and then turned back again. "Nothing to do 'till we get to the barn," he remarked quietly.

Kiel jumped at the sound of every honey bee and fly as they limped and stumbled along, and it wasn't until they'd made the first corner of the barn that he realized that it wasn't buzzing that he should have been listening for, but the slow whap-whap of monster-sized blades that slowly grew louder. The plodding, leisurely rhythm invoked a sense of tremendous size, and Kiel had no doubt about what it was.

"It's back," he warned quietly, fearing to draw their enemy's attention even though he couldn't even see it yet.

Daniel ran back along the line of refugees, looked a moment, and then nodded. Kiel saw it too; something huge was rushing directly towards them across the fields. This wasn't the previous monster returning, though. This one was its big brother, coming to finish the job with a vengeance.

If it was the big brother, however, it was begotten from a different father. Kiel stared, frozen with wonder. If he hadn't witnessed the short history of the colony's rise, he would have thought that this was some monster mutant bird, some living fossil of a long-past time when giant dinosaurs set the earth trembling. Deliberate, tree-high sweeps of huge, powerful wings carried the behemoth along on its deadly mission. Yet again, Cam was right. The colony's three days of evolution were converging with four billion years of Earth's. The uncountable collective of crablets was taking the most successful creatures of their new environment as models.

"Everybody back!" Daniel ordered, breaking Kiel's dazed reverie. They all pressed against the wall of the barn where they were just out of view of the approaching menace. Kiel and Daniel peeked around the corner. They had just seconds before the artificial bird would arrive. "Into the barn!" Daniel directed. "Stay close to the wall."

Clumsy with panic, the family staggered along until they stumbled into the darkness of the cavernous structure. Kiel entered just ahead of Daniel. His eyes adjusted, and he saw scattered bales of hay and the workshop off to the side before the light dimmed further as Daniel rolled the large door completely closed. They couldn't see, but the whoosh of monster flapping wings swelled until Kiel could almost feel the rush of wind against his chest. Nicki was crying hysterically, and Julie was on one knee explaining that if she didn't quiet down, she'd have to put her hand over her mouth.

"Down!" Daniel ordered, walking to a ladder that led to the lower level. The barn sat on a slight incline, so that the front was level with the outside, but the rear was ten feet above the ground. The lower level was completely underground at the front end, and level with the down-slope at the back.

Daniel and Kiel helped the others down the ladder. Daniel reached out and took Nicki, who screamed at being torn from her mother, so that Julie could descend. Then Daniel lowered the little girl through the hole to the waiting arms of her mom. Cam was next, followed by Peggy, and Kiel had the urge to give her a push on the top of her head with his foot to speed her up. Then Daniel handed down the shotgun and practically jumped through so that he could help his mother from below.

Kiel was the last. The cracks between the wall planks presented a segmented, sampled view of the world beyond. There was insufficient information to make out actual definition, but he could see form and motion against the milky white sky. The monster was close, and it was massive.

No time to dawdle. The wooden rungs were smooth with decades of use, and one of his feet slipped. Although he'd given up the jugs of water, he still hung on to the bat so that he missed regaining a handhold, and fell the last few feet. The bat fell on top of him, demonstrating that it could inflict damage. By feel, he could tell that the floor was not hard, but spongy and slightly wet. By smell he guessed that he'd fallen into a bed of manure mixed with loose hay.

The lower level was better lit, having windows on two sides set into mortared stone walls. The rear wall, level with the ground outside, had a double set of doors, which Daniel hastily closed. The windows were set high, just above Cam's eye-level, and he dragged a crate over so that he could see out towards the house. This was the only window still fit with glass and not covered with translucent plastic, so Kiel went over to join him.

What he saw over the boy's shoulder made him gasp. The colony beast was even larger than he'd thought. If this artificial bird were a hawk, the house would be a stack of text books. On wings that seemed to flap in slow motion from sheer size, the silver raptor came in with the obvious intent of roosting on Mrs. Bakke's home. With each mighty whoosh-whoosh of wing-flap, the maples on each side rustled and leaned as though a hurricane was blowing at them from the house, and in a sense it was.

Because the behemoth seemed to move in slow motion, Kiel could see detail. The entire structure was hollow; jointed legs, talons, wings—all were coverings over a trestle network, seen from glimpses at odd angles. Also, he could make out the mail armor pattern of interconnected ringlets. But from a hundred yards, he knew that he wasn't looking at the same arrangement that had greeted him through Mrs. Bakke's uncovered window. This pattern had to be at least a hundred times as large. Clearly the colony was using a hierarchy of identical designs: a pattern of interconnected crablets made up a ring, which was part of a pattern of rings which made up yet a larger ring, which itself was then part of a set of similar rings, and on ad infinitum. It was the sort of mindset you might expect from a replicating automaton.

All these observations were perceived in the few seconds it took the colony hawk to settle onto the house. Talons the size of logs opened to grasp the roof, which sagged in the middle, forcing the giant bird to adjust its stance. The head tilted down and scanned back and forth, taking in the structure of the perch. It dawned on Kiel that it was doing this with eyes. This was new. He had always assumed that vision was provided by each individual crablet. So, why now with the eyes? Obviously to gain definition at a distance. Each eye could gather thousands of times more light than any one crablet. He imagined an array of crablets underneath perceiving the projected image just as his retina cells did.

Satisfied with its inspection, the bird lifted its head and brought the man-sized beak down with a mighty swing onto the edge of the roof. Like a wrecking ball slicing home, the roof and upper wall gave way and the raptor bill penetrated as far as the rounded head allowed. The roof caved some more under the middle talon, apparently pinching the beak, for the beast struggled a moment to remove it. It then lifted its head for another blow.

This was when Cam shouted, "Dad!" and ran off.

Kiel saw why. He had forgotten in the riveting spectacle of the titan's arrival that the man was still there, but Brandon now abandoned the house that was crashing down around him. Instead of running for the barn, though, he was angling off east. For a brief moment, Kiel thought he was drawing the monster away from their hiding place, but he realized that Brandon probably just didn't realize that they had stopped here. The panicked man was trying to catch up with them. His chances of survival would increase with other victims for the beast to choose from.

As Kiel spun around, he heard Daniel shout a warning, and then light poured in from an open door and Cam's calls to his father disappeared outside.

Kiel looked out the window. The predator bird was taking to the air, once again sending the maple trees dancing, as the boy sprinted across the grass after his fleeing father.

Chapter 22

Kiel ran to the open door, but Daniel held up his hand to stop him.

"Everybody stay put, and out of sight!" he called, hefting his gun and stepping out into the bright sunlight.

Kiel disobeyed orders and peered around the doorframe. Daniel had moved along the wall to the corner, where a small chicken cage provided some cover from the monster who was gathering speed towards Brandon. He lifted the gun, aimed, and pulled the trigger as the blast rang out above the roaring rush of the mammoth bird's flight.

The effect was immediate. The behemoth pulled up and turned its head in their direction. Kiel very much wished he'd followed Daniel's direction to stay hidden. Even though just the top of his head was visible around the doorframe, the black, bottomless eyes seemed to bore directly into him from a hundred yards away. Held fast almost against his will by the powerful stare, he saw Brandon take cover behind a hay-baler machine.

Cam had stopped dead and stood staring up at the giant as it pumped its massive wings to hover. Then the mighty head tilted down ever so slightly. It was looking at Cam.

The boy called again to his father, his voice hysterical now with terror. Brandon crouched behind the baler—Kiel could see him clearly. His son was no more than a hundred feet away. It was impossible that he didn't hear him.

The flapping wings changed rhythm, and the colossal beast glided forward towards Cam.

Daniel was calling to him, but the boy seemed riveted in place, staring up at his impending demise. The farmer lifted the gun and shot again, and again the monster took pause. Kiel wondered if the beast perhaps thought that it was Cam who was somehow firing on it.

This notion was supported when the gigantic bird turned back to its original pursuit. Its prey had disappeared, but it was obvious where it was hiding. Kiel saw Brandon cowering, and then trying to crawl under the baler. He was still trying to push underneath when a raptor talon reached down and deftly rolled the machine over and out of the way. Brandon scrambled to his feet and tore off, but a taloned foot reached out and plucked him from the ground. The erstwhile senator candidate and intransigent husband struggled against the thigh-sized claws that grasped him, while the beast peered down at its catch. It hesitated, as though not sure of the best way to dispatch this little human. Based on the blood already pouring along the shiny silver surface and the struggles that had turned limp, its task was probably already accomplished, but for good measure it used the talon tips of the other claw to pull off the man's head as one might a grape from its vine.

Kiel's stomach knotted and he felt an overwhelming nausea. Adrenaline electrified his reactions, though, and he looked to see what had happened to Cam. The boy had fallen to his knees, and now crawled behind an azalea. This was as good as nothing. The monster dropped his dead victim and worked its wings to turn back.

Kiel stepped out and called to Cam, but he realized that Daniel was already shouting to no effect. Somehow Kiel imagined that he would have time to run out, grab his young friend, and make it back. He was half way when he realized that he had catastrophically miscalculated. Before he even had a chance to consider an alternative move, the beast was swooping down like an airliner on a crash dive. He saw an open claw as big as himself closing in. His body willed him to try to turn and run away, but some rational corner of his mind understood that this was futile and urged him to try the unexpected. He dove for the ground straight under the approaching hungry talons. The beast tried to compensate, and Kiel saw a blur rush at him, and the next instant a mighty jolt stunned him and he was lying on his back watching fireworks exploding. One of the talons must have caught him with a glancing blow to his midriff, knocking him flying like a crumb flicked idly from the table.

The bursting stars cleared and he saw that the Godzilla bird had overshot its mark and was working to lift and back up to get at him. He felt paralyzed. He lay waiting to be decapitated.

He caught motion off to one side, and the next instant he felt the concussion of a shotgun blast. Daniel! God bless him!

Kiel forced himself to ignore the mammoth predator maneuvering above him, sending blasts of wind across him. He rolled over and got up on his hands and knees. Where was Daniel? Kiel had *felt* the shotgun blast, it was so close.

Amid the hurricane roar of wings, Kiel heard Daniel cursing, shouting words that surprised him. He looked up, and the nausea returned. The giant raptor held the farmer clasped in its claw. Two talons wrapped around his waist and thigh, leaving the upper part of his body free to struggle. Miraculously, he'd managed to hang on to the gun. Kiel heard a distinct snap, and one of Daniel's legs bent in a way that it wasn't designed to do. The man screamed in agony, and the gun fired—intended or not, Kiel couldn't tell.

This seemed to interest the beast. It lowered its head and raised Daniel to get a better look at this human that made so much noise. Daniel screamed, "Go to hell!" as he pumped, aimed, and shot directly into the monster's face. Kiel saw a tiny hole erupt in the surface of the beast. Daniel pumped and shot again, and another hole appeared.

The living animals that inhabited Kiel's world would have reacted violently to such wounds, but this monster was not alive. It did apparently notice the damage, however, since it pulled Daniel away. Deciding it had had enough, it reached over with its other claw to pull off this second human's head—the established method of execution. It reached in, and Kiel saw Daniel's body drop ten feet to the ground. But as the second claw withdrew, Kiel saw that instead of Daniel's head, the humongous automation had instead gripped the shotgun, which had gotten twisted up in his shirt.

Something else caught the marauding predator's attention, and it flapped off to the side, out of Kiel's view. He heard screaming, and he was glad, since it might mean that Daniel still lived, however mangled. But then he remembered that Cam was probably still close by, and he thought he might faint from the relentless horror. Indeed, the screams were high-pitched for a grown man, and then he felt the ground thump with something powerful, and the scream instantly stopped.

Kiel had reached his limit. He was having trouble breathing again, and his arms felt too weak to hold him up any longer. He let himself collapse flat on his face. He would be next. The colony collective wouldn't forget about him. He felt the blustering wind from the giant wings, and heard the mighty whoosh-whoosh, but they faded into the distance. He thought that perhaps it was he who was fading into unconsciousness, but the sensation of the grass pressing against his cheek and nose remained vivid, undiminished.

Could it be?

He rolled over onto his back, and the only thing above him was the white feather-light curls of cirrus clouds miles up. He heard a faint moaning and soft sobbing. Somebody somewhere lived.

He forced himself up on his hands and knees again. After a moment, he gathered the strength to stand unsteadily up. After such a violent battle, he half expected to find smoking blast craters, but the only indication that death had stalked was the crumpled form of Daniel, bare-chested, lying in a heap.

Kiel went to him, apprehensive about what he would find. The moaning had stopped, and the man seemed unconscious. He was breathing, though, and although one leg was clearly broken in two, Kiel saw no blood, and was relieved that bone splinters had not poked through his skin.

The soft sobbing continued, however. Kiel followed the sound, but before he found the source, he nearly tripped over yet one more horror. A bloody body lay dead in the grass. It was Peggy. This is what had caught the monster's attention when it dropped Daniel.

His wife had rushed to his aid, no matter that there was patently nothing she could hope to do against the huge beast. Despite that, she had inadvertently found a way. It remained to be seen whether she'd given her life in vain. Kiel had no inkling whether Daniel had sustained mortal internal injuries.

Still the soft sobbing. Kiel found Cam curled into a tight ball under the azalea. He glanced around, but the colony had indeed inexplicably retreated. Off in the distance he heard gunshots—more than what just one man would produce. They were coming from ... the north. Tagget's farm! He and Daniel had seen two hovering beasts in that direction when they'd left the house. Somebody was making a stand there. This probably explained why their attacker had left—to provide support. Perhaps they were safe as long as those gunshots continued.

He knelt down next to Cam and put his hand gently on the boy's shoulder. "It's okay," he assured. "It's gone."

His young friend seemed to just tighten into a tighter protective package.

Kiel wasn't sure what to do. He needed to get the boy to cover so that he could see what he could do for Daniel. "Listen," he explained quietly, "I'm going to pick you up. We have to get back to the barn."

Hesitating just a moment, Kiel squatted down and started to gather him up. The boy, still crying, turned around and wrapped his arms around Kiel's neck. When he stood slowly up, the boy wrapped his legs around his waist, and buried his face in his shoulder. Holding him tight, Kiel trotted to the barn.

Julie stood in the doorway, waiting, holding Nicki behind her with both hands. Her eyes were still wide with the shock of all the horror they'd seen, but they also pleaded to him with desperate hope.

"Daniel's alive," he reported, pushing past her with his charge into the darkness. "He's hurt, though."

"Peg? What about Peggy?" she asked.

Kiel wasn't sure whether she could see his face in the dim light, but he shook his head tersely.

She understood, for she put her hand to her mouth with a little cry of despair. Mrs. Bakke sat on the ground against a partition, staring as though in a trance.

A moment later, Julie pulled Cam from him and buried him with a hug that tried to protect against all the world's menace.

Kiel started for the door, but Mrs. Bakke said, "Help me up."

He extended his hand and pulled her to her feet. "I have to see about Daniel," he explained, starting off again.

"I know," she replied, hobbling towards the door.

"I think you should stay—"

"I'm his mother," she said simply.

He was torn. He'd already delayed too long getting back to Daniel, and Mrs. Bakke could hardly stand with her swollen ankle, let alone walk. He yanked a bracing strip from the chicken cage, broke off a three-foot length, and handed it to her to use as a cane. "Go!" she admonished, taking it. "I'll catch up."

The farmer was still unconscious, but also still breathing. Kiel realized he had no idea what to do. For all his life, the proper—only—response to someone injured was to find a phone and dial 911. What if Daniel did have internal injuries? A burst spleen meant death within hours. But what could he do even if he knew? He couldn't operate; he had no drugs, and wouldn't know what to administer if he did. Shorn of the sophisticated medical support system, he was effectively thrown back two centuries. The only clear advantage that he had was an understanding that germs caused infection. Keep the wound clean. But there was no open wound.

He decided that the primary imperative was the same as was taught in traffic school: make sure the victim is out of the way of further danger. Danger in this case came in the form of crablets configured as rings, configured as the structural composition of an eagle the size of an elephant.

Which meant that he had to move Daniel. And that scared him silly. Dragging a man with thigh bones snapped in two across the ground seemed to him in the same league as cutting him open with a pocketknife to make sure there were no internal injuries. Also, his immediate goal was to get everybody back into the barn, but that was just a temporary haven. If—when—the beast returned to finish the job, it would surely not hesitate to rip apart the wooden structure in its quest.

If Daniel were awake and lucid, Kiel knew what he'd say: *Get to the cave.*

"How?" Kiel asked quietly, gazing down at the unhearing wounded man.

Daniel was wise; he knew this land, and that grounding seemed to provide an appreciation, a connection with the Earth as a whole. Maybe it was just a consequence of the constant decisions and problems that required solutions every day in running a farm. Or maybe it was genetic; maybe his father was just as wise. If so, then Cam surely inherited the gene, and then some.

He caught himself. Cam *seemed* like Daniel's son, not Brandon's. Perhaps it was a family-wide attribute.

But the thought of Cam buoyed his spirits. The kid was only twelve years old, but Kiel realized that he'd come to trust the youth's judgment. The boy had predicted nearly everything that had unfolded with the colony.

It hit him like the proverbial flash. Cam had already solved this problem as well.

He passed Mrs. Bakke as he ran back to the barn. "Don't move him 'till I get back!" he yelled.

"Where're you going?" she called.

"To get the ambulance!"

Chapter 23

Cam's go-kart started up with the first pull of the rope. The half-gallon lawnmower gas tank was full, and there was a plastic gallon can nearby with at least that much more. The drones either hadn't found these, or decided them not worth the bother for the small amounts. Cam mounted the bicycle seat he'd jury-rigged and grasped the handlebars. After a few seconds Kiel called, "Let's go!"

The boy looked at him apprehensively. "I've never driven it!"

There was irony here: his uncle hadn't let him try it out, and now the man's life depended on its use.

"You want me to drive it?" Kiel shouted above the roar.

Cam shook his head determinedly, and the homemade vehicle jerked into motion. The clutch he'd devised wasn't so much a clutch as a catch-and-run engagement. Once in motion, the operator stayed in motion until the destination was reached. Kiel ran ahead, sliding the large doors open, and scoping out the path around the barn to the lower level. Staying ahead of the little vehicle wasn't difficult, as Cam had geared the drive train down so that the little motor wouldn't stall out when the large ATV wheels negotiated obstacles. Kiel found that he could stroll along beside Cam with his hands in his pockets.

They decided to not even stop at the bottom level; instead, Kiel sent Cam off towards Daniel, while he and Julie dug out the old farm wagon from under bags of fertilizer. The wagon was nothing more than a rusting frame on four wheels with side walls of three horizontal two-inch boards set on four upright corner posts. The bed was barely four feet by three feet, but could be handy for hauling around . . . well, bags of fertilizer.

Together, they easily pulled the wagon, with Nicki pretending to help by pushing from behind, and caught up with Cam before he'd even reached his uncle and grandmother. The young driver took it out of gear next to his prone uncle and looked to Kiel for direction. "Let it run!" Kiel shouted. "We'll be leaving soon anyway!"

They tied the wagon tongue to the back of the go-kart frame with baling twine. Kiel added a second wrap for good measure and double-checked the knots. He was stalling, dreading the next move. Daniel hadn't regained consciousness, and Kiel knew he should probably be worried about the long lapse, but he was thankful for it because of what they now had to do. The four of them—everybody except Nicki—positioned themselves on both sides of the casualty. Kiel didn't like it. This wouldn't work.

"Hold on!" he yelled and tore off to the barn. He couldn't find what he wanted, so he grabbed a pick and pried away at the side of the barn until one of the boards fell away. Nasty nails extended from one side, but there was no time to deal with it. They'd just have to be careful.

Back at the accident site, everybody seemed to understand immediately what he intended. He placed the board next to Daniel's broken leg, and as Julie and Cam slowly lifted the broken appendage, Kiel pushed the board underneath, which wasn't easy, as the nails caught in the grass. For the first time, Daniel showed life, but the indication was more animal than human—a guttural groan, the sound of excruciating agony welling up through blankets of unconscious protection.

After tying the broken leg to the board with more baling twine, they lifted the 180-pound man into the wagon. It wasn't nearly long enough for him to lie down, so they propped his back up in one corner and lay the splinted leg flat. Kiel didn't like that either.

He fed the last of the twine around Daniel's chest and tied it fast to the top of the post. This way, he wouldn't slide down.

There was one last problem. He eyed Mrs. Bakke. Even though Cam's kart crawled along at a slow stroll, it was still too fast for her to keep up using her makeshift cane. "Get in!" he shouted to her.

She shook her head. "No, sir!"

"Why not?"

"My boy's hurt. I'm not going to risk doing more damage. There ain't nearly room for two."

He tried to argue, but he knew it was useless.

Julie touched his arm and gestured with her chin, indicating that she wanted to talk to him away from the roar of the go-kart's engine.

"It's going to take forever," she said once they could talk.

He shrugged. "I don't know what else to do. You don't think we should go to the cave?"

"Yes! It's our only hope—if we have any hope. I mean, we don't all have to go together."

He blinked. His brain was only running on three cylinders. "Of course. I should have thought of that. You go ahead with Nicki and Cam, and I'll meet you there."

Her brow furrowed. "No, that's not what I mean. I need to stay with mom and Daniel. *You* take the kids on ahead."

He stared at her. "I think it would be better if—"

"Look, we don't have time to argue. I'm asking you to do this for me."

He took a deep breath and looked up at the cirrus feather-clouds, then back at her. "Julie, do you understand what you're asking?"

She seemed annoyed—impatient; but then her face softened. "You mean the charges of child molestation?"

"Yes. Of course."

"Under the circumstances, there's obviously more at stake . . . ." She stopped and shook her head. "No, it's because I trust you, Kiel. Listen, if anything happens to me . . . you'll take good care of them?"

He sighed. "Okay. Of course. But are you sure—"

"No more discussion! We have to get moving before that creature from hell returns!"

When they explained the new plan to the others, Cam shouted, "No!" and refused to get off the go-kart, crossing his arms in defiance.

"Come on, honey!" Julie shouted. "We don't have time to argue!"

"I'm not running away and leaving you, Uncle Daniel, and Gamma!" He drew his arms in tighter and pushed up his lower lip in determination. Then without warning, he swung one leg around, jumped down, and sprinted off.

"Cam!" Julie cried, but before she could react further, he bent down, picked up Daniel's shotgun and ran back.

Holding it up in demonstration, he said, "I can protect us!" He leaned the gun against the go-kart and carefully reached into his uncle's pants pocket, extracting three shells, which he loaded into the clip.

Julie looked at Kiel in resignation. "Go on! We'll meet you there!"

He looked hard at her. "Just me and Nicki?"

After a moment her mouth turned up in the barest smile—the first one since before the initial drone attack. "Take good care of my baby."

Kiel knelt down next to the little girl who was standing with her grandmother, holding her hand. "Hey, Nicki," he said. "You and I are going to run on ahead. Your mom and grandma will follow soon after."

She looked uncertainly to her mother.

"Kiel's going to take you to a safe place, honey. We won't be long."

She looked from her mother to Kiel, frightened and worried. "Is that thing coming back?"

"Not for a long while—not before we all are safe in the cave."

Lying to little kids was so easy.

She gave a little nod, let go of her grandmother's hand and practically jumped into Kiel's arms.

Holding her tight, her legs wrapped around his torso, he was ready to go ... but where? He turned to Julie. "How do I get there?"

She pointed off to the low line of hills. "See that lone oak against the skyline? The cave is about a hundred yards to the right. You'll see it. Daniel has junk piled around it. Also, Nicki knows where it is."

He nodded and started off at a trot. "Take care of my baby!" Julie called.

The morning sun was climbing, and the warmth of day settling in. Before long, he was sweating and breathing hard. His arms were numb from holding her. He stopped, and had to practically peel Nicki from his neck. "I have an idea," he said. "Do you know how to play horsy?"

She nodded glumly.

He squatted and let her wrap her arms around his neck from behind. He stood up and, holding one leg in each hand, he took off again. This was much better, and ten minutes later they arrived. The junk Julie had mentioned comprised mostly stacked pallets of varying degrees of age and integrity, plus odds and ends of construction paraphernalia—remnant pieces of lumber, sacks of cement, and a scattering of cinder blocks. Off to the side sat a small cement mixer, every square inch caked with dried cement, as though a heavy, wet cement snow storm had blown through.

The cave itself was almost lost among the confusion of littered remnants. An indentation in the low, sloping hillside began a hundred feet up, and deepened and widened as it opened towards the flat ground where Kiel stood, so that it was wide enough to walk into directly in front of him. Inside the rounded fissure was blackness, and he could only assume that he was looking into the depths of the hill. The fact that this was more than just a crack in the limestone was made obvious by the fact that above the level of his head, someone—perhaps Daniel—had filled in the crevice with an amalgam of lumber and cement, creating a sloping roof over what was presumably the cave's alcove.

"This is it?" he asked, letting Nicki down.

"Uncle Daniel's romping room," she replied.

"Is that what he calls it?"

"That's what Gamma calls it."

Kiel understood. "Does she maybe call it his rumpus room?"

She nodded and shrugged. Adults were always hung up on semantic details.

"What does he use it for?"

She shrugged again. "Gamma says he used to come here because Grandpa didn't want him to. Cam says that he wanted a bomb shelter."

"Your grandfather wanted a bomb shelter?"

"No! Uncle Daniel. When he was a teenager."

Kiel took a few steps inside and let his eyes adjust to the darkness. He could imagine an only son on a farm getting bored and searching out innovative projects to satisfy a hunger for adventure and creative outlet. He couldn't see very far into the depths, but he began to make out something next to him on the wall; it looked for all the world like—a light switch! Bracing against a whole spectrum of possible outcomes, he flipped it up, and then jumped when the cave blinked alive with stark blue light.

Nicki came in and climbed up into an old chair. She was obviously comfortable here.

Kiel saw that the lighting consisted of half a dozen fluorescent tubes spread around the perimeter of the cave, which was about the size of a large living room. Daniel had even installed AC outlets at several strategic locations. Tracing the electric conduits along the ceiling, he found the source of electricity: six car batteries stacked on two shelves next to an AC inverter. Between these was a panel with two rotary switches—one for selecting discharge, and another for charging. Behind a little door, he found a gas generator set back inside a small cavity in the wall, vented to the outside.

Whatever exotic adventures Daniel had had in mind when he'd created this haven in his youth, he'd found a practical, if relatively mundane, use for it as a working farmer: storage. Stacked against the wall on pallets to keep them dry were plastic sacks of fertilizer and pesticide. Next to them were cases of bottled water and juice drinks. This far from the house and barn, Kiel could easily imagine this as a convenient depot while working the fields at this end of the property. In fact, Cam had told him as much.

"When's mommy coming?" Nicki asked.

"Shit!" he muttered, remembering his mission. He was totally wasting time.

"That's a bad word," Nicki observed.

"I know. I shouldn't have said it." He glanced around, and saw a pile of old burlap sacks in a back corner. "Come here, Nicki," he said. He placed his hands on her shoulders and looked her in the eye. "We're going to make a nice bed for you here using these little blankets—"

"They're bags."

"Right. But they make a nice bed anyway. I'm going to turn off the light and go and help the others. You'll be safe here. You just have to cuddle up in the warm bed and stay quiet. We'll be back in no time. But you have to stay in here no matter what you hear. Can you do that?"

" 'course!" she answered, indignant that he'd doubted. But then her face turned troubled. "You're leaving?"

"Just for a little while. When I come back, we'll all be together again. But you have to stay in this bed, no matter what happens. Understand?"

He spread some of the burlap sacks and pulled others over her when she lay down.

"Kiel?" she said as he started to get up.

"Yes, Nicki?"

"You promise to come back?"

"Of course."

"I mean, you promise."

He looked at her, so tiny and scared huddled among the old bags. He smiled, trying his best to look confident. "I would never, ever leave you here, honey." *As long as I'm alive*, he added in his mind.

"Kiel?"

"Yes."

"Is my Daddy dead?"

His heart skipped a beat. He'd managed to sideline the gruesome image in all the activity, but the child's simple question brought the reality squarely home. "He's somewhere else—I'm not sure if he's coming back."

He was pussyfooting, but this was something for Julie to talk to her about.

"Daddy's dead, isn't he? You just don't want to tell me."

He sighed and squatted again, placing his hand on her arm. "I'm sorry, honey. Yes, your daddy's dead."

She stared at him a moment, and then her mouth pouted up and tears welled and rolled down her cheeks. "I'll never see him again?"

He squeezed her arm. "I'm sorry, honey."

She used her other arm to rub the snot from her nose. "Is Uncle Daniel going to die?"

"Of course not."

He immediately felt guilty. She trusted him. Maybe people lied to children far too casually. "Actually, the truth is that I have a whole lot of hope that your uncle will be okay. Lots of people get broken bones and get perfectly well after a while. But it may depend on how quickly we can get help for him, and you can help by doing just what we tell you. You understand?"

She nodded, sucking back the snot that her arm had missed.

He got up, went to the opening, and said, "Okay, I'm going to turn off the light, but we'll all be back before you know it."

He flipped the switch, and blackness enveloped the cave, obliterating all traces of Daniel's industrious endeavors.

"Kiel?" Nicki's tiny voice came out of the darkness.

"Yes, Nicki?" he replied, trying to supress the impatience he felt overwhelming him that he was forsaking the others.

"It's okay if you call me 'honey.'"

He smiled. "Thanks. You *are* a honey."

And with that, he sprinted away before she could detain him further.

His feet pounded the ground and it seemed to him that the gunfire at Tagget's place had diminished. In fact, it seemed like just one person firing now. That was depressing.

Topping a small rise, he heard the put-put of Cam's go-kart and then saw the Bakke caravan inching along next to a stone fence at the far end of the adjacent field. At their present snail's pace, they would make the cave in maybe another ten minutes. He raised his hand and was about to shout a greeting when something caught his eye off to the right. He hissed a word worse than shit. It was a drone—not the giant raptor warrior, but the old-fashioned wing-ear flying rabbit. Even these had evolved, though. He could see two eyes and multiple tentacles that probed around the ground as it glided along, as though feeling for something it had dropped. If it continued on its current path, it would surely see the others soon.

He'd left his baseball bat in the barn. He felt naked. But despite the previous encounters, where even the small colony creations proved themselves perfectly lethal, still, there was definitely something less terrifying about them after watching a monster-sized beast crush someone flat with one stomp.

And so, only questioning his sanity after it was too late to turn back, he jumped down from the stone fence and ran shouting, angling past the scouting drone and directly away from the wounded and limping procession.

The drone had given no attention to the rat-tat-tat of the go-kart's engine, perhaps not yet associating the sound with humans, but it immediately recognized Kiel's shouts. Abandoning its tentacle probing of the ground, it lifted a few feet for a better view. Then, without hesitation, it angled over and took off after him.

Now Kiel truly questioned his sanity. He'd known that he couldn't outrun a drone. What was he thinking?

He considered trying for the cave, but knew he wouldn't make it in time, and even if he did, they weren't ready to defend it yet—he'd just be leading the colony to Nicki.

He had to lose it. While his mind was debating, his feet took him to a nearby stand of trees. He crashed through the thick brush that bordered the perimeter, feeling the sting of branches whipping and tearing at his face and arms. Once through the tangled ground cover, the woods opened up and he was running through a thick bed of old leaves. His only obstacles now were fallen tree trunks, which he either hurdled, or climbed over. He looked back, and saw that he'd already lost his pursuer. No, there it was—exiting the brush barrier. At least he was gaining on it.

He looked back again and saw that he'd been optimistic—the drone was now gaining on *him*. Once in the open woods, it had to weave among the trees, but this hindrance was easily compensated by his own tree-trunk hurdles.

It had been the thick brush that had provided the advantage. He was able to plow through faster than the drone could navigate the dense barrier. He had to find more thick ground cover. He noticed that the ground sloped downward a little to his right, so he let himself follow. Sure enough, a much welcomed wall of green leaves appeared ahead, and moments later he dove into it as though it were a pond in a forest fire.

He found that the easiest way through the tight crowd of stems and briars was on his hands and knees. This had the additional advantage that he was less visible from above. After scrambling for a while he paused and listened. He heard the burr of the drone's wings, accompanied by a continuous slapping as it caught leaf and twigs. The bastard wasn't giving up.

He pressed on, trying now to be quiet. Before long he heard another sound ahead—a gurgling. Soon he came to a small stream, and he stood up. The brush huddled close on both sides, but the rocky stream itself was like a little road cutting through the shrub wilderness. He pressed on, crossing the stream and re-entering the thick undergrowth on the other side. He stopped almost immediately. He could make distance so much easier following the stream. He backtracked and veritably flew, splashing down the middle of the rocky brook. He didn't go far, however, before realizing that the stream would provide even better access for the drone, which didn't have to wade through water. Cursing, he dove back into the thicket. But he reentered on the same side of the stream that he'd arrived. It wouldn't hurt to throw some curve-balls.

He had to be careful now, since he was potentially heading back towards the drone. He stopped and listened. He could hear the burring whir of the spinning ear-wings. The alien stalker was moving slowly sideways past him towards the stream, following his trail. Some intuition urged Kiel to wait, to sit tight a moment. Slowly, quietly, he crawled back to the stream and peeked out through the weeds. The drone hovered a hundred feet away—where he'd first broken through. It glided back to the edge of the brush, and let its tentacles dance around among the stems. After a few seconds, it moved to the other side, and the octopus appendages now probed among the weeds and shrubs there. Then, deliberately, it moved forward into the brush.

Kiel backed up, turned around, and skittered away on hands and knees, back in the direction he'd come as quietly, but as quickly, as he could manage.

The damn thing was following his scent! They'd learned how to smell, maybe mimicking the rats that lived in their cave.

With some luck, though, it wouldn't be able to follow his trail down the stream, and with more luck, it would assume he'd continued on in a straight line and would fail to find his backtrack.

It was an old trick, and he'd stumbled on it by accident, but he wasn't looking for tracking awards, just to hang on to his life for a while.

When he came to the edge of the woods, he paused before scrambling back through the perimeter growth. He listened, holding his breath, but heard nothing except birds and early cicadas. An unnatural pattern caught his eye. Someone had arranged sticks and branches in parallel rows, forming walls and a roof around four tree trunks. He recognized it at once, for he had done the same thing when he was a young boy. Cam and Nicki had made a fort here at the edge of the woods. Inside the doorway, he saw a spray-bottle of household cleaner. Nicki probably imitated her mother and grandmother, pretending that she was cleaning their little abode. In happier times, before the colony of crablets arrived, the little fort had provided a place where the kids could feel safe, a miniature haven of their own. Now, it was just a demarked place for colony drones to pick you off.

And if he hung around any longer indulging in idle musing, he would get picked off. He pushed noisily through the perimeter growth and then ran like hell when he made the open fields again.

He caught up to the go-kart before the group reached the cave, and setting propriety aside, lifted Mrs. Bakke and carried her the last hundred yards, allowing Cam to open up the throttle and finish at his maximum cruising speed of two miles per hour.

Nicki came running out to meet them, jumping up and down in excitement. So much for staying hidden no matter what she heard.

They untied the wagon and pulled it, Daniel and all, into the cave. It was a tight squeeze getting in. Once inside, Julie piled burlap sacks over him for warmth, and rolled together a couple more to make a pillow, which she gently placed between his head and the wagon wall.

Once everybody was inside the cave, Kiel examined the lighting system again, with Cam at his elbow. The inverter was a hefty 24V, 3,000 Watt model. The six batteries comprised three pairs, and by switching through the three discharge positions, he found that two sets were charged enough to maintain the inverter output, but the third set was discharged—in the darkness he found a red warning LED lit on the inverter as everybody complained about the lights going out.

He flipped back to the first pair and walked around unseating half the fluorescent tubes. No sense using more power than they needed. He figured that two fully charged car batteries should keep three thirty-Watt bulbs going for about . . . eight hours. That wasn't hugely encouraging, considering they didn't even know how much charge the batteries had. Eventually they'd have to run the generator. Luckily, Cam had thought to bring the half-gallon of gas along.

Kiel then made an inventory of the rest of the cave's contents. Besides the sacks of fertilizer and pesticides, he found a hand-pump sprayer for the pesticides, a trunk full of worn out boots and wire-mesh gloves, and four thirty-pound bags of salt, which Cam explained that his uncle sometimes mixed with the cattle feed. On a battered workbench that Daniel had built into the near corner, he found what looked like an electric fencing sword, but that Cam explained was an experiment in which his uncle had dabbled when he was younger. He had tried to build a termite gun that he'd read about in Popular Mechanics. Using a car engine coil, fluorescent light transformers, and Radio Shack transistors, he'd jacked up a clock oscillator to tens of thousands of volts. The idea was that the high voltage could penetrate the wood they infested, zapping them dead.

"Was he successful?" Kiel asked, picking up the three-foot wand. He saw that Daniel had used thick plastic tubing to insulate the conductor that extended through the end an inch. The attached wire snaked along the ground to a homemade metal box.

"He wasn't sure," Cam replied.

"I'd have thought it would be obvious—ten kilovolts isn't exactly a subtle effect."

"Oh, the gun worked like he'd intended; he just couldn't tell very well if it really killed the termites."

"Does it still work, you think?"

The boy shrugged. "He stopped messing with it before I was even born. He obviously wasn't going to let me try it out."

"Yeah, he's a careful guy," Kiel agreed studying the ingenious creation.

"You want me to turn it on?"

"It's all connected?"

"I think so," Cam replied, reaching around the back of the metal box.

An instant later, the metal box buzzed with the familiar hum of unbalanced fluorescent light transformers. Otherwise, there was no indication that the gun wand was energized. Kiel pointed it towards the workbench, but nothing happened.

"I think he stuck this in the ground," Cam said, holding up a short metal rod attached to another wire.

Kiel took the ground rod from him and immediately felt a tingling in both hands. He was tempted to bring the two probes together to see if it would arc.

Something distracted him, however. The hum of the metal box seemed to be modulating. His stomach felt like it had dropped out of him onto the floor. The sound of flying lawnmowers was becoming his hell on Earth.

Déjà-vu enveloped him when a moment later Julie and Nicki let out piercing screams.

Chapter 24

Kiel spun to find Julie holding Nicki behind her with one hand, while fending off the drone with the other. It looked like the same one that had stalked him through the woods. Guilt kicked him in the head—he'd led the unliving creature straight to their lair. It had obviously picked up his scent again.

Two tentacles danced a moment in front of her hand, and then the beast turned towards the workbench. The predator was *still* following his scent. As it glided towards him Kiel said, "Get away from me, Cam."

"But—"

"Just *do* it!"

Kiel didn't know if the boy complied, as he kept his eyes fixed on his attacker. He desperately wished he had his baseball bat. Four tentacles lifted above him like a butcher's hand reaching for a choice cut. His inclination was to swat at it with the termite probe, but a competing instinct knew that it was far too flimsy to be effective. As the grasp of the butcher's hand closed around him, he reflexively lifted both hands in defense, holding the probe and ground rod out for whatever meager resistance they might provide. Two tentacles reached around to each side of his head, while a third rose above him, perhaps intending to grab his hair. He felt two cold snakes contact the back of his neck and slide around in choking grips. These were deadly and about to strangle him, but he was mesmerized by the one hovering above him, as though this was the center of its conscious will, even though he knew that nothing in the colony had a centralized consciousness.

But the creature's imagined head hesitated. The tapered tip made as to strike downward, but froze, as if an invisible barrier prevented it from moving farther. Kiel saw that the barrier, real or imagined, extended between the tips of the termite probe and ground rod.

He'd been right after all—the crablet creatures *were* affected by electric fields.

Self-congratulations lasted a fleeting moment only as the tentacles encircling his neck suddenly tightened in perfect synchronicity, causing his whole head to jerk as his windpipe was squeezed closed.

There was a blur of motion and the drone suddenly shook, but the fourth tentacle was now wrapped around Cam's wrist and the hammer he'd used to strike.

The stranglehold around Kiel tightened even further, and he wondered that he didn't hear the popping of neck vertebrae. The tentacle that had been trying to grab his hair lifted away from the invisible barrier that was keeping it at bay, and turned to go after its second victim.

Kiel wasn't done with it, though. As it rose and turned, he lifted the two probes and laid their tips against each side of the drone's limb. The result was instantaneous and intense. The whole creature convulsed so that Kiel thought his head would be ripped from his shoulders, and the end of the tentacle flopped down, like the arm of a gunslinger shot through the heart. The appendage had a new joint where the probes had made contact. The smooth surface was warped and wrinkled there, and when the drone tried to swing the arm out of the way, the weakened section began to disintegrate, parting and separating like pulled taffy so that the intact end of the tentacle dangled helplessly, writhing in isolation.

The stranglehold around his neck did not relax, however. The desperate panic of suffocation condensed his life into a few frantic remaining seconds that might or might not be followed by continued life. He had three—maybe four—heartbeats to use his new weapon to break the chokehold.

The beast had already guessed his next move. It let go of Cam and grabbed the ground stake, yanking it away. It had run out of functional arms, though, and Kiel was free to reach over with his right arm and slap the tip of the termite probe against the side of the drone. Too late, the colony warrior realized its mistake. It released the ground stake, but the damage had been done. The tentacle that had grabbed the stake went limp, and the drone sagged, like a helicopter that had lost power.

Unfortunately, the pythons gripping his neck needed neither power nor direction from the drone's body proper. Kiel felt a moment of quiet peace, a bit of asphyxiated euphoria to send him off, and then he was falling through endless darkness.

Ж Ж Ж

"I already got that one!" Cam's voice protested. "See? It's, like, dead—oops!"

"What do I do?" Julie asked.

"Just touch the tips against—"

"Ow!"

"Keep your fingers out of the way!"

Kiel opened his eyes. He was lying on his back. The side of his head hurt. He must have fallen and hit it. Above him, he saw Cam struggling with a disembodied tentacle that was curling around his wrist. The boy tried to pry it loose, but the tip grabbed his finger so that now both his hands were immobilized. Julie cursed, and held the two probes against the middle of the coils. Where she touched, the silvered surface seemed to melt. The rest of the free-agent snake gave up, and the familiar snowfall of abandoning crablets fell from Cam. The damaged section of the coils remained, though—shapeless and limp. These were the many thousands of casualty crablets, victims of the electric zap.

Kiel sat up, rubbing his head. Julie was harassing the deformed remains of another tentacle lying on the ground. "That one's totally dead," Cam opined.

"Can't be too sure," his mother replied. "Besides, I don't want any of the cellular units escaping."

She noticed Kiel. "Welcome back," she said.

"You used the probes on my chokers?" he guessed.

"It was Cam, actually," she replied, finally setting the probes on the floor.

"Mom!" Cam objected. "You're letting them short against the ground!" He reached behind the metal box and shut it down.

"Well, thanks," Kiel said. "To both of you."

He noticed that his voice sounded hoarse. He felt his neck and winced. The damned things had rubbed the skin raw. "What happened to the—"

He saw it. The main body of the drone lay off to the side. As he watched, it slowly changed shape, but it seemed as though it couldn't make up its mind what to become. It bulged one way, then contracted and extended a baby limb off in another before pulling that back in as well.

"I think a lot of it is damaged," Cam observed, noticing Kiel's curiosity.

"Yeah," he agreed, getting up on his hands and knees so that he could get a closer look. "It's probably trying to figure out how much of it is still alive."

"Well, let's not let it find out," Julie said, picking up the probes. "Cam, turn it back on."

The boy reached for the box, but Kiel held out his hand. "Wait."

"Why?" Julie asked.

"It could be useful."

"How? You think we could torture it for information? Perhaps convince what's left to turn traitor and come over to our side?"

"No . . . we can maybe use it to experiment—"

He had an idea, but like a name that you knew you knew, but couldn't quite bring to your tongue, he struggled to pull it to the surface. He'd read about people who came back from near-death suffocation with ingenious ideas—pulling together mental threads that wouldn't have found each other among the well-worn grooves of their conscious brains.

Cam watched him closely, waiting for his insight.

Kiel had an image of cream of wheat on Mrs. Bakke's carpet, and miniscule crablets squirming under the blue arc of Julie's stun gun that was gripped by their own brethren. He'd thought that the electric arc had simply been animating the already-dead crablets, but now he saw otherwise. The stun gun had had little effect on the dry drone, but the carpet had been wet from Mrs. Bakke's broken vase, and then had been showered with the rock salt from Daniel's shotgun blast. The dissolved electrolytic salt had provided vastly increased conductivity, greatly amplifying the effects of the meager stun gun current.

And then there was the huge claw of the monster that had attacked them in the house. The goliath had inexplicably retreated when Daniel shot the claw with wimpy rock salt. But now Kiel pieced together the clues. He'd watched in horror as the claw prepared to disembowel him, and had noted the surrealistic sight of the fish squashed against its maw. The fish implied a shattered aquarium, which in turn meant water. When Daniel embedded the creature with rock salt, it felt—or at least understood—the reactive combination. If the colony creatures contained anything like instincts, the monster reacted in defense against a serious vulnerability.

They'd finally found a pale, unarmored underbelly.

Maybe.

"Cam, did you bring along any rock-salt shells with the gun?"

"Uh, I don't think so. The ones I carried were pretty heavy—either pellets or slugs."

Salt—he'd just seen a label—

"Keep an eye on the prisoner a second," Kiel said, getting up and dragging over a bag of salt.

"What are you going to do?" Julie asked.

"Find out if we have an A-bomb."

"You're going to make a *bomb*?"

"A metaphor."

"You think that salt hurts them?" Cam asked, watching him closely.

"Not salt alone. Saltwater and a shot of zap. Do we, uh, *have* any water?"

Everybody looked at each other, shaking their heads. Kiel had left his gallon containers back at the barn with the baseball bat.

"Pee," Mrs. Bakke said.

"You need to go to the bathroom, Mom?" Julie asked.

"No, you can use piss."

"For water!" Kiel enthused. "Mrs. Bakke, you're a genius!"

"When you live on a farm, surrounded by animals, urine is a daily fact of life. You only *wish* that you could forget about it. Will it be enough, though?"

"For the experiment, sure—er, I may need volunteers."

Kiel and Cam took turns peeing into the pesticide sprayer tank, taking the plastic container to a dark corner for privacy. They were both probably a little dehydrated; their efforts yielded barely a cup each.

"I can contribute," Julie offered. "I just regret not pissing on the horror directly."

Her mother held a large burlap sack to hide her, a matador daring the bull to lunge into her daughter's lap as she squatted over the container. Nicki jumped up and down, eager to join the fun, but Kiel figured he had enough now. He poured in a handful of salt and swished the noxious stew around. He thought about adding more, but decided that undissolved crystals might clog the sprayer nozzle. He screwed on the cap and pumped the handle to pressurize the tank. He had an urge to give it a trial squirt, but thought better of it.

The wounded drone had collected what parts were still functioning, and was extending one tentacle along the floor under the workbench. Cam harassed it with the hammer, keeping it occupied avoiding his whacks. "I think it's trying to get to the box," Cam said. "Maybe it understands that this is where the electricity comes from."

"Well, let's give it a good taste of it, if it's so curious."

"Good taste isn't exactly what I would call it," Julie quipped.

"Who knows?" Mrs. Bakke added. "Maybe the nasty little thing finds urine pleasantly aromatic."

"One way to find out," Kiel concluded.

Kiel let Cam do the spraying so that the boy could keep back while he leaned in with the probes. At Kiel's word, the boy pressed the nozzle lever, covering the incapacitated alien creature, along with Kiel's hands and wrists, with a fine, pungent spray. At the contact of the salt-saturated liquid, the beast froze, and then the tentacle separated from the mostly inert body and tried to squirm away under cover. "More!" Kiel shouted, even as Cam already jumped forward to soak the wiggling appendage. The fleeing monstrosity was escaping between two boxes when Kiel realized that he was missing his chance. It was too far to reach with both hands without losing his balance, but he leaned forward with the probe gun anyway, putting his left hand on the floor for balance. He barely brushed the surface of the faux-snake with the probe's tip when it jerked once and then seemed to melt where it lay. He had inadvertently completed the circuit by touching the floor with the ground rod.

Kiel tried to drag the inert victim out using the ground rod, but merely succeeded in tearing the corpse apart. The once-firm collaboration of tiny crablets now had the consistency of cottage cheese.

They pushed the boxes out of the way, and found that the last couple of inches at the far end had dissolved into a scattering of snow. The current this far from the probe had not been enough to do the little bastards in. Peering closely, he could see the myriad metal mites thrashing about in their pee-swamp as they tried to escape. He made sure his ground rod was pressed firmly against the floor, and then held the probe tip above the miniature frantic crowd. The effect was like magic. Without even making contact, he caused the horde to dance in unison, swirling and shimmering beneath his wand as though all mesmerized by mass-hypnosis. When he lifted it away, however, the charade was revealed—the snow lay lifeless. He couldn't detect a single moving crablet.

"They seem so strong," Julie commented once they made sure there were no remaining parts still operating. "It seems odd that they're so sensitive to a little electricity."

"No, I think maybe it does make sense," Cam countered. "They have to communicate."

"What do you mean?"

"They have to work together to make a working drone or . . . you know, a big monster. They have to coordinate their movements—the only way to do that is by communicating."

"They talk to each other."

"Well, I don't know about talking. Do computers talk to each other?"

"I sometimes talk to my computer using bad language."

Cam rolled his eyes. "Anyway, they must use electricity somehow to communicate. So, their fingers must be sensitive to it. It probably doesn't take much to frizzle their innards."

"Sort of like blasting a very loud sound into someone's ear."

"More like setting off a grenade next to their head."

Kiel stood watching the conversation. He was struck by their easy repartee. Most young teenage boys he knew wouldn't give their moms the benefit of a full sentence. "Looks like we've found their weakness," he interjected. "But we're almost out of energy-juice."

Cam and Julie looked at each other, then at Mrs. Bakke.

"I could probably give you a dribble," their forbear offered half-heartedly.

"No," Kiel clarified. "I mean I think we should find some water—enough to fill the tank. Is there anything closer than the stream that runs through the patch of woods north of here?"

Cam thought about it, and shook his head. Julie and Mrs. Bakke concurred.

"Well, the stream it is, then."

"Are you sure you want to go out there?" Julie asked with furrowed brows. "There may be other drones around."

Kiel certainly did not want to go back out, not after being stalked like an escaped prisoner running from bloodhounds. "I have to risk it. It's our only weapon. They're bound to figure out where we are eventually, and Daniel's shotgun will hold off those—bigger ones—only so long."

"Well, be careful," she urged. "If you see anything suspicious, you hightail it back here."

After they'd checked on Daniel, and Kiel was carrying the sprayer out of the cave, he decided that he'd actually do the exact opposite. If he happened upon a scouting drone, he'd have to run in the opposite direction. He couldn't give away their hiding place, at least, not until he'd re-loaded their clumsy weapon.

Outside, Kiel crouched down and surveyed the surroundings. All was quiet; even the gunshots at Tagget's place had gone silent, and his heart sank at the implication. No time to worry about that—he got up and trotted off, retracing his steps from the last time he'd left the cave. At the top of the low ridge where he'd spotted the arriving caravan, he saw that the stream exited the wooded area below him, spilling into a small swamp choked with rush and cattails. By the time he'd waddled his way far enough into the thick growth to get his feet wet, he realized that it probably would have been quicker and dryer to go the extra distance into the woods. That was just hindsight now, though. The problem was that although there was water plenty enough to soak his feet, he had no way to collect it into the sprayer tank. He had no choice but to continue deeper into the marsh until he finally came to open pools where he could immerse the tank and fill it. By now he was up to his knees and elbows in mud and organic swamp stew. It had been a simple idea: go and fill the tank with water. Execution never fit neatly inside the streamlined form of the notion.

Once he'd filled the tank, he then had another thirty pounds to wrestle back through the reeds, the velvet cattail drum mallets tapping out a tune of nature's indifference against his head. At some point he stopped and listened, not sure why the thought impressed itself at that time. A dragonfly buzzed haphazardly about, on the lookout for an easy insect meal. Another one searched just out of sight. The unseen predator's hunting technique demonstrated less randomness, the burring of its wings steady and sure.

Shit. The sound was indeed a burr and not the buzz of a harmless little insect.

Kiel wanted to cry in despair and scream with fury all at the same time. Instead, he flopped to the ground, feeling the cool life-rich swamp water soak his pants and shirt. It was hard to tell how far away the drone patrolled. Judging from the volume, it could have been a hundred feet, or a hundred yards. All he could do was wait, imagining all manner of wiggly things finding their way inside his clothes, and visualizing how he might use the sprayer as a weapon. The imagined scene ended with the drone bending the sprayer nozzle in half, while a hundred thousand crablets all laughed in unison.

The sound of the alien scout slowly diminished, but then circled around and grew in volume. Kiel buried his face into the musty marsh stalks and prayed for invisibility.

Whatever gods were tuned in must have decided to watch and let the drama unfold according to the abilities of the players. Closer and closer the sound of evil whirring wings charged until the anthem of oblivion stopped, hovering directly above his head.

Chapter 25

Despite himself, Kiel whimpered, and then held his breath, awaiting the cold, hard touch of a tentacle seeking to encircle his neck. The drone waited as well, perhaps biding its time until better access to his windpipe was revealed. Second upon interminable second dragged on, and still the damned alien abomination held its ground.

Kiel could finally take no more, and rolled over, attempting to brandish the sprayer nozzle, but failing because he had rolled onto the hose. Above him, a startled dragonfly retreated upward a yard, and then banked and whirred away. With it, went all evidence of beating wings.

He lay, holding his breath again and listening. Nothing. He wondered if the drone had been just his imagination, but rejected the thought—he'd *heard* an alien scout; he was sure of it. It was a sound he would spend the rest of his life trying to forget. This wasn't saying much, since that span might only be measured in hours.

Kiel waited a few minutes longer, listening so that he could be absolutely sure, while the smelly swamp water soaked the rest of him. When he finally stood up, his wet clothes were heavy with mud. At the edge of the swamp he paused and listened again before heading back up the ridge. At the top he stopped and surveyed the countryside. He found himself reluctant to look, not just because he was afraid of what he might see, but more because it would mean that he might have to follow through with his promise to himself, and running away from the safety of the cave with a killer drone in pursuit seemed almost impossible.

Far off in the direction of Tagget's place he could see dark smudges moving vaguely about on the horizon, what he presumed to be the victorious platoon of giant alien hawk-monsters. Three, five—he counted an even half dozen enemy behemoths. Once the colony had re-established power from the grid, the production of crablets and their incorporated flying war machines had resumed with a vengeance. Cam's prediction of runaway geometric multiplication seemed to be gaining momentum. The tiny specks of faux-life that had nipped the tip of his finger in the hole as he sought shelter from the rain had flourished and were morphing into a malevolence that threatened more than just a scattering of rural farms. Kiel shuddered to think where it might end.

He wiped mud from his cheek and flicked it away as he started off again. Thoughts like this served no purpose beyond hobbling them with despair. He'd turned his back to the distant gathering storm, but the hairs on the back of his neck still tingled at the knowledge.

He was a hundred yards from the cave's entrance, and could see Julie and Cam peeking out with perplexed expressions at his appearance when he heard it again. He spun about and saw it. This time there was no mistake—a scout drone had topped the ridge and was gliding down after him, tentacles writhing in anticipation of grasping his throat.

His dutiful promise called to him to run, to run away from the cave and lead the enemy off in a different direction. He was so close, though. Once it reached him, would it really not notice the entrance anyway?

Before he had a chance to find out whether his resolve was up to it, his friends decided for him. Cam came running out calling a warning, with his mom hot on his heels. It was impossible for the drone not to have seen them.

Kiel ran for the cave. His arms were exhausted from carrying the thirty-pound sprayer, and the plastic container banged his knees and calves until finally tripping him so that he tumbled headlong. By the time he'd gathered himself, Cam was already picking up the sprayer, trying to lug it back to the cave, but struggling ineffectually with the weight a third his own. Julie arrived and took it from him, ordering him back to safety. Without a word, Kiel and Julie both grasped the tank's handle and ran towards the cave with the load swaying between them.

Kiel heard the drone, the sound of the vile machine's flight swelling until it seemed to roar an arm's length behind him. They were seconds from making the cave when fiercely sharp talons suddenly grabbed his shoulder. The pain was beyond any anticipation, and he let go of the tank's handle and fell to his knees in agony as the burr of the drone's wings rose an octave while it struggled to maintain position against his weight. A second claw grabbed a forceful clutch of his hair and jerked his head back. As his view swung up, he had a fleeting image of Cam standing before him holding something heavy in both hands. An instant later a shotgun blast coincided with a hot flash near his left ear, and he was suddenly being held by just his hair. Cam was working to pump the gun for a second shot without success. The drone apparently didn't comprehend the boy's difficulty, for it let go of Kiel's hair and rose to safety, leaving him to drop to his hands and knees.

The pain in his shoulder continued unabated, and he understood why when he reached up with his right hand to feel. Although Cam had severed the appendage, the claw continued its clutching mission on its own.

Julie grabbed Kiel's wrist, urging him along. With her help, he got to his feet and staggered forward. Cam still struggled to pump the gun, and as they passed him, Julie caught her son by the arm and pulled him along as well.

Kiel had a hard time concentrating past the pain. As he stumbled through the cave's mouth, he vaguely noted that somebody—probably Cam—had dragged Daniel's termite-gun box and batteries forward to a new location just inside the cave. The boy had been busy the short time he'd been gone. He took the shotgun from Cam, but his left arm was practically useless, and he had no more success pumping a new shell into the chamber.

And then the drone, minus one claw, appeared, nearly filling the mouth of the cave. It seemed cautious, wary of losing another appendage. Kiel played on this. He lifted the gun, pointing it at the alien devil. His whole body shook from the pain, and the tip of the barrel swayed so that even if it was loaded, he probably would have missed anyway.

The drone wouldn't understand this, though. It too swayed back and forth as though trying to predict and avoid where he'd shoot.

"Julie!" he called. "Get the sprayer ready! Cam, grab two handful's of salt!"

Kiel felt faint, and the tip of the gun dropped despite his best grunting effort, just as the mother and son team called that they were ready. "Go!" he yelled, letting the heavy gun fall with a thud to the ground. "Julie first, then Cam!"

He heard the hiss of spraying water as he scrambled to find the probes. A second later, he felt a shower of salt on his face and neck. He had the ground rod in his ailing left hand, and was reaching for the gun probe when the drone moved in and got him. His head jerked up as the remaining claw once again grabbed his hair, and he saw the flash of another tentacle swing around for his bared neck. With an effort beyond what he thought he had left, he held the ground rod up just as the razor-sharp blade slammed home, hammering the metal stake into his Adam's apple and choking him so that he gasped each breath.

He heard screaming, and realized that it was Julie—she was right next to him. Out of the corner of his eye he saw her flailing at the monster, but it quickly wrapped a free tentacle around her own neck as she desperately pulled at the coils, struggling to keep from being strangled.

Her efforts paid off, though. The extra weight forced the drone to sink lower. Staring unwillingly at the ceiling of the cave, Kiel groped blindly with his right hand until his fingers found the termite gun probe. Glee at the opportunity for vengeance energized him as he slapped the tip against the drone's body.

Nothing happened.

The drone was working the knife blade, tilting it, trying to slice his neck at an angle. He felt the blade cut his skin.

"I've got it!" he heard Cam yell. Suddenly, he felt the wondrous tingling in both of his hands as the boy turned on the device, and he again slapped the drone with the gun tip. The wicked knife melted around the ground rod, and he felt the soft mash of dead crablets press harmlessly against both sides of his neck.

Keeping the gun probe pressed against the drone's body, he called forth superhuman will to lift the ground rod against the searing pain in his shoulder and slap it against the tentacle holding his hair. Instantly, his head was free, although he could tell that the severed claw still clung fast in his hair.

The drone gave up, understanding that this weapon was something it should fear. It began uncoiling its hold from around Julie's neck, but she hung on with both hands. "Kill it!" she rasped, gasping for breath.

Kiel doubted that it understood her words, but it obviously comprehended her intentions. The tentacle parted neatly in two just above where she grasped it, half of it given up in sacrifice.

Kiel wasn't done yet. It was truly beyond his ability to lift his left hand any higher, so making sure he was pressing the drone firmly with the gun probe, he gave the ground rod a toss upwards, towards the whirring wing-ear blades. The mechanical beast seemed to sigh in resignation as it fell heavily to the ground, one blade limp and bent. What was left of the main body dissolved in familiar ultimate retreat as the remaining uncountable crablets let go their holds on each other for a last-ditch attempt at individual escape.

"Oh no you don't, you son-of-a-bitch," Kiel growled. "Spray and salt 'em, Cam."

Seconds later, Kiel held the ground rod against the cave floor as he swept the gun probe a few inches above the fleeing horde. A minute later, the spreading film of micro-miniature machines lay lifeless and unmoving.

Kiel's vision suddenly fuzzed over, and he sat down heavily on his butt, dropping both probes. The snow before his eyes cleared quickly, but he didn't even have the strength to sit up anymore, and he lay back on the cave floor. He heard Julie say that she could wait, and then Cam was bending over him, both probes held out as though about to perform a blessing. His young friend hesitated, and then turned to his mother. "What if some of it stays inside?"

Julie's face appeared above him, studying his shoulder. A tentacle still encircled her neck like a thick, gaudy choker necklace. "Hang on," she said and reached forward. A second later, Kiel cried out when the searing pain jumped a notch as she tugged at the severed claw still embedded in his flesh. She let go and studied a moment more. "What if you touch the electrodes on each side? But just a quick tap."

Cam considered this and nodded. Kiel saw the probes come forward, past his head. He gritted his teeth against the expected pain, but he hardly felt any difference when Cam pulled the probes back again. Julie reached forward, and the resulting stab of intense pain now caught him by surprise. But when her hand retracted, it held a bloody talon. Cam had obviously destroyed the center of the claw, separating the individual mini-daggers. Three more unbearable stabs, and she proclaimed him free of alien invasion. The claw grasping his hair was easy, and Cam dispatched that moments later.

Cam then looked at his mother. She clutched at the tentacle encircling her neck.

"Not on opposite sides of her neck," Kiel warned weakly.

Cam understood and nodded before reaching forward with the two probes. He tapped them against the coil, two inches apart. The metal surface deformed, but the coil held fast.

"Water," Kiel instructed. "And salt."

Julie made a face when her son sprayed her head with smelly swamp water, followed by a handful of salt. But now when he laid the probes against the alien appendage, it virtually melted, falling from her as though made of wet clay.

Mrs. Bakke appeared next to Kiel, gently unbuttoning and pulling apart his shirt. She examined the puncture wounds and told Cam to hand her some salt. Kiel's eyes went wide at the prospect, and he was relieved when Julie questioned whether the mild antiseptic would even penetrate far enough into the punctures to be useful.

"Don't even have fresh water to clean the wounds, let alone bandages," she bemoaned. "They seem to be clotting already. Maybe you won't die after all."

Working together, they got him into a sitting position against one leg of the workbench. He was feeling better, just tired. Cam surprised him when he held out a power bar. "Where'd that come from?" Kiel asked.

His young friend shrugged. "My pocket."

Kiel shook his head. "I can't take that."

"You need it a lot more than me."

"Take it, Kiel," Julie urged.

Sighing, he accepted the bar, broke it in two, and handed half back. Cam started to object, but his mother told him it was okay.

"You've earned it," Kiel said. "You've already saved my life more than once. That was one hell of a shot out there. Where'd you learn to shoot like that?"

Cam blushed. "I just got lucky."

"Lucky, heck! That was precision marksmanship."

The boy's face blushed a couple of shades deeper. "I was aiming for the drone's main body."

Kiel stared at him, speechless. The boy could have easily blown a hole in Kiel's head. "It seems that I was the lucky one. You did exactly the right thing, though. I would have been dead in a few seconds anyway."

Cam just stood staring at his hands, maybe wondering that they could do something so risky; or maybe he was just tired—saturated and burned up with adrenaline.

A thud just outside the cave mouth snapped their heads around in unison. A rock, the size of a pumpkin sat where Kiel was sure there had been none before. It was followed by a thin rain of sand and pebbles. "Everybody back!" Kiel ordered, waving his hand. "Move to the back!"

Something was up there, above them on the steep slope of the ridge. Suddenly they heard a tremendous thrashing, and the rain of earth grew to a veritable dirt shower. An instant later, a flailing metal mass fell heavily to the ground, so big that Kiel saw only a portion through the small cave opening. The colony behemoth had tried to catch them by surprise, coming in over the top of the ridge, but had slipped and slid down the precipitous incline.

Kiel was on his feet, the throbbing shoulder pain relegated to insignificance. For a fleeting moment, he considered going for Daniel's termite tool, but picked up the shotgun instead. Against such a monster, the probes seemed like using chopsticks to beat off a grizzly bear. But then he remembered that he hadn't pumped a new shell into the chamber. It was a bad mistake; this should have been the first thing he did after killing the scout drone. Ignoring the tearing pain, he worked at the pump action. It wouldn't budge, as if the pump handle was locked in place. Maybe it was. He flipped the safety button on top to the other side, but the pump remained locked in position. He flipped the gun over and saw another button just behind the trigger guard. There were no markings, but he pushed it anyway.

He glanced up to find an enormous eye peering through the cave opening. As he watched, a giant hand extended through. For a moment he was stunned to inaction by the surreal image. It was the hand of a human, but made of flowing, flexible metal instead of flesh, and at least two feet across from imitation thumb to little finger. The colony was evolving—imitating birds, and now people themselves.

Kiel forced his attention back to the shotgun. This time the pump slid easily—it had indeed somehow become locked.

He looked up when he heard a shout from Cam. Instead of moving to the back, the boy had picked up the termite gun probes, and held them out in front of him as the gigantic hand reached for him. Just as the thumb and fingers—as big as the boy's arms—closed together to grasp him, Cam ducked, barely missing being crushed. The monster, its view blocked by its own arm, started to pull the hand back before it realized that it had missed.

Kiel lifted the gun and aimed for the alien's pie-sized eye peering in like some curious cat gazing into a fish bowl. He squeezed the trigger . . . and it refused to move. Shouting a curse, he remembered that he'd flipped the trigger safety before finding the pump lock. He flipped it back and lifted the gun again. The monster's elbow blocked his shot at the eye, so he waited, holding the gun ready.

Motion caught his attention. It was Mrs. Bakke. She held a piece of pipe like a cocked baseball bat as she limped forward past Cam. Another blur of motion was Julie throwing herself on top of her son and wrapping her arms around him. At this moment the monster must have realized its mistake, for it reached in again. Once more, Kiel was staring into the giant evil eye, and he squeezed the trigger. This time the gun kicked against him like a mule, and he nearly lost his balance. He recovered just in time to see the hand exit. The fingers were balled into a fist, and seemed to be clenching a bundle of clothes.

He looked over at the family. Julie lay on top of her son, hugging him for dear life. She stared, horrified, at the cave entrance.

"Where's your mom?" Kiel shouted.

Julie turned to him, her gaze seeming to look right through him. She shook her head, as though rejecting what she'd seen.

Kiel finally understood what the bundle of clothes had been.

Chapter 26

They had no time to react to the horrible turn as the other giant hand reached into the cave. The monster had repositioned itself, moving to look in with its other undamaged eye. The python fingers seemed nervous, wiggling about in what might have been twitches in a smaller body with quicker reflexes. Julie had pulled Cam to his feet and pushed him towards the back of the cave when the monster's hand wrapped around her. Kiel saw this as he pumped the shotgun. He aimed at the second eye, pulled the trigger, and braced himself as the gun kicked.

He pumped the gun before looking to see what had happened to Julie. His shot must have caused the beast to jerk, for it had lost most of its grip on Julie, but still grasped her upper arm between its thumb and forefinger as it continued to drag her inexorably out of the cave.

Kiel ran ahead of the hand and trapped woman. The wrist was as big as his thigh, and he shot into the center of it point blank. Although wielding a combined, individual crablets could hang on to their neighbors under only so much force, and a blast of speeding shotgun pellets was more than they could withstand. Kiel blew a two-inch hole right through the beast's hollow wrist.

The elephantine arm seemed to jerk, but continued to pull Julie away to her death. Kiel stepped back, pumped, and shot again, this time above the first hole. He pumped and shot a third time. There was no resistance when he pumped the fourth time, and he knew that he'd used the last shell.

But he'd inflicted significant damage to the mammoth appendage. The wrist had lost structural integrity, and bent back and forth where he'd blasted three perforations. The tattered connection was enough, however, to drag Julie along, kicking and screaming in terror. In desperation, Kiel whacked at the damaged section, using the gun as a club. The remaining strands must have been stressed to their limit, for each blow caused a section to stretch and grow thinner. Finally, the last few filaments parted simultaneously, and the arm pulled away, leaving the dismembered hand behind.

Bereft of direction and control, the colossal fingers bent and waved like the tendrils of an anemone undulating in a current. Julie sat stunned on the floor nearby, holding her arm.

The ground shook as a mighty blow struck near the mouth of the cave. An instant later, the first hand shoved back through. Rock dust fell from the damaged knuckles where the monster had struck the side of the cave opening. Kiel had apparently managed to blind the beast, and it was groping for them sightlessly. The fingers of this hand, the one that had pulled Mrs. Bakke away, were coated red with blood. When he saw this, his stomach flipped and tried to empty its contents.

Kiel ran to Julie and pulled her to the side, against the wall of the cave. He despaired that he was out of gun shells. But the hand was acting oddly. Each finger seemed to move in spasms, as though having a mind of its own. Also, the whole hand swung back and forth, sweeping across the cave floor—outside, the monster itself seemed to be struggling against some sort of whole-body spasms. Maybe they could just wait out the death-throes, if that's what it was.

Hope for such an easy solution evaded them. Against all reasonable caution, Cam shouted in defiance to the groping hand. The boy held the two termite gun probes up like twin rapiers, a lone Musketeer calling challenge to a whole squadron of the Cardinal's men. He yelled curses beyond his years, all in the name of his grandmother.

One finger, the particularly bloody forefinger, seemed to notice him. While the others continued their random probing searches, toppling crates and breaking one leg of the workbench, this one reached out purposefully towards him. It was like the hand of God reaching to give life to Adam, except that this hand was intent on taking life. Kiel and Julie called to him to hide, but he either didn't hear or ignored them. Instead, he stood firm, waiting patiently for the advancing finger as it slowly convinced its brothers to come along. When the bloody tip reached him, he stepped back, and then stepped back again. And then, like a fencing champion lunging for the touché thrust, he stepped in, leaned forward, and laid the two probes on each side of the red, rounded surface staring him in the face.

The tip of the finger melted, seeming to cave inward like a balloon deflating. Cam pressed his attack, sliding the probes down each side of the finger so that it sagged and flowed like a candle caught in a blowtorch.

He had vanquished the finger. But it was just one of five. As he had moved forward, destroying the length of the forefinger, the others surrounded him. All the monster had to do was bring the thumb and remaining fingers together into a fist, and Cam would be crushed, following his grandmother's fate. But the fingers seemed to be on their own, abandoned of control from the beast beyond the cave entrance.

They weren't rendered harmless, however. As they twitched and bent in their individual pursuits, Cam was knocked about like a pinball. Kiel picked up the pipe that Mrs. Bakke had dropped and beat against the outside of the thumb. This seemed to get its attention, and it straightened—perhaps the million constituent crablets were all straining to discern what was banging at them.

Cam took advantage of the reprieve from the thumb's batterings, and concentrated on applying his probes to the remaining three fingers. As each was destroyed, the remaining sparring opponents were that much easier to deal with. Soon, only the pinky remained. It had somehow escaped being bathed in blood, and lacking conductive electrolytes, it resisted an easy dispatch. At this point, however, the monster proper had apparently surmised that something was amiss, and pulled the finger-depleted arm back out through the cave mouth.

Cam stood watching the cave opening, shaking the probes as though daring the murderous alien to return. Tears streaked white lines through the dirt on his face. Julie sat with her head bowed, still holding her arm. Outside, out of view, came the sound of the monster thumping and crashing—Jack's furious giant at the top of the beanstalk discovering that his goose is missing.

Kiel wanted to sit down too, to wrap his arms around his head and squeeze his eyes shut. But he knew that these alien creatures were resilient. Rip off a tentacle, and it just wraps itself around your neck while its parent presses on without breaking stride. The monster was probably out there reconfiguring—maybe extruding new hands, or perhaps reverting back to the proven tentacle form.

He breathed deeply and then headed for the cave entrance. He felt like a mouse strolling out to see if the cat was poised waiting to pounce. What he saw stopped him in his tracks—not from fear, but from wonder. He was expecting to find a giant person, a body appropriately formed and proportioned to fit the hands that he and Cam had destroyed. Instead, he found a centaur; at least, that was his first impression. The thing had four legs, and a simple head with two eyes. Arms, terminating now in tattered strands of crablets, extended from the shoulders on each side of the head. The body was just a platform for the giant arms. The whole thing was no bigger than an elephant. Kiel was expecting something the size of a brontosaurus.

It was acting like neither, however. It could barely stand. Like the ruined fingers, the legs seemed to have a hard time working together. The artificial creature could have been drunk.

"You blinded it," Cam said next to him.

Kiel looked down at him. Cam was still sniffling, but the torrent of rage had passed.

"Yeah, I guess so," he agreed. It didn't make sense, though. "I don't understand why it's having such a hard time. The drones never even had eyes."

Cam was quiet a moment, his brow collected together in thought. "It's too big."

"I'll say."

"No. I mean it's too big *not* to have eyes. There's too many crablets—millions, probably billions—to coordinate by themselves."

Kiel was beginning to understand. "Specialized eyes produce visual information that has to be distributed, which means a nerve network—or something like it."

Cam nodded, his brow still furrowed. "Not just the vision, but motor control too."

He glanced at the boy. The kid's mind never took a break. "I see what you mean. Something as big as that needs centralized control. Even if there's no actual brain, it still needs somebody in there calling directions to all the parts—traffic control. When I shot out the eyes, I must have disrupted the control."

"Size has advantages, but there's a tradeoff in complexity. And complexity can be vulnerable."

Kiel looked at him. The tired young face issued these thoughts as a matter of course, simple observations that were obvious, at least to him. "Are you sure you're just thirteen, and not a grownup with some sort of growth disorder?"

A tired, sad grin lifted the corners of the boy's mouth. "The evidence is pretty clear."

"Well," Kiel said, pulling his shoulders back in a stretch before wincing with the pain that this caused, "I guess we'd better take care of this uncoordinated monster."

Cam looked up at him, the grin gone, replaced by the usual worried thoughtfulness. "You think we can get close enough with the probes?"

"We have to try. That thing will eventually repair the damage we've done. It takes longer the bigger they are, but I don't want to be here when it finishes."

As they turned back to the cave, Kiel saw something lying along the bottom of the ridge. He quickly took Cam's shoulder and herded him inside with instructions about preparing the probe assembly, then stole three burlap sacks from Daniel and went back. He kneeled by the crumpled form and stifled a sob as he absorbed how broken the old body of his former host was. Even though she was beyond feeling, it was pitiful to see her so mangled. It was defilement, a corruption of a soul by a soulless creature. A tornado can wreak such damage, but a tornado doesn't kill purposefully.

Positioning the sacks carefully one at a time, he covered the body of the woman who had welcomed him in from the cold, and then placed stones on the corners against the wind.

Back inside, Cam had lifted the heavy battery onto the termite gun box, and together they lugged the stack out to find that the damaged alien beast had settled onto the ground, folding its legs under it like a cow. Slowly, stepping cautiously, they approached the disabled alien and set the load down ten feet away. Even lying down, it was taller than Kiel.

"It's making this easy for us," Cam observed, stepping back a few feet.

Kiel didn't like it. "I don't know. I doubt it's just giving up. More likely, it needs to be immobile to do the repairs. Let's get on with it."

They returned to the cave and poured handfuls of salt in with the water of the sprayer tank. Before leaving, Kiel checked on Nicki, who was hiding in the back. The little girl clung to him, and he had to gently pry her hands from his leg and promise to return soon. Julie seemed to be in shock. Kiel wasn't even sure she recognized him, but she yelled in pain when he felt her arm where the giant thumb and finger had grabbed her. He guessed that it was broken, but it was hard to tell for sure. At least it wasn't a complete fracture like Daniel's leg.

Back outside, he was relieved to find the monster still recuperating, although it had already re-formed the stump ends of its arms, opting for talon claws rather than the more complex fingered-hands. He gave the sprayer to Cam and readied the probes. "Let's start with its arms—get the most dangerous parts out of the way. No telling how it's going to react, so once you've given one good spray, you jump back—far back. Got it?"

The boy nodded, focusing on his target: two fifteen-foot jointed arms tipped with nasty claws. They were folded together, resting across what served as the monster's chest. The metal beast hardly took notice of them, apparently not having repaired the sight in its eyes yet. The arms jostled restlessly against each other; Kiel guessed that the myriad individual crablets knew they were there, and were nervous, or what served as nervous in creatures the size of fleas.

Cam held the sprayer tank in one hand, and the nozzle in the other. Kiel yelled, "Go!" and the boy took two steps forward and sprayed a long arc across the folded arms. "Okay, back!" Kiel called, and leaned in with the probes. The arms froze as the salt water fell on them, but when he laid the probes against the nearest forearm, all hell broke loose. The entire beast shuddered, and the arms began to unfold. He kept his attention focused on the point where he'd made contact, stepping back as the arm unfolded. The foot-thick forearm melted like hot butter under the probes, and five feet of arm and claw tilted down, and fell off before the arm fully extended. Kiel stepped away from the fallen section, knowing from experience what an alien claw could do on its own.

The remaining arm was too quick for him. He ducked as he saw it swinging his way and held up the probes in defense. The gun probe jerked violently in his hand as the monster caught it in its claw. The next instant, Kiel was holding a broken stub; the rest of the probe had snapped off, and now lay clutched in the beast's talons.

Cam shouted for him to get back, but Kiel sensed that this would be a mistake. The mighty arm was directly above him, and its reach was a distance well beyond his ability to jump. Instead, as he did when the bird-beast had attacked him, he chose the opposite and stepped in towards the belly of the alien. The stub arm swung down, and he danced out of the way. His gun probe was broken, but out of reflex, he laid the ground rod and small piece of remaining busted probe against the stub arm. To his delight and relief, the amputated limb melted. The probe was just a conductor—the broken piece worked as well as the original, only with less reach.

He danced again when the intact arm, still clutching the broken length of probe, swung down to crush him. The sheer mass of such gigantic members could snuff him instantly if they caught him. But the weighty mass equaled inertia, and as long as Kiel avoided being trapped, he found that he could outmaneuver the lumbering motions. His biggest problem was avoiding getting tangled in his probe wires.

Jumping and ducking, he tapped the two conductors here and there on the massive arm. Bit by bit, the surface became pock-marked, but he realized that he'd collapse from exhaustion before he finally incurred enough damage to disable the arm. He had to find a way to keep the probes in continuous contact.

One method was obvious, and he executed this before he had a chance to realize the potential stupidity. Instead of jumping away as the arm swung down the next time, he reached out and wrapped his arms and then his legs around it. He was now hugging it as he rode it like a rodeo clown might the neck of a horse.

Instantly he saw the multiple problems: the arm might drag him beyond the reach of the probe wires; the monster could easily now crush him against its body; and even if he did detach the arm, he still had to survive the fall while mated to it. He would be like Slim Pickens, riding the A-bomb down on Russia in the movie *Doctor Strangelove.*

He could have tried to jump away, but he chose to follow through, where following through meant just hanging on. His fists were flat against the surface, and the probes were already doing their job. As the arm swung him up and down, making him dizzy, he felt his hands sink together as the monster's arm dissolved beneath them. His rodeo ride settled to a continuous vertical position, and he realized that he'd created a bending joint in the arm, with gravity providing the orienting directive. He saw that he was slowly sinking, and understanding that this was the new joint giving way, he pushed himself off, falling just a few feet to the ground. He stumbled, though, and fell onto his back. The separated arm fell heavily next to him, and the claw immediately began crawling towards him, like a zombie version of the alien. Kiel reached over and touched his probes to the tips of each of the talons, essentially de-clawing the bastard. He got to his knees and worked the probes along the arm, inflicting just enough damage to keep it from quickly reconfiguring.

"Wow!" Cam said next to him. "That was—" The boy just shook his head in wonder.

"Stupid," Kiel finished for him. "Don't tell your mom I did that. She won't let me play with you anymore."

The alien beast interrupted their respite. Shuddering and swaying unsteadily, it tried to get to its feet, probably deciding it was time to get the hell out of there, however uncoordinated its escape might be. Cam had kept the sprayer close at hand, and once he'd soaked one leg, Kiel reached up and went to work on the knee. He was almost squashed when the behemoth fell heavily forward, the damaged leg buckling beneath it.

They discussed how best to attack the rest of the billion stranded crablets, but their debate was cut short when another shudder shook the alien bulk. This time the entire mass shivered and jiggled as though from an earthquake. When the seismic shaking was done, the once-continuous surface had dimpled and warped so that it looked like a moonscape. Then each peak pulled even higher and still higher, creating one gigantic hedgehog. Kiel pulled Cam back, wondering what devilment the alien colony was now up to. Dozens and dozens of individual peaks each morphed and formed, and within seconds, a flock of flying drones lifted up and away. The mass of crablets were in full retreat.

One, however, paused and then tilted and glided towards them. Cam positioned the sprayer nozzle, and Kiel held the probes ready. The familiar tentacle-dangling form halted out of reach, though. It hovered there a moment, and then lifted up and away, following its identical colleagues off towards their home cave.

"I think it wanted to get a good look at us," Cam said.

"Could be," Kiel agreed, sitting down. He was suddenly faint with exhaustion again. "They'll be hanging up alien wanted posters of us. We've made quite a nuisance of ourselves."

The nuisance-making had only begun.

Chapter 27

Kiel and Cam returned to the cave and dispatched the giant hand that Kiel had amputated with the shotgun. It was still floundering about, maybe thinking (or whatever served for thinking) that it might grab a human by chance. The high voltage duo began by zapping small sections all along the length before starting at one end to thoroughly destroy all the crablets. This was to prevent portions from separating off to escape as flying drones. The technique worked, although they weren't able to kill all the crablets. They'd only destroyed perhaps two-thirds of the alien remnant before the rest dissolved into individual micro-beings, which slowly flowed away in the cave's crevices as Kiel swept the broken probe back and forth, leaving swaths of dull metal powder.

After that, Kiel sat down again before he fell down. His shoulder ached, but mostly he was just completely exhausted. Cam walked up and handed him a bottle of water and a plastic packet of molasses the size of a sandwich. Kiel stared at the two items as though he was being presented with ten-carat diamonds and wasn't sure if he'd get into trouble for possessing something of such value.

"Where'd you find these?" he asked, looking up at Cam in astonishment.

"At the bottom of the trunk with the boots and gloves."

Kiel took the plastic packet and examined it.

"Uncle Daniel used to add molasses to the cattle feed in the winter," Cam explained. "He bought it by the barrel—these must be samples."

Kiel took the bottle of water as well and looked at Cam, who just shrugged.

No sense looking a gift horse in the mouth. As he twisted off the top he suddenly realized that he was desperately thirsty. He lifted the bottle and guzzled, but quickly stopped. He wasn't the only one in dire condition. "Were there more?" he asked. Cam left and soon returned with two more, along with a whole handful of molasses packets. Kiel tore open one, squeezed the earthy sweet fluid into his mouth, and guzzled more water. It was like his ON switch had been flipped. All the adrenaline had dehydrated him and depleted his blood sugar. He gulped down another packet, and handed Cam the bottle to wash down the contents he too had just ingested.

They went to the back of the cave where Julie sat with her head buried in her one good arm, while the other lay limp on the floor. Nicki sat quietly next to her, her head resting against her mom's waist. When they walked over, Julie looked up briefly, shook her head woodenly at the offerings, and let it fall back down.

Kiel sat down cross-legged in front of her. Nicki watched him silently, hiding deep inside herself, from where she peered out through her eyes. "You need to at least drink some water," he said softly to Julie.

Instead of transitioning to a single mom by divorce as she expected, she had become a widow. This was not what devastated her, though. "I didn't even get to say goodbye," she said, lifting her head.

Kiel couldn't think of a single thing to say, so he just held out the bottle of water. She accepted it and drank deeply, and then handed it to Nicki, who took it obediently and lifted the liter container to her lips with both hands. "Brandon, Peggy, and now Mom," Julie protested. "Where will it stop?" As she said this, her face became even tighter, and she glanced down at her daughter, realizing that she was probably scaring the little girl even more.

"Once we get them all," Kiel replied. It sounded like a platitude. "We've found their Achilles heel."

She snorted. "You're going to kill a whole army of these . . . metal monsters with a homemade termite tool?"

He lifted his shoulders. When laid out in a single, short sentence, it did sound completely nuts. "We're going to try."

"You're going to get my son killed."

She glared at him. Her motherhood challenged Kiel against even thinking of putting him in further danger.

"Mom, we have to do *something*," Cam countered. "They know we're here. They'll come back—that's for sure." He too glanced down at his little sister, but these things had to be discussed.

His mom shook her head, rejecting thoughts of Cam heading away on an offensive. "Daniel was bringing us here because he thought we could defend ourselves," she said to Kiel. "You have a gun."

He lifted his shoulders again, and winced at the result. "Maybe he thought that we would just hide here—use the gun only as a last defense."

"This is that last defense. It's not a battle you can fight—leave it for the Army."

"The last we heard—hell, just a few hours ago—nobody even knew what was going on. It takes days to mobilize the army."

"Then we'll just have to hold out for days."

"But that's only after they understand the situation. Who knows when that will be?"

He was frustrated that she didn't understand the futility of just holing up in the cave. He knew it was probably the trauma incapacitating her, but she represented exactly half of the voting adults of the group now. And even though most of the original family adults were either dead or unconscious, Kiel still felt that she carried the deciding ballot. After all, he was the outsider, the drifter—the fugitive.

"Okay," he relented with a sigh. "I'll go and see if I can get the word out. It looked like somebody was on top of it over at Tagget's place, but . . ."

Julie just gave him a dead stare. The words didn't have to be voiced: somebody over there had understood, but they were now dead as well.

"Don't listen to him."

Julie's eyes went wide with wonder. It was Daniel's weak voice.

They got up and went to him where he lay in his cart-bed. He still looked unconscious, but then he opened his eyes and stared a moment before seeming to notice them. "Don't let him get to you," he muttered.

Kiel and Julie exchanged glances. After a moment, Julie said, "Kiel?"

The farmer frowned. "No! The idiot—Brandon!"

Julie looked at Kiel and gave him a little surreptitious knowing shrug. Daniel didn't remember.

"The government will never get here in time," he continued. "Take care of yourselves."

"We will, Daniel," Julie assured, laying her hand gently on his arm. "You just rest." To Cam, she said, "Bring the water."

"Dynamite," her brother said, his face contorting in pain.

"Just rest," she repeated.

"Wait," Kiel interrupted, leaning in closer. "What dynamite?" he asked.

"No permit," Daniel muttered, barely understandable through pain-clenched teeth. "The high shelf."

Cam held out the near-empty bottle of water, and Julie took it and held it up to her brother's lips, but when he tried to drink, he choked and coughed, causing him to cry out in pain. He banged his fist against the metal side of the cart. "Get me out of this coffin," he groaned, and pulled on the lips of both sides to sit up. His scream caused them all to jump in alarm. The next instant he lay motionless again.

Silence closed in within the small confines of the cave.

"Did Uncle Daniel die?" Nicki asked in a tiny voice.

"No—no!" Julie, assured her. "Uncle Daniel just needs to sleep. He's hurt badly and has to rest." She got Nicki to lie down on some burlap sacks, and then looked at Kiel knowingly.

"I guess that changes things," he said.

Her brow furrowed. "Not at all—you mean that stuff about dynamite? He's delirious, Kiel. You can't be taking him seriously."

Kiel just looked at her. He didn't want to argue, but he knew in his heart that waiting for help was a huge mistake.

"I think he was making sense," Cam said. "He agrees that we can't depend on the government. It's like the giant colony beasts—the larger the structure, the slower to react."

"No, honey," she said firmly. "Your uncle is delirious."

"But, if we don't—"

"That's enough, Cam."

"But Mom!"

"Cameron! I said that's enough!"

The boy's face was crimson, and his mouth a tight seal holding boiling anger inside. He pounded his fist in the air in silent frustration, turned, and stalked away.

Julie checked her brother's pulse with her good arm, and then, satisfied, repositioned his burlap blanket. "You should take the gun," she said without looking up.

Kiel assumed she was talking to him. "No. It should stay at the cave. Like Cam said, they know we're here, and you'll need it when they come back. I'll stay low—stick to cover."

"I have a broken arm," she said pointedly without looking at him. She was mad. "And Cam has already demonstrated that he can't handle it."

Her son was poking around the perimeter with his hands in his pockets, and he gave her a glare.

"He saved my life with it," Kiel reminded her.

"He missed what he was aiming for. He almost killed you."

"That's not important. He could still protect you. At close range, you don't have to be a marksman."

Now she spun on him. "You're sticking up for him to cozy up."

His eyes went wide with astonishment at the implied accusation, and his heart beat a galloping rhythm of fear and resurfacing guilt. "Is that what you think?" he sputtered, barely able to get the words out.

Her face was furious. "Oh, come off it. That's not what I meant. Don't be so sensitive."

He didn't understand why she was so riled with him. What had he done or said to deserve such anger? "Well, what do you mean, then?"

She was distracted by Cam, who had crawled up onto the broken workbench. "Get off of there before you fall!" she yelled.

Her son ignored her. Instead he slid a crate a foot to one side and climbed up on that so that he was now a good four feet off the floor.

Julie stomped over. "You're going to get it, kiddo—" she started.

Cam cut her off as he reached up and pulled aside an ancient timber wolf hide hanging near the roof that they now saw had been covering a hole. "I found it!"

"I said, get *down* from there," she warned, but he ignored her. He reached in and slid out a cardboard box. The load was heavier than he'd expected, and he lost his balance and started to fall backwards. Luckily, Kiel had walked over to see what he'd found, and caught him. He pushed him back up onto his crate and took the heavy box. He set it on the tilting workbench, opened the top flaps, and peered inside.

"Holy shit!" he cried, stepping back reflexively. He grabbed Cam by the waist, lifted him to the floor, and moved him back before looking in again.

"What is it?" Julie asked, walking over.

Kiel held his hand out to keep her back as well, although it wouldn't make much difference. "Daniel's dynamite," he answered. He put his hand in to lift a stick out, but thought better of it. An even dozen eight-inch cylinders stood vertically, each in its own cubbyhole of corrugated cardboard.

"You're serious?" she asked, alarmed.

"Oh, yeah. I guess he was hiding it because he didn't have a permit." He peered in again. "I didn't think they made them with fuses anymore."

Julie caught his hand, preventing him from reaching in. Her concern had subsumed her anger. "We don't know how old this is," she cautioned.

"Right. I read somewhere that dynamite has a relatively short shelf-life."

"The nitroglycerin can seep and pool. That concentrates it, and it becomes extremely sensitive to shock."

Kiel remembered that she had studied biology, which must have included a lot of chemistry as well. "They could be useful."

"They could kill us all spectacularly."

"Those sticks could disable a lot of giant colony monsters."

"That may be, but they're not staying in here. I want that box outside—and *be careful*. Don't jiggle it. Don't even sneeze."

Kiel wasn't about to argue. The box scared him nearly as much as whatever the colony was going to throw at them next. He lifted it slowly, as though it was a vase filled to the brim. He soft-stepped carefully to the cave entrance, and then paused and looked around outside. Not seeing anything flying or crawling, he stepped outside. He thought a moment, and then carried the box along the base of the ridge and set it down. If it went off, they'd be deaf for a while, but shouldn't be hurt. Unless the blast caused the cave to collapse.

Back inside, Cam and Julie were arguing again. "As long as they have power from the substation, they'll be in high gear making more of themselves," Cam was saying, trying against all odds to convince his mother.

"We could use the dynamite to defend the cave," she replied, obviously trying to be more reasonable than before. "That way, Kiel can take the gun."

"Mom, you're not getting it!" he rejoined. "The colony is evolving. The beasts are not only getting bigger, they're more complicated. Hands imply using tools. They're evolving intelligence. And it's not going to take them years, but days, or even hours before they're smart enough to figure out what we're up to."

Julie looked at Kiel with a level gaze. "He wants to use the dynamite against their own cave," she reported in a tone demanding he agree that this was ridiculous.

Kiel sighed and looked at Cam.

"They've either evolved or were made to learn," the teenager explained, talking directly to Kiel, assuming he would be more receptive. "It was just a few days ago that they barely learned how to fly. It's now or never."

"You want to take the dynamite . . . to *their* cave?" Kiel asked. He was just trying to understand what Cam was thinking, but the boy obviously thought that he too was challenging the whole idea.

"I know it's dangerous, but—oh, shit!" he exclaimed in frustration.

"Cameron!" Julie admonished. "That's enough!"

The boy kicked at the floor and turned away from them. Kiel couldn't think what to say to draw him in without making Julie even angrier. He looked to her for help, but her mouth was set in stubborn determination.

He felt suddenly drained again. It was bad enough that they were battling a relentless alien enemy, but to fight among themselves was just . . . stupid.

They had to get off the volatile issue of taking the battle to the colony's cave. They needed a distraction, and Kiel had just the thing. The idea had been just a vague wish until now. Daniel's whole termite contraption was too unwieldy. They couldn't always count on the colony beasts coming within reach of the collection of cumbersome pieces.

"Cam!" he called. "We need to do some engineering. We have to get your uncle's contraption off the ground."

The boy turned back, intrigued.

"We need a portable colony exterminator."

Anger faded from Cam's face and his eyes glinted at the prospect of putting his brain back into gear.

They talked it over while Julie checked again on Daniel and Nicki. It was a matter of figuring out how to assemble the power box and one of the batteries into some sort of backpack. The metal box itself made up most of the weight. Kiel guessed that the steel container served no purpose other than as a container for the transformers, coils, and circuit card. They removed all these guts, wrapped the individual components in burlap, and then bundled all of it together inside one bag.

The car battery was the real problem. At thirty pounds, it was going to be a bear to lug around. It alone weighed as much as his whole backpack had when he went hiking for three days on the Appalachian Trail.

Cam came alive as they worked through the details, while his mom sat with her back against the cave wall, staring off at something invisible to Kiel—perhaps memories of times with her own mother, or as unlikely as it seemed, her dead husband. When Cam left to step outside, she woke from her reverie and asked wearily where he was going. He looked at her in disbelief. "To *pee?*" he replied as a cynical question.

She pulled herself to her feet.

"You're not going with me, are you?" he asked, appalled.

"You don't know what's out there."

Her son rolled his eyes and walked out without waiting for her.

Kiel was disconnecting the battery that he guessed had the most charge when Julie called to him from outside. He dropped the cables and sprinted for the entrance, expecting to grapple with metal tentacles, but found mother and child standing thirty feet away staring off towards Tagget's farm. Kiel saw what they were looking at: a thin trail of white smoke reaching up into the sky. As he watched, the trail broke and dissipated in the slight breeze, but was soon followed by a new one starting at ground level and rushing up and up until it arced over and terminated in an expanding puff. Seconds later, he heard a distinct pop.

"What is it?" he asked.

"The army," Julie replied hopefully. "Finally."

Cam looked skeptical and Kiel had doubts about Julie's assessment; these missiles seemed pretty wimpy for Army munitions. "What are they firing at?" he wondered.

Julie shrugged. "Aliens. They're too far away to see."

Cam shook his head.

"It's the Army," his mother reiterated.

"They're not weapons," her son stated.

"How do you know?"

"It's obvious. There's no detonation, for one thing."

"I can hear the explosions—there!" Another finger of smoke had blossomed.

"Mom! That would barely bring down a sparrow."

"What do *you* think they are?"

He chewed his lower lip. "Estes rockets."

"*Model* rockets," she scoffed.

"Yeah," he retorted sarcastically. "I have experience, you know." He looked to Kiel. "Mr. Dickson tried to start a model rocket club last year, but there wasn't enough interest."

Kiel wasn't sure what they were looking at, but he was confident it wasn't the Army—at least, not Army weapons. One thing was certain, though: whatever they were, they probably weren't alien. The colony of alien crablets hadn't developed technology—not yet. "I guess that's where I'll go for help," he concluded. "Whoever's there might have contact with the outside world."

Julie nodded enthusiastically, but Cam's face had gone dark again. He hadn't yet learned to control his impulses. "Big mistake."

Kiel winced, hoping Julie would let it go. She didn't. "What is?" she asked, her voice edged with anticipation.

"Ignoring the fact that the colony has to be destroyed *now,* before they evolve further!"

"We've been through this, young man. We don't have the means; that's what the Army is for."

"We have dynamite!"

"Enough! I don't want to hear any more about it."

"Mom, you're not—"

"I said enough!"

He glared at her, epithets probably tumbling around in his head, but he was at least smart enough to know when to give in.

Kiel returned to the task of building a portable drone killer, and Cam moped around mostly just getting in the way. He'd lost interest in the project, and kept going to the entrance to stare off towards Tagget's farm. Kiel finally suggested that his young friend keep watch, figuring that serving as a lookout would put him where he apparently wanted to be anyway. The boy paced around just outside the entrance for a while, and then sat down, hugging his knees and gazing off to the north.

Julie wasn't much help either. Kiel had to concentrate to make sure he didn't mess up all the connections as he tore down and rebuilt the components, but Julie insisted on revisiting over and over her argument about why they should seek help. Her anger with her son obviously derived from her worry about him, and to

Kiel it seemed that she was determinedly trying to justify to herself her harsh behavior. It was also obvious that she was exhausted. He suspected that otherwise she would have already put it to rest in her mind. After the fifth round of the same rationalizing train of logic, Kiel finally had had enough and gently suggested that she should get some rest, that they should all take whatever advantage they could of the opportunity. She stared at her shoes a moment and then nodded. She went off and lay down next to Nicki in the pile of burlap sacks in the back. When he looked over a few minutes later, she was asleep.

Kiel became absorbed in piecing together a jury-rigged backpack using an apple crate he cut down. He found some woven cloth belts that he cut and attached with tie-wraps as shoulder straps. After perhaps a half hour, he stopped. Something had caught his attention. He looked towards the back of the cave, but Julie and Nicki were still sound asleep.

It wasn't any particular sound that had nudged his consciousness, but rather the lack of something. He glanced towards the cave mouth, and saw that Cam was not there. He ran outside and looked in all directions, and then called the boy's name. There was no response. Even the cicadas seemed to have disappeared.

He stood, feeling the breeze brush the hair across his forehead. There was no use calling. Cam was gone.

Chapter 28

Kiel eased himself down onto his butt, letting a rock take up the weight of his backpack as he sat in front of it. The relief to his shoulders was exhilarating; a bona-fide backpack would have placed most of the weight on his hips. He ever so gently set the bundle of dynamite on the ground, and then set his sixteen-ounce spray bottle of salt water next to it. He worried about that decision. He had started off from Daniel's cave haven with the commercial pesticide sprayer, but carrying that plus the dynamite and mobilized termite gun had been too much, even after emptying most of the salt water. So, along the way he had stopped in the woods and borrowed Nicki's household sprayer bottle that she'd left in their fort, transferring sixteen ounces of salt water from the large container. At the time it had seemed genius, but now he wondered if it would be enough.

He checked his watch. Still ten minutes to go. The colony cave should be just over the next small ridge. He suspected that Julie might be late at her end, but he wanted to be in position in case she wasn't. She'd really given him hell when he'd woke her up to tell her that Cam was gone, particularly since he hadn't noticed for upwards of a half hour. The boy's departure had turned everything on a dime. She was sure that her son was making for the colony cave on his own, and so had readily agreed to change plans and have Kiel go there as well instead of Tagget's farm. It hadn't been easy to convince her not to go along, though, and the current plan had started out mostly as a way to dissuade her.

Now he was committed. He had agreed with Cam that the colony needed to be destroyed, but now that he was sneaking in behind enemy lines, making for their munitions factory, command center, and home all rolled into one, he wondered about his sanity. Maybe he needed to be "committed" in a completely different fashion.

He checked his watch again. Nine and a half minutes. He held up his hands to admire Cam's last stroke of genius. A pair of Daniel's old metal-mesh gloves now replaced the stick-like probes. The fact that the rubber had worn off the fingers and palms, exposing the metal mesh underneath, was critical. Wires from the backpack ran underneath his shirtsleeves to clips attached to the wrists of the gloves. The two scouts that had attacked him along the way had been easily dispatched—all he had to do was spray, and then reach up and grab them, making sure afterwards that he didn't leave enough active crablets behind to collect together and return to warn the rest of the colony.

It was the thought of their big brothers—the giant birds, or hand-equipped centaurs, or who-knew-what-next—that raised the hair on his neck. That, and the image of dozens of drones descending on him simultaneously in one swarm. God forbid they should ever figure out how his weapon worked and manage to simply yank off one of the feed wires.

He heard a sound—the familiar burring buzz of drone wings. He stood up, ready. He wasn't frightened by one lone scout, but this was clearly multiple sources. The sounds remained fixed in place, coming from one distinct direction, obviously not nearby. That wasn't good, since it implied things significantly larger than scout drones. He listened. He'd been wrong: the location was not fixed, but moved slowly, sideways to him . . . in the direction of their own haven.

Kiel's heart sank. There was nothing he could really do. He'd be putting Julie in dire straits if he didn't follow through now at his end. And in any case, he doubted he could make it back before the moving objects. Daniel, who had woken before they left, would have to use the shotgun from his bed in the cart to deal with whatever they were. One saving grace was that the sounds were not that of the giant birds; the pitch was too high. From the quality, Kiel imagined something more the size of perhaps a tiger. Maybe Daniel could hold out against metal beasts that big.

He looked at his watch: time to go. He stood up, straining to lift the heavy pack, picked up his salt water, and lastly the wrapped half-dozen sticks of dynamite. Each tube was individually wrapped in burlap, and the whole bundle then wrapped together, providing layers of cushioning. Still, he handled it like delicate china. He could only hope that Julie was as careful with her half.

Topping the low ridge, he peered carefully around a stone outcrop. He'd been right—he was looking down into the little box canyon that was home to the colony's cave. He saw that they'd made changes. They had cleared away a large quantity of the fallen rubble in order to enlarge the cave opening, which would have been necessary for the larger monsters. More ominously, they'd built what looked like a track system that emerged from the darkness of the cave and led down the slope, terminating in a fifteen foot high pile of sand that fanned down the slope for a hundred feet. They'd obviously been doing some excavating.

He ducked back when he saw motion inside the cave. Moments later, the familiar burr of a drone moved out and echoed about among the canyon walls. Peeking around the outcrop, he saw the scout head out of the canyon and away around the corner. Something else caught his eye. On top of the far ridge, a few hundred yards away across the canyon, stood something unnatural, something too geometric for natural growth. It appeared also too straight—too rigid—for one of the colony beasts, which were formed and moved in smooth curves, like the Earth animals they sometimes imitated. As he watched, it disappeared beyond the ridge. It was too far to distinguish any detail, but he had the impression that it moved like a giant ant.

He was still wondering about the strange sight when Julie's first explosion boomed across the fields. Trees blocked his view of the Bakke house, but not of the debris thrown high into the air, loose beams and shingles and obliterated household items falling back to the ground in seeming slow motion in the distance. That would be her first three sticks. He held his breath. If she had screwed up and got caught in the explosion somehow, then no more would follow—boom! There went the barn! Planks spun lazily in long arcs, the smoke merging with that of the house explosion. Moments later, the third and last stick of dynamite detonated. She'd wanted to blow up Daniel's house, but Kiel had suggested that the sound alone should suffice. She would have just lit and tossed the last stick as she made for the milk-house bunker.

As the detonation thunder died away, Kiel realized that the air was now filled with a veritable roar of buzzing flight. It sounded like a million angry bees in hot pursuit. He crouched down as a dozen—two dozen at least—scout drones hurried off towards the billowing smoke. They wouldn't know what it was, but he'd hoped that the sheer magnitude of disturbance would draw them to investigate. He'd guessed correctly.

He pulled back behind the outcrop even farther, making himself as small as possible, as two giant hawk-beasts flapped majestically past, following their more maneuverable little brethren. Kiel closed his eyes and said a little prayer for Julie. She'd had faith in the paranoid obsession of her grandfather who had buried the little concrete milk house under a mound of dirt, and replaced the wooden door with a half-inch slab of steel. He assured himself that she would be okay until his own dynamite extravaganza called the monsters back.

Once the emerging stream of colony soldiers dwindled and finally stopped, Kiel carefully placed the bundle of explosives in his pack and made his way down the slope. His thumping heart urged haste, but the combination of a heavy, unbalancing pack and six sticks of dynamite required care. Luckily, he made the canyon floor before a stray scout drone suddenly burst from the cave. It paused just a moment before diving for him, tentacles spread in anticipation of an easy catch.

Kiel took his time. He was experienced now, and he was confident in his abilities, weapon, and technique. He carefully laid the bundle of dynamite in the dirt, refusing to let the approaching enemy rush him. He straightened just as it reached him, and swung his arm in an arc, spraying a mist of salt water over the tentacles grasping and curling around his head. Then, like before, he simply reached up and grabbed at each appendage in turn, melting them like ice cream under a hot spoon. As with the two prior, this drone was not prepared for the sudden disastrous turn of events. It hesitated a moment, perhaps in disbelief at what was happening to it, before lifting up and away from this human with the magical gloved hands. As before, Kiel didn't let it. Reaching up with both hands, he grasped the main body, and the drone fell flopping and squirming to the ground, where Kiel touched it here, and there, incapacitating enough crablets to prevent it from quickly re-forming. He didn't take the time to completely destroy it as he had with the others, however. Any opportunities the colony might have had for early warning were now past—he had arrived, and whatever lurked inside the darkness of the cave would know soon enough.

He found that the track they'd built for dirt disposal was wide enough to walk on. This saved him significant time, as it was much easier than climbing over the boulders of the debris pile. Inside the cave foyer, into which he and Cam had spied using the camera and laptop seemingly so long ago, another scout drone attacked him. In the dim light, he wasn't able to bring it down, and it flew back into the inner tunnel, minus three tentacles. No matter.

Kiel paused a moment before following the wounded alien beast into the inner sanctum. He heard sounds from within, the hum and light clatter of industry. Suddenly nervous about the wounded drone's advance warning, Kiel strode quickly down the tunnel. He saw light against the curving wall—a pulsing, modulating glow with a reddish, evil tinge. When he came to the inner chamber entrance, he gasped. Spread before him lay a dense, intricate factory. He saw no wheels or gears or articulating, program-driven arms, but he didn't doubt that this expanse of miniature complexity was an alien factory, an assembly line for making crablets and constructing functioning bodies from them. Where previously small robot-like crablet creatures scurried about performing crablet production, the space was now filled with a continuum of metal crablet structure. The form and functions were too alien to guess, but the entire assemblage pulsated with movement, one giant, immensely elaborate living machine whose sole goal and purpose was to reproduce its elemental units. He realized that the light was emanating from a pool against the wall where the power feed—now as thick as a tree trunk—snaked in. Whatever liquid filled the shallow pond was hot enough to glow. To his left, a third of the way around the wall, they had built a new tunnel, presumably to expand the factory activity. This would have been the source of the dirt dumped at the end of the track.

Kiel absorbed all of this in a matter of seconds. Amid the seeming chaos of alien patterns that comprised the cave factory, he saw that one section against the wall on his right was denser—solid, in fact. Something the size of a small car, but the shape of a Picasso sculpture, sat quivering and pulsing. Kiel had the distinct impression that whatever it was, it was watching him. Instinct told him that this . . . thing was central to the operation and needed to be destroyed. He had to scramble through the factory to reach it. Halfway, something grabbed his ankle. It was a piece of factory that had disconnected to form a tentacle and wrapped around his leg. One squirt and a grab, and it melted. Now more sections were detaching and reaching for him. He waved his sprayer wide and started grabbing, but then found that he only had to wave his hand across the squirming snakes—where he brushed them, they wilted.

Suddenly the attack ceased. He looked at the solid mass against the wall, what he now thought of as the brain. From the heavy core rose half a dozen weaving tentacles, each ending in a taloned claw. Simultaneously, a shrieking scream rose, building in volume and pitch until Kiel thought his head would explode. And then instantly it stopped and the cave seemed to ring with the aftershock.

Kiel was now sure of his mission. He plowed on through the waist-high factory. The claw-tipped tentacles had grown until they hovered threateningly above him. He wished that he had not abandoned his original sprayer, as it had a longer reach. The creature inadvertently cooperated by closing in the cluster of claws all around him, as though searching for the weakest point to attack. As soon as Kiel sprayed, they sprang into a frenzy of motion, stabbing and grabbing at him. His gloves served double-duty: not only did the metal mesh conduct the alien-zapping electricity, but it provided protection against the sharp talons. He placed his hands in front of his face and neck, exactly where the claws were stabbing. One by one, the talons of each claw were dulled and softened as they contacted the gloves. Only one managed for a moment to get through his defense to stab his scalp, causing him to cry out from the piercing pain.

He didn't pause once the beast was de-clawed. He gave the tentacles another good spray, and then grabbed each in turn at the base and waved his hand to contact the tip, which whipped about, desperately attempting to avoid obliteration. By the time he had destroyed the last tentacle, he was sweating and felt weak. He couldn't give the alien time to recover, though. Before it had a chance to concoct some new defense, he sprayed the surface liberally and began applying his death hands. At first he wasn't sure his termite zapper was working. He'd never encountered such a dense quantity of crablets, but when he sensed the surface quiver and shake, and felt his hands slowly sinking into the mass, he knew that Daniel's tool was not letting him down.

Kiel had worked hard—they all had—to arrive at this point. Mrs. Bakke had given her life. He intended to take as much satisfaction as he could from the evil alien's destruction. His reverie was compromised by the beast, however. Two new appendages were rising and taking shaping towards the back. He kept his eye on them, intending to dispatch them once they took a threatening form. But instead of nasty talons, they morphed into the shape of human hands. The previous grotesquely monstrous alien imitations had broken Julie's arm and killed her mom, but these were small and harmless, almost delicate in fact. Kiel found himself intrigued by their gentle gestures. The two hands paused a moment, and then clasped together, exactly as Kiel's grandmother would do when kneeling in the Altoona Sacred Heart Church.

As Kiel watched, mesmerized now, a low moan swelled from within the mass of crablets serving as billions of neurons. The moan repeated, and then again, like a cat pleading to come in from outside. It dawned on Kiel that it was trying to say something, and this made him pause while goosebumps rose on both arms. Of all the bizarre encounters with the crablets, this was surely the strangest. Hearing the alien speak was somehow horrifying, as though a monster from a nightmare managed to escape into his waking life.

It was repeating one word over and over. The beginning sounded like "ball," while the end trailed off as a rough hiss. With each repetition, though, the pronunciation became more distinct, until Kiel was hearing "Ball-ease." His breath caught when he realized that it was saying, "Please!"

It was pleading for its life.

Surprised, he instinctively lifted his hands from this entity that suddenly took on life and intelligence. This saved his life. Out of the corner of his eye, he saw sudden motion, nearly behind him. He swung his hand back just in time to stop a two-foot knife from slicing into his neck. The son-of-a-bitch monster had tried to trick him. While pleading for mercy, it surreptitiously extended a knife-tipped tentacle out the far side.

Gripping the knife blade in his metal glove, he reached down and punched his other fist into the alien's core. Instantly the knife melted in his hand. It dawned on Kiel that he knew where the bastard had learned how to beg for its life like a human being—from the same. Those clasped hands, that mournful word was the last gesture from one of its victims.

He'd had enough. He felt nauseous and just wanted to get it over with. He stepped back, nearly tripping over pieces of the factory, and this was when he noticed that he was not alone in the cave chamber. A new alien creature, one unlike any he'd seen before, stood just inside the entrance tunnel staring at him. It had a roughly tubular body with three legs on each side, each terminating with a combination hand and claw. An opposable thumb worked opposite three digits, one of which comprised a nasty talon. The surfaces were glossy, unlike the mat texture of crablet material. Finally, most telling, the joints of the legs and fingers had the appearance of mechanical construction—pin and socket rotating linkages.

The brain spoke again, but this time the words were entirely undecipherable, meaningless squeals and honks. It was talking to the interloper. Kiel understood what the earlier shrieking scream had been: it had been a call for help. This insect-like beast was surely what he had seen silhouetted on the far ridge.

Kiel charged forward, electrified hands raised to melt and destroy. The sooner he put this one to rest, the sooner he could finish his business here. The creature reared up on its back four legs, reaching out with its front two to meet the attack. It was making this easy, Kiel thought, offering him convenient contact points. When Kiel reached the glossy beast, it swung one arm at him, and he caught it in his gloved hand. Quickly, he reached out and grabbed the other four-fingered claw. The two of them—man and unliving predator—stood facing each other like wrestlers caught with stop-action film. The spindly arms, the robot-jointed hands, the sharp talons all remained intact. Kiel squeezed his gloved fingers to make better contact, but the two domed, black, featureless eyes just stared back inches from his face.

His weapon, the delivery of high-frequency electricity so lethal to crablets, had finally failed him.

In the milli-seconds it took him to realize this, he understood that the outer body of this alien soldier was not comprised of crablets. This close, he could see that the material was translucent. Inside, visible like the ghastly face of a lost explorer frozen in solid ice, he saw intricate patterns—networks of controlling crablets, buried deep and protected from electrocution. The insulating body was silicon. The drones that had escaped from the dying centaur had returned with warnings, and the aliens had made a new creature using the sand all around them.

Kiel was wrestling a killer beast against which he had no weapon and no defense.

Chapter 29

The giant glass insect made its move. It reached up with one of its middle legs to grab him. Kiel tried to reach down to block it, but the beast clung to his hand. This actually proved to his advantage, since with only one foot on the ground, the creature was unbalanced and Kiel pulled it over on its side. It let go of Kiel's hand to steady itself, and he took the opportunity to jump back.

His attacker hesitated only a moment before springing after him. Kiel turned and ran. He jumped over and around the factory structure, breaking parts as he fled. With six legs to choose from, the creature should have been faster, but it had the disadvantage of choosing to avoid damage to the assembly machine—essentially its mother.

Kiel's mind raced. What could he use as a weapon? Everything around him was constructed of crablets, cohorts of his pursuer. The brain was squealing away again, probably broadcasting directions. At one point, Kiel felt a tug on his back and wrist, and he doubled his speed. Before long, he came to the far wall and spun around.

The creature stopped ten feet away. In one of its hands, it held a long wire. For a moment, Kiel wondered where it had come from, and then it dawned on him that his assailant had ripped it from his pack. That was the tug he'd felt. The brain had probably told it to disable the crablet zapper before killing Kiel.

Terror launched him to desperate action. He reached down and grabbed the only thing available—some sort of pipe made from crablet material. He yanked it from its fastenings and swung it like a bat. The giant insect leaned back, perhaps momentarily uncertain what to do when its kindred was used against it. Kiel knew that this wouldn't deter the creature for long, and ran along the wall. His pursuer followed, keeping him from escaping into the jumble of factory again until Kiel came up against the molten pool. He could feel the intense heat on his face. His pipe weapon had gone limp in his hand as the many thousands of crablets mutually decided to go passive on him. The insect giant came in for the kill. There was nothing for Kiel to do . . . except the only thing left to do. He dipped the flaccid hose into the molten substance and then swung it at the creature's face. Glowing gobs flew in heavy arcs, and one landed squarely on one of the beast's eyes. This gave it pause as it reached up with one hand to feel.

The momentary respite was fortunate, since Kiel held just a stub of the original crablet pipe—the rest had melted. The respite also gave him a few seconds to think—more than he'd had since the giant ant arrived. He had come to the alien sanctuary for a purpose. He reached up and pulled out the bundle of dynamite from his pack. He wasn't thinking about altruistic principles of self-sacrifice for the better good; he just remembered that he had something that could be used as a weapon. He tore off the outer burlap covering revealing the six fuses twisted together. There were matches somewhere down in his pack, but the monster could lunge at any moment. He dipped the tip of the fuses into the molten pool, and they instantly hissed to life.

He now held six sticks of nitroglycerin-impregnated sawdust that were going to detonate within seconds. He hadn't thought this through; he just wanted something to use against the alien predator. What he held in his hand was going to be supremely effective, but it was also going to force that altruistic self-sacrifice on him.

To hell with that. Transferring the primed dynamite bundle to his left hand, he took the burlap wrap and dipped it as well into the pool, setting it alight. He waved this in the monster's face as he moved sideways along the pool. With one eye scorched by molten magma, and the other faced with a flaming rag, the beast seemed unsure. This was all Kiel needed, and he leaped around it, towards the entrance tunnel. He hadn't gone four steps, though, when he was yanked to a stop. His enemy had grabbed his shirt.

Kiel howled in terror and turned and jammed the burning rag into the monster's one good eye. The brain's jabbering rose in pitch and volume, and the giant ant let go of him and backed off. Intuition whispered to Kiel that it was afraid of the dynamite, and he waved it threateningly in the air. Sure enough, the beast crouched and took another step back. The brain. It must have guessed the nature of the dynamite and told its colleague.

This was his last chance. He was either going to be blown to tiny bits, or possibly struck down with a knife-talon. The former was assured, the latter only a distinct possibility, so the choice was easy. Kiel meant to lay the dynamite on the floor, but in his haste, he dropped it the last six inches and winced. He turned and ran for the tunnel, jumping factory structures as though they were hurdles from his high school days in track.

When he reached the tunnel, he turned around to look. This would have been stupid if the monster had followed him, but it hadn't. It had disappeared. No—he caught a glimpse of it as it scurried away into the new tunnel on the far side of the factory. If it did indeed find refuge back there from the coming blast, he might have to deal with it yet.

Right now, though, he needed his own refuge. Six sticks of dynamite were about to make a really big boom.

He turned and sprinted away, lowering his shoulder as he ran to let the heavy, useless pack fall to the ground. Thirty-five pounds lighter, he ran like an antelope. He was through the foyer and just over the lip of boulders at the entrance when a twelve million joule hammer slammed his back and flung him forward like so much tissue paper.

He came to with a tremendous pain burning his shoulder. A rock must have jabbed into his wound. He hadn't been out long—sand from the blast still pattered down around and on him. Other than his shoulder, he seemed to have survived, which was lucky, since the entrance was the only outlet for the expanding gases of the explosion. He'd nearly been caught still inside the giant gun barrel.

Echoes from the explosion were dying away in the distance, but curiously, the boulders around him started to shake. The next instant, a tremendous rumbling swelled until he thought an airliner had crashed into the ridge. But when a blast of dust billowed out around him, he realized that the roof of the inner chamber had collapsed. He could have danced with glee if he'd had the strength. Whatever colony members weren't killed in the explosion were now either crushed or buried—including the one-eyed giant ant.

The voice of Cam—a silent, inner voice, born from his close association with the precocious boy—reminded him that he was still too close to the cave. Kiel heeded his friend, even if he was just inside his own head. He pushed himself to his feet, gritting his teeth against the renewed shoulder pain, and stumbled down the boulder ramp. The ghost of Cam saved his life, for just then the outer foyer caved in as well, spilling rocks down over the top of the ramp, exactly where he'd fallen.

Kiel collapsed to the dirt, completely drained. The ground stopped rumbling, and the last of the fair-weather thunder died away among the line of ridges. The dust cloud settled, and after a minute or two of silence, a bird began singing again somewhere beyond the little canyon. Nature took its bruises, dusted itself off, and strolled on, whistling the song of life eternal.

Kiel decided that he would just lie where he was, maybe forever. The colony armada would arrive back before too long to investigate the explosion—this was part of the plan, drawing them away so that Julie could escape from her hole—and he wasn't sure how he was going to deal with it. But for now, for a forever of a minute or two, he was going to just rest. Lying on his stomach, with his cheek cradled in the dirt, he was content.

He realized that the bird had stopped singing. He waited but it stubbornly refused to serenade a man sorely in need of serenading. But then he heard another sound—a scraping and rustling. From the rhythm, it could have been multiple pairs of legs . . . and it was approaching.

He rolled over, gasping at the pain, and shouted in terror when he saw the face of the giant ant staring down at him. He thought for a split second that there must be two, but then he saw that one of the domed eyes was coated with solidified stone. The new tunnel wasn't an expansion of the factory—it was a backdoor.

The silicon beast raised a foreleg and struck. Kiel rolled away, and felt the thump as a talon sank into the dirt. He needed something—anything—to use as a weapon. With his good arm, he grabbed a rock just as a flash of movement ended with searing pain in his wounded shoulder. This time the excruciating agony was beyond what he could have ever imagined. The monster's foot was right next to his head, and he realized with despair that it had sunk its talon deep into his flesh. He heard his own insane scream as he swung the rock upwards, smashing directly into the good eye. The protective dome crunched and blossomed with a dense spider web of cracks. The creature turned its head one way and then the other, and then it raised the other foreleg and struck again. The second talon missed Kiel by inches. He'd managed to blind the bastard, but he was pinned down, and a couple more random strikes would dispatch him, just as he'd dispatched so many of the creature's brothers.

His assailant raised the talon for another try, but motion swung in from the side, and the silicon beast jerked back at the impact. Another blur of movement, and the cracked eye shattered into tiny pieces. The monstrous ant turned to face its new opponent, but as it pulled the dagger talon from Kiel's shoulder, he reached over and grabbed the leg with his good arm. Another blow from above battered the murderous beast and it hunkered down, blind, against the onslaught. Kiel jerked the leg for spite as a solid hammering bash found the base of what served as the abomination's head. This must have severed a vital control link, for the creature slumped sideways and seemed to go limp. It lay inert, other than faint random twitching of its six legs.

Kiel craned his neck to see who had come to his rescue. It was Julie, mouth set in determination, her left arm hanging useless at her side, as she swung with a metal bar at the disabled beast again and again, sending solid, crunching blows echoing around the small canyon.

"It's dead," Kiel said.

She stopped and stood breathing hard, staring at it, as though not trusting that it wouldn't get up and fly away. Finally, she dropped her weapon, and sat heavily on the ground. After a while she looked at him lying there. "You're wounded," she observed in a tone that suggested he might not have noticed.

He nodded. "It hurts."

She nodded as well. After another minute she added. "You're bleeding."

"Yeah."

"We should get it bandaged up."

"Yeah."

Neither moved. He lay staring at the puffy balls of cumulus clouds, and she sat staring at the dirt.

"You're supposed to be hiding in a milk house," he commented after a while.

"I know." She looked down at him. "I found this when I set the dynamite in the barn," she explained, picking up the hooked metal bar, "and it dawned on me that I couldn't just hide. I had to try to get here . . ."

"To find Cam," he finished.

She nodded and shrugged. "And you."

"You're lucky you didn't run into any drones," he said.

She looked at him again and blinked. "I did."

"You did?" he exclaimed, turning painfully so that he could see her better. "How did you get away?"

She seemed not to understand at first, and then shook her head. "I didn't. I killed it."

"You killed it . . . *how?*"

She held the metal bar against her neck to demonstrate. Kiel saw that a blade was mounted inside the hooked end. "When it tried to wrap a tentacle around your neck, you cut it in half," he guessed.

"It was a tentacle with a knife, but yes. Then I reached up and cut the one that was pulling my hair."

Kiel just stared at her. She looked like she'd been homeless for months. Her face was grimy, and her hair matted with twisted strands falling across her eyes. But underneath it all he saw a handsome woman with mile-deep character—a farm girl emigrated to the city, but still tough as nails.

He gestured at the blade-equipped bar. "Do all Wisconsin farmers have anti-drone weapons lying around their barns?"

She managed a tired grin. "No, but most have bail-twine cutters."

Kiel understood. He imagined how a farm worker would use such a tool to cut the twine from hay bales.

He noticed that the bird had again taken up its song. But a deeper, widely pervasive hum provided a backdrop. Kiel was expecting this, but anticipation did not ameliorate the dread.

Julie noticed as well. "They're coming back, aren't they?"

"I expect so—that was the plan. Help me up," he said taking her offered hand and pulling himself into a sitting position.

"You should lie down," she urged. "I can press against the wound and slow the bleeding."

"I'll be okay," he replied. His unspoken thought was that in a few minutes it wouldn't matter anyway. He wanted to be facing them when they arrived.

She gazed up the boulder ramp at the choked cave entrance. "I guess that wasn't part of the plan, though."

"Right—no place to hide, now."

"It would have just postponed the inevitable," she concluded. She took his hand in hers and squeezed it, then gazed off through the mouth of the canyon.

The distant hum had swelled to a low roar. In the narrow field of view provided through the opening to the canyon, Kiel saw what seemed like a whole battalion of drones winging their way towards them. In addition to those that he'd watched leaving, all the others already in the field scouting the area would be returning as well. All the soldiers were hurrying back to defend a home that no longer existed. He didn't expect that these alien constructions experienced emotions like anger and revenge, but even if they didn't they also wouldn't exhibit mercy and compassion.

A new buzzing component had joined the whirring roar of the approaching armada. The new sound was more variable, higher pitched, and modulating up and down like multiple engines shifting through a range of gears. It sounded like what he'd heard in the distance when he'd arrived—what he took to be alien creatures heading for Daniel's cave.

"You hear that?" Julie asked, tilting her head to better discern the direction.

At that moment the first of the drones burst through the canyon entrance. Kiel knew that it was just his imagination, but they looked mad as hell. The leading half dozen changed direction, angling down, obviously having spotted the two humans. But then they suddenly slowed, rose, and turned together towards the ridge above. Kiel looked up. A hundred feet above them, silhouetted against the deep blue sky was a wheeled vehicle upon which sat two helmeted men.

"There!" Julie shouted, pointing towards the canyon mouth.

One, two, three large-wheeled ATVs came tearing around the entrance wall, their rear ends fishtailing in their haste. Two more less sporty models hurried around keeping up as best they could. Each vehicle bore two men—a driver, and another riding shotgun behind him, where shotgun was a literal description, since each held one in both hands, ready.

A dozen drones instantly dove for their prey. The mobilized humans halted their ATVs and readied themselves. Each driver stood up in his seat and reached his hands high into the air. Kiel saw that they all wore gloves—the same beaten metalized kind that he had used. As the drones reached their victims, the driver grabbed at tentacles, or talons, or swinging blades—whatever the alien creature brandished. Once caught, the hapless drone struggled frantically, clearly distraught with what clutched it. Its frantic struggle ceased when the rear man stood up, and shot point-blank into the captured drone's midsection. As before, this only killed those crablets in the direct line of fire, but the beast was blown to pieces, which fell twisting and squirming to the ground. If an odd tentacle happened to attach to one of the men, the rider only had to grab it with both hands, and it writhed away desperately trying to escape the vile touch.

Julie let go of Kiel's hand and shouted, pointing up the canyon wall. The ATV that had first appeared was working its way down the steep ridge wall, slaloming back and forth. It made the canyon floor and sped to them, skidding to a stop, which raised a cloud of dust that engulfed the two wounded warriors so that they coughed and covered their eyes. When Kiel looked up again, the rear rider, a tiny man whose shotgun seemed outsized in his hands, lay down his weapon and pulled off his helmet.

"Cam!" Julie shrieked, and pushed herself to her feet with her one good arm as he jumped off and ran to her.

A moment later, she fell to her knees and wrapped the good arm around her son. They clutched each other fast, lost in warm love.

"Cam!" the helmeted driver called. "Incoming!"

Cam glanced up and gently pushed his mother away. "Mom, I have to get to work." He ran back to the ATV, leaving her on her knees watching.

"Mr. Dickson?" Julie said incredulously.

"Afternoon," he replied, watching an approaching drone. "Get ready, Cam. Here she comes."

The boy lifted the heavy gun just as his science teacher grabbed the attacking alien.

Kiel winced as the shotgun blast shook his bones. It was a wonderful sound. He hoped he would hear many more.

He lay back in the dirt and closed his eyes. It was good to let somebody else do the work for a while.

Chapter 30

"When I saw the rockets," Cam explained as they got off the elevator, "I knew they were Mr. Dickson's."

"Why didn't you say so?" Kiel asked, looking at the papers the woman had handed him at the discharge window. He wasn't sure how he was going to pay for this. The hospital needed all the beds they could manage for other drone victims, so they'd patched him up, pumped him with antibiotics and after one night of observation told him to skedaddle. At least he got to wear his arm in a sling for a few days as a purple heart.

"I *tried*!" Cam protested. "You guys wouldn't *listen*!"

"I wasn't listening?"

"Okay—it was Mom. She was all hung up on the Army saving us."

"It was a stressful time. We were all a little off our game."

"You're just sticking up for her because you like her," the boy accused.

Kiel glanced at his young friend and saw that he was grinning. He was glad to see the boy smile. He hadn't seen much of that since he'd arrived in the rain so long ago. At least it seemed like such a long time ago. "So you made it to Tagget's place with no problems?"

"There were a couple of drones, but I stayed hidden until they flew on."

"What was Dickson doing with model rockets?"

"He wanted to get the drones' attention."

"He *wanted* them to come?"

"He thought that they were ready to fight them."

"He *thought* they were ready."

"Well, he hadn't thought about using gloves."

Gloves . . . "He went to our cave for the gloves that the riders were wearing!" Kiel exclaimed. That explained the sound of engines he'd heard while waiting at the colony cave for Julie's diversions.

"We all went together. From there, we came straight to you guys."

"Huh," Kiel responded. He already knew that Mr. Dickson had independently come up with the idea of using electric jolts against the crablets, that he'd even experimented on one drone that he'd captured. Kiel had gotten this from one of Dickson's volunteer militia who'd been wounded before Cam showed up, and who had shared Kiel's hospital room for a few hours. The science teacher didn't have the luxury of pressing termite zap guns into service, though, and had to make do with a box of old tractor engine coils that he'd found in Tagget's shed. These didn't produce nearly the voltage of Daniel's homemade device; this was why the crablets were only tormented and not killed when grabbed.

They arrived at Julie's room, and Kiel knocked on the frame of the open doorway. She called for them to come in. Her upper arm was in a cast, and tubes fed medical juices into the part that was exposed.

"Glad to see you're alive," he commented brightly. He was only half kidding. She had collapsed before they got her down out of the canyon. The last time he'd seen her, she'd been unconscious in the backseat of Donny's car. The deputy had joined Dickson's volunteers—he'd had gone and searched them out, in fact, after confirming for himself that Sheriff Lanner had been killed.

She sighed. "It was just dehydration," she said. "I don't know why they won't let me leave."

"How about a multiple fractured arm?"

"Oh, poo. Mom came home the first day when she broke hers."

Julie looked down at her hands and her eyes swelled with tears at the thought of her mother.

"How's Daniel doing?" Kiel asked. He wasn't trying to distract her from her grief, but he wasn't sure how else to react, and he really did want to know.

"He's going to be okay," she replied, dabbing her eyes with a tissue. "They have him sedated. The doctor says that they'll have to do at least one more operation—maybe two. He won't be running any marathons, though."

"I'm sure he's heartbroken over that," Kiel quipped.

They were interrupted when a hospital staff member arrived with Nicki, who had been kept busy in the nursery pretending to help with the toddlers. When she saw her mother, she ran to the bed, while her escort admonished fearfully for her not to jump up. The little girl was just happy to be next to her mom, who put a loving arm around her shoulders. "You're going to go with Kiel and Cam and stay at Uncle Daniel's house tonight," Julie explained to her.

Kiel himself hadn't known what the plan was.

"I want to stay here with you again tonight," she pleaded.

"No, honey. I'll be home tomorrow—you'll have fun with Kiel and Cam."

Kiel looked at her for some sign of implied warning directed at him, but the comment had apparently been completely innocent. The fact that he was wanted on a charge of child molestation seemed to be no longer relevant, at least to her.

"No more drones?" Nicki asked.

"No more drones," her mom reassured.

"Uncle Daniel shot the last one," Nicki stated matter-of-factly.

"Sure, honey," Julie agreed with a dollop of patronization.

"What are you talking about?" Cam interjected.

"You weren't there," his sister accused, taking his question as a challenge.

"I know I wasn't there. Did a drone come into the cave when we were gone?"

The little girl shrugged. "It was already in the cave."

"It didn't fly in from outside?" Cam reiterated.

"No," Nicki replied, irritated that she was being doubted. "I told you, it was already inside."

"How do you know?"

"I *saw* it. It grew up in the corner."

Cam glanced meaningfully at Kiel. "You mean that it sort of came together?" her brother asked.

She shrugged again and nodded.

Cam looked at Kiel and sighed.

"All the crablets that dispersed managed to come together," Kiel suggested.

Cam nodded agreement. "Looks like we'll have to get Uncle Daniel to show us how to make another zapper."

"Okay," Julie announced firmly, giving Nicki another squeeze. "I think that's enough talk about aliens for a while."

They all turned towards the door at the sound of the raised voice of a harried nurse just outside. She was forcefully reminding somebody that until the emergency was over, visitors were restricted to family members only. Two men in suits came through the door, and the nurse hurried away muttering sarcastic remarks about how rules apparently only applied to the little people.

"Mr. Martin?" one man asked, looking at Kiel. He was maybe forty, and stood with his feet spread slightly and his hands clasped loosely together at his waist. It was a stance that implied casual authority.

Kiel's heart climbed up into his throat. If these guys were not FBI, then he was a monkey. "Yeah," he replied. He forced himself to step forward and extend a handshake. "Kiel Martin."

The man ignored the proffered hand. "We'd like to speak to you outside."

"Can I ask who you are?" Kiel asked. Out of the corner of his eye, he saw Cam scrambling to open the laptop that sat next to his mom's bed.

"Outside," was all the man said, and then stepped aside, waiting for Kiel to go first.

He didn't see that he really had a choice. Out in the hall, the men escorted him to an empty waiting lounge. Inside, they closed the door and told him to sit down, and he did, feeling himself trembling slightly. "You were the one who set off the dynamite in the cave?" the first man asked.

Kiel stared at him a moment. What were they getting at? "Yeah," he replied.

The man nodded. He obviously already knew this. "You saw the vermin lair?"

"You mean the drone lair—the colony."

Both men watched him levelly. "We would prefer if you didn't refer to it that way."

"Why?"

The first man lifted his palms. "No need to scare people."

Kiel looked from one to the other. "You aren't FBI, are you?"

The only one of them to speak so far just shook his head. "Mr. Martin, this is Barry Web. He's been assigned to stay with you the next few days until—"

"Who are you?"

The man just looked at him, and then went on. "Barry will be with you all the time. We want you to take him to the other cave where you encountered some of the vermin. You are not to talk to anyone about what happened. You need to understand the seriousness of this. I must warn you that doing so will result in your detention and eventual conviction."

Kiel stared at him. He wondered if they even knew who he really was. They continued to call him Martin, not his real name. "Am I under arrest?"

The man raised one eyebrow. "No, Mr. Martin; you are not now under arrest. However, you will need to do as told—"

"Then how can you threaten to detain me? What would I be convicted *of*?"

"Treason, Mr. Martin."

"*Treason?* For talking about what I *saw*?"

"Under extenuating circumstances, the President has the power to suspend habeas corpus. You would be held under military arrest."

Kiel stared at the stone-faced man. "It was you!"

"What do you mean, Mr. Martin?"

"The drones—the crablets—they're not aliens from some other star system. *You* made them."

"Me? That's ridiculous."

"Not you personally. The military—the US government."

"That's nonsense, Mr. Martin. Why would the government create vermin?"

"Why did the government inject hundreds of unsuspecting soldiers and inmates with plutonium in the fifties?"

The man stood up. "I think you understand what's required of you, Mr. Martin. If you'll excuse me, Barry will take it from here."

Kiel watched him walk out. Barry held his hand out, indicating that they should leave as well.

This could be disastrous. Whether the crablets really were extra-terrestrial or some insane brainchild of the military, these black-suit dicks needed to understand the danger. Every last one of the crablets had to be destroyed, and they weren't even asking him how to do it. Cam had told him that they never did find the giant hawk-beasts that Kiel had seen flying off towards the distraction Julie had made when she blew up the farm. The assumption was that these two had disassociated into individual drones, but nobody knew for sure. They could still be out there somewhere.

But Kiel knew that he wasn't in a position to protest. Although he didn't doubt that presidential powers could suspend constitutional guarantees, he would have bet money that they were mostly bluffing—trying to cow him into being cooperative. But he couldn't take any chances. He had to lie low. He'd be lucky as it was if they didn't find out his real identity.

He sighed and followed his chaperone/guard back to Julie's room. Cam was huddled next to his mom. He had the computer on his lap, and they both smiled when he walked in. "I found it!" Cam crowed.

"What?" Kiel asked.

In answer, the boy turned the laptop around for him to see. It was an article from the Altoona Herald. On June 10, Maria Stintson had appeared at the police station on 16th Street to file a complaint against Mayor Brine, alleging that the Mayor had molested her five-year-old daughter. Under questioning, she became violent when it was pointed out that the Mayor had been in Harrisburg attending a Mayor's conference on the date of the alleged abuse. Ms. Stintson had to be restrained, and eventually a doctor was called in to administer a sedative, since it was deemed that she would otherwise pose a threat to herself. Ms. Stintson's mother was located and took custody of her sedated daughter. City Solicitor Harry Wallace interviewed Ms. Stintson and subsequently announced that all previously lodged charges against Kiel Bilinski were to be dropped.

Kiel looked up to meet the silly-ass grins of Julie and Cam with one of his own. It was like a dream, only he didn't have to wake up. Julie took his hand and gave it a jubilant squeeze.

"Hey, Barry," Kiel called. "Go get your boss. We have a lot to talk about."

Blaine C. Readler

About the Author

Blaine C. Readler is an electronics engineer, inventor of the FakeTV, and a two-time San Diego Book Awards-winner. His novels, although generally considered science fiction, are always about ordinary people who find themselves in extraordinary circumstances. Reviewers, on the other hand, have described his books as eccentrically wild and irreverent, and he offers no counter-argument.

He encourages you to visit him:
http://www.readler.com/

www.ingramcontent.com/pod-product-compliance
Lightning Source LLC
Chambersburg PA
CBHW031200020726
47499CB00002B/431